A NOTE ON THE AUTHOR

Peter Jackson lives with his family in County Durham but comes originally from Lancashire. He read Modern History at Oxford and then went to work in the City of London which he found so dispiriting he had to leave. After that he undertook a number of roles (and if he told you, he'd have to kill you) before becoming a journalist. He worked on papers in the North West and North East where he was business editor of the *Newcastle Journal* before becoming a freelance.

Legions of the Moon is his first novel.

Legions of the Moon

Peter Jackson

writeleft side

ISBN: HB: 978-1-9162610-9-9
ISBN: PB: 978-1-9162610-8-2
ISBN: eB: 978-1-8382595-01

Compilation & Cover Design by S A Harrison
Front Image: *Sleeping Legionary*, Ubaldo Gandolfi (1728–1781)

Published by WriteSideLeft UK
https: / /www.writesideleft.com

For my wife, Anne

BRITANNIA

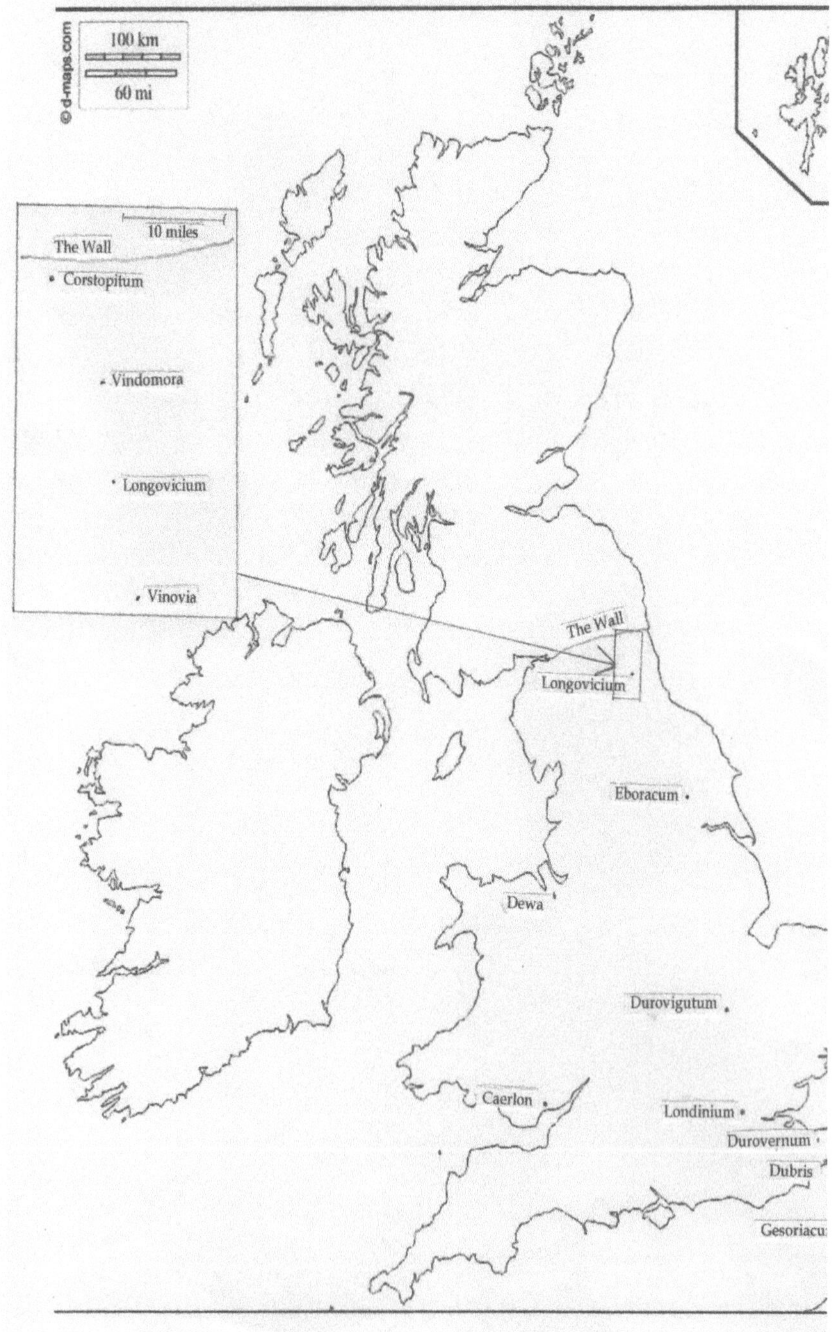
© d-maps.com
100 km
60 mi
10 miles
The Wall
Corstopitum
Vindomora
Longovicium
Vinovia
The Wall
Longovicium
Eboracum
Dewa
Durovigutum
Caerlon
Londinium
Durovernum
Dubris

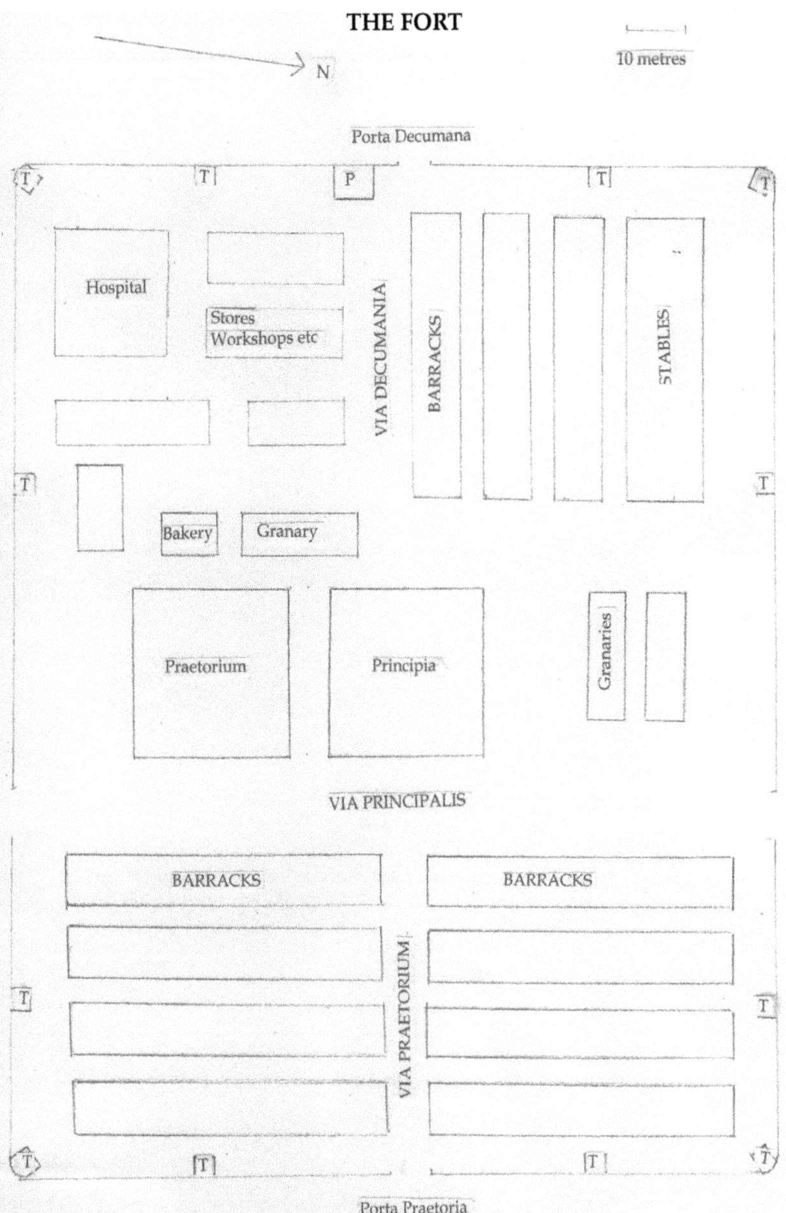

KEY

P: Pigsty

T: Turret

Principia: Fort Headquarters including Basilica

Praetorium: Fort Commandant's House

Legions of the Moon

Peter Jackson

Principal Characters

Spies
QUINTUS Suetonius Lupus. A frumentarius.
MANIUS Suetonius Lupus. His adopted son and apprentice.
TITA AMATIA Aculeo. A Roman noblewoman, resident in Britannia.
GUT CRISPINUS. An informant.
TIRO. A hired desperado.

Politicians
Gaius Caerillius PRISCUS. Governor of Britannia, senator and former consul.
Gnaeus Horatius BUTEO. Provincial Procurator.
Emperor COMMODUS.
SAOTERUS. The Emperor's chamberlain.
MARCUS AURELIUS. The late emperor (161 to 180AD) and Commodus' father.
Tiberius Flavius FIMBRIA, a general and imperial legate.
DECIMA Flavia Fimbria, his wife.
PELLIA. His concubine.

Soldiers
Lucius Antonius MERENDA. Tribune and commander of the First Cohort of Loyal Vardulli, Foot and Horse.
GAIA Antonia Merenda. His wife.
LUCIA Antonia Merenda. Their daughter.
TITUS Caelius Metellus. Second in command of the First Cohort of Loyal Vardulli, Foot and Horse with rank of tribune.
BIRCA. His betrothed and a Briton.
Appius RUFIUS Atellus. Senior centurion of First Cohort of Loyal Vardulli, Foot and Horse.
VIBIA RUFIA Atellus. His wife.
PUBLIUS FLAVIUS Fimbria. Half-brother of Tiberius Flavius and replacement second in command of the cohort.
ANTIOCHOS. The cohort's surgeon.
AMBROSIUS CRASSIPES. A centurion of the cohort.
JULIUS VALERIANUS. Legate commander of the Sixth Victrix legion.

Others
Spurius AURELIUS COTTA. A magistrate, Roman citizen and native Briton.
Sexta AURELIA Cotta. His wife.
Arrius GRACCHUS. A tax official.
Arria Gracchus. His wife.

Chapter One

Gallic witches sucked the moon down from the sky and Manius began to have deep misgivings about the mission.

Hadn't he and Quintus been relying on that moon to illuminate their way down to the ship and to light the vessel out into Gesoriacum's harbour? They were still only minutes from the fort, having collected their grumbling captain and his reluctant crew to urge them to the quay. Stumbling down the winding, cobbled streets, one of them, a lad, even younger than Manius, screamed and pointed upwards.

Manius stopped, horrified. The moon! It should have been a full disc, bright and entire between the scudding clouds. But at one edge, the blackness was nibbling it.

Manius seized Quintus, who turned his red-rimmed, drink-dulled eyes upon him.

"Look!" Manius yelled.

Quintus' shaggy eyebrows rose. He said something, but it was lost in the din of doors being opened all along the street and people pouring out, shouting. They carried pots, pans, cooking spoons and one man, with the pierced ears of a Levantine and wearing a nightshirt, even had cymbals. They clashed their implements and shouted and urged each other on.

The thin, greying captain grabbed the front of Manius' cloak and bawled into his face.

"The witches! The witches are calling down the moon so they can draw off its magical foam."

Manius nodded dumbly. He'd heard of this sorcery and as a child had been taught what must be done. So he too shouted and shrieked, to drown out the noise of the witches' incantations and so save the moon.

Still the darkness ate into the disc; then the whole was obscured, not by sorcery, but by the racing clouds.

"Don't stop! Keep it up!" urged the captain, and the crowd and his crew continued, their numbers swelled by those from other streets and soldiers spilling from the taverns.

Only one didn't shout. Quintus contemplated them with sullen contempt. Manius knew that he would sooner have let witches eat the moon; aye, and the sun and stars too, before shouting with a mob. He swigged from his wine skin and spat.

Then it ended. Perhaps they grew tired of shouting and realised that, as the world hadn't died, the unseen witches hadn't won. Or maybe it was the moon reappearing intact and safe from behind the clouds. Whatever it was, the noise fell, the shouts subsided, and the banging grew half-hearted as the crowd thinned. A muttered, reluctant consensus emerged: the sorcery had been unsettling, but it was probably safe to return to bed and to tavern. Soon Quintus and Manius were left alone again with the captain and his couple of dozen crew.

Manius eyed them. Their mood, uncooperative enough when they set off, now became downright ugly.

"What worse omen could there be?" the captain demanded of Quintus. He turned to Manius. "This is too late in the year for sailing, I told him that. The weather looks foul enough as it is. Only the gods know what effect this will have."

Quintus corked the wineskin, wiped the red dribbles from his greying beard and belched.

"We still sail. With the morning tide."

"This is madness," moaned the captain, wringing his hands. His crew muttered; their own morale undermined by their skipper's evident despair.

"Enough!" roared Quintus and the grumbling died. Manius could see his anger, always a light sleeper, was awakening. "You have our orders and you know what it means to question us."

He seized the captain's shoulders and bundled him against a wall. His face inches from the seafarer's, he hissed: "I'm in no mood for this. You must get a grip on your men. Get me and my boy on your boat, underway and to Dubris."

Will they defy him? Manius wondered. Will they choose crucifixion?

They didn't.

So Quintus succeeded in getting them onto that ship and Manius cursed him for it. Surely, he thought, the captain's right: the auspices are bad.

And that was clear enough the moment he set a reluctant foot on the ship's rolling, heaving deck, having scrambled over the bulwarks, clutching fiercely at the wet wood as the boat pitched against and then away from the quayside, while its painter strained and creaked.

The captain and his crew joined the watch already aboard in untying and hauling on sheets, retying them, scurrying across the decks and manoeuvring the great oars into the water. Manius made to go below, to the oarsmen's deck out of the drizzle from where he couldn't see the harbour's undulant water. "Heaven help me, have mercy upon me," he muttered. He'd never been to sea, and now he was about to be launched on that most dangerous northern ocean. As he made for the ladder, Quintus pulled him over to join him; to sit with their backs against the mast.

Quintus leaned into him and whispered: "We'll stay here, where we can keep an eye on these dogs. I don't trust them so far as I can spit; I'll swear the captain is a foreign-born slave. Ha, you can still see the chalk marks on his feet."

But Manius couldn't care less about the captain.

"Why are we here?" he demanded. "I've asked you a hundred times."

"Aye, and for the hundredth time, I don't know," said Quintus, still contemplating the crew. "We won't be enlightened until we have crossed. This sea: it's like life, we don't know what the point of crossing it is – if there is one – until we get to the other side." He paused to cast a brief glance at Manius. "I know it's important."

"Rome thinks it's important?"

"That's what they told me. But too important to tell me any more."

"Is that what was said?"

"Eh? I think so."

"You think?"

"I was unwell."

Manius groaned. "You were drunk?"

"No! No, but my head ached, my guts were griping."

Manius shook his head, then rested it against the mast, his eyes closed.

"Oh cheer up, boy. There's information for us on the other side, I tell you. Last night I received word that a man by the name of Arpocras will meet us in Dubris. He'll enlighten us."

"You never told me that."

"I'm telling you now."

Quintus returned to his wine, while Manius looked about and shivered. It was late in the year, well into autumn and too late to be making sea voyages, as these seamen well knew. Whatever the purpose of this mission – a posting to the northernmost ends of the Empire, to a freezing wilderness – Manius wanted no part of it. It was surely a punishment for Quintus' past drunken mistakes. No, he didn't want it, but then: for what did his wishes ever count? He sat and brooded as the sailors shouted and busied themselves and as the boat rocked out into the main harbour and Quintus finished his wine and dozed.

They anchored for several miserable hours, waiting for dawn's faint light to the horizon behind them. At last, there were more shouts and scurrying and the crew weighed anchor and manned the oars. Quintus stirred, awoke and stumbled to the bulwark to piss over the side. From there he turned to watch their progress towards the harbour's mouth, the wind and spray dampening his wild black locks to his forehead. Once they were out into the open channel and the boat was rocking with greater and more sickening violence, he made his unsteady way back to the mast to rejoin Manius. The captain roared a command and the sailors abandoned the oars and darted about the deck. They hauled on the sheets to release the sail which unfurled and filled with a great crack and made the boat heel. Manius cried in terror but everyone ignored him, too intent on ship and sea. The helmsman brought her back upright and she picked up speed, with the wind screaming in from their left.

That wind frightened Manius, but not so much as it dismayed the captain and his crew, whose ashen faces advertised their own – more significant – fear. Oh, surely this was madness.

Quintus, at Manius' side, seemed unmoved, and remained facing back towards Gesoriacum. Was it courage or Stoic indifference? Manius neither knew nor cared. Just then, he hated Quintus as the cause of him being there, hurtling onwards, with seawater crashing over the sides at every pitch of the vessel, his tunic soaked and his bowels churning.

"Are you all right boy?" Quintus asked.

Manius only nodded. If he spoke, he would weep.

Quintus squeezed his knee. "Good lad."

Manius had to turn to throw up, which he did for a long time. And this was welcome. He felt that death would be a blessing, except that Charon would never get him aboard his boat to take him over the last channel.

He was nearly insensible, with nausea and the exhaustion of heaving, when the crisis came. To this groaning seventeen-year-old wretch, spewing his stomach juices into the scuppers, it seemed to rush in from nowhere. The boat went into a violent forward plunge, deeper than any before, followed by a shudder and a wrench to leeward. The captain gave a bellow of fear and outrage and shook his fist at the helm, or Neptune, or both. Manius still sat, but he could see the waves, white-capped, churning and raging, because, for a heaving heartbeat, they were higher than he, then the ship was once more above them. This went on in a sickening, lurching rhythm and the sky above was dark, even though it must still be morning.

"We're done for!" cried a crewman, a squat, hairy, one-eyed Gaul.

"Isis Pelagia save us!" yelled another.

A hand took the shoulder of Manius' sodden cloak and Quintus hauled him to his feet, shouting into his face.

"Your sword, take out your sword!" Before Manius could move Quintus rummaged beneath his cloak, grabbed the weapon himself, and stuffed it into Manius' frozen hand.

"Look to yourself, and to me," he said, his own sword now in his fist.

Manius shook his head, clearing his senses and was then aware of some six or seven of the crew advancing on them across the slanting deck, carrying spikes and clubs.

"Over the side with them!" shouted the one-eyed one. "They've brought us to this, they're our curse. We know what they are, an offence to the gods. Over the side with them!"

They took another pace, their seamen's legs keeping balance on the heaving deck. Quintus, his left arm clutching the mast, scythed a wide sword-arc with his right, forcing them back, in sullen retreat.

"Captain!" he roared over his shoulder. "You have a mutiny."

The boat plunged and soared, the seamen stood firm and Manius and Quintus clung to the mast, swords pointed, while the spray lashed them all.

A cry from the bows broke the spell. Manius couldn't make it out but their attackers suddenly darted in all directions and busied themselves again about the sheets and sail. The captain began shouting his orders, now with urgency and purpose.

Quintus laughed and pointed. Manius looked and saw – at what distance he couldn't tell – two lights ahead and a couple of hands' breadths above the bows.

"The Pharos," said Quintus. "The Pharos of Dubris."

Maybe those lights heartened the crew, or perhaps the wind abated, but half an hour's concentration, urgent curses and clever manoeuvres with oar and sail, saw them mooring at the quay at the foot of the cliffs on which these great light houses stood. That damned boat still bobbed enough to sicken Manius but his terror had gone, leaving a vacuum of feeling. The sailors, now fawning, fingered salutes to their foreheads and, with wary sidelong glances, helped Manius and Quintus to the gangplank and handed them their baggage. The captain was all sheepish smiles.

"Well, as the saying goes, `All's right that happens in the world'," he said, clapping his hands.

He handed Manius down from the gangplank and the young man's knees almost failed as his feet hit unyielding land.

"Welcome to Britannia, young sir."

Manius hiccupped, so grateful he could have embraced him.

"Maybe now we'll find out why we're here," said Quintus.

Chapter Two

This captain, anxious to please, detailed sailors to carry Quintus' and Manius' baggage and insisted on leading them.

"You see, sirs, all these warehouses," indicating the rows crowding down to the jetties. "Normally full to the brim. Regular little Ostia, ha, ha, but this season, there's little sailing, what with the weather, as you've seen for yourselves. Not that we mind for gentlemen." He stared hard, gauging their reactions. "`Course, some of the lads might have turned a bit daft, frightened by that business last night, but they'll pay. I've told 'em: `You don't fu… you don't mess with frumentarii, not if you want to keep the skin on your back. You only say, and I'll report 'em."

Quintus ignored him. Manius conceded the occasional murmur of acknowledgment, preoccupied as he was, soaked to the skin, frozen and picking his way through the sludge and mire of a working port.

The captain left them at the mansio's entrance. He bowed and cringed, all the while cursing his sailors. Quintus, sparing him not a glance, strode through the double doors into the lobby leaving Manius to struggle after with the baggage.

For such a grubby port it was a fine building, standing as it did at the gateway to a major province, the first and last hostel for imperial officialdom. Inside Quintus bade the door slave summon the steward, who appeared – burly, bald and barely civil as he watched Quintus wringing seawater from his tunic onto the marble floor. Without looking up, Quintus demanded rooms and food for the night and horses for the following day. Impassive, the steward replied that none of this was possible without notice. The mansio was closed for the winter for all but the most important visitors, but there were inns in Dubris which would no doubt oblige.

Quintus held out a hand for the document Manius had ready.

"Our commission," Quintus said.

Wary, the steward took the document, examined it.

"Quintus Suetonius Lupus?" His eyebrows raised, he looked up. Quintus nodded. "And Manius Suetonius Lupus? This your son?"

"Adopted son."

The steward read on, skimming, muttering. Quintus interrupted: "Do you know of a man named Arpocras?"

"Mmm?" said the steward, raising his gaze.

"I said, Arpocras. A dealer in dogs."

"I did."

"What d'you mean: did?"

"He died last week."

"How?"

"Dunno. Seizure, I think. I'm no doctor."

He scanned the document further and then stopped.

"Frumentarii?" he said and swallowed.

Ah, that magic word, more potent that any witch's moon spell: frumentarii, the eyes and ears of the Emperor himself, responsible to him, reporting to him – and may the gods have mercy on those of whom they reported unfavourably.

§

Small wonder then, that half an hour later they were sweating the salt from their skins in the mansio's baths, a jar of the house's best between them – a Marmertine – and a fine dinner ordered.

"And after dinner, we'll find ourselves a tavern," said Quintus, smacking his lips over the wine.

Manius grimaced.

"What's wrong with that?"

"I'm tired. Anyway, shouldn't we discuss this fellow Arpocras?"

"What's to discuss? You heard the man, Arpocras is dead. Agents are always dying – they're very annoying like that."

But he fingered his beard, looking uneasy.

"Then perhaps we should look over our original orders, consider how to proceed in Londinium," said Manius.

"What's to look over? We're to place ourselves at the disposal of the provincial procurator Horatius Buteo and deliver a letter to the governor Caerellius Priscus, a copy of which – unknown to Priscus – also goes to the procurator."

Manius knew this was unremarkable. The procurator reported to the Emperor, not to the provincial governor and, for that reason, usually had the job, along with tax and fiscal duties, of supervising any frumentarii in a province. But Manius wasn't happy and, besides, he didn't relish, in his weakened condition, a session in a dockside tavern with Quintus.

"Shouldn't we at least think about what we might find in Londinium?"

"Think all you like. There's no purpose to it – not without this Arpocras to enlighten us. We'll find out soon enough."

"You believe we're here for some particular aim, or… just exiled?"

Quintus' thick black brows met and he cast a sly glance at Manius.

"Exiled? What rubbish!"

"Is it? Isn't it a punishment posting?"

Quintus snarled and waved the youngster away. But he made no denial. What point? They both knew that punishment was merited, because Quintus had already failed his new Emperor. Commodus' accession, only seven months ago, had begun amid furious rumours of a plot against him. One plotter, Dermius Balbus, had been arrested by the Praetorian Guard. An urgent message went to Quintus, calling him to interrogate Balbus but he'd been in his cups and, by the time Manius had sobered him, the Praetorians had – predictably – already tortured Balbus to death, also killing any chance of extracting the names of co-conspirators.

Once the panic was over, other questions had been asked. The old emperor, Marcus Aurelius, had indulged him, but Quintus had enemies in the service who'd persuaded Commodus that a long posting in a cold, distant province would prove chastening for his father's old favourite.

Quintus rumbled into his beard and Manius caught: "Britannia! More of a punishment for me than you know."

§

Commius, the mansio steward, did visit a tavern. He had to go and, as he wrapped his cape tight against wind and rain, he swore. He muttered oaths as he made his way to the docks, scurrying, despite his unwillingness, hugging the shadows of the back streets.

Nothing would normally bring him out on such a night, to that squalid, fetid hole they had the nerve to call an inn. It was late and he had to rise early to see to the furnace and to food and horses and a thousand other fucking things.

It was fucking ridiculous.

Fear had gripped him since he'd opened the mansio's back door a couple of hours ago, to the brat with the message telling him to go. It wasn't the kind of summons you can turn down, not from Tiro the Sicilian – mad Tiro.

Tiro delighted in violence, violence that always went undetected, or at least unpunished. Tiro had protectors.

Commius paused at the inn's door, listening to the voices inside. He nibbled his lip. Had he been too discreet this evening, too prudent, or not prudent enough? Fucking frumentarii. All he fucking needed. Now he had to weigh fear of them against fear of Tiro. With another oath, he pushed the door and entered the low ceilinged, smoky room, in which two or three groups sat, talking low and drinking. Several looked at him and Tibo the pimp raised a lazy hand. Commius returned the greeting and caught the eye of the tavern keeper Philox who was halfway across the room carrying a tray. Philox jerked his pig-tailed head and rolled his eyes towards the rear. Commius nodded and made his way to the door in the far wall and through that to the creaking stairs.

He climbed and stopped at the first door. A light seeped from under it. He tapped and a familiar, rasping voice told him to enter.

In the centre of the tiny room was a rough table, sitting at which, with bottle and beaker, was a tall figure, its face in the shadows cast by a lamp. A finger pointed to a chair opposite. Commius sat.

"Tiro," he said, by way of greeting.

Tiro jerked forward so his unshaven, thin-lipped face was in the light. "You've guests, I hear?"

Commius shrugged, waggled his hands, half laughed. "Just two no-account fellows, I don't see..."

"Who are they?"

"Eh? I dunno, taxmen, administrators..."

"From?"

"Gesoriacum, came today."

"I know. You're supposed to let me know about visitors from Gaul. Why didn't you?"

There was a playful, wheedling tone here which Commius didn't like. It held the promise of something bad.

He forced another laugh. "I was going to."

"When?"

"Tomorrow."

Thin lips peeled back; a snarl of yellowing teeth; an instant's fear, before Tiro's left hand snaked out, grabbed Commius' bald pate and shoved it down towards the table and towards the other hand which pressed the point of a blade against the corner of Commius' eye.

"Tomorrow could be too late. Who are they?"

"I dunno!" gasped Commius, frantic, squirming, striving to drag his head away. "I told you, I dunno, probably auditors. They wanted to know... they wanted to know..."

"Yes? What?"

"About Arpocras... how he died."

"Oh did they? And why would two auditors be asking about the death of a dog dealer, you dick? The skipper who brought them thinks they're more than auditors. He thinks they're frumentarii." The point of the blade pricked a fraction further. "I need you to tell me things like that, Commius."

Commius squirmed; whimpered. "Please... don't..."

"You don't just let anyone into the mansio. What was their authority?"

"The... the seal of the Imperial Council."

Tiro whistled. "And you thought that could wait 'til morning? Now I must ride for Londinium and it's a filthy night." He removed the blade from Commius' eye, but only to put the point in his nostril. "I would slit your fucking nose... but they might wonder about that."

He hammered the hilt of his knife onto Commius' crown. The mansio steward squealed and his eyes watered, before Tiro hurled him into a corner where he followed with liberal, expert kicks.

"I won't mark your face this time Commius," he panted. "But if this happens again..."

He strode from the room. The mansio steward lay still until he heard his footsteps complete their descent of the stairs. Then he groaned and hugged himself on the floorboards.

Fucking ridiculous.

§

The next day a new storm brought another strong wind and lashing squalls. Quintus and Manius took the road out from under Dubris' famous white cliffs, on a couple of Gallic ponies, with a third beast for their baggage. The steward, eager to please, had offered them his best horses but, neither being a confident rider, they both declined.

With slower mounts the journey to Londinium took three weary days of low light in wind and rain, riding with shoulders hunched against the weather and soaking clothes chafing the skin. Everything Manius had heard or read about this province was being confirmed. Sure, Cantium, the region through which they passed, boasted some impressive villas and estates lining the road. The country, while barren at that season, gave promise of rich produce, with fine-looking pastures and ploughed fields between the woodland. They passed prosperous villages of squat, round houses and a few small towns, boasting decent enough public buildings. But it was grey, and so cold.

It wasn't unlike Northern Gaul, but the air was fresher, keener and the wind had an edge. It came from over the great ocean where there was no more known world and it carried with it possibility – or threat. It added to something that was unsettling – or unsettled – about the place.

Manius wondered: was it in the wind? Or was it in his mind? Was he haunted by tales of the British barbarians, of their savage customs and animal practices?

They met few on the road apart from couriers, army officers and a handful of traders. The natives seemed much like the Gauls, with outlandish flowing moustaches and plaited hair. They were respectful and Quintus, who knew Celtic, had little trouble making himself understood to the few with no Latin.

One night in Durovernum they stayed in a mansio; on the other nights they found inns. It was in the Durovernum mansio, over dinner in a private parlour, that Manius again probed Quintus.

"The governor, Caerellius Priscus, what manner of man is he?"

"You've met him."

"When?"

"You wouldn't remember. You were just a child, when your father presented you to Priscus who was then a legionary legate. I doubt you were four."

"Tell me about him."

Quintus shrugged. "Typical patrician, typical politician. He's charming;

he's shrewd. The late emperor valued him and under him he prospered politically and financially and became one of the richest in the Senate. You know what Meander said: he's so rich, he has `too many goods to make room'."

Manius laughed and completed the verse: "`He's so rich, he has no room to shit'."

Quintus chuckled. "Aye well, when he was consul that cleared a little house space. What, with paying the price of office: the bribes, the games, the entertainment. But the late emperor gave him his reward, only months before he died. How? Why, with the governorship of Britannia – the plum posting."

"A plum?"

"Why the surprise? Oh do try to think boy. There are more troops stationed in this province than any other in the Empire. So? So, commanding them as governor means great prestige and opportunities for enrichment, which matters so much to our masters these days." He rubbed his thumb and forefinger together and curled his lip. "Think of all those army contracts to be awarded, all those clients coming to you to ask for an officer's post for a son or a nephew. Think of the officers who want a cushy posting on your staff and of all the profitable goods you can get shipped to Gaul courtesy of the fleet. Don't you worry, Priscus is practised enough to more than recompense himself for his consulship.

"What of the provincial procurator?"

"Horatius Buteo? An old woman, from what little I know. They say that like many weak men he agrees with whoever he spoke to last. Best line for him is Homer: `Men praise most the song which rings newest in their ears'. He's a North African; made his money trading slaves; bought himself a knighthood."

Manius well knew what Quintus thought of that, even without the accompanying sneer: insupportable that a tradesman could buy into a once honourable order; worse, that this entitled him to a theatre seat in front of those – like Quintus – from decent Roman yeoman stock. Proof – if proof were needed – of how far Rome had fallen from its noble origins. Manius could have written the speech.

But Quintus surprised him with a harsh laugh. "Still, it works well. Giving provincial procurators responsibility for the frumentarii when they're just men of business at best, or greasy auctioneers at worst, that strengthens our hand. They may be fly with the abacus but they know nothing of our work, which means they'll believe anything we tell them."

"And if Priscus is a patrician and Buteo from trade, how are they likely to get on?"

"Oh, make no mistake, Priscus will despise Buteo for what he is, but he's enough of a politician not to show it. But, no, they won't get on. Governor and procurator never do. They're not supposed to. The governor's word is damned near law and he answers only to the Emperor, but the procurator controls the purse strings, and he also answers directly to the Emperor. He's a check on the governor, hence our reporting to him."

So, they resolved – or Quintus ruled – they should go immediately to Horatius Buteo upon their arrival in Londinium.

§

Horateus Buteo, the provincial procurator, wrung his podgy hands, heart hammering. Halotus, the Bythian, an associate of Arpocras, was responsible. Halotus had arrived trembling in Buteo's study minutes earlier, couldn't sit still but kept jumping to the window, checking the street.

Oh curse the fellow, weren't his nerves bad enough – and now this. He'd feared it would come to this. He'd been dreading it for weeks. Yes, weeks since the atmosphere in the city had grown menacing. Whispers and rumours had intercepted glances that passed unspoken signals, conversations were hurriedly cut short at his approach. There'd been a sense of crisis building and Priscus, who should've been a calming influence, had only made matters worse, voicing suspicions of plots, trusting nobody and making oblique – and not so oblique – comments about Tiberius Flavius Fimbria and his influence.

Merciful heavens! What had all that to do with him? He was a provincial procurator, an accountant. He was a private man, a stay-at-home man. He'd no interest in intrigue, but only sought that his figures should tally.

"Tell me what you heard," he squeaked.

"Word's gone out," said Halotus, over his shoulder, still peering through the window.

"Word? What word?"

"Paid blades. Generous payment promised. They say you're as good as dead, to be killed this very evening."

Buteo wept.

§

The young slave was nervous in the presence of his new superior, Saoterus. For one thing, Saoterus was a freedman and they were always harder on the unfree. Second, though not yet thirty, Saoterus was one of the most powerful men in Rome, the Emperor's chamberlain and – some whispered – his bedfellow.

This was the young slave's first time in this office, perhaps the finest in the Domus Flavia, with richly painted walls, exquisite mouldings and large windows. But it was a working room, with documents scattered over Saoterus' broad desk and piled on cupboards, cabinets and even in heaps on the floor. Saoterus sat behind that desk and the young slave perched on a stool, a wax tablet on his knee, pen in hand.

Saoterus uncoiled his long body, rising to stroll to the window to look out over northern Rome, over the Velia down to the Sacra Via and then across to the slopes of the Oppian Hill, still sharp in a crisp winter light, despite some city smoke.

He spoke over his shoulder: "So, you've been sent to me from the Treasury. They say you're bright." He turned to his young secretary and added in a softer voice: "Your eyes are certainly very bright."

Saoterus' own brown eyes twinkled and he smiled. The young slave blushed and looked down.

Saoterus contemplated him, then turned back to the window.

"They also say you're discreet. I suppose you'd have to be in the Treasury. I can take it, can't I, that you'll never repeat anything you learn in this room? You do know the consequences?"

"Yes sir"

"Good. We need new blood here in the Palatium. The old emperor's people were set in their ways. The new emperor has his own methods. He doesn't like to trouble himself with detail as Marcus Aurelius did. Therefore we must make summaries for him of the important facts of a matter, that he might make a judgement. You understand?"

"Yes sir."

"Good. Then we'll start by drafting a memorandum for him. We begin in the usual style: `August Caesar, noble emperor, etcetera. We write to you concerning the situation in Britannia' and so on and so forth. You get the idea? You know what to put there?"

"Yes sir."

"Excellent. Well then, we want a few facts about Britannia. Do you know any?"

"I... I know it's a huge island, off the coast of Gaul."

"Even the Emperor knows that. Do some research. Your old colleagues at the Treasury can help. It's a rich province. Find out and write down what the tax revenues are; they must be enormous. Most of the main island is in the empire and has been for a hundred and fifty years, it's civilised and prosperous, if cold, damp and foggy. The outer regions and islands are barbaric but give only sporadic trouble. As I said, it's a rich province and that justifies its huge military establishment. Now, have you got all that?"

"Yes sir."

"Excellent. Now we move to the crux of the matter." Saoterus cleared his throat. "`The current governor is Caerellius Priscus...' we need give no background on that old fox. `There have been rumours that his loyalty to yourself, August Caesar, is suspect. We have therefore, as previously agreed, taken steps to provide a counterweight in Britannia, in the person of Tiberius Flavius Fimbria.

"Flavius Fimbria, however, is also known to harbour political ambitions and has associated with parties not necessarily sympathetic to yourself, Noble Emperor. However, the antipathy between himself and Priscus is so intense as to render any alliance highly unlikely.' Hmm, I'll probably take that out of the final draft, it's the kind of detail that only bores the Emperor. Are you keeping up?"

"Yes sir."

"Good. You're very quick. We shall get along."

Saoterus treated him to another smile and a lingering gaze. The young man gave a nervous cough. "Thank you, sir."

"We will continue thus: `Reports from the provincial procurator Horatius Buteo are confused and alarming, talking of rumours of conspiracy and treason on the part of both Priscus and Flavius Fimbria. We believe the provincial procurator's correspondence is being intercepted and we may not have the full story. Clearly we must have first-hand intelligence and, to this end, it was agreed that we should send a frumentarius: namely Quintus Suetonius Lupus. He should be in Britannia by now and we await his first reports. There were questions as to his suitability but his presence was specifically suggested by…' Er, leave that blank, I shall insert it myself." Another glance and another smile. "From him and Buteo we need sure information on the loyalty and intentions of Priscus and Flavius Fimbria. In some letters Buteo has claimed that the situation in Britannia is threatening to become dangerous. It is possible that the arrival of Suetonius Lupus may bring matters to a head. That could work in our interests, for any conspirators will wish to ensure that he makes no reports, and if he – as one of the Noble Emperor's frumentarii – were to be liquidated, then Rome would be justified in taking the most extreme measures.' Now, have that written up for me. Did you find it interesting?"

"I understood little, but what I did I found interesting."

Saoterus laughed. "A good answer. Yes you're bright, you'll do well."

This emboldened the young slave. "Do I understand, your honour that this Suetonius Lupus is being sent… as bait?"

All trace of laughter drained from Saoterus' face and when he spoke his voice was metallic. "Why ask that? Do you know this Suetonius Lupus perhaps? Have the frumentarii been at you?"

"No your honour, of course not! I… I only… "

His voice tailed off into nervous mumbling. Saoterus continued to stare at him until a thin smile returned to his lips.

"Don't try running before you can walk. When you have your draft we'll go through it together. Until then, you'd better remember the importance of absolute discretion. This is delicate matter and important. Britannia is far away but events there could bring all this… " he raised his arms to the ceiling and its beautiful mouldings, "… down around our ears."

§

Buteo stuffed the last handful of documents into the study fire and, as the yellow flames licked at the sheets and warmed his face, allowed himself a pause, no longer having to cast around – flapping and twittering – among his files for further incriminating words.

He felt sick. The heat made it worse. A rush of saliva filled his mouth and he feared he'd vomit. He felt terrified.

He shook, his skin crawled and scalp tingled. He started at every noise. And there was so much noise. His slaves were hurrying through the house, shouting, banging doors, packing essentials and preparing for hasty departure.

Dear Jupiter have mercy! As soon as Halotus had gone, he, the provincial procurator, had been like an infant, oh he freely admitted it, clutching his steward Theon and gibbering, craving consolation and direction.

And Theon – blessed Theon – had taken control, issued orders to the household to pack what was necessary, had secured safe accommodation and made arrangements to leave the city.

He heard Theon's discreet cough, familiar, but still enough to have Buteo whirling around in terror.

"Master, it's time we left."

"Thank heavens! Everything's packed? Everything's ready? Good, well done. And Arpocras, you sent word? You told him to meet the frumentarii and tell them on no account to come to Londinium?"

The old steward nodded and, as Buteo whimpered his relief, he held out his master's cloak, and fastened it around his shoulders. Then he led him like a child to the hallway where the household of six slaves stood wide-eyed and pale, clutching bags and bundles. Theon appraised them, then waved them through the door. He took Buteo by the shoulder and ushered him after.

On the dark street, Buteo turned. "Theon, which way, where? "

"I know the way sir, follow me."

They crossed the street and had started towards the Forum, when they stopped, frozen by voices, loud and aggressive, coming from ahead.

"Oh no, no," clucked Theon and shepherded them all into an alleyway to their right, down which tradesmen gained access to the townhouses on either side, but with no exit. Theon put his finger to his lips and waved his hand at Buteo and slaves alike. They cowered in the shadows as the voices grew louder. Then they saw, across the street, a dozen men brazenly brandishing flaming torches, staves and swords.

Buteo drew himself back into the darkness, pressing himself into the rough brickwork. He listened to the men heading towards his house. He didn't like what he heard.

§

Quintus and Manius reached Londinium on a day still cold enough for a cape close fastened and a scarf up to the chin, but it didn't rain and a weak sun occasionally peeped through a fleeting gap in the clouds.

Late in the afternoon, as the light faded, they left their ponies and shouldered their bags at the imperial posting house by the gate at the southern end of the long bridge over the Tamesis. They were waved through. Some two hundred paces before them was Londinium, its massive timber wharves stretching more than half a mile along the north bank, against which were crowded more than a score of ships, moored for the winter and behind them were ranks of warehouses. The whole city smoked and glowered over the broad river in the dusk, its lights shimmering on the oily black waters. As they passed over the bridge, jostled by many travellers, they could also make out on the far bank to the left a splendid palace of light stone, its terraced gardens running down to the Tamesis. A respectful distance from this palace, on three sides, were tightly packed wooden buildings.

Once over the bridge, Quintus approached a soldier, a beneficiarius who was supervising the traffic, for the whereabouts of the provincial procurator's house.

They went as directed, moving amid a greater crowd: Britons, Gauls, Greeks, even swarthy Africans and many Germans. It was a bewildering mix of dress: peasant hooded cloaks of coarse blue broadcloth, turbans, skull caps, barbarian trousers, plaid of many colours and – good to see – a party of respectable, if boisterous, young citizens with cloaks clutched tight over togas, hurrying, no doubt, to some smart dinner party. All striding out, as if eager to be indoors and warm before dark. Even a file of half a dozen slaves, dragging their chains through the mud and filth, moved smartly, needing no coaxing from their driver's lash. The air was damp and heavy with the stench of smoke and grease and, as the day died, a chill penetrated to the very bone. But indoors there was promise of relief and ease and Quintus and Manius passed taverns whose open doors revealed the crackling glow of fires and the welcome moist smell of ale. Outside, the press of the crowd thrust them into the roadway, to be driven back by rumbling wagons throwing up muddy water and by the oaths and whip cracks of the draymen. The wooden buildings were tightly packed, squeezing each other out and over the street and signs boasted their wares: wine, meat, fish, leather, oil, bread, quackery and whores. Manius noticed, discreetly cramped between a cobbler's and a potter's, a small temple to Cybele and her vile castration cult. He shuddered.

The press thinned abruptly as the road opened into the Forum, at the far end of which was a huge basilica. Manius gawped but was interrupted by Quintus: "Come boy, we don't want to be knocking on Buteo's door after dark."

As it was, they didn't need to knock on the door of the fine town house to which they were directed by an oyster seller, situated on a narrow street of similarly opulent buildings. That door was half open, the lobby inside dark, and every window unlit. Quintus shrugged and pushed the door wide. He called: "Is anyone there?"

Silence.

He looked back, surveyed the empty street, then jerked his head for Manius to follow him inside where they dropped their bags. Outside, it was now nearly dark and in that corridor they had barely light enough to see their way as they crept along, calling tremulous enquiries.

"Something's wrong," Manius whispered.

"Aye," said Quintus and he drew his sword. Manius copied with a trembling hand,

After turning a corner, they made out a flickering light from one room. It was the shrine to the household gods where a votive lamp was burning. They used that to light two more lamps and continued. They looked into each room: dining room, bedrooms, gymnasium, library and even slaves' quarters and found all ransacked. The flickering lights revealed to their staring eyes cupboards spewing their contents, drawers yanked out and upended, bedclothes strewn and pillows slashed, books and papers scattered: a house pillaged.

The kitchen was the final room and they found it like the others. Quintus swore.

"What does this mean?" Manius whispered.

"Nothing good."

"What will we do?"

Quintus shook his head. "I don't know. Let me think." He sank into a chair by the great kitchen table and reached for a jar of wine and goblet.

"Who has done this?"

"Be quiet, let me think." Then, a minute later: "We'll stay the night."

"What? What if whoever did it comes back?"

"So much the better. Then we'll know who it is. What's our alternative? We can light the fire here and get some bedding. There'll be food in the parlour… and more wine."

Manius opened then shut his mouth. This was chilling. This house had been violated, the home of the second most senior official in a major province. Only the desperate – or powerful – would commit such an affront to Rome. Surely they should immediately report it to the governor and place themselves firmly behind him and his hundreds of beneficiarii?

He kept this to himself, lit the kitchen fire with his lamp and fetched their bags from the lobby, taking care to close and bar the front door.

Quintus was right, there was food in the parlour: good food. They found oysters and sea urchins alive in brine; and a sow's innards; fine fish sauce; eggs; asparagus and some fragrant apples. Manius was no great cook, and Quintus was worse, but they made a decent enough meal, helped by a couple of jars of mellow Surrentine. They ate by the warmth and glow of the fire which, together with the lamps, entertained by flitting shadows on the plaster walls to the sound of steady drumming of rain in the courtyard behind the window. Hardly Spanish dancing girls and Syrian harpists but agreeable enough.

Manius sighed, pushed his plate away and reached for an apple. "The food was fresh."

Quintus grunted, picking at his teeth with his thumbnail. "So we know the house hasn't long been long deserted – a day, two at most."

"What happened?"

"How can I know? The house was abandoned and then ransacked. Or the other way round. Were the occupants taken, arrested and then the house searched? There's no way of knowing. But the matter's serious. Here, reach me over my bag."

He took it, unfastened the strap and felt inside for his document case. "Here's the procurator's copy of the governor's letter. Let's see what that tells us."

"It's under imperial seal!"

"And we're on the Emperor's business. We're ordered to report to the procurator and he has disappeared, it's our duty to find out why and where he might be. This," he tapped the letter, "could tell us."

He broke the seal and unfurled the document. He peered at it in the dim light, holding it close to his narrowed eyes. In a few seconds he read the single sheet. Then he swung himself off his chair and threw it into the fire, ignoring Manius' horrified squeaks.

He turned. "I don't want to be found with that."

"Why? What?"

"It confirms what appears to have been an earlier order to the governor, giving Tiberius Flavius Fimbria command of the armies in the North – Sixth Victrix at Eboracum and all auxiliary units on the frontier – and he holds that command directly from the Emperor. All other units, including Second Augusta at Caerlon and Twentieth Valera Victrix at Dewa, remain under the command of the governor."

"I don't understand. Who's Tiberius Flavius Fimbria?"

Quintus rubbed his eyes, as if massaging his memory. "He made a name for himself under the late Emperor in his first campaign against the Sarmatians and later took his seat in the Senate. A few years ago he had some role in Gaul, where there was an unpleasantness over executing some Jews or Christians – Christians I believe. He acted within the law, but it wasn't the kind of thing the Emperor approved of so he was sent to Britannia to command Second Augusta. Generally regarded as a bit of a shit… and a prick."

"What's the Emperor doing with this appointment?"

"Overturning all precedent, that's what. It's unheard of for a governor to have the command of troops removed from him. Why not replace him as governor, if he's not thought to be up to it… or to be trusted? This is a humiliation for Caerellius Priscus."

He heaved himself from his chair to fetch another wine jar.

"One thing's for sure," he said, on his return. "We've been landed in a hell of a queer set-up. Procurators disappearing, governors circumvented, emperors behaving like…" He trailed off, muttering as he poured the procurator's wine.

Manius knew Quintus had been devoted to the late emperor Marcus Aurelius and that made him loth to criticise his successor Commodus, who so forgot his imperial dignity that he even entered the amphitheatre as gladiator.

"So what do we do?"

"We'll drink some more of this admirable wine, then we sleep and, tomorrow we see the governor. We tell him the truth. We got here to report to the procurator Buteo, found what we found and stayed because it was so late. We give Governor Priscus his letter – with no mention of the other copy – and see what he has to say."

He proffered more wine which was declined. Manius already felt its effects. He didn't want to be drunk, another Quintus. Just look at him now. How many times had he had to cover for him, sweep up after him? He'd been his late father's dearest friend and Manius owed him much. But he felt no obligation to emulate him.

His adoptive father rolled himself up by the kitchen fire in borrowed blankets and fell into a hoggish slumber. Manius doused the lamps and made his own bed on the other side of the room.

Despite the wine and the day's long journey, he could only manage fitful sleep, never wholly unaware of the rain drumming outside. He rolled over one way, then the other and wrestled with his pillow, but true sleep wouldn't come. It was held at bay by thoughts of Priscus, Buteo, Fimbria, Commodus, Marcus Aurelius, his father, Quintus visiting, sitting up late with his father… drinking… singing old army songs… keeping him awake…

A noise alerted him.

That had been no dream. He'd heard something from the back of the house, near the courtyard. Had he bolted the back door?

He sat up, straining to listen but there was nothing, only Quintus snoring. He must have imagined it, or dreamt it.

Then he did hear a sound. It was distinct and came from the corridor. He scrabbled about in vain for his sword, getting to his feet and clutching the blanket. Whoever it was was raising the latch. In the red light cast by the fire's embers, Manius watched the door begin to open. He sank back against the wall beside it, his heart hammering so loudly he was grateful for Quintus' snores.

The door half opened. A broad figure, shorter than Manius by a head and shoulders, stepped into the room.

Driven by courage or the madness of wine, Manius raised the blanket and fell on the figure, throwing the blanket down over its head. He shouted: "Quintus! Quintus!"

He screamed and this intruder yelled. They rolled round the floor, with the blanket entangling them both. They rolled into the table legs and against the wall, rolled, screaming and shouting, until they were nearly into the fire itself – until Quintus' bellowing brought a halt.

"Silence, rot you!"

Manius pulled the blanket from his face, to see Quintus standing over him, sword in hand.

"Who the hell are you?" he cried. Manius turned to see a woman, portly and middle-aged, with puffy red face and a flattened nose – a slave's face. She sat up moaning and rubbed her elbow.

"Get up. Come on," said Quintus. "Help her."

Manius threw off the blanket and rose, banging his head on the table. He offered her his hand. With a suspicious glare, she took it and, straining, Manius hauled her upright. Quintus waved her into a chair.

"Now, who are you?"

"Oh, oh," she moaned, still rubbing her elbow: "Una."

"You speak Latin?" She nodded. "Una is your name?" Another nod.

"What are you doing here?"

She looked indignant: "I'm the cook."

"The cook? You mean you are Buteo's cook?"

A nod.

"Where is he? Where is Horatius Buteo? Who has ransacked the house?"

Una's eyes narrowed. "Who wants to know?"

"I want to know, woman!"

Una wriggled in sudden affront, folding and unfolding her arms. "The master told us we had to flee."

"When?"

"The day before yesterday."

"Why?"

"Men were coming to kill him, kill us all."

"What men?"

She shrugged.

"Where is he now? Where has Buteo gone?"

Una's piggy little eyes screwed up again. She shook her head.

"You'd better tell me," growled Quintus.

She shook her head and stuck out her chin.

"Woman, I'm a frumentarius, I know ten thousand ways to make you tell me."

"What's a frumentarius?"

With a heavy sigh, Quintus continued the interrogation. She refused to say where her master was, though she let slip that he wasn't in the city. Quintus assured her that they were Buteo's friends, there to help him. But Una was stubborn and loyal and refused to reveal her master's whereabouts. He clearly wasn't far away because she said she had returned to the house late to avoid being seen. She had come to retrieve her best skillet which, she observed tartly, she could see they had used. What was that in it? Here she hauled herself to her feet to inspect it – oh, the sow's innards. Oh, and they had had the sea urchins too had they? Was there anything else she could get them while she was there?

"No!" rapped Quintus, "And we're not here to talk about sea urchins!"

He breathed heavily, filling the kitchen with stale wine fumes. "If you won't answer my questions, perhaps you'll take a message to your master. Tell him Quintus Suetonius Lupus is looking for him, tell him – oh, never mind, I'll write it down." He snapped his fingers at Manius who produced a tablet and stylus. Quintus scribbled on it and thrust it at her.

"Here. Give that to your master."

She took it sullenly. Quintus made a dismissive gesture and turned, back to his bedding.

Una stared at her skillet and then at Manius, who reddened, took it and gave it a quick wipe. She snatched it then stamped out, slamming the door.

"Well, at least we've established communications with the provincial procurator," said Quintus, and pulled his blanket over his head.

Chapter Three

"My dear Quintus Suetonius. How are you?"

Gaius Caerellius Priscus, governor of Britannia, senator and former consul hurried across the mosaic and Quintus took his outstretched hand.

Quintus stood with Manius in a grand chamber of Priscus' palace, before windows overlooking the Tamesis and the wooded bank beyond. They had been led there by a succession of starched and shining centurions and adjutants, whose boots echoed as they marched them through the long corridors, passing them to the next immaculate, stone-faced staff officer: regular soldiers, who affected to despise frumentarii but were damned careful not to push that too far. Now a pair stood tucked in the corners of the chamber, observing.

The governor turned his ruddy beaming face towards Manius. "And this must be – no, it can't be – not young what's-his-name: Manius Lucretius' boy?"

Quintus confirmed it. Manius simpered, coloured and took Priscus' hand.

"Well, well how he's grown, but then they do, don't they? Hey?"

He called for wine and waved them to chairs around a spectacular orbis, its highly polished surface supported on ornate carved ivory legs. Manius admired it and Priscus' smile broadened.

"It is magnificent isn't it? Moroccan cypress, carved from a single trunk. Cost me an absolute fortune. A reprehensible indulgence, but you know me Quintus Suetonius, I have few vices; hey, hey? Ah, the wine."

A slave girl placed leather pads on the orbis under the goblets and jug. Priscus took a deep draught and turned to Quintus, his expression now serious, his manner brisk.

"Quintus Suetonius, before anything else, what's this alarming report my adjutant gives me on Horatius Buteo?"

Quintus told him what they'd found at the procurator's house – omitting Una.

"The whole house – empty and despoiled you say?"

Quintus nodded. Priscus turned to Manius, open-mouthed and eyebrows raised for confirmation.

"But this is… I'm at a loss, an utter loss." He rose, paced towards the windows and back, rubbing his chin. He opened his mouth, then closed it and beckoned one of his officers. Priscus whispered something and the officer saluted, swivelled on his heel, and marched off. Priscus resumed his seat, his lips pursed.

"I've ordered that the house be secured." He paused before leaning over the orbis towards Quintus.

"Quintus Suetonius, it would be highly improper to enquire as to your orders. But if you can share anything that would shed any light on this..."

Quintus shook his head. Priscus added: "Of course, forgive me, I understand."

"No," said Quintus, "it's not that I won't tell you; I have nothing to tell you. We were ordered to report to Horatius Buteo, but he wasn't there. All I can tell you is that I bring you a letter from Rome – Manius..."

Manius produced the letter and handed it to Priscus, who broke the seal and scanned it, while Manius, ostensibly admiring the plaster and mouldings on the walls, observed the governor's face. It was expressionless. When he'd finished, Priscus refurled the document.

He leaned back, smiling again. "Well, tell me: how is Rome?"

Quintus told him: crime was rampant, prices extortionate, no sleep at night from the racket of wagons not allowed into the city during the day, shoddily built tenements always collapsing, and when not collapsing, burning to the ground and taking whole districts with them. Priscus chuckled and said he was glad some things remained constant in a world of bewildering change.

"Talking of change: our new emperor – how's he doing?"

"I believe things go on much as usual."

Priscus stared at him and then, without looking at Manius, pointed at him. "This boy, does he have your confidence?"

"He does."

"Then let's speak frankly, Quintus Suetonius. The Emperor's young and inexperienced. There are those who'd exploit that, who have his ear. That's not good for him, or for Rome."

"Inexperienced? Didn't his father make him joint emperor for the past three years?"

"When he was fifteen! Oh really, you know as well as I that Commodus shared power in no meaningful sense. His father died too soon and that's the tragedy – for Commodus and for us."

Quintus, stroking his beard, surveyed Priscus, before replying, his voice low and slow. "Perhaps, but Marcus Aurelius is dead; and Commodus is Emperor."

Priscus held Quintus' gaze. "Yes, and don't those of us who served his father – and loved him – have a duty to make Commodus a good emperor?"

"Make him?"

"Help him, if you prefer. Advise him, influence him, whatever word you choose; you know what I mean."

"Do I? Oh, I know you want to see Commodus do what's right – who'd argue with that? But I'm not clear: how you'd like to see that achieved?"

"There are factions in Rome and I fear the wrong faction is close to the

Emperor, in ascendance in the Imperial Council. They say – and it pains me to repeat this," he glanced around and whispered, "that the young Emperor is headstrong, even vicious, and easily led."

"Who says that?"

"Many. I suspect you do."

Quintus laughed, a harsh bark. "Oh no, I'm too careful for that."

Priscus smiled. "You're a true frumentarius. Study him, young Manius – I presume you took your father's name. Aye Manius – study him well, you'll learn a lot. Quintus Suetonius, you give nothing away and I don't blame you. But I've spoken as plainly as I dare and you should take that as a pledge and as a security, because I've placed myself somewhat in your hands, have I not?"

Quintus continued to look at him.

Priscus sprang to his feet.

"I shall have a room found for you. You'll be my guests for dinner – both of you. Until then, I shall have the most rigorous inquiries made into this business of the provincial procurator. That worries me and I fear it's not unconnected to the other matters I've touched on."

He called for his chamberlain to provide them with rooms and see to their wants and, swept off amidst a swarm of staff officers.

Manius had never before met such men: urbane, polished, at ease with themselves and with others and, most of all, at ease with power. As Quintus' apprentice, Manius had dealt with fellow frumentarii and others around Quintus' rank: men who swore much or articulated little. Or, with the hired ruffian weasel-faced informer or the whining minion who'd betray for a fistful of denarii. And these were creatures to be met in the shadowy corners of greasy taverns or low brothels, transacted with in muttered, reluctant whispers. This world of palaces, fabulous wealth and self-assured command was new – and alluring.

Their adjoining rooms were well appointed. A slave was assigned to them, and after changing for the baths, Manius sent him off with their togas to be laundered, starched and pressed before the evening. That done, he sat on Quintus' bed while he looked out of the window onto the terraced garden which ran down to the Tamesis.

"So, what d'you make of that?"

Quintus shrugged. "Nothing out of the ordinary. I shouldn't worry about it."

"Worry? What we heard was treason, or close to it."

Quintus said: "Perhaps you're right. Perhaps I should've sent you from the room."

"Oh, that's just unreasonable!"

Quintus faced him. "Our job is knowledge, but sometimes the less you know the better."

"And tonight, when he starts again? Will you send me from the room, while you treat with him?"

"I'll do neither. I'll listen to what he has to say, and that's all. Look, men like Priscus – politicians – they're always plotting. It's as necessary to them as eating or breathing. We know things they don't, so they seek our support, or at least indifference. However much I sympathise with what he had to say, I've lived long enough to tread carefully."

"But you don't approve of the new emperor."

"But he is the emperor. I served his father faithfully and would've served him to the death. To betray his son would be to betray him. But if the son himself is betraying the father's work... Come, we're jumping at shadows, let's bathe."

But Manius still had his concerns and these nagged at him later, even as he and Quintus relaxed in the palace's opulent baths, within broad colonnades of Laconian marble, as they tossed a ball to and fro in the gymnasium and then rolled dice.

Quintus had been careful not to compromise himself, but he hadn't refused to have anything to do with Priscus or his schemes. Manius knew he'd revered the old emperor, Marcus Aurelius, and he also knew – how could he fail to know who'd had to listen to him so often after his third jug of wine – how little he thought of the new emperor and his friends. He also knew Quintus was getting worse – drinking more and caring less. He was capable of overstepping the mark. If he did, Manius could be implicated and, at best, what little hope he had of a career – of sharing in that glittering world of Caerellius Priscus – would be blighted. Or, worse, he could end up on the wrong end of a praetorian interrogation. By all the gods above, hadn't Quintus already managed to get him exiled to this miserable island? They returned to their rooms shortly after noon, needing rest after their disturbed night. So, despite Manius' worries, after he'd closed the shutters, he lay down on the soft bed, fell asleep and dreamt of Italy, and of sun.

He woke an hour or two later to a tapping at the door. He rubbed his eyes and listened to Quintus' snores rumbling through the wall. He cursed, rose and went to open the door. He looked up and down the empty corridor. He shrugged, about to return to his bed, when he noticed a woollen bag at his feet. He opened it to reveal the togas he had sent to the laundry; at least he could see Quintus' toga, easily identified by the pink dots of old wine stains. The slave had been as good as his word. Manius picked up the bag, surprised by its weight, and brought it into the room where he extracted Quintus' toga. He reached in for his own, but what he touched wasn't cloth. He yanked open the neck and looked upon Una's best skillet.

Manius ran next door, shook Quintus awake and stuck it under his nose.

"There's a note," Quintus said and prised a writing tablet from the pan.

"I've told you that, but it makes no sense. Is it in code?"

Quintus held the tablet in his palm, squinted at it; began tracing the letters in the wax, muttering and counting. He found a stylus and made his own notes on the tablet's margin.

"Of course it's in code, a child's code. Even you should decipher this. It's reversed, then every third and first letter transposed."

"What does it say?"

Quintus made to give him the tablet, then snatched it back. "Here, I'll read it. It purports to be from Buteo. He summons us to an address tomorrow, an hour after nightfall."

"Will he meet us?"

"I've told you what it says. Here: decipher it yourself, it'll be practice. No, do it here; I want to see you wipe that clean when you've done. Memorise the address. And you'd better remember to take that skillet with us – she values it."

§

A silver salver bearing a plump, tender kid was brought to the table. Surrounding it were lampreys, oysters, snails, asparagus, mushrooms, many kinds of fruit and jugs of a wine which, Priscus informed them, was Alban, which he personally preferred to Falernian. At this Quintus frowned and growled, but still drank deeply.

They stood, jewel-encrusted goblets in hand, in an elegant colonnaded chamber intended for such intimate dinner parties. One end was curtained off, and from there came gentle sounds of timbrel and pandoura.

Once all the food was placed they took to their couches and Priscus dismissed the servants.

"It's better that we can talk freely."

"Without witnesses?" suggested Quintus.

Priscus inclined his head with a smile and raised his eyebrows. "Oh please, do help yourselves, we don't stand on ceremony tonight."

Once they had filled their plates, he told them that the procurator's house had been found as Quintus had described it with no clues as to Buteo's whereabouts or the cause of his disappearance. One of his speculatores had been assigned to secure the property and investigate.

"You've no idea what lies behind this?" asked Quintus.

"I have. But we'll come to that. Here, you must try a lamprey. They're hardly Sicilian but really quite decent."

They ate and drank for a couple of minutes.

"You're aware of the contents of the letter you brought from Rome?" Priscus resumed, dabbing his lips with a napkin.

"No."

"No, how could you be? Well it gives Tiberius Flavius Fimbria command of half the troops in this province – those on the northern frontier – and answerable to Rome, not me."

"That is... unusual."

"It's unheard of! It's the act of an inexperienced emperor who has been badly – or maliciously – advised."

"Maliciously?"

"Quintus Suetonius, this morning I spoke frankly. I intend to continue in that vein."

Quintus nodded.

"Fimbria's family are ambitious. Even more so than the rest of his family. His friends at court constitute a party. He and his people use the Balbus affair, playing upon fears that conspiracy has aroused; they use it to cast suspicion on any potential opponents. But isn't it possible that Balbus was a creature of the Fimbria clan and that brood are the accomplices he never named? Ha, I thought that would interest you."

Manius glanced at Quintus, whose expression was impassive.

"But surely, Quintus Suetonius, I'm telling you nothing you don't already know, or suspect, but I'll spell it out anyway. Here in Britannia, Fimbria commands the Second Augusta in the West. He's popular among many officers in the army and also has a party here in Londinium. Among my princeps praetorii and speculatores, I don't know whom I can trust. He has sought to undermine my position both here and in Rome."

"Why would he do that?"

"At first I thought he wanted the governorship for himself."

"Impossible. He has never been consul."

"With the new order anything seems possible. On the other hand, perhaps he merely sought to have one of his own in the position; you and I could both come up with two or three names, could we not?"

"You said `at first...'"

"Eh? Oh yes. But later his campaign against me seemed to crystallise around the north of the province. He has been arguing, both here, and to Rome, that the situation is dangerous, close to insurrection."

"Is he right?"

"Of course not! There's always discontent amongst the Brigantes..."

"Brigantes?"

"Yes, a wild people in a wild country – barbarians to the bone and never happy under Roman rule. Strictly speaking they're a confederation, a grouping of clans: the Gabrantovices, Latenses, Setanii and others. You'll remember, there was a major rising some twenty years ago suppressed by Julius Verus."

"I remember."

"Well, after that, the Brigantes and their chieftains were deprived of much of their land. Some made their peace with Rome, have become citizens and serve as magistrates. Others haven't been so easily reconciled. Eleven years ago, under my predecessor, there was another threat of war, but thanks to a mixture of conciliation and threats on his part, this was averted."

"The situation now?"

Priscus took a hurried swallow of wine. "I honestly don't believe it to be much different from what it has been for years. Oh, there's the occasional incident and constant rumours, but nothing to worry us. But Fimbria persists in claiming a serious threat of rebellion. His aim – and now he has half achieved it – is to alarm the Emperor into giving him – as the only man who really appreciates this so-called threat – command of the army in Britannia."

"Why?"

"Hey?"

"Why? Why does he want command of the troops?"

Priscus pushed his plate aside and toyed with his goblet.

"Now we come to the heart of the matter; and you and your... your son are taken into my deepest confidence and share my deepest concerns. What you do with this is, of course, up to you. But you'll realise that I speak with the Emperor's best interests at heart."

"Go on."

Manius' hand trembled as he replaced his goblet on the table. He was party to the highest politics of the empire. For a second he believed Priscus would dismiss him, as the governor gave him a brief appraising stare, but then resumed.

"There are some forty thousand troops in this province – the largest garrison in the Empire. Imagine, if Fimbria gained command them all and took just three quarters over to Gaul, where he also has friends in the legions."

"He could make an attempt on Rome?"

"That's exactly what I'm saying. Fortunately, the Emperor, no doubt influenced by wiser heads, has left two legions answerable to me. Hedging bets, hey? But it worries me that the Second Augusta has hitherto been Fimbria's and he'll have the loyalty of its officers, though the gods only know how that man inspires loyalty – everyone else hates him. There it is, a divided command, but I suspect that, when he goes north, Fimbria will do everything in his power to provoke the very rebellion he's warning of and will say to Rome, `I told you so', and then be given overall command."

Quintus reached for the wine jug. "Have you evidence for any of this?"

"I've told you the Emperor's instructions regarding the command. How can such an extraordinary step be explained, other than by intrigue? I tell you, Fimbria has followers active here in Londinium. I approached Horatius Buteo – confidentially – with my concerns and he took my point. I believe he was waiting to set you on the scent. But, just as you arrive, what happens? Buteo disappears."

"You suspect Fimbria is behind that?" asked Manius.

He blurted out the question. Quintus fixed him with a glare but Priscus looked grateful.

"It would seem to be a coincidence otherwise, would it not, young man?"

Silenced by Quintus' disapproval, Manius stared at the table.

"Have you nothing to say, Quintus Suetonius?" asked Priscus.

"No. I must think deeply about this before I say anything."

"I'd expect nothing less."

Priscus passed smoothly on to gossip about common acquaintances in Rome, a conversation he maintained with charm and poise for an hour before declaring that he must retire; he'd have an early start in the morning. He urged them to stay and enjoy the wine; indeed, to call for more should they wish it.

Which Quintus did as soon as Priscus had gone. He didn't stay to drink it but stood, jar in hand, and declared that he too must sleep.

"But shouldn't we discuss…" protested Manius.

Quintus jerked his head toward the curtain – music still played behind it – and put a warning finger to his lips. Manius followed him in silence till they reached their rooms. Then he whispered: "Can't we talk?"

"Not tonight." Quintus put his hand on his shoulder. "Tomorrow, after we've seen Buteo. Buteo would seem to be the key." Then he and his jar of Alban left.

§

Far to the north, Titus Caelius Metellus chased the man who fled, stumbling over the tussocks of moorland grass.

This man panted, sobbing with effort and the desperate knowledge that he wasn't running fast enough, confirmed by terror-filled glances over his shoulder. He stumbled once too often and Caelius Metellus slashed the back of his knee, severing the tendon. He screamed, sank to the ground and Caelius Metellus, pausing for one deep breath, seized the man's forehead, wrenched it back and drew his sword across his throat. He held his jerking, choking victim until he was lifeless, before gently releasing him to lie on the boggy ground.

He straightened, shaking his head. Then spun, sword outstretched, at a noise behind.

He relaxed as he recognised Appius Rufius limping out of the darkness. The centurion stopped to wipe his own blade on the damp turf.

"Dead?" asked Caelius Metellus. "Is Nepos dead?"

"Aye, dead."

Caelius Metellus groaned and dashed a tear from his one eye. "Two good men out of a patrol of four dead. How do I break this to the old man?"

He beat one hand against his temple, a gesture Appius Rufius had seen on the stage. Caelius Metellus was a good officer but his histrionics grated at the best of times. And this, for Appius Rufius – surveying the body at their feet, wincing at the stab of pain in his foot and feeling a warning spot of rain on his cheek – was far from the best of times. They were out in a cold night on a wild northern heath, had lost two of their men in a bloody and inglorious skirmish and the country was alive with rebels. He wanted to get back to the fort, report the whole sorry business and climb into his bed. Caelius Metellus, however, the cohort's second in command, a tribune and his superior, had to be indulged. Dear gods just don't let him launch on a rhapsody about honour.

Appius Rufius shrugged. "Good men? Perhaps, but not good soldiers. They fought poorly and paid the penalty. Tell the old man we avenged them; that two Wolves are also dead and he'll take it as fair exchange."

Caelius Metellus grunted and sheathed his blade."He'll not. It'll be evidence I'm failing and this land is slipping away from us."

He strode past the centurion. "Come, let's get the horses. We'll take back our lads' bodies."

"And the enemy? The Britons?"

"Not unreasonable is it, that we leave them to rot?"

"Aye," muttered the centurion, following him, "and would that we could leave the whole bloody country to rot."

§

The next day, Quintus went to see one of Priscus' adjutants to make arrangements to revisit Buteo's house. Quintus collected Manius and, as they made their way back to the Forum, the youngster's insistence wore him down.

"Do I believe Priscus and his accusations against Fimbria? I don't know. He may be right. It has a ring of truth. At least it would, were it anyone but Fimbria. Why? Well, he's ambitious enough, but he's never struck me as a politician and that's why he's so popular with the army – just the kind of blustering, unthinking bully they go for these days."

"So, Priscus is wrong, or lying?"

Quintus shrugged. "Again, I don't know. It's some years since I've seen Fimbria and perhaps he's changed. Though, from what I hear, it's more likely that he's being used by others – his family or some senior members of the Imperial Council. As Priscus said, it's not difficult to think of likely candidates. His popularity with elements in the army and his command of a legion make him a key figure in this game, whether he likes it or not."

Their talk ended at the door of Buteo's house, where the commanding optio scrutinised their written authority and gave them free run of the house.

They searched all the rooms. In the office, they flicked through sheets of tax receipts and assessments. In Buteo's private suite, they examined his lengthy correspondence with relatives in Mauretania about a late uncle's estate. And, in his bedchamber, Quintus sneered over the provincial procurator's collection of erotic sketches. But there was nothing to explain Buteo's disappearance or the house's mysterious abandonment. Still, Quintus insisted on thoroughness and it was mid-afternoon before they returned to the palace. By the time they'd visited the baths and regained their rooms it was growing dark.

"Come," said Quintus. "Let's prepare."

They put on dark hooded capes, beneath which they concealed their swords, to avoid being stopped by a beneficiarii patrol, and slipped daggers into the tops of their boots. It struck Quintus: how many times had he done this? Yet another furtive night-time excursion to meet and to question. But this was different. He wasn't among people and places he knew. He'd operated all over the Empire, but never so blindly as here. He was uneasy, had been ever since Priscus had revealed so much. Why had he done that? Priscus wasn't a man to give something for nothing.

And the boy: why did he seem so nervous? Aye, look at him there now, gnawing his lip and staring into space. What the hell was wrong with him? Quintus tried to think of something to say, to cheer and reassure. He couldn't, so instead he ushered Manius out with ill-humoured grunts.

As they left, Quintus noticed that they drew one or two glances. Not surprising – as known frumentarii, all their comings and goings attracted the thinly veiled interest of Priscus' numerous staff. What of it?

Once clear of the palace, Quintus, who'd memorised the note's directions, led them up one street then along another. They doubled back, darted into a shop, then a tavern. They left the tavern by a back door, hugged the shadows in a series of filthy alleyways and came out – Quintus confident now they weren't followed – by a temple of Mithras. This stood on the banks of a wide stream which ran to join the Tamesis some blocks to the south. Now it was raining, a steady drizzle which glistened on the wool of their capes and made the pavements greasy.

Quintus stopped to get his bearings: the Tamesis was to their left.

"This way," he said and took Manius' arm. They crossed a bridge by the temple and entered a series of narrow streets of mean wooden houses; the noise of drunken, dangerous sailors and the persistent stench of beans and sour wine issued from low taverns.

They asked the way of an old cripple sitting on a stool under the dripping eaves with his begging bowl. Without speaking or looking, he pointed to his left, up the street. Quintus put a hand under the beggar's chin and tilted up his unresisting head so that milky eyes gazed sightlessly up. Quintus dropped a couple of ases into his bowl and they hurried on to a junction and the sign they sought: Via Cantorum.

The neighbourhood improved. The street was wider and the houses, while not large, were at least of dressed stone. It had the look of a quarter which had once been respectable and which now struggled to keep up appearances. They found their house which was in better repair than the others and had a freshly painted door. The windows were shuttered and there was no reply when they knocked. Quintus tried the door which opened.

"Just like Buteo's place," Manius whispered.

Quintus nodded. They crossed the entrance hall to a door which was ajar and from behind which a dim light showed. They pushed it open and entered a small room containing a plain wooden table with four chairs. On the table was a small flickering lamp. The table bore a thin film of dust in which someone had traced: "Q Suetonius. Wait. Buteo."

Chapter Four

Within minutes they heard hurrying footsteps in the street splashing through the puddles. Quintus put a finger to his lips, swept aside his cape; drew his sword and darted behind the door. The footsteps ceased, then someone stepped into the entrance hall and shook their garments with an expression of disgust. The door opened and a man's dark shape filled the frame and Quintus, lumbering from behind the door, seized the front of the man's cloak and, with his sword point to his throat, drew him into the light.

The man – portly, short, swarthy, with black, tight-curled hair – squeaked. His neatly trimmed, pointed beard was thrust forward. He squinted down his nose at the blade.

"Who are you?" demanded Quintus.

"Buteo… Horatius Buteo."

Quintus, his fist still balled around the other's cloak, pulled him closer and peered. He released his grip and patted and smoothed the garment.

"Aye, I think I recognise you. You remember me?"

Buteo's black eyes, like little currants, darted from Quintus to Manius.

"Quintus Suetonius; yes, I remember you. This one?"

Manius bowed and pre-empted Quintus. "Manius Suetonius Lupus, at your service, sir."

Buteo lunged, thrusting Manius aside, to fling himself onto one of the chairs. He wiped his brow with the damp hem of his cloak.

"By all that's holy," he groaned. "Did you have to do that? Look at the state I'm in." He held out his shaking hand. "My nerves, they're ruined, utterly ruined. I've lived in fear for weeks – and terror these past few days." He spun in his seat and gawped at Quintus. "You're certain you weren't followed?"

"Are you certain your accounts balance?"

"What… what do you mean?" Indignation vied with fear.

"That I presume you know your business and you can pay me the same compliment."

Buteo wiped his brow again. "Yes, yes you're right… I have to assume your competence. You're experienced… none more so." His eyes pleaded with Quintus, seeking reassurance. Then, he jerked forward. "But why're you here? I sent word to Dubris that you shouldn't come to Londinium. There's so much danger here. I wanted to meet in Dubris."

"Arpocras was to have told us, I take it?"

"Yes."

"He's dead."

Buteo wrung his hands and whimpered, rocking himself to and fro. Quintus told Manius to open a shutter and watch the street. He pulled up a chair next to Buteo and asked what had been happening.

Buteo ran his fingers through his hair and puffed out his cheeks, shivering and moaning, but, when he could speak, his voice was slow and considered, if still shaken by the occasional tremor. He described how the crisis had crept upon him. They must understand: he was a private man, a man of business, indifferent to politics, immersed in his accounts and, when not working, happier to retreat to his own home and his domestic concerns than to mix with soldiers and other officials. But, eventually, even he'd noticed that there was something wrong in the city – rumours of plots and counter-plots, then factions forming.

"My position was impossible," Buteo wailed, looking at them in appeal. "I had to send intelligence reports to Rome and these could no longer be merely routine accounts culled from frontier garrison returns. No, now I was being urged from all sides to tell Rome this and to tell Rome that. But I didn't know what to write because everything was contradictory. Priscus said one thing; so-and-so would say something else, but then there'd be a whisper from another quarter with a different theory."

"Was one of these theories that Tiberius Flavius Fimbria was exaggerating a threat in the North, to gain command of the army?" asked Quintus.

"Priscus said so and some agreed, but others said the situation on the border was truly serious. How could I know who was right? Figures are figures, there are either a hundred thousand sesterces or there are ninety-eight thousand sesterces and numbers are verifiable. But how do you count opinions, how do you weigh the worth of one whisper against a contradictory rumour? I'm a tax collector, not an intelligence expert. What could I do?"

"What did you do?"

"I wrote to Rome and said I needed help; I presume that's why they sent you."

Manius looked at Quintus. This was the first intimation of why they were there; but Quintus' attention was fixed on the quivering Libyan.

"Nobody wrote to tell you we were coming?"

"No, but I cannot be sure, I cannot even know all my correspondence was getting through to Rome, or all theirs to me."

"That's serious; what made you suspect it?"

"Oh, I tell you, Suetonius Lupus, by this time the plague had infected me. My appetite was gone, my sleep was gone, my tranquillity destroyed and I too began to suspect everyone. In my communications with Rome there were urgent points I raised that were never addressed. Also, I got a letter, privately delivered, from Tita Amatia Aculeo and that truly…"

"From whom?"

"Tita Amatia Aculeo; you must know her, she…"

"I know her. You correspond with her?"

"Oh, perhaps twice. You know she had the old Emperor's ear; they corresponded regularly. When I first came here, I was told she could be of use. They say she's mad; but that nobody else knows better what happens in the North."

"What did she tell you?"

"It was she who warned that my correspondence might be intercepted. She told me that there are powerful factions at work – not only Fimbria's – that their influence was being felt in the North. She was circumspect, you'll understand."

"You destroyed her letter?"

"Her courier had instructions to watch me read it and then burn it."

"Very good. How long ago was this?"

"A month, six weeks. Then things grew worse."

"Go on."

Buteo pulled his cloak around his shoulders, leaned closer to Quintus and lowered his voice, so Manius had to strain to hear and in doing so, forgot to watch the street.

"I had a warning from one of my officers, who told me he'd heard that Fimbria ordered my murder – me, the provincial procurator!"

"You told Priscus?"

"No. Tita Amatia had warned me other factions might be at work, perhaps including Priscus."

"But he would have given you protection, surely?"

"You don't know what it's like. There are rumours of factions in the army, some loyal to Fimbria, some to Priscus, each side cursing the other, demanding allegiance and nobody knowing whether his best friend is really his deadliest enemy. If Priscus were to increase my guard from his beneficiarii or singulares, they are only seconded from the army and so could well be Fimbria's men. By The Unconquered Sun, I might detail my assassin as my chamber guard – how would I know?"

"Where can I find this man who warned you?"

"Ha! In the graveyard. He was fished from the river days after we spoke. Can you not imagine my feelings then? I really began to fear for my sanity."

"Was this man the cause of you fleeing your house?"

"Eh? Not the immediate cause, no. Another fellow – Halotas, a Bythnian merchant – came to see me. He owed me a debt of gratitude over a tax matter. He told me one of his people had learnt in one of the quayside taverns that men had been hired to kill me and my household and that they were going to do it three nights ago."

"So you fled?"

"Of course I fled!" Buteo almost shouted. He collected himself, adding, "and we were right to flee. It was all true, I saw them myself as we fled. I tell you: they weren't all quayside scum, they were commanded by men of quality – officers."

Quintus contemplated Buteo, who seized his forearm.

"You were in my house and you saw what they did. And you have seen Priscus. What does he say?"

Quintus summarised their discussions with Priscus and the letter notifying him of Fimbria's command in the North.

"Ha, that was to be expected. The order had already been made, but Priscus appealed it. Was he displeased at that?"

"He made clear his disagreement."

"Has he given you any orders?"

"Only you can do that, Gnaeus Horatius."

"That's true," said Buteo, revolving the thin gold ring of knighthood on his podgy finger. "But what should you do? What can you do?"

Quintus muttered: "I know so little." Then: "Fimbria claims the North is on the verge of insurrection, Priscus says not. Fimbria – who Priscus believes is scheming treason – is heading north. It would seem that's where answers lie."

"If you went north, that would mean leaving me." Buteo's face clouded. "But, as you say, events are moving there. And, Tita Amatia's there."

"And, Tita Amatia's there," repeated Quintus.

They debated. Buteo conceded that Tita Amatia was better placed to provide intelligence than he and that, if things got too dangerous for him, his merchant friend Halotas could arrange to ship him over to Gesoriacum and Gaul

Quintus furrowed his brow, stared at the floor and spoke without looking up. "We should go north, report to Fimbria and tell him our orders are to work with him to assess the threat from the Brigantes and give whatever assistance we can." He looked at Buteo. "But you should resurface, resume your duties and demand Priscus' protection.

"What?"

"Listen, if Fimbria is the traitor and Priscus loyal, then the governor will protect you as best he can, and you'll surely be safer in his palace than in some British peasant's round house." Buteo snorted but Quintus went on. "If Priscus is the traitor and if he's told that you've met and spoken to us – and he's only to be told that when we're with Fimbria – then it won't profit him to have you harmed, knowing there are frumentarii beyond his reach who can communicate his failure to protect you to Rome."

"That's easily said by you. Harder for me!" squeaked Buteo.

He gnawed his knuckle like a sulky child, but it was agreed he'd think about it. In the meantime they were to say nothing to Priscus about having seen him. They would meet again soon for a final decision.

"You'll get word to us?" asked Quintus.

"Yes, in a day or two."

"And we'll meet here again?"

"Probably. There's nowhere safer or more convenient."

"How did you find this place?"

"I bought it last year." Buteo coloured and gave a childish half giggle. "It was for a young man I had here… he died in the summer, poor thing – oh, how I've missed him during these troubles – a weak chest… you understand how it is."

Manius was prepared for the usual curled lip or a hasty change of subject, but Quintus rounded on Buteo: "Was this known?"

"What? Well yes, I suppose so, why not? I've no wife, want no companion. Poor Vibius was happier to live here and there was nothing to conceal…"

"No, by Jove, but there is now! This place is known to be yours – is that what you're saying?

"Yes," said Buteo, his voice tremulous, as the implications dawned. And on Manius, who swung back to the window he'd neglected. What he saw made his stomach clench.

Across the street, in a pool of pale light cast from the window under which they stood, was a group of six, with swords drawn. Manius was sure they were looking straight at him.

"Quintus!" he hissed. Quintus read the alarm on his face, and, with the back of his hand, he swept the lamp from the table and took Buteo by the shoulder.

"Outside, now!"

The three scrabbled in the dark doorway, Quintus cursing, Buteo whimpering and Manius wriggling to slip between them. Together they burst into the street, like the stopper from a jar of gas-spoiled wine. This brought an exultant cry from the group in the street. Now Manius could see they were not only armed, they were gladiators, Samnites, complete with crested helmets and leg greaves armed and dressed for killing.

Quintus shouted: "Run! Run!"

And the gladiators ran at them.

Manius pelted down that street. Behind he heard Quintus making noise enough to rouse the city, bellowing like a bull, urging Buteo to flee, and cursing, challenging and taunting the Samnites and, for good measure, crying warning of fire and thieves.

Manius stopped and turned. He made Quintus out, in the shadows, shoving Buteo into an alleyway off to the left, while he made a pass – parried with ease – at the lead Samnite. The others circled, enclosing him in a horseshoe. Quintus thrust to his right and then his left and kicked at the groin of the man before him. Manius made to run back to his aid; he stopped; he rocked forwards on his toes, backwards on his heels…

There was an angry shout from the far end of the street and another armed party appeared, a beneficiarii patrol. Everything then dissolved into a chaos of running, shouting figures, thrusting, swiping, grunting and cursing and, amidst all the noise, Manius heard Quintus: "Run Manius!"

So he ran. He ran back through all the streets they'd walked. He skidded round one corner, almost straight into a band of drunken sailors. He dodged them, ignoring their shouts and fled down another lane. They pursued, calling him to stop. He rounded another corner and hid in a yard, which from the stench must have served a tannery. He crouched among the reeking barrels of dog turds until their shouts faded and he could only hear the splashing of rain in the puddles and dripping from the eaves. He waited until he'd regained his breath and he peered up and down the deserted street. Then he ran on again, through the puddles, until he picked up his route and was over the bridge by the temple of Mithras and back to familiar streets by the palace. Fear, instinct and the protection of some god had brought him safe home.

§

Buteo ran down a long winding street, his shoe soles slapping the wet pavement, a sound that steadily decreased in frequency as his strength and breath failed. Soon he was limping, one hand pressed to the stitch in his side, until, finally, he halted and leaned his other hand against the shutters of a saddler's shop close to the street corner, his head down, gasping for wheezing breaths. Gradually, his chest heaved a little less and his heart's pounding eased. As his body recovered, so his blind panic eased to a chilling fear.

Again, he'd narrowly escaped with his life. Would the gods spare him nothing? Was there no relief from this horror? And where the hell was he? He'd taken no heed of direction, too busy fleeing those murdering swine to worry about which streets he pelted down and into which filthy alleys he dodged.

He shuddered. He must collect himself. He was going slightly downhill, was he not? Well then, that must be towards the river and, even at this hour, he could hire a boat and reach the East Gate before curfew. Theon would be waiting for him there – blessed Theon.

He heard a small noise, then a pair of feet rounded the corner and, along with the wet pavement, filled his field of vision. Buteo raised his gaze.

"Oh, you!"

Then he saw the blade.

§

Manius waited in the shadows opposite the palace, hoping to see Quintus – he peered at every figure who came down the street, But he didn't materialise and, eventually, Manius gave up, his cape soaked and his body goosepimpled with cold and shock. He was admitted by the sentries, without challenge or enquiry.

In his room he dropped onto his bed. He tried to bring his racing thoughts to order. What had happened to Quintus? Had he escaped and, if so, where the hell was he? If he hadn't, what was to become of Manius, alone in this province, without protection and caught up in an affair in which assassination was a ready weapon?

Not since he'd been orphaned had he felt so utterly abandoned.

"Damn him! The old fool!"

He wanted to be free – by heavens how he wanted to be free – but not like this. Not now. What could he do without Quintus?

Only one thing: go to Priscus and tell him everything about Buteo and this Tita Amatia and then swear to serve him and become his man. There was no other way. He'd summon a slave and demand to see him there and then.

But he heard the door to the adjoining room and he leapt from his bed and out into the corridor to see a weary Quintus, in his own doorway, muddy, bedraggled and with glistening blood covering the front of his cape and his arms.

§

Quintus' gory condition hadn't escaped the palace guards, though they made no remark. Just as well, for he was in no mood to explain. Their orderly officer, however, must have reported it to the governor, as Priscus raised it with Quintus shortly after noon the following day.

"You're quite well Quintus Suetonius?" he asked, as he and Manius entered the same grand room. This time, he rose and came to greet them as soon as they were shown in.

"I ask because I received a report that you'd been wounded… last night? You were… bloodstained?"

Quintus told him he'd been visiting a tavern and, returning to the palace, had been pursued by men equipped as gladiators. Fortunately, a beneficiarii patrol had happened by. There'd been a scuffle and one of the soldiers had cut a gladiator, who'd fallen against Quintus and covered him in blood. He didn't add how, as he'd made his own escape, he'd watched the provincial procurator of Britannia squealing like a whipped eunuch and scurrying off towards the river.

Priscus frowned and summoned his princeps praetorii, who confirmed a report of a brawl involving drunks near the amphitheatre. He'd no information that they were gladiators, Samnites or otherwise.

"Any arrests?" asked Quintus, without expectation.

"All the miscreants escaped," replied the centurion, staring into the distance.

Priscus waved him away. "Inform Speculator Silanus and tell him I want inquiries made at the amphitheatre," and then called after him, as he marched across the mosaic: "And tell him I want this matter cleared up."

As soon as the echoing crash of the centurion's boots had died away down the marble corridors, Priscus turned to them with a grim smile. "Of course the inquiries will reveal nothing. My princeps is a Fimbria man, as, I suspect, is Speculator Silanus. This is alarming Quintus Suetonius. Buteo – whatever has happened to him – was a target and now, it seems, so are you. It shames me to admit it, but I cannot guarantee your safety in my own capital, even in my own palace."

"That's more than alarming, it's astonishing, If two frumentarii, on the Emperor's business, were killed in one of the Empire's great cities, can you imagine the storm in Rome? Marcus Aurelius, temperate though he was, couldn't have allowed such an affront to go unpunished. Commodus would have Londinium razed."

Priscus sighed. "I know it. I put my situation candidly before you. What am I to do? What are we to do?"

They stared at each other; Quintus searching, Priscus in mute appeal.

"Caerellius Priscus," said Quintus finally, "We should leave your palace and head north with Flavius Fimbria. We cannot watch him from here."

Quintus was observing Priscus but, from the corner of his eye, noticed Manius twitch. He'd told the youngster of this decision last night; Manius hadn't liked it then and he obviously didn't like it now. To hell with him; there was too much that pup was starting not to like.

Priscus raised an eyebrow. "I admire your bravery. But is it wise? Won't you be running onto Fimbria's sword?"

"I'm hoping not. If we're with him we can keep an eye on him and he can keep an eye on us. That might so reassure him that he no longer feels the need to dispose of us. Also, he'll be responsible for our safety."

Priscus placed his fingertips together, as though in prayer, looking at his beloved orbis. He raised his eyes to Quintus. "The truth is that I agree with you. I can guard the Emperor's interests in Londinium. Oh, Fimbria has his creatures here, but I'm not without a trick or two. No, it's in the North, where we lack intelligence. Will you report back to me?"

"I've no objection to that – unless I judge it not to be in the Emperor's interests."

"Ha, unless Fimbria talks you round you mean? No, don't bridle, I know you're too shrewd to be taken in by a blowhard like him. But listen to me, both of you." And he lowered his voice, leaning forward.

"You speak of the Emperor's interests. In the North, you'll meet Lucius Antonius Merenda. Remember him?" Quintus nodded. "He served the late Emperor's interests well. Remember how?"

"I should, I put him up to it. He killed the traitor Avidius Cassius."

"Aye, and was richly rewarded for it." Priscus looked at Manius, as well as Quintus.

"Always bear in mind that such bold action is sometimes the only way to serve the Emperor."

Then, he leaned back and clapped his hands to summon a slave. "I support your decision and will have all arrangements made. Now, I'll ensure you also have all the necessary information." He turned to the slave. "Send word for Herennius Fusus." He explained: Fusus was another staff officer and an expert on the North and the Brigantes, and, while he was prone to overstate the threat posed by the tribes, Quintus would find it invaluable to pick his brains.

Herennius Fusus arrived, plainly to hand, reflected Quintus.

He was young, perhaps three or four years older than Manius; tall and gangly, with an Adam's Apple, which bobbed with his frequent nervous swallows. He stood, his stare fixed above them, his hands clasped before his groin.

He repeated much of what Priscus had already told them, about the various clans or septs who made up the tribe of the Brigantes and their dispossession following revolts and disturbances.

"Since last winter, we've seen similar signs of disaffection sir. Those loyal to Rome have been threatened, a dozen killings, villages burned, a patrol ambushed."

"Is that it?" asked Quintus; Priscus beamed at him. Fusus cleared his throat and cast a brief, nervous glance at Quintus.

"Most commanders have reported disaffection, of horses hobbled, wells poisoned, military equipment wilfully damaged, insults to soldiers."

Quintus fidgeted. "Hardly out of the ordinary in a frontier province?"

Fusus swallowed several times.

"Sir, there've been rumours… "

"Ha! Rumours!" put in Priscus.

"Rumours," continued Fusus, reddening, "such as we haven't heard before."

"Their nature?" prompted Quintus.

"Well, the Brigantine clans have their feuds and rivalries and history – and they all blamed each other for the failed revolt years ago, so they've been slow to unite to form any serious threat?

"But, no more?"

"No more. There's supposedly a young man, known as Iovir. It's claimed that he traces his descent to Venutius, a king who fought Rome. He's said to have united the clans of the Brigantes, or at least the common people, who regard him as their king come to restore their kingdom. He has a group of particularly fanatical adherents who follow the cult of the wolf. They're said to wear the heads of wolves when they kill, and to tear and rend flesh like wolves."

Quintus smiled to observe Manius rubbing his chin and nodding, as though flesh-rending wolfmen were neither here nor there.

"Can't we seize him, this Iovir?"

Priscus scoffed: "We don't even know he exists."

"Is this true?" Quintus asked Fusus.

"Perhaps," muttered the young centurion, "but..."

"But what?"

"Well," he looked at Priscus, but then seemed to throw caution aside, "we don't think it matters. He's dangerous, whether he exists or not, do you see sir?"

Quintus sighed. "Aye, I do. But surely there are tribal leaders who've become citizens or magistrates. Cannot they rein in the hotheads?"

"There are too few. When we dispossessed the Brigantes we hardly left any with the property to qualify for office."

Quintus mused, ruffling his hair. "Anything more?"

Fusus looked at Priscus, swallowed twice and took from his tunic a small object, which he placed on the orbis. Priscus groaned and rolled his eyes. It was the size of a child's fist, crudely fashioned from clay, a representation of a hunched figure wearing a heavy hooded cloak. Quintus picked it up and examined it. "What's this?"

Fusus shrugged. "It's known as the Hooded Spirit but its significance isn't understood, though we know it has always had a place among the gods of the Brigantes. Of late it seems to have become associated with Iovir, the Wolves and imminent insurrection. These are found at the scene of any outrage and are left outside military forts, or the houses of magistrates and tax collectors. I receive at least four or five reports of them a month."

"Perhaps, Herennius Fusus, we could progress to factual matters?" suggested Priscus silkily.

Fusus coloured again and rummaged in confusion among his documents. He spread maps on the orbis and talked for another half an hour on the location of forts, on the frontier, on troop dispositions and the state of tribes beyond the border wall. Quintus directed Manius to take notes, freeing himself to let his thoughts wander.

Border policing was much the same anywhere in the Empire – surely? Perhaps not; no swift mounted Parthians, nor rolling desert wastes here. Hell, no; he'd never been anywhere so waterlogged. He'd been colder, on the Rhine and the Danube, but never damper. Rheumatism would surely cripple him here. But Britannia was still gratifyingly Roman – particularly Londinium – and rich. The important part, its fertile lowland southern provinces, had been peaceable from time immemorial. Trouble on the frontier was a few days' journey away and no real cause for concern – unless Fimbria chose to make it so. Was there something in what Priscus had had to say? Or was it all petty intrigue of the kind found in any distant province? What about Buteo?

Aye, poor Buteo.

He shifted in his seat, feeling uneasy and then, when he remembered Tita Amatia, felt uneasier still.

There was a discreet cough from Manius and Quintus realised Fusus had finished and was looking at him. Quintus thanked him, and the young man gathered his papers, saluted and left.

Priscus said: "You see what I have to contend with, hey, hey: rumours and nervy soldiers. Anyway, I hope you've learnt something – if only that."

He informed them that they were to leave the day after next, escorted by Sarmatian cavalry led by a young tribune.

"You'll go with your escort to Longovicium fort, a couple of days short of the frontier wall. Doubtless the best place because, by great coincidence, your old friend Lucius Antonius Merenda commands there. Either there, or on the road, you'll meet Fimbria, who'll be making his way from Caerlon."

He shook them both by the hand, and clasped their arms, wishing them luck. Manius began a nervous speech – on his determination not to fail the governor, which prompted a withering stare from Quintus. He had barely begun when an optio marched in to draw Priscus to one side to whisper into his ear.

Quintus watched them. Priscus stiffened and his face lost its ruddiness. He looked sharply at the optio, who nodded. Priscus dismissed him and almost staggered towards the orbis to fall into his chair.

"Unwelcome news?" asked Quintus.

Priscus drew his hand down his face. He looked tired, older.

"Horatius Buteo is dead, his throat slit. His body was found an hour ago, stuffed into the latrine of a house near the river." He balled his fist and banged his forehead. "This gets worse. Fimbria is foul. He must be stopped!"

He rose, took hold of Quintus by both arms and held him. "Be careful my old friend. By all that's holy, be careful. Look after yourself – and the boy."

Chapter Five

Manius was angry.

He was desperate to discuss a hundred things with Quintus. But Quintus ordered several jars of the palace's best wine and retired to his room, ignoring all Manius' entreaties.

For the greater part of the following day and a half Quintus drank doggedly, heroically, as only he could; pausing for a period of snoring, of stentorian insensibility. Manius cursed him in the room next door.

Manius suggested that they should devote time to considering their situation, and maybe even to examining Buteo's body. "What the hell would that tell us?" demanded Quintus. Discussion wasn't necessary; all that was necessary was that he should be left in peace.

So a furious Manius went with a slave, and hand-picked escort assigned by Priscus, to buy warm clothing: woollen tunics, thick hooded cloaks, socks, knee boots, fleece-lined sheepskins and breeches. It was Manius who dealt with the palace's stableman for horses, and asses for their baggage. And it was he who arranged with Priscus' secretary for mansios and posting houses; through which officials, they would send their dispatches back to Londinium, which ciphers they should use and when they should be changed. While Quintus drank, alone in his room, muttering and glaring at the walls.

Guards, chosen singulares who stood rigid outside their rooms, followed him within the palace and whenever he left it. Every shopkeeper he visited must have taken him for the governor's son – or catamite – accompanied by his burly escort, who barred entry to all other customers while Manius made his purchases.

This prompted a thought. These guards had been assigned because of Quintus' account of being attacked by the Samnites. It had been a half-truth, but what if Fimbria did kill Quintus? What, for that matter, if the old fool killed himself, with the palace's finest vintage wines?

Any number of things could happen which could mean Manius being left on his own. That brute fact gripped him, as he ran his errands in Londinium's smoky, rain-sodden streets: he must look to his own future.

So his duties became a question of self-interest. He went over those ciphers with Priscus and sought out Herennius Fusus to pick his brains again. He also enquired delicately, if he knew anything of the mysterious Tita Amatia Aculeo, but Fusus stared blankly at the name.

§

Manius woke late on the day before their planned departure. He dressed hurriedly and went to see the governor's secretary's chief clerk, a fussy little Illyrian whom he found in his office, hair on end, harassed by the enquiries of three clamouring junior clerks, demanding instructions on requisitions, furlough requests and pay arrears. Exasperated, he looked up at Manius, who explained that he hadn't yet met the commander of their escort.

The clerk groaned and jumped to his feet to hurry into a back office and bark instructions. He returned with a young, acne-ridden legionary.

"Go with him please," said the Illyrian and returned to his clerks.

Manius followed this lad back into the guest quarters, to a room. The door was ajar. The soldier knocked and they entered. The chamber, like Manius', held a bed and scant furniture. Clothes were scattered and books and papers covered a table. A slave was packing a saddlebag. The lad asked where the centurion was and, being told he was in the stables, said: "Fetch him."

Manius dismissed his guide and sidled over to examine the books and papers on the table, careful to disturb them as little as possible: Notes taken from military textbooks, and three works; two by Julius Frontinus and one by Pliny: *Throwing the Javelin from Horseback*. All three were old and well-thumbed.

Manius heard sounds in the corridor and moved to the window to survey the grey skies.

He turned as the door opened to see a short man, perhaps in his mid-twenties, a centurion. He was thin, his scalp covered with only a fine down and his eyes were deep set.

"Hello," he said, almost in a whisper.

"Honoured. I'm Manius Suetonius Lupus. I understand you're to escort me and my father, Quintus Suetonius tomorrow."

"Ah, the frumentarii. Pleased to make your acquaintance. I'm Flavius Fimbria, Publius Flavius Fimbria."

"I'm sorry, I didn't quite hear…"

"I'm sorry. People say I speak too softly: it's Publius Flavius Fimbria."

"Flavius Fimbria? Are you related to..?"

"To Tiberius Flavius? Yes, I'm his brother."

§

That afternoon, after Manius stamped off down the corridor, Quintus poured himself a goblet of Priscus' fine Alban and, with a satisfied sigh settled down for a serious session. After barely half an hour, a tap at his door caused him to curse and splutter and spill his wine getting to his feet.

"What the hell do you want now?" he roared, yanking open the door to reveal a slave who, stammering, handed him a letter.

Quintus snatched the note and slammed the door. He peered closely at the pitch seal, which appeared unbroken, but doubtless Priscus had someone able to tease apart and then repair a seal – a common enough skill.

He opened it and scanned the few words. He blinked, then re-read them.

"Gods!" he breathed.

He read the letter once more before holding it over the lamp and then he ground the ashes in his fist. He pulled on his boots and cloak. Five minutes later he was walking away from the palace, knowing he'd be followed by one of Priscus' men, or by a creature of Fimbria. Hell, probably by both. But he was counting on someone else tracking him and, sure enough, as he turned onto a street leading to the Forum a hand fell on his shoulder. He turned and saw a man well past middle age, with grey, greasy hair plastered close to his head and over his ears, his face lined and his thick lower lip hanging and trembling as he laboured for breath. He had been hurrying to catch Quintus, on short bandy legs which supported a belly drooping part way to his knees.

"By heaven! It is you, Gut Crispinus!."

"Quintus Suetonius, let's get off the street," wheezed the other. "The fellow following you has been tripped and buffeted by a couple of lads but I've no doubt he'll soon be after you."

He bundled Quintus into a nearby tailor's. Nodding at an old man who glanced up from his needle, he guided Quintus to a door, then – panting hard – up a short flight of stairs and into a small room, furnished as an office. Gut Crispinus squeezed behind the desk and flopped into the chair, wafting a hand to invite Quintus to sit opposite, then took up a napkin and wiped his face.

"Is this place yours?"

Gut looked about the room. "It's only a place of business."

"Last I heard you were in Memphis."

Gut shrugged.

"Got too hot to hold you did it?"

"Doesn't everywhere, Quintus Suetonius?"

"For you it seems, sooner or later."

"The prefect was a fool... no vision... I could've made him a rich man."

Quintus raised a weary hand. "Spare me."

He stared at Gut, who gazed impassively back. "How did you know I was here?"

Gut winked. "It's my business."

Quintus smiled. Aristotle would have struggled to classify the nature of Gut Crispinus' business. He was a dealer, but he dealt in so much and used a bewildering variety of means of exchange. Certainly he brokered stolen goods and he traded information and Quintus had often done business with him. But they'd first met long before Quintus had become a frumentarius, when he'd been a young man running with a rakish bunch to whom Gut, then a mere stripling – though already a stripling with a belly – had been able to supply sundry illicit pleasures.

"I take it it's the same business?"

"Ah, it's old dog and new tricks isn't it? What else can I do?"

"How long have you been here?"

"Since last summer."

"That's plenty of time for the Gut Crispinus I know to have discovered anything worth knowing."

"You mean in your line of work?"

"Like you Gut, I'm an old dog that's well past new tricks. So you just tell me all about governor Priscus and procurator Buteo and legate Tiberius Flavius Fimbria."

Gut's eyes narrowed.

Quintus laughed. "Don't worry, I haven't learnt ingratitude either, you'll get paid."

Gut grunted and leaned back. "The situation's this: it has – as a poetical gentleman like you might put it – all gone to cock."

"That's the impression I'm getting, but perhaps you could expatiate?"

Gut Crispinus added little new. The governor and a leading general were daggers-drawn, each with their own faction, in the army and the administration, while bemused citizens looked on.

"Don't people fear trouble from the northern barbarians?"

Gut grimaced. "The frontier's far away and there's probably more troops there than Britons. There's more fear of the legions heading south to involve themselves in the quarrels of Priscus and Fimbria. Soldiers get bored don't they Quintus Suetonius?" He leered at Quintus who urged him on with an angry gesture. "There's resentment among the gentry and merchants and the right sort, that there's people who should know better, but who're playing their own games and threatening intrigue and war and heaven only knows what else. That does, as you might say, piss ordinary folk off."

"Who's the troublemaker? Priscus or Fimbria?"

Gut Crispinus shrugged. "Depends who you believe."

"And who do you believe?"

"Dunno, probably six of one and half a dozen of the other."

"How d'you know I was in Londinium?"

"Ah," said Gut and winked. "Now that's an interesting one. Someone came to me, asking after you. Told me one Quintus Suetonius Lupus – you can bet my old ears pricked up at that – had arrived; was lodging with the governor and could I find out what he was up to."

That made sense to Quintus. Even if Gut Crispinus had barely had a year to weave his webs of owed favours, uncalled debts and damaging gossip, anyone seeking information would soon be recommended to go to him.

"Fellow by the name of Tiro, a Sicilian. Hard man they tell me."

"But what is he? Who does he work for? What's his interest in me?"

Gut shrugged theatrically, palms spread high, eyes rolling. "Good questions Quintus Suetonius. And I'm embarrassed I don't have good answers. This Tiro is also a close one, he don't give nothing away. Naturally, I'll try for further information on his return, but what am I to tell him about you?"

Quintus chuckled. Gut, like any good broker, was seeking two payments from both parties. Why begrudge him that? For old times' sake, or because the frumentarii were such valued customers – he'd play this Tiro false rather than Quintus.

"I don't know what you should tell him. How can I? Unless I know who he works for I can't poison the well. I need to speak to him."

"Will you take him up?"

Quintus shook his head. "He's not in Priscus' pay. Why would Priscus be seeking information he already has? If he's working for Fimbria, how can I be sure the man set to watch his cell won't be of Fimbria's faction and that the next morning I find that cell empty or containing a prisoner with a slit throat?"

Gut ran his tongue over his thick lips and nodded.

"No, Gut, I'll have to come along to your next meeting."

Gut stared. "What! What are you asking me? How do you think he'll take that? How much do you think it'll then cost me to have him put out of the way?"

"You'll lose his fee I'll grant you, but you know I'll stand that."

"I'll have to have a blade there. You know that'll cost."

Quintus nodded.

"You have a lad with you. Is he handy? Will you bring him?"

Quintus shook his head. "No, I don't want him involved... not until I know how the land lies."

"I still don't know, you're asking a lot, even of an old friend."

"We do go back a long way, Gut."

Gut rubbed his fat jowls and muttered in what Quintus recognised as a fighting retreat, "If I did, would you put in a word for me in Rome, with a view to me being allowed back? I'm too old for weather like this."

"Mine wouldn't be the best recommendation. There's a new man now, Saoterus, a freed slave, so naturally – in this insane world – promoted to the highest office. Still, I'll do what I can."

Gut nodded, but without conviction and his eyes slid shiftily across Quintus' face. He coughed. "I'd er... I'd like you to have a word with someone else." Quintus waited. "I'd like you to er... to speak to Tita Amatia for me."

Quintus stared, uncomprehending.

"She er... she's still in Britannia you know," said Gut. "Up in the North apparently."

"I'd heard."

Gut fell silent, writhing and stealing glances at Quintus.

"If you want me to speak to Tita Amatia, you must know I'm going north. How? And, what in the name of heaven can you want me to say to her?"

Crispinus wriggled and scratched his head. "Once Tiro told me you were here, I asked about, didn't take long, an ostler in the palace tipped me off he had to find horses for your journey."

"So, I'm going north. I may see Tita Amatia. If so, what's your message?"

Gut coloured, squirmed and avoided Quintus' eyes, which widened in astonishment.

Of course, all those years ago, young Gut Crispinus had appeared on the edges of their set. Some said he was a freed slave, others that he was some knight's bastard. Awkward, ugly, strange Crispinus – always on the outside, always mocked, but always useful and always allowed back. He always returned because of Tita Amatia. How farcical, that a creature like Gut could even aspire to her.

Then, her father, Titus Amatius, married off his daughter, a great match and a beauty, to Aulus Curius Caecus, a rising politician some ten years older and from another grand family. It had broken Gut's heart. And if that hadn't, what followed surely must.

"What is your message for her Gut?" asked Quintus gently.

Gut leaned forward Quintus, his rheumy eyes gleaming. "Just tell her I'm here, in Britannia. If she needs help or anything…"

Quintus nodded. "And if Saoterus allows you back? Would you choose Rome or Tita Amatia?"

Gut Crispinus grinned. "Not sure. The what-ifs…? As and when. It'll be what you might term a nice dilemma."

Quintus shook his head. That Gut Crispinus could still be moon-struck a lifetime on – and a lifetime like his for heaven's sake – was the stuff of fable. Or farce. Quintus studied the man opposite. Was he entering an early dotage? The frumentarius had known others.

Quintus brought them back to business. "When are you meeting this Sicilian?"

"Sometime around the seventh hour. I put a light in the window over here so he knows I'm waiting."

"You said you'd have a blade?"

"I'll have a man downstairs, he's handy. He'll bring him up."

"Your Sicilian won't mind?"

"He won't have to."

They discussed details, timings and price. A simple plan: Quintus was to arrive an hour or so before Tiro; when they heard him downstairs Quintus would hide behind the door and, once Tiro and Gut's hired blade entered the room, they'd disarm the Sicilian and Quintus could interrogate him. What they did with him then would depend on his answers.

Quintus left, confirming he'd return in eight hours. Back in his room in the palace, he ordered fresh wine. After all, Priscus was paying.

But he couldn't get drunk. That evening would call for a clear head. A shame, for he'd a great urge to drink; Gut Crispinus had brought back memories that blasted any bloody chance of tranquillity.

So many years ago. So many recollections seemed clear, but he'd probed enough men's memories to know how treacherous they could be. Tita Amatia; Caecus; Domitius Calvinus; young Gut Crispinus... if he closed his eyes he could see their faces, hear them laughing – braying, high-pitched or Tita Amatia's musical peals, which always closed with "Priceless! How priceless!" Aye, they'd had good times; had sailed close to the wind – Tita Amatia too close.

All that laughter – however musical – had been brought to an abrupt end when she'd been married off to Aulus Curius Caecus.

Gut had wept then, but shed more tears when the subsequent scandal broke: Tita Amatia already had a lover of her own age but of lower standing and she'd continued to see this man after her marriage, until, one day, they were caught in the act.

Quintus finished his drink and weighed the jar in his hand. He could finish that and close his eyes for a few hours and he'd be fresh enough for the evening. If Manius came knocking again, he'd ignore him, just fake snoring. He couldn't face being questioned. Not until he had his thoughts straight. Anyway, there was something going on in the lad's mind, he was truculent, resentful, and Quintus had seen that often enough – too often to trust any useful information to those harbouring such feelings.

Then there was the other problem. How to get word to Rome? A frumentarius' despatches should go with the provincial procurator's correspondence, independent of the governor's. No chance of that now. From what Buteo had said, Tita Amatia was in correspondence with Rome. Not with that shit Saoterus presumably.

He finished the jar, stared longingly at a second, cursed, fell back on his bed and closed his eyes.

§

When he woke, with a start and a splutter, it was dark. Hell and blast, had he overslept? He swung himself off the bed and left the room, careful not to alert Manius. The corridors were deserted, though there were distant echoes of voices and footsteps. He made his way to the hallway outside the gymnasium where the water clock trickled and dripped the hours. Quintus grunted with relief, it wasn't yet the fifth hour.

He returned to his room to wash his face and to arm himself. He left the palace and with the street almost deserted, it was easy enough to spot the figure who flitted from shadow to shadow some hundred paces behind, and easy enough to lose him.

Twenty minutes later he was outside the tailor's below Gut's office. He walked past it and crossed the street, noting that there was no one to be seen in that small area not swallowed by the darkness. Above, he could make out a glimmer behind the shutters. He hurried back to the door and tapped. No response. He lifted the latch and entered to find the workshop in darkness but there was some faint light from the top of the stairs ahead.

Quintus frowned. Was Gut alone? Where was his hired blade? Why not down here by the door? Stupid to leave the door unbolted. Quintus pulled his knife from his sock. He moved towards the stairs and he stumbled against something.

Quintus knelt on one knee and groped. He felt clothing and, as his eyes adjusted to the darkness, he made out the outline of a body. It was a huge hulking man, much bigger then Gut Crispinus. Quintus' fingers recoiled from a sticky dampness. The fellow had been stabbed, below the ear. Quintus grimaced and felt below the wound. No pulse.

With a grunt he heaved himself upright. He stepped over the body and made his cautious way to the stairs. He peered up and saw that the light was coming from the half open door of Gut's office. Knife in hand, Quintus climbed the stairs, his shadow creeping up the wall behind him.

At the top he paused, pushed the door and it slowly revealed, in the lamplight, Gut Crispinus, sitting back in his chair and staring with the unwavering, shocked intensity of the dead.

Quintus looked around the room. He took the lamp from the desk in front of Gut and stepped back into the corridor. There was one other door, locked. He rejoined Gut, replaced the lamp and took a minute to examine the body. He sighed and sat in the chair he'd occupied that afternoon.

He shook his head in mute apology. What a fool he had been. What a tyro.

They'd set a trap for the Sicilian, a childish, obvious trap and he'd sprung it on them. He must have been watching – or had someone watch – Gut's place.

"He noted my visit, didn't he, Gut?" whispered Quintus. "He guessed you'd invited me along to meet him, so he came earlier."

Gut's blade downstairs had been no help. This Tiro was a man to reckon with.

"But did you talk, Gut?"

Men usually did, in the end, but, looking at poor Gut, Quintus could see that his torturer had taken too much pleasure. Gut couldn't have lasted long.

"I hope not," he said. "For old times' sake, I hope not."

Chapter Six

Winter came early and hard and, even on that journey's first day, Manius, Quintus, Publius Flavius and four Sarmatian troopers were clad in barbarian breaches and swaddled in capes, hoods down, flinching from pelting rain and driving wind. They were glad to reach a village, only a few miles out of Londinium. They could take brief shelter to wait for the weather to abate.

In this settlement – half a dozen rude buildings in an enclosure – Publius Flavius tossed the villagers a couple of coins, and they tethered their beasts in the barn and squatted by the fire in one of their roundhouses where the air was thick with smoke which stung the eyes and scoured the throat. Hens clucked and strutted fussily around and a pair of children,with matted hair and, grimy, snotty faces positioned themselves to stare unblinking, while some fat slattern, whom Manius took for their mother, watched them more slyly from the other side of the room. Manius ensured he and Quintus sat far enough away from the others to allow them to whisper privately.

He was eager to talk to Quintus, who'd not only shut himself away for the previous two days, but even that morning had been too affected by all he'd drunk to answer questions, before they'd received urgent summons from Publius Flavius, who was impatient to be off.

"Publius Flavius," Manius hissed. With a shudder, Quintus dragged his gaze from that of one of the British brats and turned his glazed, bloodshot eyes on Manius.

"What of him?"

"He's Tiberius Flavius Fimbria's brother."

"I know."

"But Priscus has made him our escort, to protect us from Fimbria."

Quintus grunted. "Priscus knows what he's doing. They're half-brothers. When Tiberius' mother died, old man Fimbria married his freed slave – ye gods what a scandal that was – and Publius was the result. The old man doted on him. When he died there was a big lawsuit over the will. Tiberius won and young Publius was all but dispossessed. They hate each other. Priscus couldn't have chosen better."

The following evening, they dined with Publius Flavius in Durovigutum. This was their first real conversation with him. For the first day, Quintus had been too indisposed and, apart from his few words to Manius in that roundhouse, remained sunk in silent, sullen gloom and had retired to bed as soon as they reached their evening halt, declining even dinner. On the second day the wind howled about them so severely it was hard to converse and a plainly irritated Quintus claimed not to be able to make out Publius Flavius' soft speech.

But at the end of that second day, his head, stomach and spirits were so much improved he invited Publius Flavius to dine in the tavern adjoining the mansio.

Quintus was all affability as he ushered Flavius into the low-beamed room A crackling fire provided heat and a cheering glow. The company was loud and good-natured and the table to which the tavern keeper showed them was clean and polished by the sleeves of many revellers.

Once seated, Quintus made no attempt at conversation and set about the wine as though he hadn't drunk for weeks. Manius asked Publius – raising his voice above the din – about the handful of Sarmatian cavalry who accompanied them.

"They're decent enough," he replied. "They were seconded to Caerellius Priscus' singulares consularii, but they got into trouble – some brothel brawl – and they're posted to my new unit to get them out of Londinium."

"Yes, your new unit. You're to be second-in-command?"

"That's so. It's the First Cohort of Loyal Vardulli, Foot and Horse," he said and added, with evident pride, "a military unit, of citizens. And yes, I shall be tribune, second in command."

"A prime posting," said Quintus, seemingly finding Publius's quiet words easier to follow. "A crack unit, and six months as tribune and you'll be a knight. Did you win this through your brother's patronage?"

Publius Flavius coloured and replied.

"What?" barked Quintus, cupping a hand behind his ear.

"Yes, I believe my half brother, Tiberius Flavius, was responsible for the appointment."

"Excellent, good for you. That's what elder brothers are for, eh?"

Publius Flavius gave a weak smile and they drank and ate in silence until Quintus resumed: "I know your commanding officer, Lucius Antonius Merenda, he's a good man."

"A distinguished man, I gather."

"Distinguished?" Quintus raised his bushy eyebrows. "Aye, I suppose he is. It was thanks to him the First Vardulli got the honorific of loyalty and their citizenship."

"So I understand. That was in Egypt was it not? The Avidius Cassius affair?"

"It was."

For the rest of that meal they talked of little of consequence: literature; wine as a cure for dyspepsia; peacock meat as tending to heart failure; the propriety of women speaking Greek. It passed an easy hour, then Publius Flavius thanked them and excused himself to see to the men and the horses.

Manius wasn't sorry to see him go. Quintus, clearly enjoying his wine after two days' abstinence, might be ready to share some knowledge.

Manius reminded him that Merenda, Publius Fabius' new commanding officer, had been mentioned before, by the governor, and that Quintus had said that he'd killed the pretender Avidius Cassius.

Quintus shrugged. "It's a well-known tale. Most of it."

Gaius Avidius Cassius, governor of Syria and dear friend of the late emperor had himself proclaimed emperor following rumour that Marcus Aurelius had died. Quintus was despatched to Egypt to thwart Cassius who'd moved there to seize the grain supplies. There, Quintus gained the co-operation of Antonius Merenda, a young centurion in a Spanish cohort, who tried to kill Cassius but bungled it and only wounded him. Fortunately his loyal decurion finished the job.

"The Emperor gave Merenda command of the cohort – which was also honoured – and a grant to buy his knighthood. But, a year later, the proudly named First Cohort of Loyal Vardulli, Foot and Horse Citizens, was transferred from the fleshpots of Egypt to the barren wastes of the Empire's northernmost frontier. And Merenda's career came to a halt. The late emperor couldn't bear to hear his name mentioned or be reminded of the treachery of his friend."

§

They continued their journey, heading steadily north, towards unknown, sunless lands, from staging post to staging post and mansio to mansio. Manius was downcast. He was from a land of warmth and vivid colour, of intensity of brilliant light and heady scents and tastes, but Britannia was cold and colourless and intense only in its harshness. It offered no wonders, other than the violence of its buffeting wind, the relentless persistence of its freezing rain and the shortness of its days. It was remarkable only in its dispiriting greyness.

The long road ran over country which undulated gently, but which became perceptibly wilder and increasingly forested. They kept a wary eye on this woodland where it crept towards the paved roadway and in these places they stayed close together, and their Sarmatian troopers were alert, spears held ready across their saddlebows. Manius was also vigilant, peering into the trees, fearful of the horrors – wild animals and wild people – they might conceal.

The settlements became less frequent and meaner and in their enclosures there were fewer pigs and cattle and more sheep and goats. Manius' spirits fell further as day succeeded day and Quintus too grew even more taciturn and withdrawn; while riding he hunched over the saddle, deep in brooding thought and, in the evenings, grumbled over whatever vile dish – boiled sheep's head and leeks as often as not – was put before them.

The weather deteriorated, making the travelling hard and wearying. On one of the better days – their first blue sky since Londinium – they halted in a village to rest. They chose it because there was a working party of soldiers under a centurion, felling and collecting timber which they were piling on huge carts to be taken to feed the insatiable appetite for wood of the legionary garrison further north at Eboracum.

The soldiers were observed by a handful of the villagers, who gazed sullen as the trees bordering their settlement were attacked. One ancient woman, leaning with both gnarled hands against the stockade's fence, gave a tremulous keening as a great ash was felled and crashed to the earth twenty paces from her. A soldier said something and the others laughed. Then, a young woman walked unsteadily by, swaying under a yoke supporting two heavy pails of water. This prompted another guffaw from the troops, but this time their centurion silenced them by laying about the nearest with his vitis, delivering furious blows to backsides and shoulders.

Having seen to the tethering of the horses, Publius Flavius went to consult the centurion to enquire as to the going ahead and the distance to Eboracum. Manius watched him go, then contemplated the blushing girl with the water yoke. He turned to Quintus and asked him about Tita Amatia Aculeo.

Quintus spoke while examining the back of his boot where the stitching was coming away. He told Manius the forty-year-old tale of high-born and high-spirited Tita Amatia and the scandal of her lover.

"What happened to her?"

"The law decreed that she should be banished to an island and Antoninius Pius, in an act of unparalleled severity, made Britannia that place of exile."

And her lover?"

"He was cashiered from the army, disgraced and banished to Corsica. He was a friend of Antoninius Pius' adopted son, Marcus Aurelius, and a couple of years later he was allowed to slink back. Tita Amatia was also a friend of Marcus Aurelius, but she declined the chance to return."

"But why?"

"She married a Briton."

Manius was amazed. He stared at Quintus, turned so sharply his horse whinnied and carolled about on its tethering rope. He grabbed its reins and held it while still spluttering his disbelief that a Roman aristocrat could so lower herself – surely proof of her reputed insanity.

Quintus explained that her husband had been a Brigantine noble, born a Roman citizen, educated in Gaul and a magistrate and loyal servant of Rome. He'd been killed in a minor revolt of the Brigantes some fifteen or sixteen years ago because of that loyalty. Quintus reserved his greatest contempt for Greeks and Levantines and had a sneaking admiration for barbarians, who, he suspected, still embodied old Roman warrior virtues.

"Anyway," Quintus said, "whatever the reason, the fact remains that she's still here, living in the North. I told you she was a friend of the late Emperor and so she remained. As Buteo said, they corresponded, and she was his chief – and most trusted – source of intelligence in Britannia."

"Surely we must contact her?"

Quintus mimed clapping. "Yes, we must make contact. But listen: there must be no word of that – and no word of her – to our young friend there." He nodded towards Publius Flavius who was deep in conversation with the centurion. "He is Priscus' man and, according to Buteo, Tita Amatia didn't entirely trust our friend the governor. He's very soft-spoken, this Publius Flavius, and I don't like that in a man. No, give me someone who's not afraid his words will be heard. Anyway, be careful what you say around him, I think Priscus provided him and his Sarmatians as much to shackle us as to protect us."

Chapter Seven

Quintus swore at the crush of bodies in the tavern, before plunging in, making a lane which Manius nimbly followed. The place was full: soldiers, merchants and travellers standing or seated and bawling and laughing and between their legs ran squabbling dogs and at least one goat.

Cold rain fell on the town of Eboracum, but in the tavern it was warm, even hot with the crush, and there was a comforting smell of ale, wine and smoke. They'd arrived an hour earlier and, leaving horses and baggage at the mansio, had come in search of food and drink.

Quintus won his way through to a harassed potboy, shouted in his ear and was directed to a table where two places had just been vacated. Quintus and Manius sat and, after exhaling in relief and mopping his brow Quintus acknowledged the greeting of the table's occupant, a florid, jovial Briton of wide girth and grey beard who presented his bald crown as he bowed.

Quintus looked at his plate. "The chops – are they good?"

"Most palatable sir, most toothsome."

Quintus waved the potboy over to order. The man opposite beamed and asked whether they were newly arrived in Eboracum; did business bring them there? They confirmed: yes, they were functionaries of the provincial procurator's office. He introduced himself as Nectovelius Vindicis, a citizen and trader in wools, skins and furs, and proud resident of this bustling garrison town.

"Sirs, it does me the greatest of honour to make your illustrious acquaintance."

Manius had learnt this was the usual way with educated Britons, clearly taught in an ancient rhetorical style from old grammars.

Manius smiled and let him prattle on. He watched the soldiers who were mostly young, good humoured, joking and shouting. Eboracum was the military headquarters for the whole of North Britannia and the home to Sixth Victrix legion and Manius felt secure in its vicus, which surrounded the legion's enormous fort. Back in the comforting embrace of the Empire, even though they were to leave after two days of resting and allowing time for an early meeting with Tiberius Flavius Fimbria, at least they'd be within a few days of their destination and the end of their journey. Then, he'd only to endure the long and weary winter months in an outpost fort in the wilderness.

Their chops and beans arrived and the merchant asked them where they were bound. When they told him, he pursed his lips and shook his head.

"It is, alas, not the most auspicious of times to be northward bound," he said. "There's increasing unrest in the country, even so far south as here. Have you perhaps been apprised of the unfortunate situation in these environs?"

Quintus said that they hadn't and would welcome enlightenment. Their new friend confirmed most of what they'd been told in Londinium: about the Brigantes again threatening revolt, their chief, Iovir, and his most active followers, the Wolves – "a terrible people" – growing ever bolder and more violent; villages burned, local petty officials threatened and even murdered Most noticeable, a growing fear affecting the peaceable part of the population.

He cast quick glances right and left and leaned forward, whispering: "Only the army ventures into the hills now. There've been attacks on the road north of here and there's even talk of the Wolves abroad in Eboracum and of their spies active in the town. Do not go about after dusk gentlemen, I implore you."

Quintus nodded. "This Iovir, is much known of him?"

"He's a young man of the old Brigantine royal house. I've met none who've seen him, but I'm a loyal citizen and would have no acquaintance with such." Then he shot quick penetrating looks at them. Manius wondered: did he suspect them of being more than tax officials?

They questioned him further but learnt nothing more than bloody details of some of their atrocities and that there was a common conviction that serious violence would start with the spring. The merchant's voice grew quieter and his sideways glances more frequent. Perhaps he'd remembered his own warning about the Wolves' spies and regretted his earlier loquacity. He pushed aside his meal, leaving food still on the plate, and rose, pleading a business engagement.

"Just a further moment, please," said Quintus, placing his hand on the merchant's sleeve. "Can you recommend a good apothecary, one who has extensive supplies, particularly of herbs and medicaments from the East?"

The fellow looked relieved and gave an address "And, the last thing, I promise you. Can you tell me how we might reach Cenares?"

"Cenares...? Oh, why of course, it's some twenty miles or so west." He gave directions.

The merchant gone, they finished their meal and paid. On their way out, Manius asked why they needed an apothecary and what was this place Cenares? Quintus winked, placed a finger to a side of his ruby nose and rolled his eyes in the direction of the door.

"I'll tell you later. See over there and remember what I said about the young whisperer and our escort."

Manius looked: at a table by the door, gazing woodenly back, was the slab-featured face of one of Publius Flavius' Sarmatian troopers.

§

Tiro was barely there an hour before he recognised the Sarmatian pacing doggedly through the streets and followed him.

He watched him watching Quintus Suetonius Lupus and the boy in the tavern. Then his thin lips curled and broadened to a grin when he saw that Quintus had also spotted the trooper.

He might not have found them but for that Sarmatian. It had been a delicate business following the frumentarii from Londinium: Tiro couldn't risk staying in the same towns on the same nights – an old hand like Suetonius Lupus would have rumbled him. So Tiro stayed a day behind, asking after them at each mansio. At least he knew where the frumentarii were bound; that fool Crispinus in Londinium had been persuaded to reveal that – before the fat cunt had carked it. Still, Tiro was anxious, hurrying to catch them here at Eboracum where there was every prospect of things happening.

Now, a beaker of ale in hand, Tiro leaned against a rough oak pillar at the far side of the room, from where, intermittently, past the heads and shoulders of a score of people, he could watch the frumentarii, deep in conversation with a bald greybeard. Then Tiro became irritated by the heads roaring and guffawing and jerking to and fro between himself and the frumentarii and was seized by an angry loathing for one young legionary right before him who repeatedly threw his idiot head back and forth in laughter. Tiro wanted to seize that head and wrench it round on its scrawny fucking neck so…

What the fuck?

The greybeard was standing and writing something for the frumentarii.

Tiro drained his goblet, wiped the back of his hand across his mouth and, as the greybeard made his way, apologising and squeezing through drinkers, Tiro peeled himself away from the oak pillar and followed him into the street.

§

Eboracum's mansio offered the best accommodation and baths since Londinium. The next morning, Manius decided that a slave who waited on their table was the most beautiful creature, an utterly lovely thing of about his age, with hair so blonde it was nearer white than yellow and with wide open, innocent eyes of intense, pure blue. Those eyes met his for a moment, in which he felt what amounted almost to a kick in his innards, before fluttering lashes closed over them and they were lowered modestly. Manius gaped, stammered, babbled, asked her where she was from. She was German.

"If I could have your attention," said Quintus acidly, before Manius could ask her name.

He turned, reluctant, substituting Quintus' glowering face for that vision.

"I want you to go to that apothecary. Here's a list."

Manius glanced at it: opium, valerian, lettuce sap and earth apple. Apart from those, the other names were strange to him. He pocketed it and left. The German girl had his mind racing and his heart thumping.

With directions from the mansio steward he set off to the address the merchant had given. The snow began, first a light flurry and then flakes dancing in the wind, making him and the few people abroad hurry, heads down and hoods up. But he took care to cast frequent glances around and behind.

The low, wooden building, with similar shops and stalls facing each other, stood in a modest square. The apothecary was an elderly Greek whose eyebrows rose as he looked at the order, but he shrugged and shuffled back to the rear of his shop, among the jumble of amphorae, sheaves of dried plants and aged barrels, declaring that the preparation would be ready in half an hour.

Manius crossed the square to where hot ale was sold from a stall with an awning to keep the snow off, a couple of rough benches and a table, and here he sat with a beaker of ale, warming his hands between grateful sips. The buildings allowed little of what meagre sunlight made its way through the unbroken thick white cloud. The air was heavy with greasy smoke and through it the snowflakes began to fall more heavily. Manius shivered and took another sip of ale and then he looked up and, through the flurry, he saw the German girl.

She was wearing a thick brown cloak and, at the instant he happened to glance up, she started pulling her hood over that golden hair. She then turned and hurried away. He stared, jumped to his feet and ran to the corner round which she'd disappeared. There was no sign of her, nor round the next corner, nor the next, and, cursing, he returned to the square.

He drained his ale before stepping back across to the apothecary who held up a tiny glass bottle between finger and thumb, full of a deep red liquid. He rotated it slowly, so that what little light there was glinted off the swirling fluid.

"I've made it up as instructed, mixed in wine. No more than half this dose at any time you understand?" Manius nodded and, as the apothecary handed him the phial, he leered. "And if for a lady, then less even than that." Manius coloured, mumbled and left the shop. Outside, he examined the bottle. Was it some medication of Quintus,' something to make him feel easier after a drinking bout?

On his return to the mansio, Quintus uncorked the bottle, sniffed it and seemed satisfied. He placed it by his bed. Manius relayed the apothecary's warning which Quintus waved away.

"I know more about it than some damned Greek."

"What is it?" Manius asked, despite an eagerness to be wandering the premises in search of the girl.

"You'll know soon enough. Now we must go out again."

"You've been out?"

"I have."

"Where?"

"To a stables."

"To a stables? Why?"

"To see about horses. Why else would one go to a stables?"

"What horses?"

"The horses which, if all goes well, will take us to the estate of Tita Amatia Aculeo. Now, no more questions. We must see the beneficiarius to send our report to Priscus."

They had little to tell this man, Iriminius Carbo, beyond announcing their safe arrival in Eboracum. For his part, he confirmed there was trouble reported in the hill country to the north and that the little clay figures of the Hooded Spirit were appearing with greater frequency.

"People find them on their doorsteps in a morning or placed among their hens' eggs or in the bucket of a well. We assume they're meant as a warning. That's how people take them."

In answer to Quintus' next question: no, he had had no word of Tiberius Flavius Fimbria's imminent arrival, but he could assure them he hadn't yet passed through Eboracum. They thanked him, promised him they would notify him the day they left and returned to the mansio.

There, as they entered the lobby, they were met by the furious glare of one the Samartians. He informed them, in an aggressive, heavily accented rumble, that Centurion Publius was searching for them. "He wants you now!"

This was the edge of insubordination and it was evident to Manius that Quintus, who surveyed him from under his beetling brows, was near eruption. But the trooper said no more, and they passed on to their room, to find Publius just leaving it.

He stood blinking. All three stared until Flavius Fimbria spoke, his face breaking into an awkward smile. "There you are. I've been worried about you. I must apologise for entering your room, but I was anxious to find you. Where have you been?"

Quintus gave an answering smile. "We've merely been seeing something of the town."

"But you mustn't. Not without an escort."

"Indeed?"

He stepped closer and whispered. "It's too dangerous. I don't know what work you're engaged in, and I've no business knowing it, but my duty is to protect you," and here his eyes, like the merchant's, darted from right to left.

The drama of his words hung over them. Then Quintus clamped a heavy hand on his shoulder. "My boy, forgive me. You've been attempting to do your duty and we put you in an impossible position.

Rest assured that I shall report your diligence to Governor Priscus and indeed to General Tiberius. But here," said Quintus, taking his hand from his shoulder, balling it into a fist to give Publius a jocular punch on his chest, "let us make amends as brother soldiers should. Join us in a jar of wine. Come, I insist."

Publius pleaded duties, preparations to be made for tomorrow's resumption of the journey, his men's welfare to see to, but Quintus overrode all objections and sealed his victory by interpreting Publius' final low-voiced objection as capitulation. "You accept? Capital! Come. Manius, take young Publius to the tavern over the way, while I just step into our room for some money."

Manius had the money and Quintus knew it. But Manius said nothing and walked on with a still murmuring Publius who insisted that he must at least order the Samartians to prepare their equipment. He conveyed this to the trooper in the lobby and, by the time they entered the tavern Quintus was right behind them, beaming with uncharacteristic good humour.

They found a table and Quintus proposed two jars of wine. Publius demurred, but, again, Quintus overbore him.

Quintus, stared out at the falling snow, said he hoped the weather wouldn't worsen. Publius said he trusted that they'd equipped themselves with sufficient warm clothing and then, with sudden seriousness, told them he'd overheard his trooper challenge them.

"I know he said nothing in itself objectionable, but I must know, was his conduct insolent?"

They told him there was nothing worth remarking, but he insisted. "I'm new to the military profession and it has been impressed upon me that, mild in nature as I am, I mustn't suffer the soldiers to take advantage. You must tell me if the man deserves punishment or they may all impose upon me and when we arrive at Longovicium the contagion spread to my new cohort."

Quintus laughed. "No, truly my young friend, you can be too much of a disciplinarian you know. Ah, see, the weather's clearing." Over their shoulders to the street beyond, only the occasional flake of snow fluttered in the wind. He rose and walked to the door, taking a jar of wine and a goblet to stand looking up at the sky. Manius watched him pouring wine.

Publius stayed with Manius at the table and said: "Perhaps I'm too sensitive, but insubordination horrifies me; something happened when I was younger."

"Really," Manius replied, keeping one eye on Quintus over Publius' shoulder, observing his sly work, "and what was that?"

Publius grimaced. "It was some years ago, when I was staying with a friend at Formiae, at his parents' villa and I witnessed a slave revolt."

Quintus returning to the table placed a glass of wine before Publius. "The Atellus affair – I certainly remember it, but I never heard a witness.

Tell us about it. Here, Manius, some wine."

Publius sipped from his goblet. "It was terrible. I couldn't believe my eyes."

He took another gulp. Quintus' eyes followed the cup to his lips and back to the table. "Go on," he prompted.

"Some slaves escaped from the market, freed others… ran riot. I saw them slaughter five people."

"How terrible for you," said Manius.

"It was. It taught me how precariously we maintain an ordered society."

He drained his cup and stared at the table. Quintus poured him a refill and assured him that discipline and the habit of unquestioning obedience made such crimes rare in the army. Manius suggested that as barbarians, including slaves, became more accustomed to Roman society and its benefits they would grow to be less like beasts and learn to reason.

"There is something in what Manius says," agreed Quintus. "Don't we not see it here in Eboracum, that we have established a place of civilisation among the Britons? Don't they grow more like us?"

Publius, now blinking and swaying, seemed not to notice when Quintus added, under his breath, "may the gods help them."

"It's true," Publius said. "As the poet says: 'Forget not Roman, that it is your special genius to rule the peoples; to impose… to impose… the ways of peace, to spare the defeated and to… and to… to…'"

"'… to crush those proud men who will not submit'," finished Quintus.

Publius swayed; made a couple more poor attempts at Virgilius Maro, his head nodded, he blinked again and said he felt unwell. Manius marvelled at the speed of the apothecary's potion.

"Unwell?" said Quintus. "We can't have that, not if we're taking the road tomorrow." Publius' reply was unintelligible. "Come, let's get him back to his room."

They supported him from the tavern, grinning at the curious stares and jokes from other customers. They took him back to the mansio, his legs hardly bearing him, and to his room, which happily was on the ground floor. They lay him on his bed and covered him, at which point he regained some life, sitting up and insisting they alert his troopers to his illness.

"Yes, yes," said Quintus, "I shall send their optio to you forthwith."

Satisfied, the young centurion fell back, unconscious.

Quintus took Manius by the shoulder as they crept away. "If that whispering ninny thinks I'm going to rouse his Samartians, he's a bigger fool than I've taken him for. I've left a note for him in our room, telling him we'll be away for a day and advising him to keep quiet about it. If he says nothing, neither shall we."

§

They left Eboracum and headed west. There was no snow but the biting wind was against them and their horses moved almost crabwise, straining to keep their heads facing away from the weather. This made for a slow journey, a whole afternoon trudging a lonely, muddy track, fording streams and one large river. They urged their reluctant mounts into its icy, dark water. It was a countryside alive with water, their way crossed by small brooks and chuckling rivulets running from the barren heath above. Manius looked at the tufts of coarse grass and bronze, dead bracken bent back by the unrelenting wind and wondered: could a land as well as a people be barbaric? Could Rome ever civilise such a place?

After the river they began to climb steadily towards that heath that encroached more on the rough pasture. Manius grew uneasy. They were heading into the hills where they'd been warned the Wolves were most active. Despite the wind, Manius kept his head up and alert for any hint of threat, regretting the absence of their Samartians. But they met nobody, apart from a lad leading a cow in the direction of Eboracum, who sneaked a wary look and gave them a wide berth.

It was dusk and it had started to rain when they reached a large village of the British round houses inside a stockade. They rode slowly through and faces peered from the dark interiors of these houses. At the last, an old man came to his doorway and Quintus halted and addressed him in Celtic. Manius heard "Tita Amatia Aculeo." The old man grew agitated, furiously shaking and then nodding his head before pointing down the road beyond the village.

Quintus muttered something, frowned and grunted in pain and swung himself out of the saddle.

"This is Cenares. Tita Amatia's villa is near but this fellow insists we won't be allowed admission unannounced. He'll give us shelter while he sends word."

Manius dismounted while the old man bawled something into the interior of his home. A young boy wriggled through the tunnel of a doorway and set off at a run, in the direction the old man had indicated. Quintus and Manius stooped to enter and crouched by the fire while the old man and Quintus held a disjointed conversation which Quintus occasionally interpreted.

"He says Tita Amatia is a good mistress; that the local people hold her in great affection for her late husband's sake and because she fulfils all the obligations of a chief."

"Ask him if the Wolves have been active here."

Quintus shook his head. "That might not be wise."

They gazed into the fire in uneasy silence until the old man spoke again. Quintus explained that he'd asked what brought them here and that he'd answered they were on their way north, to the Wall, but brought messages to Tita Amatia from family in Italy.

Fifteen minutes later a figure stooped to come through the door to stand before them: a tall Briton, with red hair and flowing moustache. He bowed and spoke to them in heavily accented Latin.

"You are Suetonius Lupus?" he asked Quintus. "I am Bodvoc, steward of Amatia Aculeo's household. She greets you well and has sent me to escort you to her."

"Good," said Quintus. To Manius, something in his voice sounded ill.

They followed Bodvoc outside, thanked the old man and gave him an as. Bodvoc set off at an easy stride, walking between their horses, taking them up the road; then off on a tree-lined drive to the right through creaking gates mounted on stone pillars. This led through ploughed fields where ahead, in the failing light, Manius could make out a large and impressive villa of black stone, two stories high, with a colonnade running along the length of its front and, behind it, extensive farm buildings. As they neared, it was less imposing, its grandeur destroyed. Water leaked from cracked guttering, weeds pushed through paving stones and doors and window shutters were spotted with dots of orange fungus and were rotting.

They approached under dripping trees which stood among nettles and dock. Manius saw a face at the main entrance for an instant before it was withdrawn. At Bodvoc's signal, they dismounted and he put his fingers to his mouth and whistled, driving crows protesting from the branches. Two slaves ran from the farm buildings behind the villa to lead away their horses.

Bodvoc took them to the front door and, lowering their hoods, they followed him into an entrance hall which was illuminated only by the dying day coming through the door behind. The corridor leading to the villa beyond was dark and cave-like; the air coming out of it cold and damp. Manius shivered.

Then, from out of the dark interior, two more men appeared to open a door to the visitors' right, off the entrance hall. Bodvoc gestured for them to enter and they passed into a large room lit by a couple of oil lamps, showing walls whose plaster was bubbling and flaking. Its only furniture was a bench running along three of the walls and the floor tiles were cracked. Manius scarcely had time to take this in, for his attention was fixed on the knife that one of Bodvoc's companions presented to his breast while the other similarly threatened Quintus.

"What in hell…?" demanded Quintus.

Bodvoc stepped forward and plucked Quintus' sword from its scabbard. "A precaution," he said, before disarming Manius.

"You might just have asked," grumbled Quintus. "And now you can get this fool to take his damned dagger…"

He broke off, staring at the door, where a woman stood. Dressed as a high-born Roman, she was past middle age, thin, her coarse and wiry hair was piled high, its colour a mix of brown and grey. Her blue eyes were fixed on Quintus, whose face had turned the colour of bleached linen.

"Quintus Suetonius Lupus," she whispered.

Quintus' silence seemed to stretch, until she put her head on one side. "Tita," he said, with a slight bow and a meekness in his voice Manius had never heard before.

There was another silence while they contemplated each other, a silence Quintus again broke. "Madam, will you tell these ruffians to put their knives down?"

She didn't reply and the blades remained at their breasts.

Ah yes, her madness. Was she confused as to their allegiance? Manius said with a half laugh: "We're the Emperor's men, on the Emperor's business!"

She fastened her gaze on him and its coldness stopped his heart. "Who's this?"

"My son," said Quintus, "my adopted son."

"Your son, by all that's sacred! Who'd have thought that? Tell me, a father and son can have no secrets. Does he know?"

"Does he know what?"

"About me?"

Like some beast tormented in the games, he lowered his shaggy head and shook it. "No… no, he does not."

"He does not? You surprise me. Didn't you always say that whoever seeks to understand the present must first understand the past? Do you remember saying that? Do you? No answer – well, I'm sure you will, if only you put your mind to it, for you have a great mind. Everybody said so. No, it's not right Quintus Suetonius, and you're a virtuous man. So can you explain why this boy, your… son shouldn't know the truth?"

Another sullen headshake.

"Tell him then."

"Tita, why are you…?"

"Tell him!"

Quintus gave a last quick glance at the terrible woman and turned to Manius; cleared his throat and spoke, with painful reluctance. "You know… you know I told you about Tita Amatia… this lady… Tita Amatia Aculeo… and her banishment from Rome, from Italy? I… I mentioned another, a young man, a young officer, who was, er… also bound up in the business?" Manius nodded. Quintus swallowed. "That was me."

Manius gawped at him and then at her.

"Did that weigh on your mind all those years?" she asked, her voice raised, grating. "All those years, did you feel guilty that you escaped with such a light sentence – and that commuted – while I was sent here, and left to rot? Did you not reflect that yours was the greater guilt? You, after all, were the dashing young soldier who seduced such a child, took her reputation, her family, her home, her country. Surely that must have tormented you? Tell me it tormented you, that you burned to fly to my side and rescue me, or at least to share my fate – tell me that!"

There were red spots in her cheeks, her eyes wide and moist and her voice a screech. Truly a mad woman.

Bodvoc and his two ruffians clearly understood their mistress's anger, and their eyes too shone with hatred. Quintus looked down, from shame or prudence, which only seemed to quicken her rage.

"Nothing to say? No words from the silver-tongued seducer who turned a young girl's head with his honeyed cooing? Perhaps you're overcome with emotion, perhaps you're so moved to have finally confronted your crime and its victim. Aye, that must be it, you're relieved to have confessed yourself. Yes it must be a great relief to have unburdened yourself now – just before you die."

She shouted the last terrible word and Bodvoc drew back the hand that still held Manius' sword to Quintus' belly.

Manius gasped: "No!"

Chapter Eight

Tita Amatia leaned over the table with a jug and filled Manius' goblet with ale.

"I'm sorry," she said, "but you – insofar as I know you – didn't deserve that." She jerked a thumb at the glowering figure, reclining on a couch at the end of the table. "He did."

"Why?" barked Quintus.

"You ask why? I told you: because you abandoned me and left me here, even when you were released from exile."

"You could have come home. You were given the chance!"

"And little thanks to you."

He gave a half splutter, half growl. "You're mad, you always were."

Manius believed him. Twenty minutes ago this crazed hag subjected them to a cruel sham before ordering her man Bodvoc to stay his hand. Then she threw back her head and released a great cackling laugh. Manius had moaned, convinced she was toying with them and they'd be slain in that cold, damp temple of insanity. Quintus unleashed a stream of such ferocious oaths that Bodvoc was again ordered not to kill.

She clapped her hands, as if calling children from play, to announce that dinner had been prepared in their honour.

Now here they were in a dining room that backed onto a courtyard in which the wind dashed an overgrown shrub against the window. The room, in as sorry a state as the rest, was ill lit by a few lamps and a fire. The food and drink on the heavy marble were in keeping with that villa of grandeur-fallen-into-decay. They had murky ale, not wine, served in fine goblets, colourless boiled cabbage and grey, mottled pike on a silver platter. The knives had ivory handles but one or two were repaired with bone.

Two slaves served and left and, as soon as they had gone, Quintus and Tita resumed their recriminations. As Manius chewed his pike, staring ahead.

"Anyway," she said. "I forgive you." She laughed at Quintus' expression. "Yes, I forgave you years ago. After all, I married a good man and was happy."

"Then why, in the name of the Unconquered Sun, did you make me – make us" – a savage nod here at Manius – "undergo that little performance?"

Another laugh. "Impulse: to remind myself how you behave when threatened."

Quintus threw down his knife. "How so very like Tita Amatia Aculeo, how very unchanged you are. Well, you've had your entertainment at my expense, but also at the boy's."

She placed a claw-like hand on Manius' forearm. "But I've apologised to him, haven't I? Anyway, is he not a Roman? Can't he face death?"

Quintus gave her a long look and ate with quick, angry movements. Manius kept his eyes on his plate, praying the woman wouldn't speak to him. He only wanted to get Quintus on one side to plot their escape. As to how – his mind raced in that room where the quiet was so intense, emphasised by the scraping of knives on plates, the crackling of the fire and the clawing of the shrub at the window.

Eventually Quintus asked Tita to refill his goblet. This led to an awkward exchange about Rome and common acquaintances. She was up-to-date: she not only exchanged letters with the late emperor but continued correspondence with those who'd been close to him and she named some who'd been members of the Imperial Council and were still close to the present Council.

"So," Quintus said, gruffly in a lull, "you might tell me about your life in Britannia."

She contemplated him, her head tilted and then, without faltering, described how for months after her arrival she'd languished in Londinium.

"Suicide was never far from my thoughts," she declared brightly. "Happily, the then governor, Gaius Papirius Aelianus, was an old friend of father's. He was sweet and he and his family cared for me and I was accepted into Londinium's society."

After a year she'd been introduced to Epillus, British nobleman – but Roman citizen – a Brigantine chieftain. She'd admired and respected him and, when he offered marriage, a union promoted by Papirius Aelianus, she'd accepted and had come north to live with him among his people.

She gazed through the fire and toyed with her goblet as she described how she'd grown to love him and his people. But her dear Epillus had died, after more than twenty years of a blessed, but childless, marriage. Serving as a Roman magistrate, he'd been killed in a Brigantine uprising.

They all stared into the fire. The silence was threatening to become awkward when they were interrupted. Bodvoc appeared at the door with a low cough, took one hesitant pace into the room and bowed.

Tita Amatia spoke in Celtic, glanced apologetically at her guests and switched to Latin as she rose and advanced toward him: "What is it?"

He coughed again. "My lady…"

He stopped, barged violently aside by a careering brown bundle which burst from the door behind before hitting the floor to skid to a halt at Tita Amatia's feet. There it uncurled into a young girl – perhaps fourteen – dressed in a brown woollen peasant dress and with long, lank brown hair. She grasped Tita Amatia's legs and turned a tear-stained face to her, speaking, between agonised sobs.

Bodvoc cursed, grabbed at the girl with one hand and swept the other back to cuff her.

"Leave her!" snapped Tita Amatia.

She knelt and took the girl's arms, soothing her. The girl's sobs subsided into sniffles, and then gently Tita Amatia questioned her. Manius shot a curious glance at Quintus who returned a slight shrug.

After some minutes Tita Amatia raised the girl to her feet, whispered something, stroked her cheek and handed her back to Bodvoc who led her away. Tita Amatia watched them go, then returned to her couch clenching and rubbing her hands together and biting her lower lip.

"You followed that?" she asked Quintus.

"The dialect and the local accent are difficult, and in her distress..."

Tita Amatia gave a thin smile. "Aye, distress..." She dropped onto her couch, toyed with her goblet, breathed heavily and looked up. "She's from a village to the south. Last night she fell in with a soldier. He raped her. She hasn't told her parents but ran to an aunt who brought her here."

"Why here?"

"Don't I ask myself that every time? She wants help and redress and I must do my best."

"How?"

"Comfort and feed her. Tomorrow I'll send for her parents and have her explain to them. They'll not regard it as any great matter so long as they get recompense. For that I shall apply to Julius Valerianus in Eboracum – he's legate of Sixth Victrix. I'll persuade him a thousand sesterces will prevent trouble."

"Trouble?"

She shrugged. "You know as well as I, where there are soldiers there's rape. My people understand that too – in normal times, but these aren't normal times."

There was another silence which she broke with a change of subject. "I corresponded, as you know, with Marcus Aurelius. I valued his compassion, his friendship, as I believe he valued mine."

"He did," murmured Quintus.

"Did he? I'm glad. I know he also valued the information I sent, on what his governors were up to. Anyway, he'd invited me home before and I'd declined, being happy building my life here with Epillus and, after he died, he repeated the invitation."

"And you declined again?" Manius asked.

She smiled at him. "I see you wonder why. You're a true Roman young man and marvel that anyone could refuse Rome's glories and the beauties of Italy for this province. In truth, I'd grown to like it here. Rome had ejected me but my husband's people welcomed me. They'd also grown to trust me and respect me. They do respect women, you see. They even allow them to rule; permit them more than rearing children and entertaining guests. So, no, I'd no wish to leave, I couldn't." She emptied her goblet and refilled it. "Also perhaps I was afraid to return."

"Afraid?"

"Is that so surprising? I'd been away for more than twenty years, my family were dead and my friends had forgotten me" – she shot an arch look at Quintus – "and I doubt my rough provincial manners would've passed muster in polite society."

Watching her taking another swig of ale, Manius doubted it too.

Quintus cleared his throat. "And how do you… fare, with no husband, no master of the household? The estate – is it a good one?"

She bridled. "My husband made this the best estate in the North. True, the land isn't good for grain but what we do grow is readily bought by the army, as are our cattle, sheep and horses. Only think of the beasts so many thousands of troops need and of their demand for hides, for leather, tents, shields, clothing, harness, gut for the artillery, wool for their uniforms."

She noticed Manius eyeing the bubbling plaster and the damaged mosaic. She laughed. "Young Manius is a sceptic. He wonders why, if I'm so rich, I don't live like Priscus and show off my magnificent orbis costing several hundred thousand sesterces – oh yes I know all about that, don't you worry.

"He blushes prettily this boy of yours. Young man, let me explain to your uncomprehending Roman mind: I live like this because I choose to. It would be ridiculous to do otherwise. After a day riding the estate in the cold and rain you want ale, not wine. You need to discuss business with your steward and you serve him plain food because he prefers it. My slaves aren't chained together in the fields, they're not locked up with the animals at night, they come and go as they please. If they wish to refer some problem to me or to Bodvoc they come into the villa, trampling mud and dung behind them. When it's cold you don't light the furnace to heat a huge villa which is largely unoccupied and which uses too much wood, which my people need. No, you light the fire in the room where you sit. Epillus and I hardly ever entertained, and I certainly never do now. These couches have been brought from the lumber room in your honour. I admit, sometimes I look round and feel that I should repair and make new, but then, then there's another harvest, or a murrain in the cattle and, somehow, one year becomes another."

"Tell me, Tita," asked Quintus. "Why didn't you take your husband's name?"

She laughed again. "Snobbery, Quintus, sheer snobbery – oh, on his part not mine. When he married me he was swollen with conceit at joining such a patrician family – the poor fool – so he styled himself Epillus Amatius Aculeo. Imagine my delight in writing to tell father, picturing his reaction at his revered family name being taken by a man born a barbarian. Priceless!"

Manius had never met such a woman. Clearly mad, but not dangerous. He savoured how she discomfited Quintus.

"Tell me about yourself, young Manius. Is Quintus a good father? Does he still drink too much?"

"Leave the boy alone!" said Quintus, more in weariness than anger.

She continued to look at Manius with her smiling eyes. "Very well, your father would have me change the subject. So, let's talk of serious matters. What brings you here?"

"The Emperor's business," said Quintus, before Manius could speak.

With deliberation, she turned to him. "I supposed that much, but why? And here?"

"We were sent to Londinium to place ourselves at the disposal of Horatius Buteo. Because of your warning he feared that his communications with Rome were being intercepted. He requested help and they sent us."

She nodded. Manius wondered – she had the ear of the late emperor and was close to some of his son's present counsellors – had she written to suggest that Quintus would be the ideal frumentarius to send to the provincial procurator's aid? Quintus' face betrayed nothing.

"Yes," she said, "interrupting imperial communications is truly serious. The gods would cover their eyes."

"Well Buteo's letters won't be read any more," said Quintus, and told her about his murder, their meetings with him, and their conversations with Priscus and the governor's suspicions about Tiberius Flavius Fimbria's treason. "It was decided that we should come north. Buteo believed that you might have information and said you told him – or implied – there were undercurrents and that Priscus himself might not be as he claims to be."

Tita Amatia summoned the slaves to bring more ale and clear away the dishes. She rested her elbows on the table and rubbed her hands together. "I've no certain intelligence, you must understand that. But I know something of Priscus and of Flavius Fimbria. One is a subtle politician and the other an objectionable boor but not someone whose loyalty has ever been in doubt."

"He's ambitious."

"Show me the man who isn't. Priscus may be right in his judgement of him, but, equally, he may be wrong. I do know this: Fimbria doesn't overstate the dangers in the North. I fear the Brigantes will rise.

"I know my people are unsettled and afraid. Thirty years ago Rome deprived the Brigantes of the greater part of their land. My husband was unusual in having land. Without land how were the chiefs ever to qualify for office and become knights? How were they ever to be bound to Rome?"

"This Iovir, the leader of the Wolves, what do you know of him?"

"He's dangerous."

"So, he exists?"

"A phantom couldn't inspire such fear or loyalty, nor unite the petty chiefs as he can. Some say he's descended from Cartimandua the Brigantine queen in Claudius' time, others from Venutius and that he was brought up among the Caledonian tribes north of the frontier."

Quintus stroked his beard; stood, walked over to the fire and held out his hands in its heat. He spoke over his shoulder. "Tell me: why don't you trust Priscus?"

She studied her fingernails. "Often women don't trust particular men. Perhaps we can't say why, can't put it into words, but we're usually right, more often right than men are about men, or about women for that matter."

Manius saw Quintus roll his eyes, but he mastered his irritation and pleaded. "Tita, we're not children any more. Can you give me no more than that?"

She looked up from her nails, directly at Manius, but he didn't think it was him she saw; under her make-up, she coloured. Manius was certain her eyes moistened.

"Very well," she said. "I'll try to give you more, I'll try to demonstrate with such and such a reason why I'm led to this or that conclusion, but that conclusion will be the same as that reached by a different route. There is real reason to fear rebellion among the Brigantes. Tiberius Flavius Fimbria fears the same. So do Priscus' staff officers. So why does Priscus set his face against it? No, don't answer me yet. You set me on this path of reasoning, let me at least finish.

"Priscus was loyal to our late dear Emperor. So were we. Marcus Aurelius was a great man, but he let blood blind him and made Commodus his heir – and Commodus, we know, is poisonous. He will be a bad emperor."

§

Tiro stamped and beat his arms across his chest as his breath turned to vapour in the night air. For the thousandth time he craned his head round the doorway which sheltered him from the snow, to peer through the falling flakes up and down the narrow street. Where was the old bastard?

He detested the cold. It froze his blood, made him lethargic, like a lizard, slow of thought and loath to move. Maybe that was good. He'd been a bit too quick to move recently. Taking this fucking job for a start. And that fat cunt in Londinium, he'd gone too far there, got carried away. Not this time, no blood this time. The cold would make him subtle.

If it didn't fucking kill him first. Where was the cunt?

At last! Footsteps padding through the snow – and some movement: a shape emerging from the shadows resolving itself into the figure of a man, bent, clutching his cape to his neck and picking his way with short, cautious but rapid steps.

It drew closer and Tiro made out the grey beard disappearing into the folds of wool. It was him, Nectovelius Vindicis. The name written above the shop door, opposite which Tiro had been waiting for more than a freezing hour. He'd tracked him there from the tavern and had made discreet enquiries among the neighbours, confirming that grey beard was this Vindicis, a leather trader who lived above his shop with wife, grown up daughter and one elderly slave woman. Tiro had gambled that by now they'd surely be in bed and that he'd have the old man to himself.

Vindicis reached his door and fumbled at the latch. Tiro crossed the street in four swift strides and put a hand on his shoulder. Vindicis gasped, spun round, his eyes staring.

"What… what?

Tiro relaxed his grip. "Nectovelius Vindicis?"

"Y… yes."

"I must speak with you."

"But… who are you?"

"Lucius Sempronius Asellio. I'm from Londinium, on the governor's staff."

"The governor!"

Tiro nodded. "I am in Eboracum on a most important matter."

"But… what have I to do…? I don't understand. At this time?"

"Yes, there's no time to lose."

"What do you want?"

Alarm hadn't entirely left Vindicis' eyes but Tiro could see it being supplanted by suspicion and some irritation. He began to regret the subtle approach. He bent closer and hissed:

"Can we just go inside?"

"Inside? Why? It's late."

"I have to ask you about two men you spoke with today."

"Who?"

Tiro suppressed an urge to seize his throat and shake him, Instead, he gave an impatient growl, leaned across Vindicis, put his thumb on the latch and pushed open the door, gently forcing the other, bleating protests, across the threshold.

Tiro was hit by the pungent smell of leather. There was dim light from a dying fire in a hearth to their left and he could make out a counter before them, then other forms took shape – cupboards, a table and two chairs by the fire.

He pushed Vindicis towards them. "This won't take long. Answer my questions and you'll be in bed in twenty minutes and I'll be on my way. Why don't you liven up that fire."

Vindicis shot him a resentful look but turned to do as he was bidden while Tiro eased the door shut. He watched the other put a log on the hearth and kick it into the bed of embers sending sparks crackling and shooting and lighting the room with an orange glow and throwing their shadows stark against the wall. That burst of light also revealed the anxiety in Vindicis' pallid face and the eyes which couldn't meet Tiro's.

"Sit down," said Tiro, taking a chair himself. He held his hands out to the flames and contemplated Vindicis.

"You're alarmed. That's understandable. I apologise for coming at this hour but business – the Emperor's business – demands it."

"The Emperor's business? Me?"

Tiro grinned and rubbed his hands together. "Not what you expected, I daresay."

Vindicis shook his head, his eyes now staring into Tiro's.

"The thing is," continued Tiro confidentially, "I must know about those two men you spoke to in the tavern."

"But… they were tax officials."

Tiro shook his head. "No, they aren't tax officials, they're crooks… villains."

"You mean they're malefactors?"

"Malefactors? Yes, malefactors. It's my task to bring them to justice. I must know what they said to you – and what you said to them."

Vindicis clutched and stroked his beard, his eyes again avoiding Tiro's. He stood and walked a few steps. Tiro watched with rising irritation.

"How do I know whom I should believe?" whined Vindicis. "How do I know it isn't you who are the malefactor… as you say… a crook?

Tiro tried a reassuring smile. "If I was a rogue, would I be sitting here talking to you like a reasonable man? Wouldn't I rather be threatening you with a knife, offering to slice you slowly and then start on your wife and daughter upstairs?" Vindicis halted in his pacing and Tiro continued silkily. "Of course I would. But I won't because I'm a government man. Now, will you sit down and tell me what passed between you and those two?"

Vindicis moved slowly to the chair and sat gingerly upon it, as though it might trap him. "They asked me for an apothecary."

"An apothecary? What the hell for?"

"For eastern medicaments."

"Is that all?"

"Also for directions to Cenares."

Ah, yes, Cenares. He'd been told – that's where the mad old bitch lived.

"Why Cenares? What business have they there?"

"They didn't tell me. That was all they wanted to know and all they had to say."

Tiro studied him. The log was burning well now. He no longer felt cold. In fact it was warm. He bent to reach into his boot for his knife.

§

A bad emperor, she'd said. Treason.

Not far from what Manius knew Quintus' own view to be, but shocking to hear it so baldly stated. He didn't think that he showed any reaction but it seemed to suit her to pretend that he had. "I've horrified you Manius," she said. "Perhaps you'd rather leave the room than hear your Emperor so traduced."

"No madam, I'm not horrified."

"Well, you had your chance."

If it didn't horrify Quintus, it annoyed him. "Really Tita! What has this to with anything? What has this to do with Priscus?"

"Why, isn't it obvious? This is the way I feel about Commodus, despite my love for his father – no, because of that love. I'm sure it's the way you feel, and I suspect it's the way Priscus feels. And, if I'm right, then where's his loyalty to the Emperor now?"

And, thought Manius, she was right. Hadn't Priscus as good as told them so? This woman might be mad but she was no fool. Quintus plainly took her seriously. He left the fireplace and swung himself onto the couch beside her, sitting on its edge, elbow on the table.

"You're suggesting it's Priscus who's planning a move against the Emperor? Surely, he'd then need the North to be quiet?"

"Of course. He could hardly take the legions to Gaul and march on Rome, leaving Britannia in flames behind. No, the army would never follow him then. But if he came to terms with the Brigantes and promised to restore their lands, under a king who'd rule as a client of Rome and secure the frontier – and free thirty thousand of our troops to make him Emperor?"

Quintus laughed. "So, it's not all woman's instinct is it? Not just some strange sense that makes you distrust Priscus? No, you've got it all reasoned closely."

She pouted. "Perhaps I have, but, believe me my friend, that comes after the fact that I don't trust Priscus." She drank, before adding: "Nor it seems do some in Rome, or why would they give Flavius Fimbria command of the frontier legions? Think – if I'm right – how that must disrupt Priscus' plans."

Another realisation struck Manius: not only could she have been responsible for them being sent to Britannia but perhaps she'd also urged Rome to give Flavius Fimbria the northern command?

Quintus spoke as though thinking aloud. "So why would Priscus have approved our coming north so readily?"

"I too wondered that. Maybe he wants the frumentarii on the frontier, spying on Fimbria, rather than in Londinium, watching him."

"And is he right? Have we been outmanoeuvred?" He stood and strode between the table and the fire, stopping with his backside to it. "No, I think we've done the right thing. If you're mistaken, and if Flavius Fimbria is the villain Priscus makes him out to be, we must be close to him. If you're correct and Priscus is plotting against the Emperor, then we should still be in the North where things will be decided. The question is: what can we do? We have no one we can trust. Can you help?"

"I hear much of what happens among the Brigantes, and I have sources in Londinium. I'll give you more as I receive it."

"How will you convey it?"

"I've people who'll find you, have no fear. Do you know where you're bound?"

"A place called Longovicium."

"I know some people in those parts. But, doesn't your old comrade in arms, Lucius Antonius Merenda, command there?"

"So I've been informed."

"You'll be able to swap memories of your triumph in the Avidius Cassius affair. Don't look so sour, I'm sorry if I seem a little caustic." She turned to Manius. "You see Manius, as you age you wrap painful memories in irony to take away their sting and, if you're not careful, it becomes habit. Don't you find, Quintus Suetonius? But, no, you were always like that." She gave another cackling laugh, which set Manius grinning, despite Quintus' snarl. "And there my acidity was particularly misplaced. The Cassius affair was a great stroke. You saved the Empire. I was proud of you."

Quintus started and coloured, but she added: "The Balbus affair, on the other hand…" and she shook her head as Quintus glowered.

"Are you a witch? Is there nothing you don't know?"

"Very little." She shook her head again. "I hear you were as drunk as a tavern rat. Oh Quintus Suetonius, you should've married. You need a woman to watch over you; to make your life less of a misery than you make it yourself."

Quintus gave a great `Bah!' and slapped the table. "As you know so much, you'll, for sure, be able to discover everything about the Brigantes and the Wolves. We were discussing these matters, not idle tittle-tattle from Rome. May we return to the point?"

She directed a swift sly smile at Manius. From here the talk went over the same ground.

Eventually the subject exhausted, their hostess drew it to a close by calling, not for more ale, but for wine, two jars of Falernian, at which Quintus chortled his appreciation.

"I've been saving these," she said, "until such a special occasion, when I could once again have pleasant talk of Italy with someone."

"I thought you were in love with Britannia?"

"One never forgets a first love, does one?"

There was a short, awkward pause, quickly followed by, "do you remember this?" and "do you remember that?" Manius observed their evident pleasure at the memories and in the shared laughter and sighs. He tried to picture them as young. Quintus had told him that she had been running with a fast set of depraved young nobles. Surely he can't have been one of them? And, she'd claimed that he'd seduced her. By the heavens! There was a picture his mind refused to paint.

"Do you remember when we stayed with Voconius Romanus and he took us to the source of the Clitumnus?" she asked. "Oh, you should see it Manius. There's a hill densely cloaked with ancient cypresses and, at its foot, a spring gushes out through several channels and they run into a pool, so clear you count all the coins that have been thrown in. The water flows out and within moments it is a broad swift river upon which two boats can sail side by side. On either bank there are ash and poplars reflected perfectly in the cold, sparkling waters. You must see it Manius and, if you ever have a girl whose heart you wish to win, take her too. It's better than rhinoceros-horn."

"Tita," said Quintus, waving a playful finger.

She swivelled on her couch and contemplated Manius with a disconcerting intensity. "But, somehow, young man, I don't think you'll need rhinoceros horn to arouse a girl's interest. You're handsome and there's a depth that intrigues. You're intelligent, that's obvious and maybe harbour something deeper, something calculating and sly, which isn't unusual in an orphan, for they must learn to look out for themselves. Useful in your occupation too, I would've thought."

Manius was embarrassed, but she seemed to lose interest and returned to Quintus. "And in Rome, do you remember how we used to walk on the Embankment, enjoying the breeze on a summer's evening? Do couples still do that and are there still fortune tellers and all the performing animals?

Quintus smiled and said there were.

"And do you," she asked, looking at him from under her eyelashes, "sometimes go there and think of me?" He smirked, placed a hand on her forearm and said it had been known. "And then," she asked, "do you slope off to find some whore in the Subura?"

"Tita!" he exclaimed; saw that she joked and they both laughed.

Manius made his excuses and went to find a slave to show him to their room.

§

Quintus watched Manius leave with alarm. He eyed her uneasily and she returned his look, a slight smile on her lips.

"I came across Gut Crispinus in Londinium," he blurted. "Remember Gut?"

"Gut! In Londinium? By heavens! Of course I remember him." She laughed. "He was an admirer of mine."

"Not any more he's not. He's dead." Deliberately brutal, but he had to steer the conversation away from more dangerous waters.

"Dead? What happened?"

He told her, briefly and dispassionately: how his own blunder had led to Gut's murder. He also passed on Gut's final message for her. Tita

Amatia gazed at him as he spoke and her eyes remained on him for some seconds.

"Poor Gut," she said flatly.

"Aye, poor Gut. He had his faults but he was a good man in his own way – true to his friends."

Tita Amatia snorted. "Oh Quintus! It was Gut Crispinus gave us away all those years ago. Hadn't you guessed?"

"What!"

"Oh, yes. Of course, he knew about us, everybody did – apart from my family. He was jealous. He told my father."

"How do you know this?"

"Because my loving father took great delight in telling me, to impress upon me what a shabby bunch of degenerates my friends were."

"Gut Crispinus! The treacherous fat bastard..."

"It was a long time ago. If I hadn't quite forgiven him, I've long since ceased to care. It's flattering – such treachery must have sprung from great devotion."

Quintus was speechless. Here was much to digest. They were both silent.

At last she said: "Why did you wait until now to tell me? Doesn't the boy know?"

Quintus shook his head.

"Why not? Why haven't you told him?"

Again, Quintus shook his head. "I don't know. Perhaps I'm too accustomed to keeping my own counsel. I've learnt the wisdom of that and it's habit. If... if I'd told him about Gut... well, one thing leads to another and then to... to us."

He looked at the floor, embarrassed. When he raised his eyes he saw Tita Amatia's were shining and she blinked hurriedly. She jumped to her feet and paced the floor. She stopped and spoke without turning. "The man who killed him – who is he?"

"Gut said he was a Sicilian and his name – or one name he goes by – is Tiro."

"Whose creature is he?"

"I don't know. I doubt it's Priscus. It could be Flavius Fimbria; it could be Rome."

"Rome? How?"

Quintus shrugged. "Things are complicated now on the Palatine. I won't echo your feelings on our new emperor but let us say things aren't done as they were in his father's day. There are those close to the purple who revel in setting one part of the state against another. But that's speculation – I don't know."

"Tiberius Flavius Fimbria is heading north you say?"

"He's expected any day in Eboracum, but we shall push on and wait for him in Longovicium."

Tita Amatia returned to her couch and folded her arms across her chest. "I too shall go to Longovicium. I shall await Flavius Fimbria in Eboracum and accompany him."

"What in Heaven's name for?"

She smiled. "I want to keep an eye on you. The boy's not up to it."

"Haven't I enough to worry about? Or is this some joke?"

"No, no joke. If this Sicilian is working for Flavius Fimbria I shall discover where he is. Then I'll settle scores for Gut. He may have betrayed me but he was one of ours and there are too few of us left. Oh, do stop spluttering, it's of no great moment. You know Flavius Fimbria is married to Decima Valeria Corvina, as was. She was the baby sister of Marca, you must remember her. If she's travelling with her husband it'll be perfectly natural for me to go to see her, and him, in Eboracum and to travel north with their protection. I have lands near the frontier I must inspect. Why are you so cross? You have no agents in the North. I can provide those."

Quintus shook his head. "There's danger."

"Nonsense! I've lived among these people most of my life, I know them. Anyway, where would I be safer? With the army or here alone?"

A kind of weariness washed over Quintus, a familiar feeling even if he hadn't experienced it for more than thirty years.

"You will complicate my task."

"How?"

"Hell and fire Tita! I have too many balls to juggle – the boy, now you... What if you come across this Sicilian?"

"I shall report it to you," she said with sudden girlish submissiveness which didn't convince.

"You swear you'll do nothing rash?"

His blood froze as she rose from her couch with an arch look and advanced on him.

"It's a long time since I did anything rash Quintus."

Chapter Nine

Manius awoke before light when a slave brought a basin of hot water. He hauled himself from the bed, into the shocking cold air and saw Quintus in bed opposite, rubbing his face, muttering. Manius remembered being woken by him during the night, blundering in, tripping, stumbling and whispering oaths. Now Quintus avoided his eye, as the slave told them his lady would be pleased to see them for breakfast.

They exchanged grunts as they splashed water on their faces and hurried, shivering, to dress. The slave led them along a corridor, across a courtyard and into a small dining room.

There was a welcome fire in the hearth and Tita Amatia sat at table, no longer in the formal wear of a Roman lady, but in a coarse broadcloth tunic and, under that – to Manius' amazement – breeches. Around her legs, lifting their heads to slobber her down-turned face, were two great hounds, tails scything the air and paws tapping on the stone flags.

She pushed them down and greeted her guests. Quintus mumbled, while she wore an expression of amused, yet discreet, satisfaction. Determined to notice nothing, Manius busied himself patting the dogs, until she ordered them away and invited her guests to the table for water, bread and honey.

"You return to Eboracum today? You shan't go as you came, without escort. I'll send Bodvoc with you. Keep your military tunics with your belts and swords concealed beneath your cloaks. There's no sense tempting fate. The Wolves might not respect my name, nor even fear Bodvoc."

"You are too kind Tit… madam," said Quintus. "Perhaps you'd remind your Bodvoc to return our swords."

She gave her cackling laugh. "I'd forgotten how you were disarmed."

Their weapons were restored when they went to the stables to be reunited with their horses, which seemed refreshed and lively under the care of Tita's cross-eyed groom, despite the high wind and further flurries of snow which depressed Manius' spirits if not theirs. The villa seemed less foreboding, the grey dawn revealing nothing ominous but only highlighting its disrepair: a hanging gutter here, a boarded window there and a shutter swinging in the wind on one creaking hinge. To Manius, this dilapidation now seemed jaunty rather than threatening.

They stood with her and Bodvoc, ready to depart. Quintus looked awkward, while her eyes sparkled. Finally, with violent clearing of his throat, he turned to Manius. "Go with Bodvoc for a little way beyond the stock houses while Tita Amatia and I confer."

Manius went gratefully, riding with the impassive steward to wait ten minutes for Quintus to join them. Some miles after Cenares, once satisfied Bodvoc was sufficiently ahead, Manius whispered – in Greek to be doubly careful.

"Tita Amatia gave us useful intelligence last night did she not?"

Out of the corner of his eye, Manius thought he saw Bodvoc stiffen in his saddle. Surely, it must have been surprise at an unfamiliar tongue.

"No," said Quintus, "she didn't. By now you should've learnt to distinguish intelligence from opinion. Her opinions however, are to be taken seriously. What she says contradicts Priscus, but he may be lying; she may be wrong. It muddies the waters."

After a pause, he continued nonchalantly: "Anyway, she may be able to revise her opinion for she intends to join Tiberius Flavius Fimbria in Eboracum and accompany him and his party north." Before Manius could reply he added: "She believes she may be able to learn more and apparently she has property near to the frontier."

Manius said nothing. It was unbelievable, but Quintus and Tita had once been lovers and seemed to have renewed, to some extent, their old affections. Seemed, for, as Quintus always emphasised, things were seldom as they appeared. All the same, he'd keep to himself his suspicions that she'd been responsible for them being sent to Britannia and for Tiberius Flavius Fimbria's appointment. Where did she truly stand in all of this?

In Londinium, Manius had had to contemplate having to look to his own interests and that Quintus might be a crutch on which he couldn't always lean. He'd feared a hired killer's knife, or wine, might bring Quintus' end but what if love were his Nemesis. Manius had to suppress a laugh, but it couldn't be discounted. Better to keep certain thoughts to himself. As an animal stores food for winter, perhaps he should have his own secret stock of suspicions and theories. It wasn't as though he was keeping intelligence to himself. Hadn't his teacher just said: opinions aren't the same as intelligence.

§

They reached Eboracum at midday, wet, cold and eager for a bath and a meal, and, in Manius' case, to building acquaintance with the German girl. Bodvoc left them once the vicus was in sight, only raising a lazy hand to acknowledge Manius' thanks.

"Surly bastard," grunted Quintus and kicked his horse into a trot to reach the mansio before the sleet returned. They were within a hundred paces of the West Gate, passing a small round temple on a patch of short cropped grass by a brook. In better weather it would have been a pleasant spot, but they wouldn't have given it a second glance, had not a man dashed towards them waving his arms and shouting. They recognised one of Publius Flavius' Sarmatian troopers. He ran to them, sending up a spray of half melted snow, and shouted that they should dismount. Quintus cursed his impudence, but the trooper jabbed a finger at the temple, babbling. Manius caught a few words.

"He says Publius Flavius is in there."

"I couldn't care less," said Quintus. But, with an angry shrug, he prised himself painfully out of the saddle. Manius did likewise; they handed their reins to the trooper and approached the building that was dedicated to the Liberator.

They entered. The air was sweet with incense and through its drifting fumes they saw a couple of pilgrims sprawled on mattresses on the stone benches lost in drunken slumber. Another – familiar – figure sat, his head in his hands, and an ancient dream reader sat by him, coaxing from him what he'd dreamed while he slept, craning for the slurred response.

"Allow the Liberator to free your memories," the reader wheedled his client, Publius Flavius Fimbria.

Manius guessed that a distraught Publius, desperate to discover their whereabouts, had gone to the temple and paid a few sesterces for the revelation that comes only with wine-induced sleep. He and Quintus waited in respectful silence, for Publius Flavius Fimbria to have his dreams interpreted and future foretold.

But his future was to remain veiled, for he looked up and his eyes slowly focused until they fixed a smouldering gaze on Quintus. The dream reader turned to see what was distracting him and gestured. "Go, shoo, go…"

But Publius rose, pushed the old man aside and approached. They retreated, until all three were on the snow outside. Publius stood, his chest inches from Quintus who stared back impassive.

Publius had plainly drunk heavily to spur his dreams – and that on top of Quintus' potion. He was pale, unshaven; his eyes red. He was also in the grip of an intense anger and he jabbed a quivering finger at Quintus' breast.

"You nasty, poisoning criminal." His voice was still soft but hissing with venom. "I insist you tell me where you've been, Otherwise I swear I'll have you dragged north in chains and cast at the feet of Tiberius Flavius Fimbria."

Manius was startled. This figure, trembling with biting rage had always been so placid and soft-spoken. He took an involuntary step back.

But Quintus lifted a ham-like fist and closed it slowly over Publius' finger. "Take this out of my face or I'll break it. That's better. Now, let's be clear how you and I stand. We both know that, if you offer any violence or insult to a frumentarius, your brother will have you cashiered, which he's probably aching to do, and if he doesn't, the Emperor will."

Publius, who had taken a pace back, now advanced on Quintus again, his mouth open for some furious retort.

But Quintus went on: "Also, whoever ordered you to guard us like runaway slaves won't be impressed when they learn you lost us. So, if you're wise, you'll keep your mouth shut. As to where I've been, that's a matter for me and the Emperor. Have you further reason to detain me? No, then I'm going to take a bath."

§

Manius hadn't anticipated a cheery travelling party the next day, but was surprised that Publius' anger was unabated. He ignored Manius' greeting as they saddled their horses but only yanked furiously on the girth strap, glaring through him, before stamping off to hiss at his Sarmatians. But Manius was more concerned that his German slave girl had disappeared. He'd spent much of the previous afternoon and evening inquiring of the mansio steward and other slaves as to her name and whereabouts, but this elicited only blank looks, shrugs and head-shaking. Now, he kept his eyes open in the streets around the mansio, for some glimpse of her. There was none and he was miserable for hours after they left Eboracum.

Publius didn't speak to them, during that day, nor at most of the subsequent forts at which they stayed. The journey to each was a painful crawl, for the weather now was fearful. Snow fell steadily, blinding them and drifting deep on the road, wearying horses and slowing progress. This was the first real snow Manius had known – and he knew it as an enemy, a dull, but relentless enemy, impervious to his curses and his pleas but always there, sapping his strength and constantly reinforced.

Where snow was absent, there was ice: puddles, ponds and meres glazed and once, even a small waterfall frozen, its torrent suspended in glittering knives, surprised and held while they tumbled over the rock.

The country grew wilder and the road began to climb, through heathland and woodland. Where the trees encroached, their escorts kept a watchful eye and Quintus and Manius hitched their cloaks off their thighs and loosened their swords in their scabbards. But vigilance was hard with snow falling thick into their faces and half closed eyes and encrusting damply on hoods and collars. Often they could hardly see for fifty paces and several times Manius' heart pounded when they lost sight of Publius and his Samartians.

Otherwise, Manius had time to think and plot how he might return to Eboracum. The lure of the German girl behind and the madness of what lay ahead made him resolved to part company with Quintus and Publius Flavius.

But how?

He wrestled with that, weighing, then rejecting the impracticable – outright refusal to go on, flight during the night. Finally, he fastened on a solution: he'd feign an illness, so Quintus would have to leave him at one of the forts, to follow on when he recovered.

Like hell he would.

He'd give them two days start and then return to Eboracum to spend the winter with his German, posting the occasional report to Caerellius Priscus. He could draw on imperial funds to buy the girl and keep them. It wouldn't cost much and he'd argue he'd unavoidably been cut off in Eboracum for the winter, yet still done what service he could, spending on necessities which would reasonably include a slave.

But his sly smile disappeared as soon as he surveyed the road ahead. Quintus wouldn't entertain the idea of him following them alone in this country with no escort. Could he argue that when he recovered he could use his authority as a frumentarius to compel a garrison commander to provide an escort? Perhaps.

He played with the idea, torn between its possibilities and its dangers, conscious that they were steadily increasing the distance between themselves and Eboracum. He resolved to attempt it.

So he began some ostentatious shivering, rubbing his forehead with a suppressed moan and lagging as far behind as he dared, keeping up when hailed with a wan smile.

Publius Flavius took no notice and Quintus only spared the occasional impatient glance. His symptoms had to worsen. He refused food in the mansio one evening – and begged scraps from the kitchen when Quintus had retired. The following morning, during a rest, he scuttled behind a hawthorn and made retching noises.

"What's wrong with you?" demanded Quintus.

"I think I have a fever."

Quintus grunted and told him he'd feel better after a night's sleep and some wine. Manius said he was sure Quintus was right.

"Don't worry about me."

But the lad did cause Quintus unease. If he fell ill, it would be a severe complication. He cursed. He should've foreseen it in this weather. The boy had never been strong. Still, strong enough to be lusting after that German wench, the young goat.

To hell with him! He should be concerned about himself. He'd older bones to stiffen in this accursed climate. Aye, and now Tita Amatia to bring sentiments more suited to a lovesick – or lust-sick – whelp like Manius. He urged his horse into a trot, to hurry towards that night's destination, to wine and warmth and away from his thoughts.

§

Manius refined his plan. He'd suggest he be left at a fort, to resume his journey with Tiberius Flavius Fimbria and his party when they arrived. They were supposedly only a few days behind. Then, easy enough to avoid the general and slip back to Eboracum. If Tita Amatia was with him that would call for more care but was hardly insurmountable.

But Manius couldn't screw up the courage. Several times he opened his mouth to speak and once Quintus looked at him.

"Well? What is it?"

Manius shook his head and said nothing.

As it was, his decision was made for him.

§

On their third day out of Eboracum, the snow turned to blizzard and again they lost sight of their escort. They exchanged anxious looks. The snow was particularly heavy and a sudden gust threw it hard against them. They realised – to Manius' horror – that they had strayed, when they saw the trees appearing suddenly out of the snow.

"We've missed the road!" Quintus shouted through the muffling flakes and waved an arm at the thick white canopy under which – the gods only knew where – was their road.

They reined in their horses so sharply that they reared and whinnied, echoing Manius' fear at their sudden arrival on the edge of true barbarity. They calmed the beasts while Quintus cursed and Manius muttered prayers to Silvanus who ruled amid those trees, that he might spare them and allow their return to civilisation.

"This way!" shouted Quintus. "We must go back."

They turned their horses and forced them, stumbling, the way they'd come, but it would have been hopeless had they not, after a couple of eternal minutes, seen dark figures take sudden shape in the whiteness. Manius had barely registered them before he heard the rasp of Quintus' sword leaving its scabbard, to be sheathed again as they recognised their escort looming out of the blizzard.

Manius gushed thanks to Publius for having returned for them but received only a hostile glare. Quintus chuckled and assured him – in the officer's hearing – that Publius would have left them to die in the snow or at the hands of barbarian forest dwellers, had he not been entrusted with their safety.

That night they were thankful to reach sanctuary at Vinovia fort, home to an infantry cohort, an isolated place on the north side of a valley above a river. There Manius abandoned his plan. Nothing on earth would persuade him to start back along that road alone to Eboracum. Even the beautiful German wasn't worth that. He'd missed his chance the day before. He wouldn't forget that lesson.

Once settled in their quarters, he told Quintus that he felt much more himself and would join him for dinner.

When they sat down to their meal they weren't alone; Quintus had ordered an icy and reluctant Publius to join them to discuss whether to go on or wait for some improvement in the weather.

"We could wait here until your brother catches up and move to Longovicium with his larger escort? According to the prefect he hasn't yet passed through."

Publius sat on the tavern bench with his arms folded across his chest and his lips pressed tight. Quintus poured wine and pushed a goblet across the table. "You can play the spoiled child some other time. At the moment we're discussing the Emperor's business and I – and he – expect you to behave like a Roman officer. I ask again: do we press on, or do we wait?"

While Publius glowered at Quintus, Manius reflected that he liked the idea of a larger escort but was uneasy that it belonged to a man who might not want two frumentarii to make it alive through this wasteland.

Breathing heavily, Publius shook his head. "No, we've no reason to suppose the weather will improve. We've barely entered winter. It's less than half a day's ride to Longovicium. If we start at first light, we'll be there by nightfall, even with this snow."

"And you've no wish to give your big brother cause to say you were waiting for his protection, eh?" said Quintus and, ignoring Publius flush of anger, added: "That's understandable. As our escort it's your decision. We ride on."

§

Manius cursed them both for that decision next morning, before light, by the stables, standing by their horses, whose breath was making clouds while all of them stamped with cold,. He cursed them even more when a distant howling of wolves – one, then two, then a chorus – had the horses wild-eyed and skittering, tugging at their bridles. At least they were real wolves, not Brigantine savages. Still his hands shook as he hauled himself into the saddle. His dread for those barbarians had grown since they'd nearly lost themselves in the woods the day before. He'd seen the Brigantines – docile; working the fields and they were little different from the Gauls. But he feared the unknown men that were out there in the hills and heaths of this wild country, who were more terrible for being unseen.

Manius' heart leaped into his mouth as his horse's rear hooves momentarily slipped on the icy cobbles of the mansio's yard, dropping him a sudden jolting foot before the beast regained balance, leaving him damning it and his fate and his bones and muscles that protested with the now constant stiffness and aches.

It was snowing as they left and it continued all morning, not as heavy as the previous day and not enough to blind them, but enough to make the road difficult to follow and hard to ride so that they made slow progress, over hills and down into great valleys before crossing swollen streams to climb again. They couldn't afford to stop for a meal, being anxious to reach their destination before nightfall.

They met nobody, military or civilian. Who else would travel in such conditions? Furthermore, they came across no villages or signs of humanity, apart from the road, following which was often less a matter of sight than of intuition. Milestones were too far buried under the snow, so they could only estimate the distance covered. By late afternoon, with the sky leaden and threatening to darken, Manius feared they'd done little more than half the journey. Publius had said it would be less than half a day's ride, perhaps a day. But how could he know? He was as unfamiliar with this territory as they? Manius whispered his fears to Quintus.

"I'm sure he's right," Quintus said. "This is the most heavily garrisoned place in the Empire; one fort cannot be very far from another."

"But we've been making hardly more than a mile in the hour. What if we don't get there by nightfall?"

"Be easy boy. If we don't make it before dark we shall have to spend the night in the open."

"We'll freeze."

"Not if we light a fire. There's no shortage of wood."

Aye, no shortage of sodden wood which they would have to collect from the forest's edge and which – if they ever did manage to light it – would throw up a glow to draw the barbarians from those dark forests. Manius shuddered, prayed and squinted into the snow, longing to see a fort.

It wasn't long after that, when the light was beginning to fail, that the road, which had been following the line of a valley down to their right, now took a steep dive into a tributary valley across their front, the other side of which they could barely make out. To their left was heath and scattered, wind-bent trees, while, on their right where the ground sloped sharply away, branches of gorse peeped out of mounds of snow.

An instinct, or some divine warning, alerted Manius that something was wrong. His breath caught in his throat even before he detected a movement among those mounds. He peered, and then one of the Samartians shouted. Six figures clutching spears and wearing strange headdress sprouted from those bushes.

Quintus seized Manius' bridle; shouted: "Hoy! Hoy!" and pointed to their left at another twelve or so on horseback, only yards away. They must've risen from the snow itself, all brandishing the long British swords. They too wore those headdresses, which Manius now recognised as wolf masks.

Chapter Ten

They drove their horses through that thick snow to escape their ambushers. But Manius had hardly moved before he saw an arrow shaft appear below its shoulder, then circles of blood in the snow, one after another, in a line, increasing in size. The horse whinnied, faltered, seemed to recover but then its left foreleg gave way and Manius pitched forward, to land on his back, the breath driven from him, gazing up at the darkening sky.

That sky was filled by Quintus, leaning out of his saddle over him, his arm outstretched. "Up boy. Take my arm. Quickly now!"

Manius shook his head to clear it. His horse was feet away, rolling and screaming in the snow. Quintus bellowed at him; Manius raised himself and grabbed his arm and Quintus tugged and then, with a roar, came sliding from his saddle to sprawl across Manius, winding him afresh.

They flailed around in the snow, trying to rise and tripping over each other, cursing and panting, throwing back their cloaks to get at their swords. Around them horses reared and protested; men shouted and grunted and blades clashed. All was whirling figures and confusion. Just as they regained their feet, one mounted figure galloped at them, closely followed by another. The first threw back his head, gave a wailing, prolonged cry and fell from his horse, his pursuer's sword released from his back as he went. He crashed at their feet and Manius recognised one of their escort. His killer, with his wolf's mask pushed back onto his head and his eyes wild, drove his mount towards them raising his sword. Quintus took an emphatic pace forward and swept his sword before the horse, thundering: "Dog! Dog! Dog!"

Wary, the horse faltered despite the angry urgings of its rider. The clamour of battle was all around them and the lonely road of only minutes before was now alive with riders and horses careening round each other and bodies falling. Manius swallowed, tightened his trembling grip on his sword and placed his back to Quintus, waiting for the blow to fall and praying: "Let death be swift."

There was no blow. He strained to look at the battling figures, puzzled. Their party – only seven strong – had been attacked by a score; yet the fight was still hot. But, even as that thought formed, the urgent movement stopped, with the suddenness of a Syrian dance when the music gracefully brings all vigour to a gentle close. All the horsemen ceased their frenzy, drew heavy breaths and gazed about them, lowering their swords and javelins.

One rider, swathed like the rest in furs and leather swung himself out of the saddle and strode up to them. Even though his sword was sheathed, Manius, still shaking, half raised his own weapon, but felt Quintus' hand on him, lowering his arm. The stranger pulled back his fur hood, took off the helmet beneath and ran a hand through the tight black curls which topped the features of a young man, not much older than Manius. A patch covered his left eye, but not all of the puckered scar that surrounded it. His good eye briefly held Manius' own before its gaze passed over his shoulder to Quintus.

"Roman?"

"We are," panted Quintus. "On the Emperor's service, bound for Longovicium."

The stranger laughed. "For the Emperor's service it's as well my patrol was out. Not so good for these bastards though. They were so damned intent on you fellows they didn't see us until we were among them. Ha ha!" He stepped forward and gave Quintus a hearty buffet on the shoulder.

"Neither did we," said Quintus. "And you are?"

"Titus Caelius Metellus, second-in–command tribune of the First Cohort of Loyal Vardulli, Foot and Horse, garrison of Longovicium, at your service."

Manius was still trembling and his heart pounding but he grinned.

Titus Caelius moved among his soldiers – a troop of about thirty – giving instructions to secure the enemies' horses, to pursue a couple of Wolves who'd escaped to the West – "but only so far as the forest lads, stay out of the trees" – to reclaim javelins, care for the wounded and – "No!" bellowed Quintus shoving Manius aside to bustle forward to where a trooper was bending over a groaning barbarian on the ground with his wolf mask twisted to one side. The trooper turned, eyebrows raised, at Quintus' angry approach, even as he slid his knife across the barbarian's throat. The man writhed and kicked and his blood gushed into the snow.

Quintus stamped and cursed over the Wolf coughing his life away, and shouted at his bemused executioner. "Fool! Fool!" Titus Caelius strode over with Manius close behind. Quintus rounded on him. "What are you doing? Are you mad? I must question prisoners."

Titus Caelius frowned. "Who are you?".

But Quintus raised his fists to his brow, before turning to stomp over the battleground in search of live barbarians. Manius plucked Titus Caelius' sleeve and whispered: "Sir, we're frumentarii."

Titus Caelius spun round and looked Manius up and down.

"You?"

Manius stammered confirmation, but after a brief stare from his single eye, Titus Caelius turned and barked an order to spare any surviving prisoners.

"Too late," said Quintus returning. "All dead."

Titus Caelius bowed his head. "Sir, I regret that but my men hate these people. They've seen their horrible misuse of their own prisoners including some from our own cohort. And, believe me, these barbarians wouldn't have spoken whatever you did to them."

"You've not been to my school," snarled Quintus.

"I truly am very sorry."

Quintus grunted and growled and flapped his hand in angry resignation.

Publius Flavius Fimbria approached, leaning on the shoulder of one of Titus Caelius' troopers, helmet in hand and a vicious bruise on his forehead. He seemed dazed as he addressed Titus Caelius in an even softer whisper than usual and the latter's face creased with the effort of listening. Eager to help, Manius introduced Publius.

Titus Caelius' eyebrows raised. "Flavius Fimbria you say? Tiberius Flavius Fimbria?"

"No, no," Manius said, "Publius Flavius Fimbria?"

"Oh I say, are you related to the general?"

Publius explained his relationship to his half brother and that they had no information as to the general's whereabouts. Touching his bruise and wincing, he added that he had arrived to take the position of second-in-command of the First Cohort of Loyal Vardulli, Foot and Horse.

"So you're my replacement. Well, well, you were expected, but we'd little idea how exalted you'd turn out to be." Publius frowned and Titus Caelius grasped his hand and laughed: "Forgive me, we cavalrymen are an informal lot. Come, let's get you to the fort where the surgeon can tend your head."

He shouted fresh commands to his optio; Quintus was reunited with his horse and Manius was found another and the troop formed up, with the two of them and Publius joining Titus Caelius at its head. They made their way down into the valley before them while Titus Caelius explained how he'd taken out the patrol in the hope of meeting Tiberius Flavius Fimbria, but chanced upon the Wolves attacking unknown travellers.

While he talked, Titus Caelius kept a keen eye on the flanks and rear of his troop. But not for long. After reaching the valley bottom and fording a stream, it was a bare minute's climb up the other side before Manius was savouring the welcoming aroma of smoke and the earthy smell of the sweat and dung of many stabled horses. Then they were facing the snow-covered earthen ramparts of the vicus surrounding the fort of Longovicium. This dominated the tiny settlement, its walls, perhaps the height of three men and – even higher – the great towers on either side of its main gate, loomed up, black against the gathering darkness.

§

Titus halted outside the fort's main gates where the mansio stood on the road, which was lined on both sides with buildings set back in enclosures bounded by ditches and, in some of these enclosures, Manius could make out the dark shapes of beasts and the strutting of hens. On the right, the occupants of the shops and workshops were putting the shutters over the fronts which gave onto the road, one by one, blotting out the light that came from within. Apart from the mansio, the buildings were single storey, thatched and made of earth and straw faced with lime. Unpaved streets, lined with more buildings, ran off either side the road making a reasonable sized village.

They agreed, when Titus suggested, they'd welcome the chance to wash and change in the mansio before meeting his commanding officer. Once inside, the steward explained that he was hosting many travellers and it would be necessary to share a chamber. Their expressionless stares told him they were past caring. He smiled and had a slave show them to their room, acknowledging with a bow, Quintus' request for a jar of wine.

This arrived as they were peeling off their wet furs and breaches and Quintus watched keenly as Manius took the jar, uncorked it and, with an unsteady hand, poured himself a goblet which he emptied in one draught.

"Here, give me that!" Quintus snatched the jar from Manius, replenished his goblet and retreated, clutching the remainder to his chest. The wine warmed Manius; did something to blur the terrible, vivid images of the fight in the snow. A knock at the door made him start, setting the remaining wine sloshing in his cup.

Quintus, half out of his breeches, shouted for the visitor to wait, but the door was opened by a centurion of middle years and grizzled, grey beard, who watched Quintus hopping and cursing. He waited until Quintus had regained his balance and dignity and introduced himself: Appius Rufius Atellus, senior centurion of the Vardulli, come to welcome them and to escort them to the tribune commander, Lucius Antonius Merenda.

"Senior centurion by all that's holy!" said Quintus. "Antonius Merenda does us great honour." He approached the man and surveyed the medals on his armour and wrists with approval.

"The tribune does hold you in high esteem, Suetonius Lupus, but I did personally ask to come to greet you, for old time's sake, though I'm afraid you don't recognise me," said the old soldier and, with a smile, removed his helmet, which he held cradled in one arm. Quintus stared into his brown, wrinkled face under the short-cropped grey hair. "Your name again," he demanded and, when the centurion repeated it, gave his harsh barking laugh. "Appius Rufius Atellus! By heaven forgive me! How could I forget you? So, you're still with the cohort and senior centurion. Well done man. Manius let me introduce Appius Rufius Atellus, an old friend, he was..."– and here Quintus faltered – "... er... Appius Rufius, meet Manius Suetonius."

They exchanged civilities while Manius wondered: who was this man? Old friends or not – they'd little to say, apart from each asking how the other did and the centurion revealing that he had a wife in the vicus and that he found Britannia far colder than Egypt or Spain.

Quintus smiled. "The skirmish we've just been caught up in was hot enough."

"Aye, I've heard," Appius Rufius laughed. "But even hadn't Caelius Metellus happened upon you, I'm sure the barbarians would have rued the day they tangled with Quintus Suetonius Lupus."

So it went for some minutes, Manius grinning self-consciously while both men laughed heartily, neither saying much of consequence or referring to their shared past.

"But come," said the centurion, "we mustn't keep the commander waiting."

He led them from the mansio – walking, Manius noticed, with a heavy limp – through the darkness of early evening, to the great gates of the fort where two sentries came to attention. Then they took the fort's main street, the Via Praetoria. Light came from the windows of the barracks lining it, soldiers stood in doorways chatting and an optio, marching a file of infantrymen past them, saluted Appius Rufius. They arrived at the Principia, greeted again by stamping sentries and from there passed into the heart of the fort and of the cohort.

They proceeded through a colonnaded courtyard into the great basilica, silent, dim lit and – to Manius – awesome: a vast, stone hall, dominated by a statue of the late emperor. Off this was a small shrine, in which, despite it being partly screened and illuminated only by feeble lamp, Manius could glimpse the standards of the cohort and more busts, which he guessed to be of the imperial family. Their boots echoed on the paving, before Appius Rufius brought them to a halt at a door next to the shrine, at which he knocked.

They entered, at a bark from within, into a large room, From behind a desk rose a tall, slender man of about forty with dark hair streaked grey, and a close trimmed beard. He held himself rigid and this, combined with bulging eyes, gave him a fixed look of surprise. Lucius Antonius Merenda, tribune commanding the First Cohort of Loyal Vardulli, Foot and Horse, and senior commander of Roman arms in the region of the north eastern frontier of Britannia. Thus he was formally introduced to Manius by his senior centurion, after he and Quintus had exchanged greetings, shaking hands and clasping forearms and agreeing how good it was to see each other. But Manius detected a certain wariness on Merenda's part.

They took their seats and Appius Rufius, after a stiff nod to his commander, took his leave.

When the door closed, Quintus remarked that it was good to see the centurion still with the cohort and risen to such an honoured rank.

Merenda shifted in his seat and stroked his beard. "Yes, a fitting end to his career, he has been a distinguished soldier."

"He is coming to retirement?"

"I'm afraid it's a forced retirement, for health reasons."

"Health? He seems sound enough."

Merenda frowned. "You'll have observed his limp. His right foot is arthritic."

"So he wants to retire?"

"He'd like to serve out his remaining five years, but I'm afraid his infirmity makes that impossible."

Quintus raised an eyebrow, which prompted the tribune to add brusquely: "You see him on a good day but on others he can't walk, let alone march. What use is that?" Merenda slapped his hand onto his desk, making Manius start. "It's not a decision I've taken lightly. I've discussed this with the surgeon so often I can quote by heart the authorities on arthritis. Rufius Atellus' foot has lost function and therefore so has he, at least as a soldier."

"This is a mixed cohort," said Quintus, "the cavalry perhaps?"

"I've some seven hundred men and only two hundred are mounted. The senior centurion cannot confine himself to horseback. As it, is my second in command, young Caelius Metellus loves horses so much – damned near as much as the dice – that I'm always having to remind him we also have infantry. By the way, you rode with his replacement, Publius Flavius Fimbria – how d'you find him?"

Quintus chewed his thumbnail before speaking.

"He seems competent enough – doubtless he has much to learn but who hasn't? I'm sure you're skilled in training young officers. I would urge you, however, to insist he learns to raise his voice, or else his soldiers are bound to miss some vital command."

Merenda frowned and looked at Quintus as though suspecting a joke. Manius had the feeling he was a man with little humour.

"What commander wants his general's younger brother as his second? I mean no offence, Quintus Suetonius, but having one," he looked at Manius, "or two spies here is enough. I don't want three."

Quintus guffawed. "There's no love lost between Publius and his brother. He won't be running telling tales."

Merenda muttered that he'd heard that but wasn't much happier having a second in command and a general who were daggers drawn.

Quintus smiled and shrugged, then added: "As for us, we're not here, to spy on you, old friend, but to work with Tiberius Flavius Fimbria. You've proved your loyalty as few have. What have you to fear from the presence of a couple of frumentarii?"

Quintus maintained his innocent smile while Merenda fingered his beard.

Quintus broke the silence. "So tell me: what's the state of the country?"

Merenda flapped a hand. "There's unrest, of course; but we must never let these people believe we fear them; that could provoke what we seek to avoid."

"There was serious trouble outside the gates of this very fort."

"You weren't harmed were you?" snapped Merenda.

Quintus only contemplated him until he gave a heavy sigh and added: "Yes, the roads are increasingly dangerous, communication with forts north of the frontier wall has been lost." He cleared his throat. "Sorry to sound harsh, but I'm worried for Tiberius Flavius Fimbria. He's probably on the road somewhere between here and Eboracum, in filthy weather and in a country alive with barbarian assassins."

Manius sympathised. As senior commander north of Eboracum he was responsible for the safety of the road over which his general was presumed to be travelling.

"We must assume," said Quintus, "that he's safe under some roof. He'd hardly be travelling in the dark in these conditions."

Merenda's expression grew uneasy at that possibility and he said eagerly: "So, you think no more patrols tonight?"

Quintus shrugged. "You know your own trade, but I think it hard on your men to little purpose. How are they, by the way? Have they been affected by these Wolves?"

"You mean disaffected?"

"Yes."

"No. You must remember that four years ago we were in Egypt and the cohort only raised a couple of years before that in Spain. These men are largely Spanish: Vardulli, with a few Egyptians and only a handful of Britons."

"Good, that's one thing less to worry about."

Merenda didn't look less worried. "You know him – Tiberius Flavius Fimbria?"

"We've met."

"Is he as bad as they say?"

"He can be… difficult, but he's a good soldier."

"That's what I hear. I also hear he doesn't suffer fools gladly."

"He'd be the first to admit that."

Merenda rubbed his beard, sighing. He rose and paced behind his desk. He stopped, swivelled to face them. "Well, you'll want food and sleep. I won't keep you. I apologise that we cannot accommodate you in the fort but spare rooms in my house are being held for our esteemed general and his entourage."

"The mansio seems perfectly clean and comfortable."

As they left, Quintus and Merenda exchanged more pleasantries and resolved to speak again soon.

In the doorway Manius was brought up short and stood frozen.

He stared into the face of the most beautiful girl he'd ever seen. The German slave girl was no more. No, true beauty lay not in blonde hair and blue eyes, but in eyes of the deepest, olive black and hair of the same colour that shimmered like silk, and in a skin of lightest brown and in lips of…

"Come along, come along," said Quintus grabbing his arm, and nodding at this vision whose magnificent eyes followed Manius as Quintus dragged him across the basilica and back out into the cold winter air with Manius tripping and stumbling as he looked back.

§

They entered a tavern, a raw place, with rushes on the floor, rough wooden tables and benches, air thick with wine and ale fumes and the loud chatter of soldiers. Manius was too preoccupied to care, he was thinking of her.

Quintus seized his arm and hissed in his ear: "Have you grown so accustomed to Publius Flavius' whisperings that you've lost the ability to listen?" He released him with a snort, muttering about a lecherous, moon-struck young imbecile.

Embarrassed, Manius hastened to change the subject.

"The senior centurion Appius Rufius – how do you know him?" he asked, as soon as they'd found seats at the far end of the inn's crowded single room, into which they sank stiffly and gratefully.

"Ah yes," said Quintus. He paused to look around before bending over the table. "Now that did rock me on my heels." He paused again to accept the serving boy's suggestion of two bowls of stew and ordered a jar of wine. "But, I should've remembered Appius Rufius. A frumentarius who can't remember is worse than a soldier who can't march. Poor Appius Rufius, like me, he's getting old. He can't march and I can't remember. Maybe they should pension me off. Ha! If only they would."

Manius waited, until Quintus brought himself back to the point.

"Where was I? Remember, I told you about Antonius Merenda and the slaying of Avidius Cassius? How a decurion had to finish the job for him? Aye, well that was Appius Rufius?"

"You didn't recognise him?"

Quintus shook his head. "Moneta, forgive me for forgetting him. But, Heaven, how he has aged."

The serving boy thrust their bowls onto the table and tossed the spoons down beside. Quintus glared after him, took up his spoon and gave his stew a dubious poke before continuing: "I suppose it's no surprise he's stuck with the cohort and had his promotion too. But Merenda's an ungrateful bastard to kick him out before he's done his twenty-five years. And how will Appius stand with his pension?" Quintus shook his head. "It's a sad, bad business."

They ate and Manius' mind drifted to the black-eyed, black-haired girl.

§

Quintus' eyes drifted across the various soldiers and officers, never lingering, despite one or two hostile, suspicious – perhaps even fearful – return looks. Why should that be? Were they known to be frumentarii? Had Merenda been indiscreet?

A figure approached through the crush: Titus Caelius' face lit up in recognition. He slapped the shoulder of a still preoccupied Manius, who whirled round.

"Titus Caelius!" he cried and rose to greet him with an enthusiasm that irritated Quintus. Titus pressed him gently down and sat beside him. "I say, you don't mind?" They shook their heads and he ordered more wine, calling to the boy and joking with the tavern master. He asked how they did and trusted they'd suffered no ill effects from the Wolves.

"Is the mansio to your liking? It's rough and ready I know, but this is practically the frontier."

"It's fine, honestly," said Manius.

"I'm glad. I know it has an extraordinary number of visitors.

"Surely at this time of year, there can't be so many on imperial business."

"I dunno… I suppose this is such a no account kind of place, the mansio has few rooms and those are taken by people like yourselves who'd normally have been in the old man's house but now he has to reserve accommodation for Tiberius Flavius Fimbria and his staff."

"And who are our fellow guests?" asked Quintus.

"Let's see: two families – a local magistrate Aurelius Cotta and wife and a couple from Gaul, Arrius and Arria Gracchus, with two charming children. The husband is a tax official. Imagine: screwing money out of people and forever counting the damned stuff." He shuddered theatrically; Manius laughed.

"You don't like money?" asked Quintus.

"I'd be a thorough hypocrite if I said so. No, I don't pretend to be any great Stoic believing – what is it? – 'virtue is sufficient for happiness.' But I'm a pretty simple sort of a fellow and so long as I can pay my way I'm content." He smiled wryly. "Not that I can, at the moment. I'm afraid my money has been shaken away with the dice. But there's always pay. A soldier needs no more and I shan't ever want to be anything other than a soldier."

"You favour the cavalry I gather?"

Titus laughed. "So, the old man told you that did he? It's true, I love the cavalry. I was just trying to explain it to Publius Flavius. I say, isn't he a quiet chap? Anyway, I was showing him his quarters and helping him unpack – poor fellow's still groggy – and came across his copy of good old Pliny's *Throwing the Javelin from Horseback* – you must know it?"

"It was a classic, even in my day."

"Yes. Heaven knows I'm not one for books or that kind of stuff but I do like that. It sums up the whole cavalry spirit: having to think and act on the move, reacting and taking your chance, seeing when the enemy's flank is exposed, sensing he's about to break and then throwing in your charge and seizing the moment. Yes, that's what it's all about."

"And it takes much practice," said Quintus. "The late emperor once said," – here Quintus closed his eyes to aid his memory – "'Practise even what you have despaired of mastering. For lack of practice the left hand is awkward for most tasks, but has a stronger grip on the bridle than the right – it is practised in this.'"

"The old emperor said that? Well he knew a thing or two. Oh, yes, without that strong left hand you can't throw the javelin." He mimed the action and sent Manius goblet flying and its contents over a nearby optio. Titus leapt to his feet apologising, ordering fresh wine for Manius and handing a coin to the embarrassed soldier.

He resumed his seat with an apologetic laugh. "Anyway, that sums it up: what it is to be a cavalryman. Ha, ha, ha! You know what they say? A cavalryman who's still alive at thirty is a blackguard."

He ran on in similar vein and even Quintus smiled. Babbling, wooden-headed soldiers were a reassuring constant in a shifting world.

"I love horses, always have done," concluded Titus, apologising for his enthusiasm and then turned to Manius: "Do you like the Races? Whom do you support? Are you a Green or a Blue?"

"Green," stammered Manius, relieved when Titus slapped him on the back, declaring him a "good man". He asked Quintus who replied: "If I was at all inclined to blind partisanship I'd say I only had energy enough to devote to the Imperial Ballet School."

Titus goggled. Manius hastened to deny any interest in the ballet.

"But you're leaving the cohort," said Quintus. "Where are you bound?"

"I'm to command the mounted singulares of the governor," said Titus, with evident pride.

"When do you leave?" asked Manius.

"In the next day or so."

"So," said Quintus, "you're to be bodyguard to Gaius Caerellius Priscus?"

"The governor? Yes, you know him?" Before Quintus could reply Titus rose, begging his forgiveness and weaved across the room bumping into a potboy. Quintus watched him approach a young woman, perhaps a few years older than him. She was red-haired and pretty but corpulent. To Quintus' surprise, Titus took her hand, led her across the room and presented her to them.

"Let me introduce my wife-to-be, Birca. My dear, meet my new friends, Quintus Suetonius and Manius Suetonius. She was on her way home and looked in to see if I was here. I've persuaded her to have a cup of wine with us."

Quintus was surprised. This Birca was presumably a gentlewoman if she was betrothed to a tribune and knight. Yet, here she was, taking her ease with men in a tavern. And she spoke with such assurance – of the weather, the wine, of the dogs that squabbled in a corner – that Quintus was reminded of Tita. Aye, and hadn't she talked of the British women and the freedom, even power, their men granted them?

"You'll be sad that Titus Caelius leaves for his new posting," said Quintus to her. "You won't be travelling with him in winter surely?"

"No." Despite her size, her voice was light and melodic. "I've no fear of winter travel, but it's better that I settle business here and let Titus establish us a home in Londinium."

They learnt she'd been born into a well-to-do merchant family in Eboracum and had met Titus while he'd been on secondment to Sixth Victrix – Quintus guessed she'd become his mistress – and had accompanied him on his return to Longovicium.

Quintus felt a rare sympathy for her. "You live here in the vicus?"

"Only a few doors away and excuse me but I must return or the fire will be out." She downed her wine said a hasty farewell. Squeezing Titus' hand, she turned to manoeuvre through the tight crowd now gathered in the tavern. Titus slipped a coin to a nearby trooper and told him to see her home. He watched after her fondly.

Quintus asked: "So an escort is necessary, even in the vicus?"

Titus frowned. "I may be overcautious, but, well she is… precious… to me."

"That does you credit. You can't be too cautious even here, if what Antonius Merenda tells us is true about the rebellious state of the country here about."

Manius raised his eyebrows. Quintus was thankful he'd the sense not to object that Merenda hadn't painted so black a picture. Titus took the bait.

"It's true, the situation gets worse by the day. An attack so near the fort shows how audacious the villains have grown. Only the other week Appius Rufius and I took a couple of troopers out on patrol and were ambushed by half a dozen Wolves. We lost both troopers – good men, fine horsemen – and Appius Rufius and I were lucky to escape. The old man wasn't pleased, I can tell you. Little wonder he worries about the lead mines in the hills. We've no way of protecting them and their wealth is important to Londinium, and to Rome, or so they tell me."

"He's also worried about Tiberius Flavius."

"Of course. A Roman general would be a great prize for the Wolves. Aye, I'm afraid the old man has much to worry about. Lost lead production, a country in turmoil and maybe a general ambushed by barbarians – none of it bodes well for an ambitious officer."

"So, he's still ambitious is he?"

"What soldier isn't? He makes no secret of his desire to return to Egypt to command the legion there."

"Why not?" shrugged Quintus. "He has a crack unit here, the legionary command in Egypt is a knight's command, so he qualifies and he's familiar with the province."

"Absolutely, so he can't afford any disasters. No wonder he frets and prays to Mithras."

"Does he?"

"Oh, he's always in the mithraeum, leading his lodge as father."

"You're not a follower?" asked Manius.

Titus guffawed. "No, Mithras is decidedly not my crown. By Jove, imagine the old man's face if I presented my sorry self in his lodge." His laugh boomed enough to stop the dogs bickering. Even Quintus had to smile at the idea of this cavalryman in such a sober cult.

"Tell me," said Manius, while Titus was still chuckling, "when we were leaving Antonius Merenda's office, a girl entered – black-haired, about my age."

Titus grinned. "Oh, you've met Lucia Antonia, beautiful daughter of the cohort's commander – beautiful and doesn't she know it. Be very careful there young Manius; the old man worships her and woe betide any young goat he finds sniffing around."

Manius stammered about only being curious but Titus laughed again. Quintus glowered and changed the subject. "How does the cohort view the appointment of Tiberius Flavius?"

Titus' brow furrowed. "Generally well disposed. Flavius Fimbria has a reputation for being hard – bloody hard – but things are coming to a head up here: we need leadership, someone to get a grip y'know. Everyone says he is a competent general."

"So the army would follow him?"

"Of course," said Titus, his tone cautious.

"Him, rather than the governor?"

Titus smiled, drained his tankard and rose. "I say, these are dangerous questions from a frumentarius."

Quintus looked at him. "As the poet says: 'There are no dangerous questions, only dangerous answers.'"

"Maybe so, but I'm not a big one for poets and this is over my simple soldier's head. I must go, I've a guard to inspect. I shall do my duty," and he added this over his shoulder, "as, you may be sure, will the army."

They watched him go. Manius said: "You've scared him off."

"You think so?"

"I like him."

"There's no room for liking in this game."

"I mean, he seems decent enough?"

"D'you know the rules on marriage for officers of senatorial and knightly rank?"

Manius shook his head.

"They're expressly forbidden to marry women from the province in which they serve. I doubt poor young Birca knows that."

He let Manius ponder that while they drank another jar. Let the young fool know what manner of man his new friend was.

"Anyway," said Manius at length. "We were fortunate that he happened along when he did or we'd be meat for the Wolves."

Quintus drained his goblet and wiped his mouth. "I can't quarrel with you, but I wonder how great a part luck really had to play this afternoon."

"What d'you mean?"

"I don't believe those barbarians – however hairy their arses – were squatting in the freezing snow for hours on end on the offchance that some Roman general might happen along."

"Go on."

"Somebody told them – and I have to believe it was probably somebody from this fort."

Chapter Eleven

Quintus woke from heavy sleep. He lay still, alert for what might have disturbed him, any threat. He remembered – he was in the mansio in Longovicium. Yes, sharing a room with Manius. He made out through the gloom the boy's shape in an adjacent bed. The lad was breathing gently. Had he made some noise? Or maybe Quintus had been having some dream – already forgotten – which had shocked him. He closed his eyes, trying to regain that sweet semi-oblivion.

He couldn't; the need to piss was too great. He sat up, swung his legs out of the bed, winced at various aches and massaged the back of his neck. He stood and sucked in his breath at a sharp pain across his back. He must have done more damage than he realised falling from his horse. He picked his way to the window to peer between the shutters. It was getting light. He dressed, making no noise and, leaving Manius asleep, went to the bathhouse.

It was another cold day and the heat inside the baths was welcome, making his flesh tingle. At that hour there was only a portly, grey-haired Levantine in the caldarium, who gave him a curt nod through the steam and then left. In the tepidaria, Quintus lay back in the warmth, contemplating the play of light on the rippling water, the chuckle of the tiny waves against the tiles and the musical drip of condensation from other chambers. His mind was lulled, as though removed and floating, independent of anything but its thoughts.

Thoughts of the Wolves' ambush. He strove to recall any detail that might be significant or useful. No, it had all happened too fast. Then those bloody fool soldiers had put paid to any interrogation. At least the boy hadn't disgraced himself – he'd hardly been an Achilles but fear hadn't frozen him or made him shit himself; that was something. He was still young.

Ah youth. How swiftly age rushed on. The poets had exhausted that subject. But what was new was the feeling of unease that now attended ageing. The world was changing for the worse, and it would be unmerciful to old men. Marcus Aurelius had been a good emperor, yet, even under his rule, something must have been rotting the Empire's very heart. So soon after his death this had become obvious – his vicious son; the upstart, unspeakable Saoterus; the Balbus plot; and now everything going to cock in Britannia. The whole empire suddenly seemed vulnerable, as did he, and yet here he was, at its outermost limits, working again to save it.

Why did he bother?

He smiled. He'd no choice. He'd no family estate, no investments and no pension. No, he had to work on – for cockroaches like Saoterus who'd cornered the market in such benefits.

He wallowed a little longer but his mood was spoiled. He hauled himself out of the tepidaria and returned to the caldarium to sweat again. After half an hour, his mind regained some tranquillity, the stiffness in his back eased and his body had gone, by pleasurable stages, from too cold to too hot. He made his way to the frigidarium and plunged into the pool, where he gasped, splashed and snorted until he was aware of someone entering. He surfaced to see Appius Rufius Atellus sit by the poolside, place his foot in the water and massage it, sighing. He nodded at Quintus, who climbed from the pool and took a towel from the shelf to wrap around himself.

"Mind if I sit by you?"

Rufius Atellus grunted, removed one hand from his toe joint and waved at the tiles in perfunctory invitation. Quintus asked him how he did.

"Well enough."

Quintus tried again. "Is this snow likely to ease?"

The centurion still looking at his foot and rubbing it, said: "Quintus Suetonius, I've barely been in the province for four winters and that's not enough to read the weather."

Quintus nodded, raised his towel to wipe his face then asked how he liked the country and the people.

Still without looking at him, Rufius Atellus told him that the people were much as others and, as long as they behaved he could approve of them, but once they threatened the peace, they became a nuisance.

"Do they threaten the peace?"

Now the other faced him. "I lost two men the other week. You were attacked yesterday. What do you think?"

Quintus shrugged. The centurion looked at him, then dipped his toe into the water; and massaged it again.

"Your foot troubles you, Rufius Atellus?"

He continued rubbing the joint and said, with an edge of impatience. "Yes, my foot pains me; it's arthritic and because of it I must retire, which is well enough known and I can't believe that the great frumentarius Suetonius Lupus isn't also aware."

"How do you feel about that?"

"I've seen it coming and made my plans."

"Which are?"

Rufius Atellus sighed, as though considering inviting Quintus to mind his own business but answered. "My wife and I will return to Spain to set ourselves up with an inn. It's sooner than planned but I'll have longer to enjoy my retirement."

"But you'll receive your pension?"

"I shall get my statement of release, my diploma; as for my pension, it seems I must appeal to the governor. I'm not intending to do that. I've served Rome well and loyally and the Emperor can pay me what he thinks he owes, I'll not beg."

"Surely Antonius Merenda will support your case? You did him a great service once."

Rufius Atellus returned Quintus' stare and stopped rubbing his foot. "Men don't always like being done a service, especially not for something they've taken the credit for."

He withdrew his foot from the water and stood. Quintus gazed into the pool, pondering. The centurion continued: "I've spoken frankly because I don't want you asking all and sundry about my affairs. I'm assuming what I've told you won't become the talk of the barrack blocks."

Quintus said: "You know me better than that."

§

Tita Amatia swore silently and prayed for patience. It wasn't the riding; on most days, for the best part of forty years she'd spent some hours in the saddle around her estate. Nor was it the weather. It wasn't snowing and, though there was another cruel frost, she'd long since grown used to Britannia's cold. No, it was her companion who sickened her.

She glanced at the matronly figure with the pinched features, red-rimmed eyes and peevish expression who rode beside her. Before Tita Amatia had embraced Decima Flavia Fimbria in Eboracum, she'd remembered her in Rome as a jolly, carefree girl. She had loved that little thing, but heavens how she whined now.

Above the steady crunch of their horses' hooves in the snow, their blowing and snorting, the creak of saddles and jingle of harness, Tita Amatia could always hear her friend's self-pitying sniffs. She wasn't the only one; she caught Tiberius Flavius Fimbria's angry backward glare in the direction of his wife.

When Tita Amatia had joined the Flavius Fimbria's twenty-strong entourage in Eboracum some days before, Decima Flavia had seemed cheerful enough, greeting her with tears and rapturous laughter. Expressions of delight and questions and reminiscences had fallen over one another. Her boor of a husband had been less welcoming.

"No madam, it's out of the question that you should ride north with us. I cannot be responsible for your safety."

Tita Amatia had told him he was ridiculous, that he – "you damned fool" – had no responsibility for her and made it clear he wouldn't hear the last of it if he refused her. He, doubtless wary of the Amatius name, had yielded with ill grace, but had barely been able to bring himself to address a word to her since. His wife had been delighted but that had soon been overborne by grievances and Tita Amatia was made to share all her unhappiness.

Not that Decima Flavia hadn't good reason.: in fairness, the ride was long and hard and she was well into middle age., they'd slept in the open, making Decima Flavia whimper through the night with the cold and the conviction that howling savages would soon be upon them.

For all that, Tita Amatia felt the general's wife could have borne the hardship and her fear of barbarians had she had the love – or even respect – of her husband. She all too plainly had neither.

An outraged Tita Amatia had learnt from a tearful Decima Flavia on the first day out of Eboracum that a pert, plump, olive-skinned girl, whom she'd taken to be a slave, was in fact Flavius Fimbria's concubine. He was flaunting her and publicly humiliating his wife. The man was renowned as a boor and a cur, but this was too much.

Now she caught that little strumpet – Pellia, who rode a couple of places ahead with one of Flavius Fimbria's staff officers – casting a quick backward look of smug triumph. Tita Amatia longed to whip to her.

She tore her gaze away from the girl in disgust. Her eyes fastened on the red cloak of Tiberius Flavius Fimbria, some twenty paces in front, near the head of their little column. He cast frequent angry looks about, as though defying barbarians to attack, or his wife to weep.

At that moment, he turned in his saddle, fixing all behind him – even his whore – with his characteristic look of stern disfavour.

Ridiculous, preposterous little man. Surely to heaven he couldn't represent a threat to the Emperor. And yet… his soldiers seemed to respect him. Perhaps he had something that escaped her. Quintus was a good judge of character – on the whole – and he had a low opinion of him. Quintus… had he been sent because she'd suggested it – what could have possessed her? – or was Saoterus playing some game of his own? Quintus… He'd looked older. How could he not? He was wilder, more unkempt, gruffer and more ill-mannered. Those failings had always been latent but if he'd found himself an intelligent and strong-willed wife...

She was distracted.

A horseman came trotting past, heading for the front of the column to talk to Flavius Fimbria. It was the ill-favoured fellow who'd joined them shortly before they'd left Eboracum, he was swarthy with a hungry, hawk face and watchful eyes. She didn't like the look of him. Had he turned up in Cenares, she'd have had Bodvoc loose the dogs on him. But he seemed known to Tiberius Flavius and the two were often – as now – in conference.

She addressed Decima Flavia. "My dear, who's that man talking to your husband?"

The other sniffed and blinked her red-rimmed, short-sighted eyes.

"Oh him, I never saw him before Eboracum. I don't believe he's a soldier. I assume he's some messenger Tiberius Flavius uses. I don't much like him, he has an insolent look, don't you think? But then, he's Sicilian, apparently."

"Sicilian?" said Tita Amatia. "What's his name?"

Decima Flavia shrugged. "I've heard my husband address him as Tiro." She sniffed again and her voice rose towards an all-too-familiar petulant falsetto. "My husband is intimate with too many low-born creatures for me to be familiar with them all. I don't see why…"

Tita Amatia nodded but ceased to listen. She contemplated this Tiro.

She wondered how she might kill him.

§

Manius lay, listening, feeling something was wrong. He half opened his eyes, looked to his side, then sat up. There was no Quintus. He'd not woken to the sound of his snoring. Where'd he gone? He guessed the baths and considered joining him. No, he'd look around Longovicium – maybe he'd meet the heavenly Lucia. He got up, splashed water on his face, dressed and went to explore.

The settlement sat outside the walls of the fort and was protected by its own earthen rampart, now covered with thick snow. Manius made for the steps up to this by the road on which he'd first arrived. He stood aside to make way for a tall, slender man with a bald crown who was descending. They exchanged nods and smiles and then Manius climbed onto the rampart and, on there, circled the vicus, surveying the neighbouring land.

Longovicium was surrounded on three sides by valleys. To the south the road ran back half a mile to ford a stream, before climbing more steeply up, perhaps a mile and a half, to the summit – which Manius could just make out – where they'd been ambushed by the Wolves. To the east, only a couple of hundred paces from the rampart, was a thick wood and this sloped away, down into the greater valley which ran north and south, parallel to the road. To the north the road rolled off into the distance, hugging the greater valley side and to the west was a flat and featureless plain until a forest again bound them in about four hundred paces distant. From this forest ran an aqueduct cutting across the plain to the fort.

As he stood, the snow stopped falling and there was a lone break in the grey clouds through which sunlight came in rigid, golden shafts. Briefly, there was a clarity in the light and every tree was distinct – even those half a mile away. Everything seemed close, sharp, and quiet. There were only two colours: the white of the snow and the black of the trees and forest. Then the clouds closed over and the light became smoky and the day seemed to fade like dusk.

Manius shivered, feeling alone, and of little consequence. A sense of wellbeing that he'd had since rising deserted him.

Were the barbarians made barbaric by the wildernesses or did their barbarism make them choose barbaric places? Or, perhaps being, by nature, what they were, they'd been placed by the gods in such places as punishment. But no, Rome's was a story of conquering and civilising barbarians and Rome could hardly be acting contrary to what the gods intended in creation. He'd ask Quintus.

In the mansio he found Quintus sitting on his bed, tugging a comb half-heartedly through his thick, tangled locks.

"I've been having a look round the vicus," said Manius. Quintus fastened him with an inquiring eye from under his comb.

"I was wondering about the country hereabouts and its people."

Quintus yanked the comb from his hair and flinched. "And what are the fruits of your mental labours?"

"Do you think the barbarity of the land makes the Brigantes barbaric or do they choose a barbarian land because they're barbarians?"

Quintus contemplated him. "Does the corruption of Rome make Romans corrupt or have Romans corrupted it?" Before Manius could answer, he added: "Come, let's go to the tavern to eat."

§

They sat with ale and bowls of the same mutton stew they'd sampled the previous night, Manius asked Quintus what he planned now they'd arrived.

"We wait for Tiberius Flavius Fimbria. If the Wolves kill him on the way, then that makes our task easier in deciding between Priscus and him."

But the decision wasn't theirs. A couple of hours later when they were dicing in their room, they heard excited shouts, commands and the blare of trumpet. They hurried out into the snow that was again falling heavily, to find a handful of cavalrymen at the gate, commanded by Titus, who explained breathlessly that his patrol had come upon Tiberius Flavius Fimbria and his party on the road. He'd left the bulk of his troop to escort the general and had returned to notify Antonius Merenda, so that the whole cohort could be paraded in his honour. He invited them into the fort to witness it.

They positioned themselves at the junction of a side street and the Via Praetoria, to the bellowing of centurions, decurions, optiones, and tesserarii. The contuberna of ten pouring out of the barracks – armour clanking, more barked commands – to line up, feet shuffling, forming their centuries along the Via Principia. Within minutes, the whole cohort,stood rigid, lining both sides of the street. The clamour was replaced by silence, broken only by a horse neighing in the stable blocks and the babble of water from the aqueduct. Antonius Merenda, with Publius Flavius Fimbria at his side, appeared on the steps of the Principia. He was in full uniform, helmet on his head and unease written across his face. The cohort was immobile; each man stared to his front. Snow melted on helmets and settled on cloaks.

Manius shivered under his woollen tunic, missing his own cloak. Happily they'd only minutes to wait before a chorus of trumpet and horn, shouted commands, a clash of weapons and a party of horsemen came trotting into view. At their head rode a man in a general's red cloak and, by him, Manius recognised Titus, riding to attention. Barely a score of riders followed, hardly any in uniform and a handful were women. Manius whispered to Quintus that one was clearly a lady.

"Just like Flavius Fimbria," Quintus replied. "Brave enough to scorn a decent escort and selfish enough to not care about exposing his wife, household and staff to same danger. He should remember Thucydides: 'Ignorance breeds confidence, reflection leads to hesitation.'"

But Quintus seemed distracted. He stood on tiptoe peering. "Is she there?" he muttered.

Then Manius caught sight of her, a figure made shapeless by thick furs and hooded cloak, who threw back that hood and dismounted in a fluid movement, shunning the helping hand of a legionary. Tita Amatia Aculeo handed her reins to the soldier and looked around as though at her own villa.

"Yes," said Manius. "I see her."

"So, she's come," said Quintus, with a tremor, then coughed and added: "stupid sow."

Flavius Fimbria dismounted and Antonius Merenda went to greet him. He presented Publius Flavius Fimbria, as his second in command, to his brother who returned only the briefest of nods before hurrying into the Principia with Merenda. Servants darted to help the woman – the general's wife – from her horse. Another woman – Merenda's wife, stepped forward to meet her. She was accompanied by the beautiful Lucia Antonia.

Appius Rufius bawled another command that was taken up by the other centurions and the cohort broke up into its components, which each headed back to their barrack blocks, doubtless to huddle round their fires. Manius and Quintus too made for the warmth of the mansio and Manius jostled against someone he recognised as the tall, thin balding fellow who'd been descending the vicus rampart that morning. He smiled at Manius.

"Let me introduce myself. I'm Arrius Gracchus; I'm lodging in the mansio with my wife and children."

He explained that he and his family were on their way north, to Corstopitum, where he had a post to assume. However, his wife had taken a fever and that, and the weather, had prevented further travel. He was friendly and eager and he bobbed his head and smiled a good deal.

"I had to see this. I've never been a soldier but military ceremony does appeal. The discipline, the spectacle of several hundred men acting with one mind, is extraordinary."

"That was hardly the pinnacle of military display," said Quintus dryly.

Arrius was all eagerness to agree. "Oh no, of course, I do realise that. In fact I was sorely disappointed to have missed the ceremony last week – a dedication of a new altar to the imperial cult in honour of the new emperor. But my wife was too ill and I had to attend her. Indeed, she was so unwell she couldn't eat the meat from the sacrificial bull so generously distributed. I hope that people understood. That's partly why I was so anxious to be here, in order to make amends as it were. But I would anyway – as I said – for the sheer pleasure of the spectacle."

After much nodding, bowing and smiling – they left him in the mansio vestibule and Quintus shook his head.

§

They'd not been back for half an hour when there was a tap at the door. Quintus opened it to a young lad, awkward and standing on one leg.

"Yes?"

"Suetonius Lupus?"

"Who wants him?

"Lady asked me to give you this." The boy thrust a writing tablet into Quintus hand, then scampered off. Quintus closed the door, reading the message scratched into the wax: "I gather you have arrived. We should meet, but you must know that a Sicilian Tiro is on the staff of Flavius Fimbria. TAA."

Quintus gazed at it, frowning.

"Who's it from?" asked Manius, who lay reclining on his bed.

Quintus rubbed the wax clear. "Tita Amatia, just to confirm her arrival."

He'd barely crossed the room to his own bed when there was another knock.

"Are we to have no peace? Enter, whoever the hell you are!"

This was an optio, with a request that Quintus should wait upon Tiberius Flavius Fimbria. Manius remained lolling on his bed as Quintus made for the door. Quintus looked at him.

"He only said you should go," said Manius, but Quintus beckoned him to follow.

They returned to the fort with the optio, again entered the basilica's hallowed interior and Antonius Merenda's office. This time it was not the cohort's commander behind the desk, but the general, the legate Tiberius Flavius Fimbria himself.

Manius grew nervous. Fimbria was short, but like a big man compressed into a smaller man's body, as if raging to burst free. He had a commanding eye that pierced with angry accusation. Glaring at them, he left them standing. The optio remained at attention. The general's fearsome gaze rested on Manius.

"Who the hell's this?"

"His name is Manius," replied Quintus.

"I didn't ask for two of you. Manius? Only one name? Is he a slave?"

"He is my assistant, and my son."

The general looked at Manius as though he'd physically challenged him, then shifted his attention back to Quintus. "So, Quintus Suetonius, are you past it then? They say you are."

"Not to me they don't. I'm happy that the late emperor was satisfied"

"Not entirely. Anyway, he's dead and the new one has yet to make up his mind." He chewed on the end of a stylus then threw it to the desk with an oath. "I suppose you're all I've got. You may be a drunken old sot, but at least you're not disloyal, or stupid – when you're sober."

Quintus inclined his head in acknowledgment.

"So, you've come from Londinium and Caerellius Priscus. What are his orders?"

"Our orders are from the Emperor."

"And what are those orders?"

"To take orders from the provincial procurator. But he's dead."

"What?" Tiberius Flavius paled.

Quintus explained; he didn't mention their own meeting with him.

The general picked up the stylus and gnawed on it before waving the chewed end at Quintus. "Mark me: this is Priscus' doing."

"He rather thought it was yours."

"What? What did you say?"

"He believes you want to lead the army against him and against Rome and that disposing of the procurator as the Emperor's intelligence chief in the province would be a necessary first step."

The colour rushed back to Tiberius Flavius' face. He rose and shook his fist at Quintus. "The lying bastard! Priscus is a lying bastard! He wants the troops; he wanted to stop my command; he wants the troops to march on Rome himself. Lying bastard!"

Suddenly speechless, he waved his fists in the air. Then he remembered Manius.

"You boy!" he roared. "Get the fuck out!"

Manius felt a fleeting sense of injustice, but pushed the optio aside in his anxiety to get through the door.

§

Tiberius Flavius Fimbria raged and paced and waved his arms until he paused and glared at the door through which Manius had escaped.

"It's wholly inappropriate that you should make a young pup like that privy to such matters," he shouted and, getting no response, added another shout, "Snot-nosed young pup!"

Quintus grew irritated, not by the attack on Manius, but by a grown man behaving like a petulant child. But he remained impassive and the general, after another angry glare, moved on to fume about Priscus, stamping to and fro. He stopped, placed both fists on that desk and leaned towards Quintus.

"It's too much, Quintus Suetonius, it's too much I tell you. That snake Priscus plots against me and Rome and defames me into the bargain."

"You have my sympathy."

Tiberius shot him a suspicious glance. "I don't need your fucking sympathy." He slumped into his chair. "I'll tell you something else I don't need: that vinegar-tongued old harridan Tita Amatia Aculeo who's surfaced from heaven knows where, obviously sent to spy on me."

"Why do you say that?"

"It's obvious man! It's well known she's been in contact with Rome these past years. She's been sent to spy on me. Why else would she pop up like some malevolent sprite? What? What are you snorting at?"

Quintus shook his head. "This is too absurd. It can't be widely known that Tita Amatia Aculeo has been in correspondence with Rome – certainly not in Britannia where the woman has been a recluse for years. If it's true, it can only be known in Rome and you can only have received such information from there. If she's a spy of Rome's haven't you asked yourself why it should reveal that to you?"

Tiberius Flavius looked sullen. He muttered and clenched his fists. Quintus' probe had been successful; he pressed home his attack.

"You have a man called Tiro. Who is he?"

"How did you know that?"

"As you said: I'm not stupid. When I'm sober."

"Tiro is my man. What of it?"

"Is he really your man, or was he recommended to you – even sent to you – by Rome?"

The general's sudden start told Quintus he'd hit home again. "You see, I know how Rome and people like Saoterus work. They don't trust anyone: their frumentarii, including me; and, you can be sure, Tiberius Flavius, they don't trust you. I'll tell you something else about such people – they don't understand our trade, but they think they do, they think it's easy.

"So, here's my guess: Saoterus sent me to support Buteo, to help him find out who threatens the Empire – you or Priscus. Simple enough you'd think, but too simple for Saoterus. No, he'd want his own man, someone beholden to him, to report directly to him, someone like Tiro. So he puts him to work for you. Of course, he doesn't bother to tell you that, nor does he bother to tell our Sicilian friend that I'm being sent. The inevitable result – bloody chaos."

"How? What's happened?"

Quintus rubbed his eyes, then pinched the bridge of his nose and spoke wearily. "I've never met this Tiro, but I know him like a brother,

I've come across so many of his type. People like Saoterus love the Tiros of this world who make them wet themselves with excitement like some rich tart meeting a bit of rough. Tiro's a cutthroat amateur, only dangerous in his amateurishness."

Tiberius Flavius grinned. "You just don't like the competition."

"Pah! Don't make me laugh. What I don't like is a competing line of communication. It only ever ends in tears. I had one good agent in Londinium who could've delivered something useful on Priscus, but your friend Tiro killed him."

"What? I know nothing of this!"

"No, you wouldn't. Tiro doesn't really work for you. As I said, he's Saoterus' man and, apart from keeping an eye on me, or even on Tita Amatia, he's here to watch you."

Quintus studied the general's reaction and savoured it.

§

Manius headed across the basilica, treading soft although any noise would have been drowned by the bellowing still coming from that room. He was going to return to the mansio, but after a few paces he halted. That terrible man might call him back to corroborate anything Quintus might say about Horatius Buteo, or about Priscus, or to take notes. Or just for the renewed pleasure of shouting at him. He must stay and wait for Quintus.

He prowled the basilica, peering through the screen, at the imperial busts, impassive, sightless, yet with an illusion of life and movement in the flickering half-light cast by the lamps. For, even in mid-afternoon there was little natural light in this great hall save that which came through the colonnaded entrance. It was, as it was meant to be, a place to awe, where ghosts or gods might walk. Manius shivered and stepped back onto a wooden trapdoor set in the floor's paving. It was bolted and padlocked and presumably led down to the strongroom under the shrine.

The softest of sounds made him look up. It was the beautiful Lucia. Her slippered feet tripping across the pavement had alerted him. It was like a physical blow. She was coming toward him with the light behind her shining through her thin cloak and dress and delineating her slender body.

She smiled. His heart froze and his throat closed. She passed within feet of him, and cast a brief, curious look before heading for her father's office. Manius tried to speak but could only make a strangled noise.

She turned, smiled again, her head tilted. He only managed to shake his head.

"He's not in?" Her voice was so soft, so musical.

"No," Manius squeaked.

"Oh."

"The… the general is in there, Tiberius…"

"Oh him." She frowned but reverted swiftly to that enchanting smile. "Father must be at home."

She approached and his heart drummed. "You must be one of the frumentarii? Everybody's talking about how we have frumentarii in the fort. How exciting."

Manius swallowed and nodded.

"But you're very young." And again that smile; a little look back over her shoulder and she left.

He stared after her, but closed his mouth and jerked upright as another figure came striding into the basilica: Titus, leading a file of six soldiers, their stamping boots shattered the calm of the hall. They marched, eyes fixed ahead, apart from Titus, who spared Manius a smile as he passed. He halted them before the door of the office and rapped on it. It opened to allow Quintus to exit. He looked at Titus. "You may go in."

As they returned to the mansio, Manius asked what Tiberius Flavius had said.

"Lots. Swearing mostly, but he did calm down eventually. I'd quite forgotten how ill-tempered and excitable he is. It always astonishes me when a man his age can so shamelessly behave like an infant. Before his father's eccentric remarriage, he was an only child and doubtless not beaten as he should have been. If you ever have children, don't make that mistake, or your offspring will grow up to be as splenetic and insufferable as he. Oh, he said he's to stay here for the foreseeable future and concentrate some units in the neighbouring forts. We'll act under his instructions for now. Anyway, that's what Priscus originally wanted us to do."

Manius remarked that awful man Tiberius Flavius doubtless was, he'd seemed genuinely outraged by Priscus' suspicions.

"Priscus also seemed honest?"

"So who's telling the truth?"

Quintus shrugged. "Maybe both. Maybe each is loyal but suspects the other of treachery. Perhaps both nurse ambitions and are manoeuvring. We cannot know yet. Anyway, before I forget, we're invited to dine tomorrow night. It's Merenda's dinner in honour of Tiberius Flavius but the general wants us there."

"Me too?" Manius asked, wary of again being thrust unwanted into Tiberius Flavius' presence.

"What? Oh, yes, yes, of course," said Quintus, with a vagueness that alarmed Manius. He was on the point of protesting that he wouldn't be embarrassed again when he recollected that Lucia would be there.

Chapter Twelve

Manius scraped the bronze strigil down his thigh, a ripple of oil and sweat pulled along its leading edge. He repeated this on his other leg, so that now his whole body throbbed warmly. He lowered himself into the caldarium's hot pool to intensify the feeling and to soak away the remaining oil. He breathed the steam in and splashed water through his cupped hands over his hair, blinking and shaking his head.

This morning it was he who'd left Quintus snoring. He wanted solitude. He wanted to think about Lucia. He could barely think about anything else.

If he went to the dinner, he'd see her. But Tiberius Flavius might object and humiliate him in front of her. Insupportable.

He was lulled by the steam, reflecting on Tiberius Flavius. Priscus had already been proved wrong about the threat of rebellion in the North. That vivid experience of disaffection among the Brigantes – those filthy savages had nearly taken their lives. Perhaps Priscus had maligned the general. Wasn't that just what Tita Amatia had believed?

He stretched his arms along the edge of the pool, allowing his extended legs to float. They came to within an inch of the surface, then sank, until he kicked to make them rise again. He repeated this, staring at his toes, his mind probing and teasing.

Whatever the true situation, the real question was: how might this affect him? How might he reap some benefit?

He must possess Lucia. He was determined on that. Priscus, Flavius Fimbria, insurgent Brigantes – none mattered an as compared to her. But how could he ever make her his? That her father would countenance any sort of liaison – let alone marriage – was laughable. Merenda was a knight, with ambitions to rise to legionary command, doubtless planning to marry his darling off into the senatorial class. Farcical for an obscure frumentarius, adopted son of a notorious, disreputable eccentric, even to dream in that direction.

Or was it?

His legs sank, jerking his arms off the pool's edge as a happy idea struck him with sudden clarity.

What if this young frumentarius had a bright future?

In truth, as he'd long recognised, it was far from bright. At best he'd take over from Quintus when he grew too old, but then what? Frumentarii were feared, even respected, but never respectable. No, he'd end up like

Quintus, doing the Emperor's dirty work and finishing up a cynical, bibulous misanthrope. But what if he had a patron, a man with influence and connections? Then there was no limit to how high he might rise. And here the gods had brought Manius to just such a man – Tiberius Flavius Fimbria.

He'd need bright young men, particularly those schooled in intelligence. And here was Manius Suetonius Lupus – already working for him. Quintus and he were to report to him; surely Manius could find opportunities to impress with his quick mind?

He conjured pictures: the general regarding him with grudging respect as Manius made some acute observation or presented him with valuable information. He could do that already, he could discreetly tell Tiberius Flavius about their meetings with Buteo, and Tita Amatia, even their discussions with Priscus? Now that would be information Tiberius Flavius would value: the secret, treasonable conversations of his rival.

Fuck no! Manius shocked himself. Quintus would kill him for certain. He'd regard it as gross betrayal.

But if Manius did it in such a way as to do Quintus no harm? And that's how he would do it, for he did owe Quintus something. But not his entire future, nor could he sacrifice – for Quintus or anybody – any chance of Lucia.

He was roused from these thoughts by the appearance of Titus Caelius.

The tribune was humming and unwrapping a towel from round his waist. He peered with his one good eye into the steam and noticed Manius in the pool.

"Young Manius, how are you?" he asked, sitting on the poolside. Manius heaved himself out of the water to sit by him, asking him how he did. Titus shook his head. "I've spent weeks putting my affairs in order here and trying to give my successor an easy start. I swear: every sack of grain and jar of wine is accounted for, all furlough sheets, duty rosters and sickness returns up-to-date and signed, all diplomas sealed, all the tedium of military life taken care of. Heavens, I normally hate this scribbling. But, it's funny, this time it gave me pleasure, like finishing a chapter as I look forward the next one – and then this." He waved his hand.

"What?"

"Why, this!" Titus said, with an incredulous smile at Manius' incomprehension. "All this… mess." He waved more vigorously. "The infernal Britons and their infernal timing. I'll be leaving the cohort just when there's some real soldiering." He paused, he squared his shoulders and gazed into the steam and said: "A chance for honour and glory." He held his pose then slumped, his face twisted, and he muttered: "What awful luck!"

"You had some soldiering the other day."

"What? That business with the Wolves? That was barely a skirmish – beneficarius' work."

"You really think something's going to happen – more than beneficarius' work?"

"My dear fellow, it already has! Last night a rider made it from Vindomora. The lucky devil made it through the Wolves and the snow and was chased for three miles. With grim news. The northern Brigantes are over the Wall in strength and have risen in the hills, attacked the lead mines and freed the slaves In this weather, for heavens' sake! I tell you Manius, these fellows must know nothing of war. Anyway, the word's already all around the vicus and there are murmurings among the locals. We're sending a troop to try to get through to Vinovia to have their prefect bring most of his cohort to reinforce us."

Titus shook his head again, then clutched it in both hands and groaned. "Oh, I've worked hard with this cohort, especially the horse, and they're good. I know any decent officer would say that about his men, but believe me Manius, it's true. These lads are ready for anything and they'll make short work of the Brigantes, you'll see. What a chance for a fellow to prove himself! Isn't it always the way? Opportunity given to the high-born, to the Flavius Fimbrias of this world. What a time to leave."

"Is it safe for you to go, with the country in this state?"

"Oh I'll take a good mount. I wouldn't flee them willingly you understand, but it's a matter of duty, y'see. Anyway, I know the country and once past Vinovia I'll be safe. The old man – the commander – has decided that I go tomorrow; he cannot sit on a governor's summons any longer, not now my replacement's here."

They were both sweating now, so Titus suggested they go through to the frigidarium. They entered the colder chamber and Titus jumped into the pool. Manius observed that his back and chest bore two or three pink, shiny scars – long ones.

Manius slipped into the cold water, gasping. He dunked his head and swam a couple of vigorous strokes to get his blood flowing. Their conversation troubled him. Once in the fort he'd felt safe enough, but now he realised that the danger was still real and growing and this experienced and capable soldier was leaving. Publius Flavius hardly inspired the same confidence.

Titus scrambled from the water, shaking himself like an otter. He swore, saying that he'd forgotten some final duty. As he left, his voice – still apologising for having to hurry away – came echoing back into the frigidarium, Manius completed his bathing and took time drying himself, weighing what Titus had said and his own plans.

He headed back to the mansio. Dawn was broken but the day offered only a dirty grey, oppressive light. The dullness of sights – grey stone of the fort, the snow and slush underfoot and mud-coloured vicus buildings – contrasted with the sudden onrush of pungent smells: of animals, smoke and cooking. After the moist warm air of the baths, Manius was struck by the dry pinch of the frost and he folded his arms to suppress a shiver. He walked head down, deep in thought but something – sound or movement – caused him to look up.

To see Lucia.

Delight, tempered by acute timidity, gripped him. She had a basket over her arm, a slave girl by her side and a soldier walking a pace or two behind. Manius stood immobile. He managed a frozen, idiotic grin, she returned a sweet smile and stopped, waiting for him to cross the street. In a daze, he approached and wished her good day.

"I don't know your name," she said; then, in response to his bleat. "I'm sorry, what was that? Oh, Manius."

"Yes, Manius Suetonius Lupus."

"Do you know my name?"

"Lucia."

"So, you've been talking about me?"

"No… someone told me… I…"

She giggled, placing a hand on his forearm. His arm jerked, and she laughed and withdrew her fingers. "No, I was only teasing. Forgive me, I'm shockingly forward, but we don't get much society here, not … proper society. Are you at the dinner party tonight? I know the other one is, the old one."

"Quintus?"

"Probably. Well?"

"What?"

"Are you coming?"

"I… er… believe so."

"You absolutely must try the barley cakes, I'll be making them."

Manius promised he would and tried to think of something clever to say, but she smiled and went on her way as he gazed after.

§

Quintus was closing the mansio door when he met Manius. The boy's cheeks were flushed and his eyes were bright. He was fidgeting, hopping from one foot to the other.

"What's wrong with you? Stop dancing. D'you want to pee or something?"

Manius tittered. "No… it's just… I heard some news from Titus Caelius in the baths."

Quintus fluttered his hand. "I know. I've a summons from Tiberius Flavius Fimbria to discuss it."

Quintus started towards the fort's gates and was surprised when Manius fell in beside him. Hadn't the boy had enough of the irascible general?

"I'd better come with you," said Manius. "Two of us can better remember anything he says. I'll see to our togas later. You remember I'm coming to the dinner don't you?

Quintus was replying distractedly when they had to stand back for a cavalry troop clattering out of the fort's gate.

"They'll be going to summon reinforcements from Vinovia, Titus mentioned it," said. Manius

Quintus studied them as trotted by, shoulders rising and falling. They looked seasoned and capable.

This time they found Tiberius Flavius in a large chamber in the Principia. It accommodated a long table, under which were tucked some dozen chairs. Four men were standing between it and the door. Quintus nodded to Antonius Merenda who was talking in a low voice to Publius Flavius, then to the other two – Titus Caelius and another who stood a little apart. The stranger was broad-chested, grave and of early middle age. Merenda introduced him as Spurius Aurelius Cotta, the British magistrate from the neighbouring settlement and a fellow guest in the mansio.

In confidential tone Merenda added: "I invited Aurelius Cotta to the meeting. As a local magistrate, landowner, and a man of Brigantine noble birth, he can give provide valuable information and counsel."

There was a grunt from the end of the room, and for the first time Quintus noticed Tiberius Flavius already seated at the head of the table.

"You're here!" he barked. "Perhaps we can get down to business." He motioned them to be seated.

As chairs were scraped back and places taken – none at Tiberius Flavius' end of the table – the general stared at Manius, who reddened. Quintus prepared to justify his presence but Tiberius Flavius said nothing. A victory of sorts, reflected Quintus.

While Merenda repeated the introductions, Quintus examined the room, noting that the walls were freshly painted white and the wood of the window ledges gleamed with beeswax. Either Merenda ran a tight ship or the legate's visit had spurred him to tighten it.

Merenda had barely finished when Tiberius Flavius slapped his hands onto the table and pushed himself back and to his feet with an exasperated grunt.

"This is intolerable! Stifling!" He strode to the nearest window, wrestled with the catch and threw it open to allow in a blast of freezing air. He resumed his seat and Quintus pulled his tunic close about him with a shiver.

Tiberius Flavius turned to Aurelius Cotta. "We'll start with you then. What can you tell us about the state of your people?"

Aurelius Cotta said dryly: "I'm not sure I accept a description of the Brigantes as my people, particularly those who threaten the peace. However, I've probably got a sense as to how the land lies."

"Get on with it," muttered Tiberius Flavius.

Cotta eyed him before continuing. "What I have to report isn't good. To the East, in my own area, the Wolves are increasingly active; they've stolen cattle from winter quarters, burnt several farms and threatened a number of petty officials and their families. I've also reliable reports of several young hotheads who've left their villages and are thought to have joined the Wolves."

A blare of military horn filled the room. Cotta cast an irritated glance at the open window before continuing.

"As for the West, the situation's far graver. We've all heard about the attack on the lead mines, and of a war band of several hundred Brigantes which is attracting recruits, even in this terrible weather. These probably included the same young fools who've left their villages in my jurisdiction."

His voice was measured. Everyone was attentive, appreciative and respectful.

All but Tiberius Flavius, who contemplated him with open disfavour. He'd been toying with a stylus, now he threw it onto the table. "Is that all? We know all that. Can't you tell us more? What about the northern tribes beyond the wall, can't you enlighten us about them?"

"Only that they are the Textoverdii, a turbulent and clamorous branch of the Brigantes. Now…"

Cotta had to pause again, this time interrupted by bellowed parade ground commands, the stamping of a hundred feet and then a repeated ringing, which sounded like a hammer at work in the fort's foundry.

"Oh, for fuck's sake!" cried Tiberius Flavius, "Will someone close that damned window?"

Publius obliged, shutting out the din. Cotta resumed. "Until now the Textoverdii have been alienated from the rest. If they've made alliances with the other septs, it's serious. More than that, I cannot tell you."

"Oh come on man, you must know more!"

Aurelius Cotta frowned and stiffened. "I've told you everything I know. These Wolves are a secret conspiracy and they keep their activities hidden. I remind you again: I'm a citizen and a magistrate?"

Tiberius Flavius snorted and turned to Merenda. "Do you trust him? Buggered if I do."

Aurelius Cotta glared at the general. Merenda, with a nervous glance at Cotta hurriedly answered Flavius.

"Spurius Aurelius Cotta's trustworthiness is beyond question, sir. He's a respected citizen and on at least three occasions in the last year has advised me on settling disputes and this has helped keep the peace. Until now. He'll be as useful to us as another cohort at the moment."

Tiberius Flavius regarded Merenda with a cold eye.

"How long have you been here?"

"What… why, the cohort's been here four years," blustered Merenda. The general's lip curled, he placed both hands palm down on the table and gazed at the surface between them. "Officers should always be wary of growing too close to those among whom they are stationed. Particularly when their loyalty is suspect."

Merenda flushed red while the colour drained from Cotta's face. Tiberius Fimbria asked about the cohort. Had many of the men had local wives? How close were they to the locals? How was their morale? Merenda assured him that only a handful had taken wives, that he'd hardly any native recruits and that morale was good, and naturally enhanced by the imminence of pay on the fourth stipendia.

Tiberius Flavius seemed a little mollified. Quintus suspected that, having managed to give deep offence, he'd have been satisfied – but for his half brother.

Publius Flavius Fimbria cleared his throat and in that characteristic whisper, which brought a spasm of irritation to Tiberius' face, said: "I've been with these men barely two days, but I'm favourably impressed. They seem disciplined and in good heart. I..."

"What the hell do you know about it?" snapped his elder brother.

Publius coloured but ploughed on. "I was merely trying to be a dispassionate observer, from outside, one who..."

"Keep your bloody dispassionate observations to yourself until you know what the hell you're talking about, which you would, had you joined the army years ago."

"I didn't join because I couldn't afford it," said Publius, his own voice rising.

"I offered you and you refused!" shouted Tiberius Flavius, getting to his feet, fists clenched. "Forty thousand sesterces I was going to put up to make you a legionary centurion, but you refused. Too proud! Only the gods know what you have to be proud of – apart from your father!"

The rest had fixed their stares on the table but for Quintus, who watched Publius' hand go to his sword, worn, as a centurion, on his left. Then he observed the hand of Titus, seated on that side, dart over Publius' hand to restrain it.

Antonius Merenda burst into speech: about the need to make contact with neighbouring forts, about assessing the earthen ramparts of the vicus and their state of repair about the possibility of arming the veterans – about anything other than the Flavius Fimbria family quarrel.

Quintus came to Merenda's aid. "You talk of the vicus' rampart. You mean to remain here, thrown on the defensive?"

Tiberius Flavius swivelled towards Quintus, with animation but with his anger seemingly having suddenly dissipated, forgotten. He spoke before Merenda could reply.

"I accept it contradicts all sound military doctrine to wait within our fortifications while rebels roam the country. It emboldens the enemy and encourages others to join them. But this isn't a normal situation." He jabbed at the table to emphasise his various points. "The snow'll make our cavalry useless. We can't attack the centre of the rebellion because we don't where it is. No, we wait for reinforcements. While we grow stronger, the rebels weaken, without food or shelter. We must only march out when we've clear intelligence on the enemy and his situation. That's your trade Quintus Suetonius. What's your view?"

Quintus rubbed his beard.

"We must work with what little we have. The enemy are drawn from the local population and we must look for information there. Someone will know something, you can count on it – of a son or a neighbour's son who has, as Aurelius Cotta describes, slipped off to join the rebels. Above all, does anyone know anything about their king Iovir? Have all the men question anyone they know in the vicus. Somebody will know something, you may depend on that. Bring it to me."

Heads nodded. "By Jove, he's right," said Titus. "Why shouldn't we employ citizens and others who're loyal? They can be our scouts among the populace. I'll speak to Birca and have her go to her friends and servants. Appius Rufius' wife is local, she can do likewise."

"It's sound advice," agreed Tiberius Flavius. He turned to Merenda. "See the men are spoken to."

"Also be mindful that the vicus can harm as well as help," said Quintus. "If any of the inhabitants have contact with the enemy, they can also provide him with intelligence on our strengths, plans and dispositions. The men must be warned that while they seek information they mustn't betray any."

There was more nodding and murmurings of approval.

§

All viewed Quintus with new respect and Manius was proud but remembered: it was he who should shine in Tiberius Flavius' eyes.

The general spoke next. "Yes, the vicus is important, for the reasons Quintus Suetonius has given. Also we can't afford disaffection there. The Wolves may be at work among this rabble and persuade them to rise against us. Be on the look-out for any signs."

As everyone repeated their sage nods, Manius seized his chance. He swallowed, coughed and, in a higher voice than intended, spoke. "Perhaps people should also be alerted for sightings of the Hooded Spirits."

Six pairs of uncomprehending eyes turned on him and his face burned.

"What in hell's name's he talking about?" Tiberius Flavius asked Quintus.

Manius stammered: "They're small clay figures, c-cloaked figures. The Wolves have been leaving them, it's believed as a warning or a boast."

Tiberius Flavius looked about. "Is this true?"

Merenda and Titus confirmed that such figures had been found at the scenes of outrages but none in the vicus. Aurelius Cotta volunteered that the Hooded Spirit represented an old god of the region, Epaticcu: a neglected minor god, but adopted and revered by the Wolves as the genius and spirit of the Brigantine nation.

"Very well," said Tiberius Flavius. "Make this...this Hooded Spirit another object of inquiry."

Manius felt satisfied as Tiberius cast a curious glance at him before closing the meeting.

"There's nothing more we can profitably discuss. Quintus Suetonius Lupus at least" – and here a dirty look at Aurelius Cotta – "has provided good advice for the cohort's officers to act upon. Remember gentlemen, the vicus must have no doubts about Rome's power and the rebels' defeat. We must always demonstrate our confidence and tonight's dinner, which Antonius Merenda had been good enough to hold in my honour, must go ahead."

"It certainly shall," said Merenda and, adopting an ill-fitting roguish humour, added: "If it didn't I would face – heh, heh – a revolt on the part of my wife and daughter far more serious than anything the Brigantes might threaten. But seriously gentlemen," holding up his hands to still polite laughter, "for all that Tiberius Flavius Fimbria has said about presenting a bold front, I think it wise for guests from the mansio to stay within the fort tonight at least. I don't wish to provide escorts back to the mansio in the early hours of the morning, as that might itself suggest unease on our part."

The general agreed and the meeting closed.

Manius blinked as they came out of the basilica onto the broad steps and sunlight flashed on the snow of the roofs opposite. They started down the steps and Aurelius Cotta fell in beside them, chatting with Quintus. Manius was impressed that he spoke easily, without any evident injured pride or smarting at the insults he'd suffered.

"This discontent or unease among the Brigantes: has it been building long?" Quintus asked him, placing a restraining arm on his companion's shoulder as a soldier led a laden mule across their path.

"In truth I don't know. I should've been more alive to changes in mood, and in the ways in which men speak, and, more importantly, the ways in which they cease to bother voicing their grievances, because they've become convinced that those grievances won't be addressed."

"That's dangerous."

"It is. I admit I was one of those who thought the governor Caerellius Priscus correct. To my regret, I told Priscus this. I was wrong and it's only lately I've seen how wrong. There's been a distinct shift in mood, a feeling that things cannot go on as they are."

"What lies behind it?"

"Oh, you no doubt know the history of previous rebellions and lands confiscated, but things have gone beyond that. There are abuses by tax collectors and a crass insensitivity by others who should know better." Here Aurelius Cotta cast an angry glance back in the direction of the Principia. He lowered his voice. "Perhaps I do myself no favours in the light of what has so recently been said, but I cannot forget my own blood, nor deny my natural affections, so I'll say that the Brigantes are a proud people and, if treated with honour, they'll respond with loyalty. I like to think that I and my family are proof of that."

Quintus patted his shoulder. "Spurius Aurelius, I've no doubt that you are and that what you say is true. I, at least, will take what you've said seriously. We must talk again."

Aurelius Cotta gave a firm nod. "I shall look forward to that Quintus Suetonius."

With another, briefer nod to Manius, he left them in the mansio vestibule. Once he was out of earshot, Manius asked Quintus what he made of him.

"I approve. He seems noble and sensible. As to what he had to say, it's all useful but perhaps most useful is that he revealed he has been in communication with Caerellius Priscus."

"Is that important?"

"As I said: perhaps."

Chapter Thirteen

The girl took Tita Amatia's dress, held it dangling and brushed it with brisk, powerful strokes before folding it. Tita Amatia watched with approval. This girl, Blathin, was competent and conscientious; short and sturdy and her young face was cheerful.

They were in the room Tita Amatia had been allocated in the praetorium, next to that of Tiberius Flavius Fimbria and his lady. Blathin was the slave appointed to wait on her. The room was bright with lime-washed walls and simple furniture. It had a military, utilitarian air but that didn't worry Tita Amatia who little cared for decoration or ornamentation. It was warm and clean.

Blathin soon overcame her nervousness and now chatted like an old friend.

"I like being a chamber slave. It's only my second go, I once looked after Miss Lucia when Numeria was poorly."

"And what do you normally do, my dear?"

"I help in the kitchens and clean… whatever I'm asked really."

"So the Merendas have entrusted me to a beginner."

Blathin's eyes opened wide and her lips formed an O, but Tita Amatia smiled and the girl gasped before doubling over in giggles.

"You're doing very well, dear, I'm pleased with you and if you continue as you are I'll tell your lady you're too good for skivvying in the kitchen."

Blathin's face burned deep red. She resumed her folding, tongue out of the corner of her mouth in concentration, redoubling her efforts to impress.

"D'you come from the vicus, child?"

"No ma'am, from Vindomora, in the next valley." Blathin stopped folding and gazed at Tita Amatia, her voice hushed in wonder: "Is it true, ma'am, you come from Rome?"

Tita Amatia smiled. "A long time ago. Cenares is home now."

"Cenares?"

"Near Eboracum."

"I've heard of that. Is that like Rome?"

"It's a city, but not so great as Rome, nor Londinium."

"I'd like to see it."

"You will, especially if you become a lady's chamber slave."

Blathin sighed. "That'd be an adventure."

Tita Amatia laughed. "Dear me, it's not that exciting."

"Oh, but ma'am, think of your journey, with those Wolves out and you travelling with the general, the legate. Think what might have happened."

"Child, if we worried about what might have happened, we'd never sleep at night. Anyway, travelling with the general didn't increase my danger. It couldn't, unless these... Wolves knew he was on the road, and how could they possibly?"

Blathin resumed folding but hoisting a nightdress to cover her face couldn't conceal a quick, sly little smile.

"They couldn't possibly have known, could they dear?" insisted Tita Amatia.

"Oh ma'am," whispered Blathin. "You'd be surprised what they know."

"How can they know?"

"Sorcery."

§

The sorcery had gone. Tiberius Flavius Fimbria didn't feel it, as he looked into Pellia's eyes. His heart didn't beat any faster or his stomach flutter.

All he felt was irritation. At this stupid bitch.

Yet she stood there, in his office, plainly sensing his indifference, gawping at him as though her gaze could make him relent and love again. She'd insisted on seeing him and he'd had her brought here, rather than go to her room in the praetorium where Decima could get wind of it and start her bloody nonsense again. Shit!

He turned away and looked out of the window. He cleared his throat. "Pellia, I'm busy. Is it something important?"

"But Tiberius, I've hardly seen you since we got here. Pellia get lonely." He gritted his teeth, picturing the pout that accompanied the whining baby voice. A wheedling finger found his fist behind his back and try to unclench it. He wheeled round.

"Pellia, is there anything specific you wanted?"

She stuck out her lower lip and looked down. "Will you come to my chamber tonight, after the dinner?"

"No. In fact, I meant to have word sent to you, you cannot come to the dinner."

She nodded and looked up, her eyes now swimming. "I knew it'd happen. It's her? She made you?"

"I make my own decisions. It would be... unseemly, before my officers."

There was silence but for Pellia's sniffing. He strode past her and paced, finishing up once more before the window.

"It was a mistake to bring you here. You shouldn't have persuaded me. It puts me and my wife – and yourself – in an impossible situation. When it's safe and the weather permits I'll have you taken back to Eboracum."

Something flashed past his ear and the window before him shattered. He jumped back with a cry brushing the front of his tunic. He saw Pellia reaching for another paperweight. The gust from the broken window was already scattering his papers, papers he'd carefully sorted and secured under weights. Now they were all over the fucking place. He roared and dashed at her. She dropped the paperweight and squealed as he slapped her face.

"Pellia!" he bellowed and pinned her wrists to her side. The door burst open and a legionary with drawn sword stood in the doorway, wide-eyed.

"Sir… I heard…"

Tiberius Flavius swore, gave a cry of anger and disgust and shoved the girl staggering into the soldier.

"Take her! Take her to her quarters and see that she stays there."

The legionary sheathed his sword, adjusted the helmet that had been knocked sideways, and gabbled his understanding, before bustling the weeping Pellia away.

Tiberius Flavius glared at the closed door. The fluttering papers provoked more swearing. He closed the shutter on the broken window, retrieved the paperweights and began collecting up the scatted documents. There was a knock at the door.

"Merciful gods, am I to have no peace? Enter, damn you!"

This time the door opened to reveal a nervous optio. He saluted and presented a note which had been left for the general by his man.

Tiberius Flavius frowned. "My man? Oh him. Very well, you may go."

Once the door had closed he read. His eyes bulged. He closed his fist tight over the message until the bark fragments splintered and crumbled and his knuckles ached. He regretted sending Pellia away. He needed to beat someone.

§

"I'm facing death," thought Tita Amatia.

She smiled at the feebleness of her own wordplay. She was facing the entrance to Longovicium's cemetery and, having struggled a few hundred paces through the snow, her breathing was laboured, her limbs protested and she felt her age. She paused to recover, looking back at the white expanse to the vicus rampart and the glowering black walls of the fort behind it. It was a white emptiness, marked only by her own footprints and the much larger ones she'd followed. She pushed the iron gate, which gave a low squeal. But it yielded, the snow which should have been massed behind it had already been forced back.

She wore her hooded, fleece-lined, toggled coat, but still the cold bit and she shivered as she entered the graveyard. She could see little ahead: the stones and monuments were planted thick and many were of head height. Every one, whatever the size, stood for a soul at large. Truly the land of the dead: the grey of the stone, the white of snow and cloud; no wind, nothing moved and all she could hear was her own blood pounding in her temples. This was like a walk through Hades itself.

She followed the footprints through the maze of monuments to a single gravestone, tall and set apart.

Tita Amatia wasn't afraid of the dead. She'd met dangerous men – and women – and they'd all shared one characteristic: they'd all been very much alive. The dead had never threatened. She approached the monument and bent to read the inscription.

A figure bounded from behind the stone, arms flapping. It cawed: "Haha! Haha!"

Tita Amatia contemplated it. "Don't play the fool."

Quintus lowered his arms and mumbled an apology. "You've lost your sense of humour."

"I've grown up!"

Quintus smiled, then looked critically upwards.

"The moon's already out, I don't believe it ever leaves the sky here. It's appropriate. You know there were some Greeks who believed the moon to be the home of the dead. Where I grew up the country folk believed it to be the home of all the troubles released by Pandora, they called them the legions of the moon."

"Anaxogoras wrote: 'Everything has a natural explanation. The moon is not a god, but a great rock and the sun a hot rock.'"

"Anaxogoras confused what a thing is with what it's made of." He looked down and scuffed the snow with his boot. "Anyway, we shouldn't meet here, it's ill-omened."

"Rubbish. I chose it because others are as superstitious as you. We won't be overheard." She looked round. "At least by none who can tell tales."

"Any reason to fear eavesdroppers?"

"There are ears in the fort."

He brushed snow from an overturned stone and sat on it, motioned her to join him.

"Explain yourself."

She told him how the slave Blathin had hinted at the Wolves having informants within the fort. "I pressed her, but the girl grew dumb."

He grunted. "I'd suspected as much. They must've known Flavius Fimbria was on his way."

They agreed there were too many possible sources to make speculation worthwhile, at least without more information.

"Our main concern – let's not forget – is Tiberius Flavius," said Quintus. "It's him we're here to study, not the Wolves. We're well placed for that. I'm part of his council, while you're in the praetorium. Between us we can gauge his loyalty."

She nodded and shifted to give her backside some relief from the cold, hard stone. Quintus glanced at her, curious.

"At least tonight we should get some opportunity," he said.

"Tonight? Oh the dinner. No, I've cried off – pleading indisposition – I've had enough of Flavius Fimbria to last a lifetime." She caught his look of exasperation. "Well, at least a few hours. I can't watch him flaunting his whore tonight in front of Decima. Don't worry, I'll resume duties tomorrow, but I cannot stomach that man tonight. He's such a selfish, angry, strutting..." she flapped her hands, groping, "... ballbag."

She glared defiance at Quintus, who raised his eyebrows. She stood.

"I'm dying of cold and this stone will do untold damage if I sit on it much longer."

"You chose this place. You haven't yet told me about this Tiro."

"My note said it all. A Sicilian called Tiro is on Flavius Fimbria's staff. He looks the type. It must be him."

Quintus frowned. "He's another distraction."

"One easily disposed of."

"You've grown hard, Tita Amatia."

"No, I told you, I've merely grown up."

§

Tita Amatia hurried to her room. The cold had penetrated her bones and she was eager to wrap herself in furs and huddle round a fire. She entered the quadrangle onto which her room faced, head down, picking her way with swift short steps over the icy pavement. Then she heard a raised voice.

Just ahead was an open window of the room given to Tiberius Flavius and Decima Flavia Fimbria and it was his voice. The sound of it irritated her – that and the conviction that he wouldn't have consulted Decima before exposing their room to the freezing air. Tita Amatia had long observed that those more sensitive to heat than cold claimed precedence.

She reached her own door which was next but one to theirs. Her hand was on the latch when his angry bellow made her pause. She'd catch her death, but she might as well hear what the fool was raging about this time.

"How dare you? How bloody dare you?"

Oh dear, what had poor Decima done now to annoy the boor?

But the next voice was and harsh rasping – a man's voice. Tita Amatia forgot the cold and sidled along the wall. Fortunately the window shutters were closed.

"What?" came Fimbria again. "I asked how you dared send me a note summoning , yes, summoning, me to a meeting? `We must meet'. Who the hell do you think you are?"

Tita Amatia, inches away from the open window, drew back when she noticed her frozen breath drifting across it.

"Sorry if I offended. I thought it urgent we meet. There's a frumentarius here, Quintus Suetonius Lupus. I followed him from Londinium. He has an assistant, a boy. I…"

"I know all that you cretin! I know Suetonius Lupus. I'll tell you something – he knows you. Ha! I thought that'd shake you. Yes, he told me one or two things about you... What? You presume to question me? Very well – he told me you killed a man in Londinium."

Tita Amatia held her breath. The voice rasped: "What of it?"

"Don't you take that tone with me Tiro. I'm told your victim was valuable."

A hoarse laugh. "I doubt it."

"Your role isn't to kill as the fancy takes you. It's to do as I say. Do you understand?" A low murmur; Flavius Fimbria continued. "Saoterus sent you to me. Suetonius Lupus says you still communicate with him."

"How would he know?"

"So, it's true! You're here to spy on me. You greasy…"

"So I work for him? So do you. Where's the problem?"

"Me! A Flavius Fimbria, work for that jumped up little slave shit?"

Tita Amatia heard Tiro's snigger. "You'd call him that to his face would you?"

There was a grunt of furious surprise and a ringing slap. Silence, then a breathless Fimbria. "Get out! You're dismissed. Don't let me see you again – heaven help you if I do."

Tita Amatia stepped back as the door latch rose. She scurried to her own door, hauled it open and stood as if just exiting. Tiro scarcely gave her a glance. He was rubbing his cheek, muttering. She caught: "You'll not see me, not 'til it's too late."

He stamped past.

§

The accommodation Merenda provided in the fort was modest: an apartment at the end of a barrack block with two linked cubicles furnished only with bunk beds. Thankfully there was a small hearth and glass in the windows and Manius had stayed in worse inns. He'd sleep easier within the fort's walls, even on a straw-stuffed mattress,

Once settled, and after Quintus returned from meeting with Tita Amatia – and a tactful Manius didn't enquire – they prepared for the dinner, or rather Manius prepared them. He ensured their togas were clean and smooth, then spent time on Quintus' thick, tangled hair, plastering it to his crown with water and oil. He looked absurd, but Manius needed to devote time to himself. He had to look his best for Lucia. He scrubbed, shaved, oiled and scented himself and took immense pains creating fashionable ringlets around his ears and forehead. But he couldn't get his toga to hang right. Either it draped over his feet or exposed too much ankle and had him near sobbing with rage at his failure to perfect it. Quintus could only sneer.

It was a relief to both, when the light faded and a slave came to lead them from their block close to the north gate, through the streets between the barracks, stables, workshops and granaries to the centre of the fort, where the principia stood beside the commandant's praetorium.

They entered through an archway, past a small bath house, porter's lodge and store-rooms, into a pleasant, porticoed courtyard. This little sanctum of domesticity was in stark contrast to the rest of the utilitarian fort. Snow had been shovelled aside to reveal a modest lawn, in the centre of which was a babbling fountain. Despite the ice and frost which clung to and disfigured the figures of Romulus and Remus and their she-wolf, the water still flowed from her teats. Along their left were a series of rooms and, at attention before one door, was Appius Rufius. Quintus asked what he was doing.

His eyes flickered to Quintus, then back to his front and he spoke from the corner of his mouth. "I'm guarding the chamber of Tiberius Flavius Fimbria and his lady."

"You, the senior centurion of the cohort?"

"It's our tradition so to honour important guests on their welcoming dinner nights."

"An honour indeed. Pity you'll miss the dinner."

Appius Rufius gave a brief smile. "I'd rather stand here and freeze than endure that. Don't you concern yourself, the steward will bring me something hot when you've all rolled off pissed to your beds."

Quintus chuckled and they moved on to the far end of the courtyard where bright light shone in a wide doorway, illuminating a handful of figures in conversation gathered around Antonius Merenda who introduced his wife: Gaia Antonia, who was olive-skinned, large, and had a bright, enquiring face. The commandant and his lady seemed ill at ease, glancing over the shoulders of Quintus and Manius. They were so preoccupied that Quintus had to ask who the beautiful young lady was standing behind them. They laughed nervously, apologised, and introduced Lucia; Quintus, with a smile, said how charmed he was. She acknowledged him with sweet modesty, shooting a puzzled look at his hair. She gave Manius a shy smile, but he could see her eyes were sparkling and his heart and innards danced. Gaia Antonia explained that this large, airy room was the summer dining room where they would enjoy their honeyed wine before moving across the courtyard to the winter dining room which, being next to the kitchen, was far warmer.

They moved into the room which was lit by more than a dozen wall lamps whose flames shimmered on the gleaming white painted walls, Manius tarried to whisper to Lucia: "I look forward to the barley cakes." Her swift turn to give him another dazzling smile had him congratulating himself on his silver tongue. She made as if to reply but then fluttered her eyelashes as she looked away with another coy smile. Manius glowed as he caught up with Quintus, among people who were standing in two or three groups, holding fine glasses which were being replenished with yellow wine by a couple of slaves. There were a dozen or so guests but conversation seemed subdued and hesitant. Manius noticed Titus, who stood with Publius Flavius and another man who was small, portly and dark. Quintus and Manius made their way over, pausing only for Quintus to relieve a slave of three glasses, one for Manius, one to down on the spot and the other to keep until the slave returned.

Publius Flavius, who evidently hadn't forgiven Eboracum, promptly made whispered apologies and left to join a military looking pair in a corner. But Titus greeted them and introduced his other companion, Antiochos, the cohort's surgeon. Quintus, for all his antipathy to Greeks, was affable enough, no doubt, reflected Manius, cheered by the excellent mulsum they were drinking.

They chatted about that, the weather and Titus' planned departure the next day. The surgeon Antiochos was voluble, telling them how much he admired Londinium and describing the happy months he'd spent there on the previous governor's staff.

"No doubt you wonder what brings a successful physician – much sought after by the very best families of Rome and a pupil of Galen himself – to the very edge of the Empire?" sighed Antiochos.

Quintus only contemplated him and Antiochos continued, suddenly melancholy: "In truth, it isn't so charming to practise medicine in Rome. Bah! One doesn't practise medicine but rather politics, countering the slanders and intrigues of rivals. I resolved to become a military surgeon so that my professional life would be one of medicine pure and simple and no more back-biting, rumour mongering and toadying. Now people respect my opinion and value my expertise. Also, I can experience a variety of diseases, new herbs and remedies and even different gods. You wouldn't believe, for example, how prevalent rheumatism is here, while malaria is unheard of. There's so much for me to observe and to record that I shall write a book, perhaps several."

Manius could see from Titus' glassy stare that this was much rehearsed. Manius began casting frequent, casual glances over his shoulder at Lucia. At last, she turned, met his glance and smiled but then turned back to be introduced to Tiberius Flavius, who was entering with a finely dressed lady, tall, and somewhat older.

Now that the guest of honour had arrived, all conversations ceased. The general and his lady took up station so that all could be formally presented. Tiberius Flavius gave Manius only a curt nod, but, when he was introduced to Decima Flavia Fimbria, he was struck not only by her easy graciousness – she asking him kindly how he liked Britannia; whether this was his first winter – but also that her heavy makeup couldn't conceal a tell-tale puffiness under the eyes. Manius remarked on this in a low voice to Titus as he rejoined him in a corner.

"The general's lady looks as though she has been weeping."

Titus looked awkward and cleared his throat. "I... ah... believe the lady has good cause to be unhappy."

"How so?"

He looked even more uncomfortable. "I shouldn't repeat gossip, it's unfair, unmanly, dishonourable."

Manius hastened to say how much he agreed, how he despised talking about people behind their backs. They settled into an unsatisfactory silence, each contemplating the floor.

After some seconds Manius coughed and said: "Titus, of course, you know my position, I haven't any interest, absolutely no interest, in idle tittle-tattle, but if the lady's unhappiness had any bearing on the general... "

Titus kept silent, his face working. Eventually, with reluctance, he spoke. "I suppose you're used to receiving confidences?"

Manius nodded.

"You would treat anything with discretion?"

"The utmost discretion."

Titus whispered."You observed the arrival of the general yesterday. Did you see in his entourage another woman, apart from Decima Flavia and her slave, a young woman, mounted on a grey?"

"A Levantine lady?"

Titus smiled. "A Levantine for sure – Cappadocian I gather – as for being a lady... she's Tiberius Flavius' concubine. He brought her despite the humiliation that means for his wife and – I happen to know – even wanted her here tonight."

"No!"

"Oh yes." Titus cast a quick look round before continuing: "That, however, was a step too far: Decima Flavia flew into the most passionate rage, telling him if that happened, she'd kill herself and disgrace him. She's a Durmia Potita, of the Valerian clan – not a family to cross. Imagine what the scandal would do to his career. Anyway, he backed down but she insisted that he send this girl, Pellia, away and conduct his affairs with greater discretion. To stop the tears and shrieks, he has had to agree. A general ordered by a woman."

"How can you know all this?"

"I wish I knew none of it. I could never be a frumentarius. Perhaps if I were less scrupulous I could rise higher." He shuddered and, as moved to answer the summons of a frantically waving Merenda, hissed: "If you must know: remember I have a guard on their bedroom door."

Manius was regretting taking advantage of a simple soldier and outraging his sense of honour, when Quintus, who'd been talking with the general's wife, joined him, replenished glass of mulsum in hand. He explained that Decima Flavia was another old friend and they'd been renewing that friendship. When Manius reported his conversation with Titus, Quintus' face darkened and he glared across the room at Tiberius Flavius, who was talking to the Merenda family and Titus.

"I told you. I told you he was a shit and a prick."

The atmosphere was uneasy as they filed across the courtyard to the winter dining room. There were only sixteen of them but they shared sufficient ill will to stifle easy conversation. Hadn't it been for the figure of Lucia a few feet ahead, Manius would have envied Appius Rufius, still at attention in the freezing air.

He found himself walking across that quadrangle with the tax collector Arrius Gracchus whose eyes were flitting to and fro over the party, craning to see over the heads of those before him. He caught Manius' glance and tittered.

"Excuse me, I've become separated from my wife. We don't often mix in society and she'll be nervous without me. Ah, she's just ahead." He wiggled his fingers in the direction of his unseen wife, then turned with a smile.

"It's Manius Suetonius isn't it? You're the son of the other gentleman?"

"Quintus."

"Ah, yes, Quintus Suetonius. May I ask, what brings you to Longovicium? Are you perhaps… on official business?"

Manius should've been evasive. Telling Titus – on first acquaintance – that he and Quintus were frumentarii, had been indiscreet. To be known could limit their effectiveness and even invite danger. But, what the hell! By now, many knew, even – for heaven's sake – Lucia. Why be circumspect with Arrius Gracchus?

Also, Manius felt awkward and shy. He was going into a dinner that included a wonderful, beautiful girl and a general who could spit venom without provocation or warning. He felt inconsequential and vulnerable and had an urge to aggrandize himself, even before such a nervous little nobody as this Gracchus.

"We're frumentarii," Manius said, narrowing his eyes at the tax collector.

Manius had hoped to impress, but never anticipated Gracchus' painful gasp and his face draining of colour as his hand came to his mouth. He stopped dead, until he was propelled forward by Aurelius Cotta stumbling into his back. They exchanged apologies and Gracchus gave his nervous titter and composed himself. But he didn't speak to Manius again.

The winter dining room wasn't grand. The table and the couches and seats around it left little space for the slaves to serve and the lamps cast a half light, giving the room an intimacy. The guests were shown to their places: Tiberius Flavius and his wife, who could hardly be split, were together at the place of honour opposite the Merendas who headed the table. The general's half brother was as far from him as possible, to Antonius Merenda's right; Lucia was on her mother's left, and on her left, in the next available space at greatest distance from Tiberius Flavius, was Aurelius Cotta, with his wife. On one long side of the table, after Publius, were the Gracchus couple, then Manius, Quintus and Titus. On the other side, below the Cottas, were the couches of the surgeon Antiochos and the two military men, who, Manius gathered, were centurions, one tall and fair, the other short and thin, almost childlike, but with grey hair. Neither had much to say, so Decima Flavia endured most of the meal in silence, for she and her husband exchanged hardly a word.

Doubtless to counter the cold outside, the furnace had been well fed and Manius was soon sweating in his dress toga and the tall fair centurion was mopping his brow. Merenda, observing Tiberius Flavius' angry fidgeting, signalled to a slave to open the doors ajar, which brought relief.

The Merendas had clearly put considerable trouble and expense into this meal. Manius brightened as they began with Picenian bread, eggs, snails, lovely crisp radishes and – a welcome taste of home – salted olives. Apart from the Setian in their glasses, most impressive were the oysters, which prompted murmurs of appreciation and, when complimented by Quintus, Gaia Antonia preened herself. "Yes, they're from Rutupiae, the best in the province. We always like to order from there but it's such a short season for once the winter gales set in no ships make it up the coast." For Manius, the best were the little barley cakes, and he ate several, while trying to catch Lucia's eye. But she was in giggling conversation with her mother and Cotta's wife.

Her father was conferring with his new second-in-command Publius, but Manius observed his frequent anxious glances at the far end of the table, where silence ruled, apart from Tiberius Flavius' monosyllabic replies to the odd remark from Titus. Opposite Manius, the Cottas chatted to Antiochos, while the two centurions chewed stolidly, staring at the opposite wall. The Gracchus couple only exchanged the odd whisper. She was a small, nervous birdlike woman, who reddened and twittered when Manius addressed her. Quintus piled into the food and the wine, while Manius adopted an attitude of stern reserve, his brow furrowed and a frown on his lips, to appear to Tiberius Flavius a serious, reflective young man and, to Lucia, as someone with deep thoughts and heavy responsibilities.

The only sounds were low or whispered voices and the odd clink of glass against plate. There were one or two hushed, nervous references, from Antiochos and Aurelia Cotta, to the Wolves, to the threat of rebellion and to the imminence of siege, but these were quashed by warning glares from Merenda, Even the slaves seemed infected by the mood. One moved to fill Manius' glass, and his hand trembled so badly Manius feared he'd spill wine on his clean toga. Other slaves whispered to each other in the shadows in the room's corners and in the doorway, on edge; fearful.

With a grim, secret smile Manius reflected that it hadn't begun as a happy dinner party.

But worse was to come.

Chapter Fourteen

Spirits revived with the arrival of the second course: boar, venison, fattened goose's liver, crab, eel and a bowl of exquisite sauce, a garum. Again, Gaia Antonia simpered under the weight of compliments.

"Superb, my dear lady, superb," piped the little Greek Antiochos. "This is a feast worthy of Apicius."

"Who is Apicius?"

It was a squeak from Manius' left. He turned to see the burning face of Arria Gracchus, holding a hand over her mouth, trying to force back the words only intended for her husband.

"My dear," he said, "Apicius was a famously rich man who was a lover of fine food and his table sometimes boasted such marvellous dishes as crane, flamingo and even ostrich."

Conversation died for some minutes to do justice to the food and drink, the best Manius had had in Britannia, even surpassing that served by Caerellius Priscus. Only after minutes of lip smacking, appreciative murmurs and polite belches did Tiberius Flavius speak.

"Tell me, who're the local gods? You… you young man, what's your name – Manius Suetonius – you seem expert."

Manius froze, a boar-chop half way to his mouth. Shit! His face burned, the eyes of the company upon him. He swallowed and cleared his throat, his mind paralysed. Then salvation.

"It's Coventina," said Lucia. "She's goddess of water and much loved here. She has a holy spring that rises only a mile away; it has magical and medicinal properties. Isn't that so Antiochos?"

The surgeon answered that he'd treated many soldiers who'd found tribute and oblation to Coventina to bring swift and lasting relief, particularly to bladder disorders.

"I, Antiochos, would certainly not discourage anyone seeking her aid, not in this region where she bears sway, for, as Galen teaches: the patient must be treated in relation to the world around him and not as something isolated, in a vacuum."

Lucia looked nonplussed. Manius feared attention would now shift back to him, the general's nominated expert. Happily, Antonius Merenda spoke, probably to divert attention from his daughter's forwardness.

"Mithras is gaining a following, not just in the army, but among British citizens such as my friend Aurelius Cotta here." Pausing only for Cotta's acknowledgment, he launched into a monologue on the cult and how its strict principles of discipline and integrity could benefit a province such as Britannia.

"You've no Christians then?" demanded Tiberius Flavius and, receiving uncomprehending shrugs and head shakes, added: "Good, I cannot abide them, as would attest those who knew me and Rusticus in Lugdunum and Vienna. Oh, we soon satisfied their lust for martyrdom."

This prompted another uneasy silence and he reverted to ill humour. He greeted Antonius Merenda's fond reminiscences of life in Egypt with a sneering remark about the soft life the army lived out there which left it flabby and ill-disciplined. He followed up with a leering observation on the huge-breasted black women of Meroe, which had Lucia and her mother reddening with modesty and Antonius Merenda with outrage. An exchange of nervous looks signalled an awful realisation that the general was drunk and that he was the kind of drunk who was determined to be offensive – even more than when he was sober.

Thankfully, he fell silent, his head lolling and his eyes struggling to focus on the table, oblivious to the cold, disdainful gaze of his wife. Slowly, with many a wary glance at him, the company resumed conversation.

Manius paid little attention, only aware of Sexta Aurelia Cotta's animated chatter to the Merendas about property. He was preoccupied: had Lucia made her interruption about Coventina because she saw his predicament and had wanted to save him? The well-bred drawls of Aurelia Cotta and the monosyllabic grunts of Quintus – in reply to Titus' remarks on British horseflesh – were a vague background, to his musings.

The conversation became general – even animated. Antiochos joined in and Titus, probably wearying of Quintus' unresponsiveness, put in the odd comment. Manius too began to listen, while covertly observing Lucia.

Aurelia Cotta was canvassing opinion on whether she and her husband should buy an estate bordering one of theirs in the south of the province, it being more convenient to visit one large estate rather than two smaller ones.

"We'd only have the expense of one steward and one villa. That's not to mention the savings in household staff, gardeners, workmen and even hunting gear."

She looked put out – and the rest of them surprised – when the taxman Arrius Gracchus demurred.

"Dear lady, I'd be wrong not to point out a danger. A large estate in one location lays you open to risks confined to that region – hailstorms, early frosts, drought. Whereas, with two estates in two locations, you halve your chance of ill luck."

"Aulus Arrius has to deal with many estate owners in many regions," confirmed his wife.

Quintus growled: "What of the major consideration? Is it going at above the market rate, in which case our friend's point might weigh more heavily, or is it going for nothing, in which case you'd better snap it up."

Aurelius Cotta grimaced. "It seems a bargain at three million sesterces, where once, I swear it would've fetched five, but the owner has neglected the estate and he's foreclosed on his tenants to meet rent arrears. So, no, three million isn't cheap, it's fair." He threw up his hand. "I don't know. What does anyone else think?"

Then came the familiar whisper of Publius Flavius. His speech was prefaced by a hiccup. His condition was fast approaching that of his stepbrother.

"I've never had an estate, though I would have liked one. At one time I thought... by way of a promise... but... others had a different view..."

Almost everybody, apart from the Gracchus pair, must have known the history between him and his stepbrother, and Manius observed their horror. Merenda groaned and sank his face into his hands. Others turned to gauge the reaction of Tiberius Flavius Fimbria. It wasn't good.

His head snapped up. His bleary eyes focused and fastened on Publius, while his mouth opened and closed as he fought to articulate words bubbling inside him. Manius noticed his wife place a discreet restraining hand on his, but it was no use.

"You little turd," he said, his own voice at this stage hardly more than a horrible whisper. "You dare talk about inheriting an estate. You should think yourself lucky you're not a fucking slave like your whore of a mother." He hauled himself to a sitting position on his couch, sweeping aside Decima Flavia's arm and jabbing his finger, shouting now. "You wormed your way into father's affections just like she did! If it hadn't been for his memory, I'd have thrown you out into the street; I should, you cunning little slave-spawned bastard!"

He rose, gathering his toga about him, shaking his fist. Manius feared he was going to launch himself on Publius and there was a terrified squeak from Arria Gracchus. But Tiberius Flavius stood, until he mastered himself and, chest heaving, raised his arm and pointed at his stepbrother.

"I'll have no more to do with you, until tomorrow – when you can look forward to being cashiered for impudence."

He strode from the room, with a thunderous face, hurling aside the luckless slave who made to fully open the door. The room echoed to the slamming of that door, following by the clatter of a silver tray, dropped by the slave, spinning on the tiles before coming to a stop with a final rattle. Decima Flavia looked around and, after opening her mouth as if to make some apology, seemed to think better of it, rose and hurried after her husband.

Quintus punctuated the ensuing silence with a soft belch and reached to refill his glass.

No one wanted to look at the chief victims of the general's rage: Publius and the Merendas. Manius toyed with his wine glass, gazing at its stem, as though it were some oracle which would repay careful study. To his left, Arrius Gracchus was paying similar attention to the fingernails of his right hand. The only sounds were the nervous clearing of a throat, the slave getting to his feet and scurrying away and Quintus chewing.

Arria Gracchus broke the spell, with a low whimpering which rose to a series of gasping sobs. This was followed – and it tore at Manius' heart – by Lucia crying and, between sniffles, whispering apologies to her mother and Aurelia Cotta. They consoled her, while casting dark looks in the direction of the general's exit. Gaia Antonia, who, as hostess, must have felt like weeping bitter tears herself, could be heard to mutter: "disgraceful", "ill-bred" and "filthy drunk".

The tax collector Gracchus was the first to speak, with a melancholic boom. "Wine makes fools of us all."

"You're right!" cried Titus. "But sometimes it can lighten the heart and dry away tears." He took a jar from the table and circulated, filling their glasses and, with bluff, good humour cajoled them into taking wine with him. His clumsy flattery and remarks about tears spoiling beauty being an affront to the gods, made Arria Gracchus and Lucia sniff, wipe their eyes and smile.

He even coaxed a weak smile from his commander Merenda, who still had his head in his hand. Publius Flavius was another matter. His face colourless, he stared, but did take the wine and drank. Titus tried to take wine with him but gave up; Publius' drinking was going to be a solitary business.

To Manius, the evening's details became a blur for he also drank, initially to steady his nerves following the eruption of Tiberius Flavius, then to avoid the necessity of embarrassing conversation and then to ease the making of it. And he drank for Titus, who urged them to be merry. But for him, Manius was convinced excuses would have been made and the party would have drawn to an awkward close.

The mood soon changed. There was merriment at Titus' feeble jokes, but with an edge of hysteria and an element of determination, even defiance: glassy stares, smeared eye make-up and mouths open for laughter that was too forced and too prolonged. Maybe it was in reaction to Tiberius Flavius, or perhaps because outside the walls of the fort and the ramparts of the vicus was a country in the grip of a barbarian revolt.

Manius smiled at Titus playing some trick that involved balancing wine glasses and filling them; laughed at him bungling it and wine spilling across the table. Antiochos, supporting him by singing a clownish song and then Aurelius Cotta told an amusing story about a baker in Concangis.

Merenda joined Titus in urging more food and wine on the company, either through duty, or infected with the same fey mood. When they finished what was on the table, he called for silence and went to the end of the room and, while they all stood with heads bowed, he made the offering of wheat, salt and wine to the household gods. He maintained the silence for some minutes, then drew a deep breath, clapped his hands and called on the slaves for cakes, honeyed bread and more wine.

The conversation again fragmented; neighbours spoke with neighbours. The Gracchus couple, looking discomfited by the amount drunk, spoke to each other. The centurions talked about cavalry remounts while the Cottas drew the Merendas and Antiochos back into discussing their prospective new estate. Publius spoke to no one and Titus, Quintus and Manius were able to confer.

"So," said Quintus to Titus, "are you prepared for your departure?"

"My bags are packed. I shall say my farewells to Birca and be away with the dawn."

"Couldn't Birca be here tonight?" Manius asked.

Titus' face darkened. "Sadly not. Our relationship is an irregular one and certainly not recognised by the army. It would've been difficult enough to persuade the old man to allow her in and there was no chance with the general here. Heaven knows what he would've said. I say, wouldn't it have spoiled the evening even more, had I been obliged to fight and kill him?"

"I must confess," said Quintus, "given the man's nature, I find it hard to understand his popularity with the army."

"Soldiers generally like plain speaking, but perhaps one can speak too plainly." Here Titus cast a meaningful glance in the direction of the two centurions, who, though deep in conversation about grain stocks, could have overheard. "But excuse me, I must go to the latrine."

Everybody during that evening – and Manius was to recall this – paid at least one visit to the latrine. He must have gone three times, twice to pee and once to vomit and Quintus – whose bladder might have benefited from an offering to Coventina – went several times. He certainly noticed Publius blundering from the room. He was gone for some time and the tall centurion asked with disapproval whether he'd made his final departure without his commander's leave. Merenda shrugged: that was the least of his worries. But Publius returned minutes later, and, while still pale, looking as though the fresh air had done him good – his gait was steadier and his eyes brighter. He noticed Manius looking at him and said: "I had to go to my quarters for a clean toga, I threw up over the other."

They sat there for two hours with people coming and going, from the latrine, or maybe just to take fresh air or to swap places with neighbours. Wine flowed and slaves moved among them, replenishing jars, mopping spills and replacing napkins. Manius began casting glances at Lucia hoping to exchange a look, but she was tired, swallowing yawns and he only succeeded – twice – in catching the disapproving eye of her mother.

Shortly after, Merenda got to his feet to draw the evening to a close.

"Honoured guests," he began, his words slightly slurred.

The doors flew open, letting in a blast of cold air, to reveal a white-faced young optio, wide-eyed, flurries of snow swirling around him. He looked at Merenda. "Sir, sir..."

"What is it? What do you want boy?"

"Sir, oh sir, come, please do come quickly."

Merenda looked about, confused. Titus stood. "What's amiss? Why do you disturb us?"

The young optio swallowed, swayed on his feet and pointed dumbly over his shoulder. He found his tongue. "The... it's the... general."

Titus took Merenda by the shoulder and brushed past the optio, out into the courtyard. Quintus likewise grabbed Manius and hauled him after them.

Manius' eyes took some seconds to adjust to the darkness and he heard a cry before he saw, across the courtyard, the figures of Titus and Merenda. Quintus and he made straight for them over the grass, past the still giggling fountain. They were huddled over a figure slumped under the portico, leaning against the wall by a door. They were joined by the optio who had a lamp in his hand which he passed to Titus. Titus held it over the prone figure of Appius Rufius whose eyes were staring but sightless, a gaping hole in his throat thick with blood, black in the semi light, congealing on his cloak.

Merenda groaned, raised himself and pushed open the door by which the senior centurion lay. The room into which they stared was fully lit, lamps blazing on all four walls.

Manius first saw Decima Flavia Fimbria. She was lying on a bed against the far wall, one leg bent under her, one arm trailing on the floor and her head lolling to the side. Her eyes were closed and she moaned. Titus gasped and pointed at that wall opposite Decima Flavia, to her husband, or what was left of him.

Tiberius Flavius also lay on a bed, sprawled, his arms and head thrown back displaying his naked chest and belly and the grey, glistening mess that spilled out onto the bed linen.

Merenda put a hand to his mouth. "May the gods have mercy on us," he moaned.

There was a sound behind them. It was Gaia Antonia, her mouth open and gasping on the verge of screaming.

"Get out!" shouted Titus. Then to the optio, "Get her out man, get the women out!"

The optio bundled her back.

Behind them all, Publius Flavius Fimbria gazed into the room, white faced, with eyes shining and teeth exposed in a grin.

Chapter Fifteen

A breeze ruffled the feathers of Antonius Merenda's priestly headdress and fat snowflakes floated about his face, a face that was grey, tired and much older than it had been the day before.

They stood around him by the altar, in the courtyard outside the basilica: the men who had been at last night's dinner – except Arrius Gracchus and Publius Flavius, the latter confined to his quarters under guard. With the cohort's remaining senior officers, they had proceeded behind Merenda, with due solemnity, from the shrine of the standards, and now, numbed with shock and cold, in the dim morning light, they watched Merenda hold aloft the curse tablet and call upon the gods to avenge murder.

"Let them not sit, nor eat, nor drink, and let this curse not be removed until their blood be spilled, whether they be slave, freeman or woman," he said, voice trembling, face upturned to the gods and to the ashen sky.

Manius pictured Publius Flavius pacing his room, tortured with guilt at having destroyed his own brother. No one, who'd seen his face last night, could doubt that he'd committed the unnatural deed. Nor had he denied it when challenged but had put a hand to his mouth and tittered, a chilling sound which had added to the horror, larding awful crime with insanity. Titus had ordered that he be led away and placed under guard.

Titus, Quintus and Antiochos had then taken command, ushering the women back to the dining room, removing the bodies and tending the unconscious Decima Flavia. Merenda had been paralysed, unable to comprehend or react to the terrible occurrence in his fort, his cohort and his command. Manius had staggered about the Praetorium's quadrangle, throwing up, along with Aurelius Cotta, Arrius Gracchus, and even the two centurions, until Titus had bellowed at them to pull themselves together. Then it was all running soldiers, wailing women and urgent commands – a confused parade of impressions which Quintus had brought to a close by putting his hand round Manius' shoulders, ordering him to bed. Not that he'd slept. The shock and puking had sobered him and he'd lain shivering under his blankets, until Quintus had roused him at first light to attend this ritual. The cockerel's squawk recalled him to the present. Merenda drew the knife across its throat and offered its twitching body, with wine and bread, to the gods. Quintus drew Manius to one side as the entrails were being examined.

"They'll learn less from those guts than we did from Flavius Fimbria's," he whispered.

Manius gagged and shuddered and Quintus grinned. "That little Greek surgeon has been poking about inside him. Ha! Probably, can do as much now as he can for anyone alive, the greasy quack."

He pulled Manius into the colonnade's shadows, out of earshot. "Listen, things have grown interesting and we must have our wits about us, gather as much information as we can while memories are fresh. I'm away for a council with Antonius Merenda, but beforehand I'll speak with Tiberius Flavius' tart, the Levantine – what's her name?"

"I can't recall."

"Never mind, I'll find out. You speak to Decima Flavia – if she's up to it. But go carefully, I only want the facts of what she can remember, save anything else for me, I know her. Understand?"

"Yes… but…"

"But what?"

"Why? What for? Publius Flavius killed his brother."

"Probably, but since when was information superfluous in our office? Go. Do as you're told."

Manius was glad to have something to think about other than Tiberius Flavius' eviscerated corpse. But he'd hardly moved when Arrius Gracchus came scurrying on tiptoe through the colonnade.

"Am I too late for the ceremony?" he gasped. "I overslept… so late last night… the shock…"

They told him he'd missed the cursing. He wrung his hands. "Oh no, I've been such a sluggard, if only I could've awoken. But after that horror, sleep was out of the question until nearly dawn. In fact, I had to get up and pace the streets of the fort. Can you imagine?"

Quintus nodded absently.

"I wasn't alone in my distress. Poor Aurelius Cotta must've been in a similar state to have also been out."

"What d'you mean out?" asked Quintus.

"Out in the fort. I saw him by the north wall."

"Really? Doing what?"

Gracchus shuffled his feet, wringing his hands. Quintus' eyes narrowed. Gracchus coughed. "He was just standing by the wall."

"Just standing?"

"Well…"

"Well?"

"I really don't know, it was dark. I just got the impression he…'

"He what?"

"That he'd thrown something over the wall. But I may have been mistaken, as I say, it was dark."

"Did he see you?"

"I don't believe so. I didn't want a conversation, it was late."

Quintus stared at Gracchus, who was red-faced and swallowing. "I so wanted to be at the ceremony to support poor Lucius Antonius Merenda. How is he?"

"Deeply unhappy. How could he be otherwise? A general, a man who was legate and senator, murdered under his protection. Perhaps he'll do away with himself."

Gracchus' mouth and eyes opened in horror. "Surely not!"

Quintus shrugged. "Why not? As Epictetus says: `The fire smokes and I leave the house'."

Gracchus bit his lip and wrung his hands some more while Quintus regarded him with curiosity. Then he noticed Manius. "Well, go on boy, what are you waiting for?"

Manius left, shoulders hunched, feet scuffing the ground. Quintus watched him with frowning disapproval. He turned as Gracchus tugged his sleeve.

"I hope you'll not mention to Aurelius Cotta that it was I who saw him. I'm sure it wasn't significant."

Quintus nodded absently and turned, heading off to the neighbouring Praetorium. He wondered about the little taxman and his tale – a tale so readily told. Was it true?

He made for the rear of the Praetorium, where the building backed onto a tall granary which blocked out most of the light, just the kind of out-of-the-way place to house an embarrassing concubine. He enquired of a man shovelling snow, hurling it, with great grunts, against a wall. Quintus brushed aside his attempts at conversation, extracting directions to a room, where he found a slave girl leaving, bearing a wash basin.

"Is your mistress in? I must see her – in an official capacity."

The woman gave a sullen look, bade him wait and went back into the room. Seconds later, she poked her head round the door and told him her lady was only just risen. Could he return in an hour?

"No," he said and kicked the door open, sending the girl spinning back into the room. He strode after her and jerked his thumb over his shoulder. "Get out!"

He contemplated the figure on the bed, who was bleating and holding the covers to her chin.

She was young, not much more than Manius' age and nothing special to look at, particularly not without make-up to cover a podgy face disfigured by recent weeping. The room was littered with clothing spilling out of bags and strewn over furniture and floor. He swept a shawl from a stool, pulled it up and sat beside her. Her eyes – half fearful, half resentful – followed him.

He stared, sizing her up. When she began to squirm, he said: "I am a frumentarius. Do you know what that means?"

She nodded, doubtful.

"You know what happened last night?"

She sniffed, swallowed and nodded again.

"What's your name?"

"Pellia," she said, her voice choked.

"Ah yes, Pellia. You're from Cappadocia I understand. A long way from home. How d'you come to be in Britannia?"

He judged her to be a girl schooled to have to answer peremptory questions from those in authority, but who'd thought such days behind her. With a sulky pout, she explained, in a low, resigned voice, that she was a slave, had been sold and shipped to Rome when twelve, bought by a brothel keeper and sold on to a customer who, two years ago, had lost her in a game of dice to Tiberius Flavius. She'd climbed in his favour and he had – she insisted – treated her as his true wife, so much so that he'd had to bring her to Britannia.

"Did he free you?"

She stuck out her lower lip and shook her head. Then her eyes brightened.

"But he's to free me in his will – he promised."

Quintus smiled, but she insisted: "He swore by his ancestors."

"I'm sure he was true to his word. But tell me about last night: where were you?"

She regarded him with petulant obstinacy. Quintus frowned. "Pellia, the poet writes: 'You were born a slave: you have no voice.' Don't take that too literally."

She looked uncomprehending, but jumped and squeaked when he thumped the pillow by her head and shouted: "I asked where you were!"

"I was here!"

"In this room?"

"Yes, yes, I ate alone."

"What then?"

"What do you mean?"

"After you had eaten, what did you do?"

"I slept."

"Immediately after eating, you slept?"

"Yes… well… what else was there to do?"

"Did you see or speak to anyone?"

"Not after my girl had taken away my dishes, no."

"Why didn't you come to the dinner? Tiberius Flavius told me you were coming."

Her eyes narrowed, wary. "He changed his mind; said I shouldn't go."

"Why?"

Pellia muttered. "What was that? What did you say?"

"I said: she made him."

"His wife?" She nodded. "So was he fonder of her than of you?"

She gave a bitter laugh. "A poor concubine that'd make me. He feared her; feared her family's power."

"He was going to put you away, wasn't he?"

Her eyes widened. "He told you that?"

Quintus contemplated her, until she could no longer meet his eye.

"Do you have more questions?" she whispered.

He sighed. "No, not for the moment, but I may later." He rose and made for the door. She called after him: "What happens now?"

"What d'you mean?"

"What happens to me now?"

Quintus shrugged. "If Tiberius Flavius kept his word, when the lawyers have finished with his will, you'll be freed. If not – and until then – I presume you're the property of his widow."

He left her wailing.

§

Tiro froze, then eased back into the trees, leading his horse. He wrapped its reins round a branch, whispering that if it made a noise – and if he survived its betrayal – he'd flog the hide off its fucking back.

Once it was secure and nuzzling in the snow, he drew a deep breath, then his sword, careful not to scrape against the scabbard.

He returned to the forest's edge and peered to his right. The Briton was still there, thirty paces away, his back to Tiro. He was dressed for war, helmet on head and leaning on his spear, a rebel sentry and a poor one. He hadn't noticed Tiro's slow approach even here, barely half a mile from Longovicium. He'd stationed himself too close into the trees so that a spur of forest hid the approach from the fort – the direction he should've been watching.

Tiro smiled. A greenhorn, and worth a try.

He re-sheathed his sword and took a couple of slow paces toward the Briton, careful not to crunch the snow. Then, he clutched his throat and staggered, giving gurgling chokes, eyes staring, The Briton whirled round, spear at the ready. He was young, his beard barely grown. Good.

Tiro took more paces, erratic, his legs bent, knees giving way. His choke became a gasping rattle before he fell backwards, staring at the grey sky.

He heard a bleat, then footsteps running towards him. Tiro focused on one dark crease in the clouds, striving not to look at the trembling spear point, nor the nervous, boyish face behind it.

The boy peered. The spear point wavered, the boy bent. Tiro lunged, both hands grabbed the haft of the spear and wrenched it to his left. The boy cried, was drawn down towards Tiro who darted one hand into his tunic for his knife, which, with a final pull and lurch forward, he stabbed into the boy's eye socket.

There was a low moan and Tiro rolled aside as the body pitched forward, face first into the snow.

A greenhorn.

Tiro dragged the body into the trees. Then he kicked over the trail it had left in the snow. He straightened, alert. He heard something.

Fucking idiot!

Of course, this fool had been standing sentry for a reason. Tiro crept about fifty paces, keeping just within the forest, until he saw them – perhaps sixty Britons, all armed. They were gathered around one of the arches of the aqueduct where it exited the forest. They had a ladder against it and one – a hulking ape was hacking at it with a pickaxe, to shouts of approval and encouragement.

Tiro weighed his options: go further into the forest and bypass them? No, he'd never get a horse through those trees. Wait for the barbarians to leave? There could be dozens – hundreds – more out there.

He had to return – back to Longovicium, the place he'd fled barely half an hour ago. He'd resolved – he wasn't hanging around there – no fucking fear, not after last night. That bastard Fimbria had got what was coming, but Yours Truly wasn't going to stay to get fingered for it.

He had bluffed his way past the sentry on the gate – "urgent dispatches for Eboracum" – then he'd slunk into the vicus to wait for dawn. A mistake. Big fucking mistake. The delay had meant running into the barbarians.

Tiro waited and watched, then cursed and retraced his steps.

§

Manius walked through the fort, juggling one urgent and unbidden thought after another. Lucia! How was she enduring the shock? What if her father killed himself? Would that make her obtainable? Then, images of Tiberius Flavius, horribly dead on his bed and of his brother, his murderer, giggling at his handiwork while men shouted and women screamed. Manius remembered his plans to impress Tiberius Flavius and become his creature and he gave a bitter laugh.

A porter in the Praetorium quadrangle's entrance archway looked puzzled. Manius composed himself.

"I'm here to see Decima Flavia Fimbria," he muttered. The porter nodded and jerked his thumb at the door to the room where they'd found the butchered legate.

Manius closed his eyes and clenched his fists. He strove to remember all he'd been taught, conjuring Quintus' words.

Questioning demanded experience, cunning and skill and Quintus was the master in extracting information. For all his bluster, Manius had never known him resort to torture, though he'd threaten it. He despised it as the crude tactic of the mere mechanical. No, Quintus deployed his talents for cajolery, intimidation, bluff, pseudo-sympathy and false naivety to create contradiction, confusion and, eventually confession.

Manius groaned. He hadn't yet a tenth part of those skills, but, maybe, with a grieving, stunned widow, his apprentice abilities would suffice. After all, Quintus must have thought so.

He tapped on Decima Flavia's door. A commanding female voice with a British accent called from behind him.

"What are you doing? What do you want?" He turned to see a middle-aged woman, thin angular features topped by tight waves of iron grey hair. Where the hell had she sprung from?

"I… I'm here to see Decima Flavia Fimbria."

"Well you can't. Nobody can."

"I'm Manius Suetonius Lupus, here with the tribune's authority."

"I don't care who you are, you can't see her."

"But…" He contemplated the unyielding stare and compressed lips, remembered how little he wanted that interview, "… I've been ordered to speak with her."

"Young man, you can tell whoever ordered you that the lady has yet to regain her senses. The surgeon will not permit her to be disturbed – nor will I."

"Er… and you are?"

"My name is Vibia Rufia Atellus. I'm nursing her."

Rufia Atellus. My gods! The widow of Appius Rufius! Her husband had been found with his throat slit only a few hours ago.

Manius stammered commiserations, which she received without expression. He stared at her, awkward and babbling his surprise that she was nursing Decima Flavia. Was there no one to help her… would she like him to see if he could find some help? She shook her head. "I need no help. I'm content to do this alone. My husband failed to safeguard the general; the least I can do is to care for his lady."

"I'm so sorry… so very sorry about your husband. I… I only met him recently but he struck me as… er… a fine soldier. I'm sure he'll be much missed by his cohort. I…"

He recoiled as her eyes flashed and she approached him, jabbing her finger. "Ah yes, his cohort; his cohort was only too ready to see the back of him. He was to be formally discharged today, to receive his diploma, a fine bronze copy, paid for by the subscription of his fellow centurions. Yes, guarding the general was to be his last duty. Did you know that?"

Manius muttered that he didn't know a great deal about military affairs and supposed he ought to leave her to go about her nursing duties. Then, with much relief, he saw Antiochos enter the courtyard, carrying a rough woollen bag. They exchanged greetings, Manius still with a nervous eye on Vibia Rufia, whom Antiochos addressed, asking after her patient.

With a visible effort she calmed herself. "The poor lady is still insensible but seems easy and the swelling is reduced."

"Excellent, as I predicted. I shall just attend to this" – Antiochos hefted the bag lightly in his hand – "and then I shall look in on her. I'm much obliged for your help, Vibia Rufia. Perhaps if you could find time to pray to your Coventina..."

"Coventina?" Her eyebrows raised. "I cannot see what good that would do. The lady has – as far as we know – nothing wrong with her bladder. No, I shall invoke the aid of Nodens – far more appropriate."

Antiochos gave his silky smile and bowed. "You know your own gods best. However you think fit, Vibia Rufia."

With that, he bade her farewell, took Manius by the arm and led him towards the porter's lodge.

"You wished to see me?"

Manius explained that he had been wanting to talk with Decima Flavia, as Antiochos drew him into a room opposite the porter's lodge.

This was a large storeroom, lit from high windows. Beams of light in slanting pillars of shimmering dust motes threw parts into sharp clarity against deep shadows. It contained cupboards, shelves with rows of amphorae and benches bearing boxes and sacks, except one, on which was a long shape, wrapped in a sheet.

"Is that...?" Manius whispered.

"That's him. This place isn't heated and no food is stored here. Do you want to take a look?"

"No! No, really, that won't be necessary."

Antiochos nodded. `No, that probably wouldn't serve any purpose. So, this is a frumentarii matter is it? And you want to speak to his wife – widow? Not possible at the moment."

"So I understand."

"She was knocked on the head last night, presumably by Publius Flavius Fimbria before he destroyed his brother – or after. There's nothing broken, and, as you just heard, she's doing well. I expect she'll come round soon."

"And her husband? Have you examined him?"

"Slit from belly to chest"– Antiochos demonstrated the blow – "and then I think a thrust into the heart."

"Don't you think Decima Flavia ought to be moved to the infirmary... from that room? You know... where..."

"... Where the deed was done, you mean? It might upset her a little, but I really don't like moving head wounds. Anyway, we've had the walls and floor scrubbed. There is nothing visible, nor any stench, to distress her."

"Vibia Flavia must be a rare woman," remarked Manius, shaking his head in wonder.

"Yes, you're right, it's truly admirable and I'm glad of her help. Say what you like about the British, I, Antiochos, say their women have great healing skills, and I gather Vibia Flavia is adept at making potions. It's far better to have one woman nurse another, especially a gentlewoman. I shudder to think of some of my capsarii treating her. You wouldn't believe what ham-fisted oafs they send me. I try to train – ha – I might as well be training oxen."

"You'll notify us the moment she regains her senses?"

"Of course," said Antiochos, then fixed Manius with a keen look. "But you must know I can only permit questioning if I judge that the lady's health will permit it."

Antiochos turned to the general's covered body. "Better check there's no corruption," he muttered. "Here, hold this for me, will you."

He handed Manius the woollen bag which was heavy. Antiochos raised a corner of Tiberius Flavius' shroud and Manius glimpsed a beard stark against white flesh. Antiochos bent over the body and sniffed before replacing the sheet. "It will keep."

Manius made to hand the bag back. "This is heavy, what is it?"

"Take a look."

Manius put the bag on a bench and peeled back the neck.

"Ughhh!" he cried and let the bag fall, releasing its contents. He staggered back wiping his hand on his tunic as he watched the severed head bounce, thudding and rolling before coming to a halt at the end of the bench. From there, the indignant, staring eyes were fixed on him.

Antiochos sprang forward and, with one deft movement, scooped the horrible object back into the bag. "Forgive me. I forget myself, I'm accustomed to dealing with fellow red-handed medical men, with brutish capsarii. Forgive me."

Manius stood gasping, pointing. "What… who?"

"You cannot have heard. This poor unfortunate is Aulus Hirtius Glabrio, a decurion: a good soldier and a fine horseman, if a little prone to eye infections. He was sent out with a troop yesterday to try for Vinovia. Somebody tossed his head over the wall during the night and it was discovered a few hours ago: obviously a message for us from the Wolves. We must assume the rest of the troop is dead. Perhaps their heads will follow."

"So, they never made it to Vinovia?"

Antiochos shook his head. "No, he met his fate on the outward journey. There was no time for it to be otherwise. It seems the country is truly risen. We're alone, my friend. During the night most of the male population slipped out of the vicus, no doubt either to join the rebels or to avoid being trapped with us."

"Trapped?"

"The barbarians are gathering. You can see them from the vicus' ramparts, sneaking in the edges of the forest, watching us.'

Manius was aghast. He'd heard of such things, but never had he been in a place where Rome seemed so fragile. The vicus was deserting them. He remembered Quintus' theory that the Wolves had information from inside Longovicium. They had enemies without and within and, at such a time, one brother killed another. Manius' hand shook; he clenched it down by his side, to hide it from Antiochos. But Manius suspected the situation was also wearing the surgeon's nerves, for all his insouciance. Antiochos looked angrily at the bag and then tossed it aside so it flopped onto the place where Manius judged Tiberius Flavius' stomach had once been.

"Why do they bring me that, the fools? What can I do with it? I tell them: it's a head. What more can I tell them, what more can I do? I can't help him now, certainly not without the rest of him." He gave Manius a keen look. "You look too pale. You need wine. Go, go and drink a glass of good Falernian – no, two glasses."

Manius left, glad to be out of the presence of Tiberius Flavius and Hirtius Glabrio. He needed to speak to Quintus.

But he had one more encounter in the Praetorium that did him more good than all the Falernian from Campania. He was passing through the quadrangle's gateway when he met Lucia. She was pale and had been weeping but was still beautiful. She gave a weak smile and they stood without speaking. Then he asked after her and her family.

"Mother is unwell. She doesn't admit it, but she didn't sleep last night – none of us did." She raised her chin, defiant. "But I'm a soldier's daughter; I'm strong."

"I'm sure you are."

They fell silent again, Manius searching for something to say that was sensible and sensitive. Instead, he heard Quintus prompting him.

"Your mother must have many people to comfort her – yourself, your father, friends… the Cottas. They are your friends? You know them well?"

Lucia shrugged. "I suppose so. They don't live far away and we often visit each other. Aurelius Cotta sees father at least once a month on business."

"And… er… what sort of man is he?" asked Manius, examining his fingernails.

"Cotta? I don't know. He's old and formal and full of business – like all the men father knows." Manius was about to ask more but Lucia added, in a low, sullen voice: "That man: Publius Flavius Fimbria – do you think he'll kill himself? Mother says that would be the decent thing."

"I'm not sure. I should think he's denied the means until we can be certain of what happened."

"Can there be any doubt?" She grew animated, eyes flashing and hands waving. "He and his brother – horrible man, though I know I shouldn't speak ill of him now – last night. He killed him in a rage. Surely he did?"

"Yes, yes," Manius said, taken aback, "but we must look at every possibility. Tiberius Flavius was a general and the Wolves would've wanted him dead, perhaps…"

"The Wolves! That's ridiculous."

Her obvious anger alarmed him.

"It's unlikely, of course, but…"

"Is that what you and the other man think? What's his name?"

"Quintus. Er… no, we've formed no opinion, that is to say, we're sure – almost certain – it was Publius Flavius."

"Tell me about this Quintus." Her voice was steadier. "Is he your father?"

"Stepfather."

"Is he old? Father says he's cunning and ruthless. Is he strong? He looks strong."

Manius told her that Quintus had a great reputation and yes, he supposed he was strong, but … well… let it only be said, he had come to rely on Manius more and more for work of an increasingly important nature.

She nodded. "Yes, I know how it is. Mother has begun to give more household duties to me. That's what I'm trying to do now – buy fresh eggs, but the egg seller is nowhere to be found. But then the whole place seems half deserted."

She scuffed the snow with her shoe. "The vicus is so dull. Egypt was wonderful, but Britannia is so grey, so dull."

Manius was about to observe that, lately, it had seemed far from dull, but thought better of it.

"I'd love to see Italy and Rome. You're from Italy aren't you? Whereabouts?"

"Tuscany."

"Tell me about it. What's it like?"

"It's not at all like this. It's warmer… not just the temperature, I mean everything. Do you understand?"

"I think so. You miss it don't you?"

"Yes, I do."

She looked at him, her shining black eyes unblinking. Manius was about to describe the source of the Clitumnus, or at least as much as he could remember from Tita Amatia's, when they were interrupted.

"Lucia!"

Gaia Antonia Merenda stood in the Praetorium's entrance. She looked haggard, drawn and irritable. She ordered Lucia to hurry inside and to see to the slaves clearing the winter dining room. She favoured Manius with a parting look of angry suspicion.

Heart thumping, Manius returned, with a spring in his step, to their rooms in the barrack block and, on the way, he met Quintus. He was about to account for his morning when they heard a commotion.

They exchanged glances and followed the clamour coming from the corner of the Principia where a small crowd had gathered around the tank. This was normally fed with water from the pipe of the aqueduct but now there was only a feeble drip of decreasing frequency.

"They've cut the aqueduct!" a soldier cried. "The barbarians have cut the aqueduct." He was silenced by a centurion who dealt him an appalling blow across the mouth with his vitis.

Manius tugged at Quintus' sleeve, drawing him back. "Couldn't it just have frozen?" he whispered.

"The water in the tank isn't frozen," Quintus also pointed to the eaves of the Principia, where the thick snow was dripping as it thawed.

Under the blows of the centurion and a couple of optiones, the shouting subsided to a concerned murmur. A runner was sent into the Principia to alert the commander.

Quintus pulled Manius away. "Come, I've no desire to be dragged into another of Merenda's councils. I'd rather spend time in fruitful thought, with a cup of wine."

Back at their quarters they met Tita Amatia, shivering and impatient at the door.

"There you are. Let me in out of this damned cold."

Once in the tiny apartment they lit a fire and a couple of lamps, which did something to relieve the gloom of Manius' tiny room whose only natural light came from one small window near the ceiling.

Manius told them about his interview with Vibia Rufia Atellus and Antiochos. Quintus made no comment but gave a low whistle of admiration when Manius told him about Vibia Rufia and grunted at the account of the conversation with the surgeon.

"That Greek had better tell us the moment Decima Flavia comes to."

"Did you know about the decurion?" Manius asked.

Tita Amatia said no but Quintus stretched his hands out to the fire and nodded. "News was brought while I was with Merenda, along with that of the defections from the vicus. You can imagine how that cheered him."

"Is he very despondent?"

"A broken man. He sees his prospects of commanding the Egyptian legion in tatters."

"But couldn't it fall out well for him? Surely Caerellius Priscus will be pleased at Tiberius Flavius' death."

"Oh for heavens' sake boy! Pleased! Priscus will be delighted, but in public he'll wear a long face and shake his head and say how disgraceful that a legate and general should be slain while under the army's protection. He'll make Merenda a scapegoat. I know it, Merenda knows it – and you should know it."

Manius glowered at the flames while Quintus went to pour himself wine.

"Pay no attention Manius," said Tita Amatia. "He's in one of his moods. Oh yes, he had those when he was young, didn't you Quintus? Hah, he grunts. Well, when you were young there was something intriguing and dangerous about them. Now you're just a cantankerous old goat."

Manius turned, rubbing his jaw to hide his grin from Quintus' glare. As she said, Quintus was in one of his moods; something had annoyed him. Tita Amatia ignored him, moved from the fire where she'd been warming her hands and took up another wine jar which was by the hearth. She uncorked it, peered critically into two goblets which stood by but shrugged and filled them, handed one to Manius, who, still not fully recovered from the decurion's head, drank greedily.

Quintus gulped at his own, gasped and wiped his beard with the back of his hand. "Let's return to serious matters," he said, with a poisonous look at her. "No, Merenda's best hope – and he embraces it like an only son – is that Fimbria's murder sprang from a family quarrel. He could hardly prevent one brother slaying another. That's his hope and it's not a bad one."

"And surely Publius did do it?" said Manius.

"So it would appear. He denies it. He swears it was none of his work, though he's not fool enough to pretend he mourns.

"Others had cause to hate his brother," said Tita Amatia.

"Anybody who met him had cause to hate him, we know that. His wife more than most; his mistress had a grievance. So did Cotta."

"Cotta? The British magistrate?"

"Aye, Flavius Fimbria humiliated him in council and after the killing, he was seen in suspicious circumstances." He told her Gracchus' story.

Tita Amatia frowned. "That's half a tale and you say Gracchus wouldn't put his name to it."

"No, and whatever Cotta was up to, if anything, it hardly changes the weight of evidence against Publius Flavius."

"There's another with motive. The Sicilian, Tiro. I overheard him and Flavius Fimbria quarrelling – a bitter falling-out and Tiro left his master with something very like a threat."

She described what she'd witnessed. Manius opened his mouth but Quintus waved him to silence – "No, no Tita, you're obsessed with that Sicilian" – and Manius wondered what that meant – "There can be little doubt that Publius Flavius is the man. You remember his toga, Manius? – the one he said he puked over last night? I asked him to produce it and he can't. We sent a couple of men to his quarters with him to fetch it but they searched the place and couldn't find it."

"It would've been covered in blood?"

"Yes, well done. Had he butchered Tiberius Flavius, that toga would have been red with gore. Had he been innocent, the only soiling would have been Gaia Antonia's first-rate meal. But he can't produce it, probably because he still had sufficient wits about him last night to shove it in the furnace."

"Is he under arrest?" asked Tita Amatia.

"What point? He can't go anywhere. He's merely suspended from duties, pending an investigation."

"There's to be an investigation?"

"Oh yes, Merenda wants the whole affair investigated, documented and sealed and ribboned, in the hope he can show that Publius Flavius was duly discovered to have been the criminal and" – turning to Manius, waving a stubby forefinger – "you and I, my young friend, are to do the investigating. We're the Emperor's eyes and ears and this matter has a political aspect, the job's ours. The way Merenda sees it, though he doesn't say so, is that if we say Publius Flavius did it, then he did it, and let's face it, he probably did."

"Where do we begin?"

"We begin," sighed Quintus, flopping down onto the lower bunk, "by conferring with your new friend Titus Caelius."

"With Titus? Isn't he leaving?"

"He is not, not with fresh snow thick upon the ground and Wolves and barbarians roaming free. Merenda refuses to let an experienced officer go to certain death or capture – not with the country up in arms and his new second in command relieved of duties. No, he's to stay and – contrary to all precedence and procedure – we're to work with him."

"Ah, so that's why you're in such a mood," said Tita Amatia.

"I am not in a mood!" He rubbed his eyes and sighed again. "Anyway, don't I have cause? D'you think I want some half-witted cavalryman under my feet while I negotiate this delicate matter. Nothing can ever be straightforward, people always have to interfere. I'm not angry… I'm… weary."

"Why are we to work with him?"

"Why? Probably so he can keep an eye on us," said Quintus and leaned for the wine jar.

"I don't understand."

"Don't you see? Surely even you must see: if Publius didn't do it, we're suspects."

"What!" Manius stared, then turned to Tita Amatia. Lips pursed, she nodded.

"Think about it boy. If that murder wasn't personal, it's political and who are more political than frumentarii? We've come straight from Londinium, from Priscus – and there's political for you – and didn't our esteemed governor as good as ask us to rid the Empire of this troublesome general? Yes, that's right: we need to find the murderer if only to save our own skins, whether it was Publius or someone else."

He filled Manius' trembling goblet. Manius drank deep. So this was why Lucia had been asking about Quintus and enquiring how strong he was.

Chapter Sixteen

The barbarians moved in the tree line to the west and east of Longovicium, at first in ones and twos, but soon in fours and fives. As their numbers increased, some lit fires and some even began to fashion rough shelters among the trees. Manius observed them from the ramparts: their long, plaited hair and flowing moustaches. There were women among them and even children gambolling in the snow at the forest's edge.

The rampart was the earth bank, of a man's height, which circled the vicus. Its top, a couple of paces wide, served as a walkway around the settlement and a platform from which to defend it. It also served as an outer defence to the fort itself which stood in the centre of Longovicium.

Manius fell into conversation with two soldiers who were tending a piece of artillery, their tunics tied for work with the right sleeve secured under the armpit to leave the shoulder bare. They were Spaniards: Urbo, a shrewd veteran of around thirty, and Lucco, perhaps five years younger and open and merry. Their weapon, which they cosseted and crooned over, was, they explained, a scorpion, which they'd just transferred from storage to the rampart with the help of some of the common soldiery who, said Urbo, spitting, shouldn't be trusted with an ox cart, never mind such a significant piece of equipment, which – the clumsy, stupid bastards didn't appreciate – wasn't normally entrusted to an auxiliary unit.

They began wiping with cloths at the two skeins of hemp and leather, each the thickness of an arm, which held the bow arms on either side of the piece.

"Has to be kept dry, you see sir, otherwise it loses its tension, which is its power you see," explained Lucco. "We coat these in tallow while she's in stores, but it's good to give her a wipe down."

They patted the machine and whispered a prayer to its spirit.

"Need all the protection we can get," he said, patting the scorpion again.

"What do you mean?"

"From those buggers." He jerked at the barbarians.

"But there seem so few compared to the cohort…" Manius indicated the soldiers who stood every few paces along the rampart, each surveying the trees with a professional eye, as their shields, without their leather covers, winked in the weak sunlight.

"Don't worry," chuckled Urbo, without humour, "there'll be hundreds more of those bastards in the forests, on their way. These are just a scouting party."

"Surely they'll be no match for the cohort."

Urbo spat again. "In a fair fight we'd kick their arses, no fear."

"But, you don't think it will be a fair fight? Why?"

Urbo grimaced and Lucco cut in: "These people have terrible magic – black magic." Then he went "Po, po, po," smacking his lips to avert the evil eye.

Urbo explained: the Britons had powerful, evil gods, especially the horned Cernunnos, who dwelt deep in the forests and to whom, in secret, sacred groves, the barbarians sacrificed human flesh.

Seeing Manius' horror, Urbo added: "It gives them great power you see sir. That's why they're so lost to virtue as to do such things as you and I and any decent person never would. They do it for the power it brings."

"What power?"

"Well, bless you sir: power over the weather for one thing. We've never seen such snow, but it comes from Cernunnos, at their bidding. And it gives them power over the minds of men, even good men." He swivelled, looking round. He crooked a finger at Manius, beckoning him as he lowered his voice. "Take the general – horribly slain last night, and old Appius Rufus – done in they say by another Roman, driven mad. But driven mad by what, I ask you? By black magic, that's what. They've put a curse on us."

"The gods preserve us."

Manius remembered Gesoriacum and the witches' attempt on the moon. An omen, just as the sailors had warned. They should never have left Gaul.

§

Titus embraced Birca. She smiled at him and he kissed her. They'd shared a late morning meal in her cottage. Already she'd wiped the table and washed and dried the dishes.

She turned her head and he released her. She took his helmet from a shelf.

"You must go."

He sighed. "I'm afraid duty demands it."

Titus was anxious to return to his station on the ramparts, observing the gathering barbarians and overseeing the disposition of the cohort. He put on his helmet, allowed her to fasten the strap and bent to kiss her again, which now proved awkward. They giggled.

"Go," she said, tapping his shoulder. "But be less mindful of your honour and heroics. We only have to come through this and we can be together in Londinium."

He was still smiling as he made his way towards the vicus' south gate where he'd ordered a decurion to assemble a cavalry turma. He and they would see how determined the barbarians were – whatever Birca had said about being careful.

Careful! Fat chance. The country was in revolt and the fort as good as besieged. This was more serious than he'd ever known.

Serious yes – but also intoxicating. Danger brought chance for honour, and opportunity for distinction. He had to distinguish himself: he'd no family, no connections nor powerful patrons to open doors or to grease the axle.

He shook his head. He was being an absolute ass, letting his heart rule his head – as usual – and how many times had Birca warned him? No, this rebellion delayed, even endangered, his new command in Londinium. And where better to distinguish himself than under the eye of the provincial governor?

It also pitched him into an awkward political situation. Here, of all places. The murder of a legate, in his cohort, was bound to reflect on him as well as Merenda. And to cap it all, the old man had taken it into his head to give him a role in the investigation. Him! Ye gods that was funny. It would taint him to be associated with frumentarii, notoriously a set of hard, unscrupulous bastards. Manius seemed a nice enough lad, but the other fellow – he was another matter. Still, he needed all the friends he could get, didn't he?

His thoughts were interrupted by raised voices. A few feet away, a red-faced optio was arguing with a civilian and shaking his fist. Since the terrible occurrence of last night, the cohort was on edge, men were nervous and tempers frayed. Whatever this was, it'd better be scotched.

"What's going on here?"

The civilian, a dark, gaunt fellow – Titus knew him from somewhere – looked him up and down, slowly and insolently. The optio, a short, round veteran, turned an even darker crimson and swallowed.

"This man sir," he said, like a child appealing to a parent. "He should be with the galearii but he's not having any of it." He held a helmet, sword with belted scabbard in both hands and waved them.

The civilian spat. "Military slaves are galearii. That doesn't include me."

Titus studied him before answering. "In the present emergency, any man with a military function – freeman or slave – is to be armed and serve in the ranks. Many with no army connection have volunteered."

"I haven't."

"And who are you?"

"I'm on the legate's staff."

"I thought I recognised you. You're Sicilian aren't you? Well, Tiberius Flavius Fimbria won't be needing any staff now. And if you're staff, surely you're army?"

"My function wasn't military."

"Well it is now."

"Nice try. I've got rights, I'm a citizen."

Titus appraised the man. He considered punching him. He knew the type: an awkward customer, a typical barrack-room lawyer, but also a dangerous character – something in the way he held himself.

The Sicilian continued: "So if you've got nothing…"

Titus held up a hand. "Look, we're all in this. If the barbarians take this fort… "

"What?" said Tiro with a mixture of disbelief and derision.

"Go and a look. See how many there are. If they take this place, none of us will live."

Titus took the helmet and sword and thrust them at the Sicilian. The man paused, then he took them.

§

Tita Amatia tapped on the door of the Flavius Fimbrias' room. She heard nothing apart from the faint tinkle of the quadrangle's fountain behind her, then a low voice from inside. She raised the latch and entered.

There were the two beds, one empty and stripped, the other occupied. She glimpsed the hair against the white pillow, but her attention was taken by the woman, rising from a stool by that bedside, hurrying towards her, mouth grim and angry pink on her cheeks. She stood before Tita Amatia, her angular frame quivering. This, who she guessed to be Vibia Rufia, placed a finger to her lips and her other hand on Tita Amatia's shoulder.

Tita Amatia surveyed that hand as though it were something a slave had neglected to dust, then turned her cold glare onto its possessor. There was a brief, wordless conflict. Vibia Rufia withdrew her hand. Tita Amatia stepped past the other towards the bed. She looked down on her old friend Decima, who was unconscious, white and barely breathing. She wore the troubled expression of deep sleep, which, to Tita Amatia, at least, was better than the determined petulance that had characterised her recently.

"You see, she still sleeps," hissed Vibia Rufia. "Come. I'm her nurse. She mustn't be disturbed."

Tita Amatia looked at the British woman gesturing at her to leave.

"You are impertinent. I'm her friend. I shall visit her again this evening."

Vibia Rufia opened her mouth but Tita Amatia spoke. "Don't cross me."

She was loath to yield, but it would be absurd to cause a scene by the sickbed. She satisfied herself with a last glare as she swept past the self-appointed guardian.

The door was closed behind Tita Amatia with a decisive clunk which made her purse her lips. But then a figure entered the quadrangle:

Quintus, hands clasped behind back, head down, deep in thought. She smiled, called and crunched her way over the snow.

"You've been to see Decima?" he asked. "How is she?"

Tita Amatia grimaced. "Who can tell? She's unconscious but looks comfortable." She glared back across the quadrangle. "She seems well cared for, I'll say that much. Were you going to see her? I wish you luck."

Quintus shook his head. "I wish I'd time. I'm going to see Merenda to persuade him not to encumber me in this investigation with his halfwit officers, I..."

He looked over her shoulder. She turned to see Aurelius Cotta. He smiled and approached. Quintus introduced him.

"Tita Amatia Aculeo? Your husband was Epillus Amatius?"

Tita raised her eyebrows. "He was."

"I met him, many years ago. I admired him."

She looked with fresh interest at this sober, cultivated Briton.

"Have you been to see Decima Flavia?" he asked.

Tita Amatia nodded.

"How is the lady? Will she recover?"

"That's for the Fates. I've seen her only briefly. She's plainly very unwell. But I'm optimistic."

Cotta nodded. "A terrible business, truly terrible."

"Shocking. And your own wife? It must've been awful for her – for both of you." Tita was thinking of the report of Cotta being abroad later that night. "You were both there, I understand. I'm glad I wasn't. I swear I wouldn't have been able to sleep a wink afterwards."

She looked at him. He gazed back.

"Did er... your lady manage to sleep?" prompted Tita. "I've a draught I could lend her."

Cotta smiled. "You're too kind but that won't be necessary. Marca managed to sleep."

"And you?"

Tita thought the corners of his mouth twitched. Had she been too obvious? Quintus remained glowering at her side. Cotta opened his mouth, closed it, smiled openly and spoke.

"Sleep has long been a problem for me, it's frequently troubled. Since childhood you know, I've suffered from sleepwalking. You seem surprised. That's to be expected. The usual reaction is revulsion, a fear that the sleepwalker is possessed. But Lucretius explains it rationally."

"The simulacra you mean?" said Quintus. "Sleepwalking as some misperception or distorted image of reality acting on the mind?"

"Quite." Cotta smiled again. "Nothing is as it seems."

"Lucretius was a dolt – an atheist."

"You think so? I rather admire him. But you must excuse me. I promised my wife news of Decima Flavia."

He bowed and returned without hurry into the main fort.

"You know," said Quintus, from the corner of his mouth. "I believe he's sporting with us."

§

Manius was pondering Urbo's conviction that they'd been cursed when he heard his name called and he looked down into the vicus. Titus was on horseback at the head of a troop of cavalry. He leapt from the saddle and scrambled up the rampart to join Manius. Urbo and Lucco knuckled their foreheads and resumed work on their beloved scorpion.

"So," Manius said, "you're not leaving us then?"

"Eh? No, splendid news, is it not?" Titus rubbed his hands. "Ha! My departure for Londinium is postponed, until this insurrection is over. Antonius Merenda wants every man he can get to defend the fort and vicus. We're calling out the veterans from the vicus, some five or six, and the galearii are to be put into the ranks."

"What about the aqueduct? Surely we cannot withstand a siege without water?"

"Oh, we have a well in the fort. The water's drinkable, though it won't be as sweet. But there'll be no baths I'm afraid, old cock. Apart from anything else, we can't afford the wood. We'll need what we have to keep from freezing."

Manius' spirits fell further. The situation seemed to get worse by the hour. He looked at Titus' soldiers waiting astride their mounts, which were fidgeting and snorting, their breath steaming in the air.

"And what are you doing now?"

Titus waved towards the barbarians at the forest's edge – and Manius swallowed to see that even since he'd last looked their numbers had increased. "Keeping an eye on that rabble. I'm not one to sit on my backside while rebels roam free. With luck, I'll get chance a to exercise these lads."

Manius regarded his turma again. Would they be as keen on being exercised? Then he noticed another figure, some fifty paces beyond, carrying the vitis and wearing the helmet of a centurion. Manius stared, straining to identify the features under the helmet. Then this centurion addressed a signifier at his side and Manius' impression was all but confirmed. The signifer cupped a hand behind his ear and leaned toward the speaker.

"Surely… that's not…?"

"Publius Flavius? Absolutely."

"But… isn't he confined?"

"As the old man said: to what end? He can't go anywhere. None of us can and, as I said, we need every man."

Titus gazed towards the forest and his manner became awkward and constrained. Without turning, he spoke. "I say, you know that I'm to work with yourself and Quintus Suetonius to investigate the murder?" Manius nodded. Titus continued: "This is bloody awkward and I want you to know it's none of my doing. The old man sprang it on us, heaven only knows why. I can think of nothing I have less of a taste or talent for. But an order's an order y'know and I must make the best of it. How are we to go about it though? That's the thing. I'm sure the two of you must know what to do. Me? I'm only a soldier; but shouldn't the three of us meet soon to… well… decide how to proceed? Don't you think?" Manius nodded again. "It's just that your… father… seemed reluctant to talk about it earlier."

Titus went on, still gazing at the forest: "He… your father… seemed to suggest there was nothing to discuss…" He trailed off, mumbling. Manius regarded him in expectant silence. Titus' face worked, then he burst out: "It's just I'm not sure! It seems to me… well, the gods know I'm no frumentarius but I cannot see that the whole affair's so clear."

Manius muttered about the necessity of a thorough investigation and an official report.

"Yes, yes, I know all that," said Titus. He looked earnestly at Manius. "Manius, can I trust you?"

"Of course."

"I suppose I'll have to." Titus glanced at Urbo and Lucco, still tending their scorpion, took Manius by the arm and walked him a few paces away. "Look, Publius Flavius is the fellow who seems to have done it and his guilt appears clear; I hardly know him, so I can't be accused of favouring him. In truth he seems a queer, quiet fellow to me but, dammit, surely he deserves a fair view of this. Yes, I admit it does look bad for him, but there are others who could be suspected."

"Who?"

"Who?" Titus rubbed his chin, the bristles rasping. "Manius, you'll think me very stupid and I confess I haven't got these ideas straight in my head, but Publius Flavius denies it… I see you're smiling, and I know that denial can hardly be seen as proof of innocence, but if he did do it, in such an obvious way, would he bother denying it?"

"Perhaps," Manius said, doubtful. "You mentioned others?"

"How about Aurelius Cotta? Didn't Tiberius Flavius insult him? Isn't he British? – They're a passionate and violent people. Then, there's what's-her-name, the concubine whom Tiberius Flavius was going to put away. She's a Levantine and they're fiery and vengeful. Even his wife Decima Flavia, he humiliated her."

"Oh, surely not!"

"Women are subject to fits, Manius, to hysteria, believe me. They don't think and behave as men. How do we know what goes on in their heads?"

"Surely not something as horrible as that!"

"Perhaps you're right. I only mention it to show there are other possibilities, even…" he held his head down and shook it, as though trying to cast out a thought. "This is terrible, I have conflicting duties, to my cohort, but now also to you and Quintus Suetonius if we're to investigate this together."

"Titus," prompted Manius, "you were saying... `even...'"

Titus swallowed and cast a cautious glance around, then lowered his voice "... even Lucius Antonius Merenda."

Manius laughed but Titus returned an even stare. "You are joking?" Titus shook his head. "But this affair could ruin him. He may have to kill himself."

"Look, Manius, I'm no politician and I may be a fool but I do hear things, y'know. It's no secret in the army that the governor and Tiberius Flavius Fimbria were bitter rivals and that Caerellius Priscus believed the general to have treasonable intentions. Don't worry, I don't expect you to confirm it. But it strikes me – and I'm only a simple soldier – but, well, the fact is that my commander has killed once for the Emperor... who better to do it again?"

Manius hadn't thought of that. He'd been too shaken after the murder and then too discomfited by Quintus' revelation that they might themselves be suspects. But Titus had. A simple soldier, sure enough, but it had taken a simple soldier to see what frumentarii should've seen. Another thought – if Titus had been speculating on who, other than Publius Flavius, might have committed the act – then might Quintus also be on his list of suspects? Or himself?

They looked at each other and Manius was casting around for how he might answer when Titus turned at a shout from further along the rampart. A soldier was pointing to a body of barbarian horsemen who'd approached to within a hundred paces to hurl insults. Manius noticed with a shudder that several wore wolf masks.

"That'll do!" shouted Titus and was down the rampart at his horse's flank and on its back in one movement. Manius marvelled at the contrast with the man who'd been so awkward, feeling his tongue-tied way through their conversation.

Titus called to the decurion who echoed the command and the troop trotted out through the vicus gate. They formed line, facing the barbarians, the horses whinnying and forehooves scraping, their riders' faces impassive. Titus, supporting himself with a hand on one of his saddle horns, raised himself, waved his javelin and shouted an order. Manius thrilled, expecting one of those famous cavalry charges, but he was disappointed, and so, he could tell, were Titus and his turma. The snow was too deep to allow more than a laboured trot and the troop's draco barely filled with wind, bobbing uncertainly behind its bronze head and making no whistle. The enemy turned their ponies and retreated jeering. This was repeated several times over the next half an hour. The barbarians approached the Roman cavalry, who would attempt a charge, only to be thwarted by the snow and called to halt and reform by Titus.

But, as Urbo pointed out, Titus was too wily to allow himself to grow frustrated and his troop to be lured close to the forest's edge.

Manius grew bored and realised how cold he was. So he returned to their quarters, hoping Quintus wouldn't be there, or, if he was, that he'd be in a better mood. Manius was disappointed in both hopes. He found Quintus sitting on his bunk, crouched over the hearth, clutching a jar of wine and he'd evidently brooded on his grievances and nursed them to a rude health. Manius was barely through the door before he was cursing Merenda for having ordered that Titus join them in their inquiry. He'd been to see Merenda that morning, had appealed against that order and had been refused.

"Merenda had no right to make any such direction, the arsehole. I shall raise this with Rome, by the heavens I will."

"Couldn't you have refused him?"

Quintus didn't meet his eye and his grumbling approached incoherence as he mumbled something about ignoring him, though whether he was referring to Merenda or Titus, Manius wasn't sure. There was something evasive about him and Manius wondered: had he seemed to accept Titus' involvement for political reasons, albeit with ill grace? After all, if they as frumentarii were under suspicion, perhaps better to broaden the base of those who'd pronounce Publius Flavius the guilty party.

"It's absurd," said Quintus. "What does this Titus Caelius know of our work? What skills has he?"

Manius paused. Titus had invited him into his confidence and he was determined to accept, but he'd make one last effort to bring Quintus along with him.

"You may be surprised to learn that Titus Caelius has some interesting thoughts." He readied himself for an eruption. Quintus merely glowered and invited him to go on. Manius explained how Titus believed there were others with motives to kill Tiberius Flavius Fimbria.

"Oh, so the great thinker has started his investigation, has he?"

Manius sighed. "If thinking is the same as investigation."

Quintus glared and pointed. "Listen boy, Merenda may think your friend Titus Caelius has a role in all this, but I don't. We're frumentarii and, whatever Merenda may say, we don't have to work under the eye of some wooden-topped soldier. And you should be ashamed of yourself. Couldn't you have thought all that out without his prompting?"

"The point is that he worked it out, so perhaps he may be useful."

"Oh what fearful rubbish! For all Titus Caelius' pretty theories, Publius Flavius remains the man who did it. Are you seriously suggesting that some halfwit concubine tripped out at night, slit the throat of a veteran centurion, cut the guts out of her lover and only protector and, somehow, managed to knock his wife on the head into the bargain?"

Manius had to confess – to himself – it did seem weak.

"And was that his comprehensive list?" Quintus demanded.

"What… what do you mean?'

"Did he have any more suspects, or was that it?"

"I think that was all."

"Oh, well what about Arrius Gracchus and his wife? They were at the dinner, they went out to piss, as far as I recall. Didn't Tiberius Flavius boast about his treatment of Christians in Lugdunum and Vienna? How do you think the Gracchus pair would have felt?"

"They're Christians! How d'you know that?"

Quintus hauled himself to his feet, his finger in Manius' face. "I know that because I've been doing this job for thirty years, since before you and your precious friend Titus Caelius were wiping your own arses." He stopped and his eyes widened and he grabbed Manius' tunic. "You keep that to yourself, d'you hear. Keep anything I tell you to yourself. You don't tell anyone, and that includes Titus Caelius. Understand?" Manius nodded. Quintus released him and flopped back onto Manius' bunk. "As far as we're concerned, Publius Flavius did it. That's what Merenda wants and that's what we want."

Manius could see there was no reasoning with him. The wine was talking for him, that and the accumulated bitterness of the years. No, it had been stupid to tell him what Titus had said. He'd be more circumspect in future. It was tragic, but there it was – Quintus had had his day.

But how had he known about the Gracchus couple? Was it even true?

Manius was weighing this when a principalis brought a message from Merenda: Decima Flavia Fimbria had regained her senses.

§

The young slave hurried up the hill from the Forum, towards the Palatium shouldering his way past street hawkers and beggars. He couldn't be late – surely he wouldn't be late. But there was never any telling what mood Saoterus might be in and, if he declared his clerk slave late, then he was late.

A capricious emperor had created a capricious court, that's what people were saying. There were even whispers that Rome was returning to the turmoil of the emperor Domitian, to those dark days before the present dynasty. Although the whisperers soon held their tongues or changed the subject if they realised Saoterus' favourite was in earshot.

He glanced at the overcast sky. Those clouds carried the threat of rain, or worse. It was barely light and he'd left the quarters assigned to imperial slaves without eating, as his stomach reminded him, tormented by the seductive aroma of fish being freshly grilled by the vendors bawling their wares by their braziers. No time to stop. No, and no time to be thinking of his belly.

Should he inform Saoterus of the whispers? The emperor's chamberlain would react badly, that was certain, and how could it profit the young slave, who would have to name names and make enemies? On the other hand, Saoterus doubtless knew these whispers were abroad and he'd regard anyone who failed to report them with dark suspicion.

The young slave nodded to the expressionless praetorian at the Palatium gate, who stood aside to let him enter, favouring him with a smart salute – extraordinary from a praetorian to slave. How soon word got round in this city. It must be well known now that this young slave was a particular darling of the chamberlain Saoterus – himself a former slave, as if men needed reminding of how the lowly might rise.

He entered the now familiar office building in the Domus Flavia, trotted along the corridor and opened the double doors to his room, the antechamber to Saoterus' office. He stopped short in the doorway. Saoterus was already there, standing, his long body bent over his desk, arms behind his back. The young slave had a view of his thinning brown pate before he looked up and smiled.

"Ah, there you are."

"Am I late?"

"Late? No, I don't think so. I'm early. But, seeing as you're here, come, we have work to do."

He beckoned the youngster and put his arm around him, letting his hand rest on his backside. He guided him through to this own office. The slave's mind raced: had he left anything on his desk he would rather the chamberlain didn't see? Saoterus seemed in a good mood, but the young slave had learnt that that could be a ruse, the silky affability suddenly being replaced by a foul-mouthed rage.

But not this morning. Saoterus took him to the window, hugged him and pressed his head onto his shoulder.

The chamberlain sighed. "We must work. Pass me that letter on the desk."

The young slave took the rolled document which he handed to his master who unfurled it.

"This is from that old fox Priscus. He has much to report. Buteo is dead – murdered. It seems he was right to be so frightened."

"The provincial procurator! Who murdered him?"

"That remains a mystery."

"But does the Emperor know? What did he say?"

Saoterus smile thinly. "Commodus isn't best pleased. He takes it personally. For the moment, however, he's leaving matters to me." He pinched his lower lip, allowed the letter to refurl and handed back. "Things are happening more quickly than I anticipated. Priscus tells me Lupus Suetonius is heading to the north of the province with Tiberius Flavius Fimbria, which is confirmed by Suetonius' own report and by another agent I have shadowing them both."

The young slave gasped. Suetonius smiled. "I didn't tell you about him. Always keep something up your sleeve, I've learned that the hard way."

Saoterus turned from the window to the desk where he stood, staring into the distance. "But I'm not happy. Events are moving off stage, into Britannia's frozen fogs. Yes, the Empire's fate is shrouded in fog."

Chapter Seventeen

They approached the praetorium as Merenda and Titus came towards them.

"Hell," breathed Manius.

He hadn't expected Titus. He should have. Wasn't it natural to bring him to question an important witness? Natural but potentially awkward. Quintus was all too capable of embarrassing Manius, making him take sides between him and Titus.

Quintus merely gave Titus a black look. Titus reddened. Quintus and Merenda exchanged nods. The tribune eyed Quintus with disapproval, probably detecting the wine on his breath. Manius' own greetings went ignored.

Merenda addressed Quintus. "Antiochos informs me that the general's lady has recovered consciousness. She should be able to name her assailant, her husband's killer."

"And if it's Publius Flavius, you want as many witnesses to her testimony as possible. I don't blame you."

Merenda's mouth twitched, then he strode into the courtyard. They trooped after him. Titus tapped on that door on either side of which Tiberius Flavius and Rufius Atellus had died. A voice answered and they crowded through to see Decima Flavia Fimbria on her bed.

Manius glimpsed her haggard white face, framed by the ministering figures of Antiochos and Vibia Rufia. The newcomers shuffled forward. Quintus beckoned Antiochos and the surgeon approached so Quintus could whisper in his ear. Antiochos frowned and shook his head. Then Quintus summoned Vibia Rufia and took her and Manius and ushered them back into the courtyard, leaving a startled Merenda and Titus with the injured woman and the surgeon.

"Vibia Rufia Atellus," said Quintus, closing the door behind him. "I must commiserate on your loss. I knew and admired your husband." She inclined her head. Quintus continued: "You're brave to face the world and to be tending Decima Flavia."

"Nonsense! I told this young man, my husband failed the general, so I must serve his lady."

"That does you much credit. Tell me, has the lady spoken since she came to?"

"Anything she says remains between us, unless she permits otherwise." Quintus was opening his mouth, but she added: "She has said nothing."

"Antiochos tells me she has made no mention of her husband. She doesn't know?"

"It would seem so."

Quintus thanked her, before opening the door to allow them all back into the room, to Titus' evident relief while Merenda goggled in indignation. Quintus approached Decima Flavia, knelt and asked her how she did. She lay, looking at the ceiling, then her eyes, half-closed moved to contemplate him, as she replied, her voice weak and cracked: "I've been better, Quintus Suetonius."

He smiled. "And you'll surely be better again soon." He paused. "Decima Flavia, you know you were attacked last night? Can you remember anything?" She closed her eyes, opened them with a grimace. "I remember something of the dinner, but nothing... nothing more."

"Nothing at all?"

"No... nothing." Her eyes opened wide, she raised her head and gave a great hiccup, vomiting over her chin and the bedclothes.

Vibia Rufia shoved Manius aside with a bony elbow. "That's enough, the lady must rest." Quintus allowed her to take his place, to mop Decima Flavia's chin and stroke her lank hair back from her forehead. Antiochos shooed them once again into the courtyard, leaving the two women together.

As soon as the door was closed, Merenda demanded. "Is she in danger?"

The little Greek began a shrug but stopped and looked grave. "I've consulted my Dioscorides and we agree on the treatment. Nothing is ever certain, particularly following a blow to the head, but there's every reason to hope for a recovery."

"And her memory?"

"If the lady recovers, her memory will return. Until then, she must have rest and peace and all we can do is tend her wants and pray to Asclepius."

"Or Nodens," Manius suggested, eager to make some impression.

Antiochos shot him a glance. "Whichever... both."

"She hasn't yet been told of her husband's death," said Quintus.

"What?" said Merenda. "She must. That's only decent."

They stared at each other and finally at Antiochos, who looked startled and disconcerted. He coughed, opened the door to Decima Flavia's room a hand's breadth and called for Vibia Rufia. From within, came the feeble voice of Decima Flavia: "What is it? What are they talking about?"

Vibia Rufia joined them. Her expression was icy as Antiochos whispered that she must tell the patient – with delicacy – of her husband's death. Vibia Rufia studied them, with lips compressed before re-entering the room. Quintus placed a hand on her shoulder. "I must come with you." And they both returned to the sick chamber.

"What? What?" said Merenda. Then shrugged and looked at Antiochos.

"There must be a funeral at some point. The general's body… is it?"

"I examined it this morning. We're safe for some days."

"Good. We cannot dispose of him without due ceremony – after these barbarians are dispersed."

"Of course. And Appius Rufius?"

"What? Oh… where is he?"

"In the hospital."

"Have him buried outside the vicus. We can't have bodies lying all about."

Manius made excuses and left. They hardly seemed to notice, apart from Titus, who smiled. Manius reflected, as he went, that perhaps he'd underestimated Quintus: the old fox had just contrived two important interviews, without involving Merenda or Titus.

§

Quintus approached the bed, with Vibia Rufia at his side. Decima Flavia gave a weak smile. "I'm sorry Quintus that I vomited on you."

"You didn't Decima. If you had, it wouldn't have mattered. All that's important is that you get well."

"I'm afraid I remember nothing of last night… I don't know…"

"Never mind any of that my dear."

Once more he knelt beside her. He contemplated the wan face. Without make-up and so vulnerable, she looked childlike. With a jolt, Quintus saw again the girl he'd known in another age. He was being haunted by ghosts lately – ghosts he'd thought laid to rest long ago.

"Quintus," whispered Decima Flavia. "What is it?"

He sighed and took her hand.

§

Manius passed through the entrance and heard a low, urgent voice. He looked up to see Lucia, not five paces away. Again, that dual pang of pain and pleasure. His stomach lurched.

"Lucia Antonia," he gulped and bowed.

She took a couple of hurried paces towards him, wringing her hands, and blurted: "I've been waiting! Have you seen Decima Flavia Fimbria? Is she alert?"

He told her what he'd witnessed. She bit her lip. He ached to embrace her. It was a moment of stillness, but then a breath of wind wafted grains of snow from the eaves of the porter's lodge and ruffled Lucia's hair before a couple of crystals landed on it. Manius was about to gently brush them away but before he could, they melted.

"Poor lady," she said at length. "Do you think she'll mourn?"

"I don't understand…"

"Will she really mourn her husband? He was beastly, bringing that concubine and flaunting her."

"They say he was going to put her away."

"You've seen Decima Flavia and you've seen the concubine."

Manius saw the twinkle in her eyes, then understood, reddened and blustered. "But the general had ambitions and his wife – widow – has a powerful family."

"Would such base motives for faithfulness incline her to mourn him?"

"Well," Manius said, picking his way, "there may be no passion, nor even affection, but to lose a husband – in such a manner..."

"That's regret, not mourning. Perhaps she'd mourn the death of passion and affection. Yes, I could understand that because I couldn't live without them."

He moved closer, looking into her eyes, and whispered: "I'm sure you won't, Lucia."

She stared, and then she laughed and spun away, towards the Praetorium. At the entrance, she turned with sparkling eyes, giggled and disappeared. Manius stared, his heart thumping. He'd been urbane and polished. Then, why were his cheeks burning?

§

Manius was still wondering a quarter of an hour later, as he lay on his bed, his hands clasped behind his head, staring at the bunk above. His thoughts were interrupted by Quintus' entrance.

First, Manius noticed he was in better humour. Second, that he was followed by two soldiers laden with helmets, mail shirts, swords, shields and belts, which, at Quintus' command, they dumped in a pile. Quintus dismissed them and they filed out.

Manius sat up. "What's this?"

Quintus clapped his hands and rubbed them together before the fire.

"We're ranked with the galearii. So we'll be called upon to help hold the ramparts. We're army after all. For that reason I've arranged for you to refresh your limited skills, training with wooden weapons against an optio – an ardent, athletic optio, ha!" Quintus continued to chortle while looking round the tiny room. "Have we no wine?"

Manius shook his head, happy at Quintus' crestfallen expression.

"You've been longer than I expected. How did you fare with Decima Flavia?"

"If I've been a long time, it's because I was detained by Merenda and Titus Caelius and the little Greek, who all asked me the same question; and then tried to involve me in talk about bodies." He gave a mock shiver. "Leave that to the Greek I say. I quoted Epictetus: `You're a soul carrying a corpse'. Only the Greek laughed, but then it's his language, the smarmy little article."

"Most amusing, but what of Decima Flavia?"

His face lengthened and he sighed. "There was hardly any reaction. Either, in some part of her mind, it was no news, or else she cannot yet comprehend it. Once I told her: `Decima, my dear, your husband is no more', she stared at the wall and a tear – one tear, mark you – rolled down her cheek and she fastened a tight grasp on Vibia Rufia's hand. I could do no more; could ask no questions, I left."

They sat staring at the blazing, crackling logs in the hearth.

"Did she love Tiberius Flavius?" Manius asked at length.

"How in the name of Hades should I know? I doubt it. I don't suppose Tiberius Flavius' own mother could have loved him. Perhaps I'm too harsh, for Thrasea writes: 'Anyone who hates faults, hates mankind.' Ha! But then I do hate mankind."

"Surely they loved once; they were married?"

"And you look for love in marriage, do you?"

"Is that unreasonable?"

Manius anticipated a cutting response but Quintus paused and coughed. "No, perhaps not. Your father and mother loved each other and didn't Tita Amatia also learn to love her husband? Yes, there can be love in marriage. It can grow out of the necessary intimacy, of shared endeavour, running a household and raising children. But it's not what the institution's based on."

"But is there no place for passionate love?"

"That's to be avoided; no, rather to be fled from, as you'd flee a plague-ridden city." He gave one of his humourless laughs. "Look what it did for me and Tita Amatia."

"But…"

They heard a blare of trumpets. Manius leapt from the bed. There was a great hammering on the door, which was thrown open revealing a grim-faced optio.

"To arms!" he shouted, "The enemy attacks."

§

Manius struggled with armour and helmet, scrabbling at straps and buckles, dropping a scabbard and swearing over a tunic rucked under mail. Quintus fussed over him, tightening leather and rearranging Manius' fumbled attempts. Then they were running, along with others pouring out of barrack blocks, through the streets of the fort, Manius, tripping with scabbard caught between his legs and with one hand steadying his wobbling helmet.

At the Porta Praetoria, Quintus demanded from a principalis where Publius Flavius Fimbria's century was stationed. They were directed to the east rampart and, once there, were ordered by a harassed optio to the spot Manius had stood that morning with Urbo and Lucco, who manned their scorpion.

Manius adjusted his helmet. Then hearing a great noise, he surveyed the land beyond the rampart. The forest's edge was lined with hundreds – maybe thousands – of barbarians standing shoulder to shoulder. To right and left, their line curled to circle the entire fort and vicus. But here, on the east, with the forest being at its closest, the enemy only had a hundred paces to cover before they were upon them.

Manius contemplated their red, angry, hairy faces and their bodies stripped to the waist, even in the snow, and their long, wicked swords. They stood, legs apart, resolute, long hair untied and waving in the breeze and weapons and armour glinting. Among them were womenfolk, dressed in black, their wild hair streaming as they brandished flaming torches. They wailed and screeched, adding to the sing-song incantations of several white robed men, whose heads were crowned in greenery.

"Quintus."

"What is it, boy?"

Manius voiced his only coherent thought. "My helmet hurts."

"Are you wearing a bonnet?" Manius shook his head. Quintus cursed. "It was with the gear, didn't you put it on? Stupid boy, your helmet is useless without it."

"I think I left it. Shall I go back for it?"

Quintus gripped his arm. "Stay where you are, you young fool! To leave the line now means crucifixion." He summoned an optio and explained. The officer swore and produced a scarf, which he and Quintus wrapped around Manius' head, before replacing and tight strapping the helmet.

"How many are there d'you think?" Quintus asked the optio, as they tested Manius' chinstrap. The optio spat and said he thought a couple of thousand, maybe more.

"Heaven knows how they survive in this weather. How do they eat? Shut your stupid mouth!" he roared at Urbo, who had – too loudly – whispered: "Black magic".

The glowering optio paced, behind the ranks, slapping his cane against his thigh. He made way for another figure who greeted them. Manius recognised Aurelius Cotta under the helmet,

"So, you too are among the galearii?" said Quintus.

Cotta smiled. "No, a volunteer. But then, as a citizen, what choice do I really have? If this fort falls, what fate awaits me and my wife?" He squinted at the enemy whose caterwauling had grown. "It's as I feared: the Textoverdii are among them. The Brigantes are a nation again. Well, they'll be a short-lived nation, the poor fools."

A crow flew from the forest and circled, cawing above them. The troops were clearly distressed at this awful portent and the optio shook his cane at Urbo, daring him to voice his fears.

"`The best and only omen is to fight for your country'," murmured Cotta, quoting the original Greek and Quintus looked impressed. "You'll excuse me, I must find Publius Flavius Fimbria and report for duty."

Quintus watched him go. "Whatever game he's playing, a well-educated Briton goes there. You must admire them."

"Who?"

Quintus waved at the barbarians. "These Britons. For all their breeches and savagery there's something noble about their courage, pride and simplicity. They're what we once were. They have the qualities which made Rome great, qualities we've lost – to vice, corruption, effete luxury, freedmen-made-equestrians, to Greeks, painted whores and mincing pansies."

Manius marvelled. Even now Quintus could ride his hobby horse. But Manius was more interested in the horrors before him – so much that Quintus had to shake him.

"Pay heed. Rely on your shield. Your mail will stop no arrow, but your shield will." Manius nodded and swallowed. "Until the enemy is close, keep your eyes on the sky. You can see arrows and you can see javelins, the only things you cannot see are slingshots and that's what makes them frightening to the greenhorn, but don't worry, they do no real damage – unless they hit you in the eye. So… perhaps then… best not to look up. Ah, see, there's our friend Publius Flavius wandering the rampart. He has to be close to his men to be heard no doubt, ha, ha. See the dark looks they give him. I wonder if that's Merenda's intention?"

"What… what do you mean?"

"Publius Flavius killed a well-respected centurion. Is Merenda hoping some soldier will slip his blade into Publius' kidneys? Rid him of a problem eh? Is that why he released him and gave him this command – Appius Rufius' old century?"

Before Manius could reply, there was a command from the optio. They all stiffened to attention as Antonius Merenda mounted their section of the rampart and, after a nod to Quintus, spoke to Urbo. He pointed to a figure several paces in front of the barbarian ranks, a man with the wolf headdress, who seemed to be a chief. Urbo nodded and he and Lucco bent, working their machine, causing the apparatus to creak. Manius observed the sinews twist and stiffen and the bow arms bend and ease rearward. When they stopped, Urbo and Lucco slid the scorpion's rear sideways an inch. Urbo, his tongue sticking from the corner of his mouth, squinted along the machine's length. He nodded to Lucco, who released the lever. There was a great whirr and a jarring thud and Manius saw something move through the air, shimmering. A white-robed priest, a little to one side and behind the Wolf, had his head clipped off.

Manius opened his mouth. Quintus clasped his hand over it. He hissed: "Absolute silence in the ranks."

But a huge bellow came from the barbarian line, which surged towards them.

Chapter Eighteen

In the moments it took the barbarians to reach the rampart, Manius clutched at his javelin, dropped it, fumbled for it with trembling fingers and dropped it again. The optio's cane cut across his calves and he snarled something about rocks. "There boy! There!" Quintus jabbed a finger at a small heap of stones. Manius followed him in snatching one up and hurling it at the approaching enemy. He threw rocks, along with the whole line, gasping with effort and gibbering with fear. The barbarian charge slowed as they raised shields against this hail.

But the stones ran out. The Britons roared and charged on. Manius moaned, his hands wringing the haft of his javelin.

"Throw your javelins!"

Manius' weapon landed uselessly on the snow between two of the enemy gathering at the base of the rampart, then the barbarians scrambled up the few feet of slope towards him.

He knew to keep himself tight against Quintus on his left and Urbo on his right, to hold his shield up and his sword out and to look into his enemy's eyes. That enemy, who seemed little older than Manius, was shorter, but his bare chest rippled and his forearms bulged. But Manius' long arms compensated for the other's longer sword and he had the advantage of jabbing down. So they went at it: jabbing and slashing. Manius took blows on his shield and returned feeble pokes, which, the barbarian parried while he grunted and Manius sobbed with effort, arms aching and lungs labouring. Sweat trickled into his eyes; he dashed at it with the back of his hand, readying himself for more blows. He was aware of Quintus beside him, fighting a strapping blond warrior. But Manius fixed his gaze to his front. From all along the rampart he heard metal against metal, metal against wood and panting and snarling, howls of pain and oaths.

The only blood he saw was Quintus cutting his opponent's forearm, causing him to swear and suck at his wound before hurling himself again at Quintus. But Manius was occupied, as his man gained a foothold on the rampart and pressed his shield against Manius' own. Panicking, Manius found the strength, with a shout, to force the enemy down. But back he came and the wearying cutting, hacking and parrying resumed.

Manius dared not slacken the furious pace but knew he couldn't keep it up. The muscles in his arms were screaming and leaden. He was dying by degrees.

Then a shout – and the whole enemy line stepped back from the foot of the rampart, to stand, chests heaving, glaring up at the Romans. A terrible wailing came from their women at the forest's edge and their priests resumed their incantations. The warriors regained their breath and jeered at the defenders, with obscene gestures.

"Are you well, boy?" wheezed Quintus. Manius nodded, breathless. Quintus grinned from under his helmet and squeezed his arm, as the barbarians gave a great shout and charged again.

Manius fought another furious duel with the same foe, prodding against his shield and taking his blows against his own. But after several exchanges the Briton swept his long sword low against Manius' legs and nicked his shin. Manius kicked out and caught him, sending him tumbling down the slope. Wearied, Manius had to watch the Briton scramble back and receive his fresh assault. But then the Brigantes again fell back all along the line and stood, regaining their breath to hurl their threats and insults.

"Quintus, how long will this go on?" Manius pleaded.

"Until they stop. Or we break."

Manius knew what would happen if they broke. The exhausting, largely bloodless beating of line against line would be over, the enemy would be among them and would slaughter every living thing within the fort and vicus. Including Lucia, he thought, when the barbarians charged again.

This time his assailant struggled, his legs working furiously. His previous attempts had crushed and crammed the snow, rendering it hard and polishing it smooth. He slipped, fell and slid to the bottom, bringing his comrades on either side sprawling beside him.

Quintus and Urbo roared their laughter. Manius, near hysterical, joined with high pitched whoops, cut short by another slash across his calves from the optio's cane.

Manius and Urbo fell silent and looked to their front. Quintus chuckled The optio raised his cane. Quintus stared at him.

"Silence in the ranks!' said the optio and moved down the line, muttering, "Fucking frumentarius".

Quintus winked at Manius.

"Urgh!" shouted Urbo.

Manius turned and shrieked to see his opponent flying up towards him, crouched on his own shield and borne aloft with a great heave by his two companions. He careered into Manius who fell into Quintus and they both rolled down the inside slope of the rampart into the vicus.

Manius lay, dazed and winded, while Quintus wallowed in the snow, cursing and struggling to regain his feet. Gazing up, Manius could see half a dozen bare-chested figures. Gods preserve us! They're on the rampart! Manius gave a cry and one glanced down – his muscular young adversary, whose eyes narrowed before he gave a slow smile and pointed

Manius out to his companions, whom he then led sliding down, hallooing with swords raised.

Quintus grabbed Manius' shoulder. "Come with me, boy!" He dragged him to his feet, towards a building at the vicus' edge. "This way! Quick, you fool!"

Manius had lost his shield and they were confronted by angry, determined faces lit in triumph. Two hacked at Quintus' shield and two more hovered with swords pointing seeking opportunity. Manius' young enemy raised his sword over him, a savage grin under his moustache. Manius flinched, holding out his own weapon in feeble, trembling parry.

There was a clamour to their right. The enemy's eyes flickered that way, his weapon still poised. Manius drove his blade into his throat.

Manius had a brief impression of him, staring, gurgling crimson bubbles before falling back. Then, two or three horses cantered from their right with their riders roaring. The remaining barbarians fled around the corner of the building, deeper into the vicus. A rider reined in in front of Manius and his horse reared and squatted on its haunches, its forelegs circling in the air, as the rider leapt from the saddle.

"Manius, Quintus, I say, are you all right?" It was Titus. He waited for no reply but with a "follow me" ran, half slipping in the slush, after the barbarians who, trapped in a broad alleyway with no exit, turned, half crouching.

"Ha!" yelled Titus and launched himself at them, his long cavalry blade sweeping aside theirs, as he cut, slashed and jabbed in frenzy. The Britons backed away. Quintus was soon by Titus' side, slower, but with a controlled, cruel ferocity behind each thrust. Manius skipped about behind them, looking for an opening. He was shoved aside by two of Titus' troopers, who thrust past and over Titus and Quintus with their javelins and the barbarians were slain with swift efficiency.

"Back!" roared Titus, "To the line!" And he led them tearing back to the rampart, now a turmoil of battling, hacking figures. One pulsating mob moved a few feet one way, then the other. Manius saw their optio go down under the fearful smash of a blade against his helmet. Titus and his two troopers scurried up the bank, roaring like bulls with Quintus puffing after them. Manius stared and noticed the horses of Titus and his men, the beasts wide-eyed and nostrils flaring, casting about for escape. He plunged among them, seized their reins and held them, his arms near yanked from their sockets by their rearing and bucking.

On the rampart, Titus was fighting like a demon – and laughing. He slashed down two enemies while beside him his troopers and Quintus pushed back the rest and gave him room to wield his blade.

He lowered his sword. Quintus put an arm around his shoulder.

"Ha!" shouted Quintus.

"Ha, ha!" echoed Titus and they slapped each other on the back. The rampart was theirs, the enemy had retired and the whole line relaxed.

Even the horses stopped tearing at the bridles and only whinnied.

"Well done all of you," Titus shouted, then he noticed Manius and slid down the bank to embrace. "I say, bravely done. Those beasts could have done themselves awful harm. For sure, I'd rather have faced Boudicca's chariot than those lashing hooves."

Manius coloured, murmured and handed the reins to the troopers. He gave a weak smile as Quintus told everyone how he'd slain a barbarian with a well-timed thrust.

Titus congratulated him and returned him to the line, with a final slap on the back, to survey again the howling Brigantes, now heartened by their near victory. Quintus was similarly reinvigorated, chortling over their fight, declaring, that, while he still resented Titus' assignment to their investigation, he truly was an admirable fellow.

"Is he not? Why can't Rome nurture more like him, instead of the scum who float to the surface these days?"

Manius gave a weary shrug.

§

Tiro watched the barbarian labour up the rampart towards him, breathing hard, his sword extended, his eyes fixed intently on Tiro.

"C'mon you bastard," whispered Tiro.

He took a sudden backward pace, allowing his adversary onto the rampart. The barbarian seemed surprised, then shocked, as he watched Tiro's sword slide into his belly. Tiro withdraw his blade and shoved the dying man down the slope. A roar of admiration came from the soldiers flanking him.

"Well done!" said their optio. "See how the galearius fights, that's how to do it."

Tiro gave a tight smile. He pointed to the blood covering his inner elbow, then clutched it, swearing. "The bastard cut me." Tiro bit his lip and groaned. "It's my sword arm, I just need a bandage."

The optio cursed and jerked a thumb at the vicus. "Go find a capsarius. Don't be long."

Tiro nodded and, holding his arm, made his way down from the rampart. He hurried through the vicus. Soldiers, messengers and other wounded were moving in all directions. None paid him any attention. He reached a lane that seemed deserted, which he confirmed with a swift glance around, then darted into an alleyway. He took his hand from his elbow and wiped the blood on his tunic.

It wasn't his, it had come from the slain barbarian. Shit! Weren't they just snot-nosed plough boys and broken winded shepherds? But they did fight like desperate men. They'd taken up arms against Rome. That meant death, so they might as well fight. Stupid barbarian bastards! And there were thousands of the hairy fuckers! Sure, Rome would win, but Tiro didn't fancy the chances of this particular garrison. Hadn't that tribune said this morning that they were as good as stuffed? Even if not, there was always the chance of a stray arrow or a fluke spear thrust. Well, Tiro had no quarrel with the Britons. Tiro was getting out.

This time, he'd make sure. He'd hide in the vicus. Most of these houses had already been abandoned. He'd conceal himself in one, change his gear. He was only a galerarius – and a bloody voluntary one at that – his name wasn't taken, no roll call would reveal his absence. Then, at nightfall he'd slip over the rampart and through the enemy. It'd be easier in the confusion of siege than it had been that morning.

He was outside a cottage. No sign of life. He tried the latch and the door opened. Inside, beams of weak, winter light slanted through picking out a corner of a table and a patch of the stone paved floor. His elongated shadow stretched across that floor towards the opposite wall. It vanished as he closed the door.

He coughed. "Anyone in?" Silence.

There was another door to the right. He opened it onto a room with a bed. Empty. He toured the main room; found a loaf and a goatskin of wine on a low shelf. Tiro was hungry. He tore a chunk off the bread, it was hard, some hours past its best, but he chewed on it. He found a goblet and sloshed wine into it. He contemplated the chairs tucked under the table but took the loaf and his drink and sank down to the floor, his back against a cupboard. Better there, below line of sight of any optio or centurion peering through the windows on the look-out for shirkers.

Tiro bit and chewed and planned. He could get out of the vicus and through the barbarian lines, he was sure of that. What then? Ride south, of course, out of this hellish wilderness. Where to? Londinium? He'd been known there as Flavius Fimbria's man. Flavius Fimbria! What a twat he'd turned out to be. Well, he'd got what was coming to him, no mistake.

How'd he fare in Londinium? Once Priscus heard Fimbria was a goner, he'd make a clean sweep of all his supporters, and who'd stand up for Tiro? If he got back to Rome, how'd Saoterus regard him? That one was a past-fucking-master at covering his trail and might see yours truly as a bit of an embarrassment. No, return to Londinium, ahead of the news, get paid and fuck off out of it, to Spain, to Extremadura, that was the back of beyond, he'd be well out of it there for a while.

Tiro swigged from his goblet, then froze as he heard hurrying footsteps. He cocked his head, reaching for his sword, knocking over his wine. A shadow rushed past the window, the footsteps ran by with it and faded. Tiro breathed again. Now it was quiet outside. But there was a noise inside, faint. What the fuck? He looked down, saw the wine pooling over a crack where two paving slabs joined. It bubbled there, dripping through. He pressed on the stone. It rocked, it was loose. He took his sword and prized the blade into the crack at the further end of the slab. He levered and the stone, which was about a foot square, rose. He took the edge in his other hand and pulled. Then he dropped his sword, took the slab in both hands and pivoted it to one side, wincing at the scraping. He lay it down, next to the hole it revealed.

The opening extended under the surrounding stone slabs and a bundle filled it. Tiro peeled back the neck of a sack. His eyes widened. He whistled. Then a shadow fell across the hole.

Tiro whirled round to see a pair of women's shoes. He looked, from the feet, up the dress to the smiling face. Tiro also smiled; rose and looked into that face. He grinned and pointed at the hole then looked at it. That was a mistake.

The blow struck below his ear. He felt a sharp pain. He went down on one knee.

"Bitch!"

His head burned and he clamped his hand to his neck. He pulled it away and saw it was crimson. She stepped back, still smiling. He struggled upright, dizzy. The room swayed. He put a hand to his forehead. The room grew darker. He took a pace, tried another, but couldn't. He swayed, dropped to his knees. Then the stone floor rushed towards him.

§

Manius watched, tired, as the armourer and his assistants moved among them distributing fresh javelins.

"They're not for throwing," shouted their optio. "Not this time – not if you value your miserable lives. Use them to fend the bastards off."

That change of tactic marked a turning point. There followed attack after attack. Manius lost track of how many. Wearied and wary, he readied himself for each onrush as barbarians struggled up that rampart slope, then poked his javelin at his howling opponents and grunted and gasped with the effort. But none of the assaults prevailed. With the Romans prodding them back, the British could only hack, in useless rage, trying to beat defending javelins aside. They bellowed in frustration and, whenever they fell back, hurled snowballs to burst against Roman shields.

Still, if it hadn't been for the fading light, they might have triumphed, for Manius and his comrades were dizzy with exhaustion. But as the sky darkened, and a brief blaze of orange to the West silhouetted the fort, the barbarians fell back, carrying their few wounded to the forest's edge, where, with their women and priests, they shouted and chanted. After half an hour the clamour died. The barbarians pulled on their tunics and some lit fires and settled to eat, while others melted back into the forest. The rampart's defenders sat on their haunches, weary, dirty and hungry. Manius, who had fought his first battle, felt only numbness.

Antonius Merenda arrived, accompanied by Titus and Publius Flavius. The soldiers made to get stiffly to their feet, but Merenda signalled them to remain as they were, although he did order a detail to descend to gather up their javelins and stones.

"How goes the rest of the line?" Quintus asked him.

"It held, but had they attacked this morning, they'd have overrun us by now."

Titus broke in. "Lucius Antonius, your honour, I can't agree. The cohort can hold the ramparts. Our fellows have the measure of them."

"Your confidence does you credit Titus Caelius, but you must see – that the enemy are too many. They can reinforce, but we get no rest and the men can only fight for so long."

Titus, the light of battle still in his eye, began to argue, but his commander held up his hand. "No. Tomorrow we must think about abandoning the vicus. Its perimeter is too wide and the rampart too easily assaulted. The fort will be easier to defend. Ah, Antiochos," he greeted the surgeon's arrival. "Have you news?"

Antiochos reported eight killed with another in the hospital likely to die before the night was out. There were also a couple of dozen injuries such as fractures, concussions and a few sword wounds. He and his capsarii had bandaged and balmed about another forty who'd be fit for duty in a day or so. Merenda scowled and looked at the forest. He heaved a heavy sigh and addressed Titus: "Give it another hour. Then, if it's still quiet, stand down half the centuries for food and sleep. Rotate them after four hours." He turned to go, then remembered Quintus. "Quintus Suetonius, you and your… boy, might as well go and eat now. You're unused to this. You're excused duty when this century is called back. Return in the morning."

"I thank you. I confess I'm feeling a little stiff. We also have other things to attend to. Tell me: how is Decima Flavia Fimbria?"

Merenda seemed at a loss. Then a shadow crossed his face as he looked at Antiochos.

"The lady does well and responds to my treatment" said the surgeon. "The nausea is subsiding and I'm convinced her memory will begin to return within days."

Everyone seemed careful to avoid Publius Flavius' eye, but Manius, in the shadows, observed him. He remained expressionless in the face of his imminent denunciation as a murderer.

§

Twenty minutes later, Quintus and Manius were in the fort, queuing for ale and porridge at a long trestle table by the porta decumana. A great cauldron was suspended over a brazier which threw a red glow against the wall of the fort behind it and against which the enlarged shadows of the servers moved. Quintus and Manius lined up with scores of others detailed for their meal, exhausted men, faces sweat-begrimed, their hair damp and plastered and their eyes red-rimmed.

Images of the day jostled to the forefront of his mind and Manius exchanged only an occasional distracted word with Quintus, who was served before him and went to sit close by while Manius waited his own turn. Similarly, Manius was too preoccupied to notice those who ladled porridge into his bowl and poured his ale, until he heard a familiar, gentle voice.

"It's Manius isn't it?" The podgy hand holding the ladle belonged to Birca, Titus' betrothed.

He returned her greeting and stuttered: "Bu... but what're you doing here?"

"I volunteered. I thought it only my duty as..." she gave a coy smile, "as the future wife of a Roman officer."

"Titus Caelius must be very proud of you."

She frowned. "He scolded me when he found out, said it wasn't fitting and that his commander wouldn't approve."

Manius muttered something noncommittal. Her face lit up again. "And Titus tells me that you've been a hero and fought bravely."

"Oh, Titus Caelius is kind but..."

"I shall tell Lucia Antonia Merenda."

Manius reddened and she gave a throaty chuckle, which wasn't unkind, but he was glad to take his meal and move on.

As he left, he saw that the figure with ladle and jug next to Birca was Pellia, the late general's whore. No slave could be left idle at a time such as this. She clearly recognised him as an associate of her oppressor Quintus and shot him a look of defiance and resentment. He moved off. Frumentarius he might be, but standing in the sludge, bowl of porridge in hand, with a crushing sense of his own mortality and fragility, he felt only her equal and knew she must have sensed it – a small humiliation that further depressed him.

He found Quintus and they returned with their meal to their barrack block apartment where at least they had enough wood for a fire which threw out a hemisphere of light in which they sat, the only sound being spoons scraping bowls and the crackle of flames. Manius ate mechanically, too tired to savour the food, but Quintus shovelled it in then downed his ale and wiped his mouth.

"So, Merenda is abandoning the vicus – the only sane strategy. Aye, let's sit safe behind these walls while the barbarians freeze."

"So why not before?"

"Pride – Roman pride and Merenda's pride. Abandoning a settlement and property to rebels for even a day isn't the Roman way. But it's the only way for us. Merenda will have to swallow his pride – even if it looks bad for him, in addition to everything else that's happened."

Manius' tired mind lit upon a question he'd been meaning to ask. "How do you know that the Gracchus are Christians?"

"Know? I don't know. I observe. I note things, then form a plausible picture. You've noticed their absence from any sacrifice, their opposition to drunkenness and abhorrence of suicide. All marks of a Christian, or perhaps a Jew. But they don't have the look of Jews."

"If you're right; doesn't their cult make them unlikely murderers?"

"I've told you that Publius Flavius is the killer. It's just that if we seek to cast the net wider, it can be cast wider than Titus Caelius imagines. One could frame a charge that Gracchus sought revenge for Tiberius Flavius' actions in Gaul, or, wanted to secure the safety of himself and his family from a persecutor of the Christians. Whatever these people claim, remember they're fanatics."

"Will you expose them?"

"To what end? The late emperor had little interest in persecuting them. They present no threat to Rome whatever Tiberius Flavius and his kind believe. One day this supposed fact concerning Gracchus may be useful. Why squander it now? We've more important things to think about."

But Manius was too tired to think about them, so he gave an ostentatious yawn and began to undress. Quintus went muttering into his own chamber, where he began swearing and throwing baggage around. Manius called out: "What are you doing in there?"

"Making sure there's no wine. You go to sleep."

Manius drifted off, but woke again, perhaps an hour later, judging by the dying embers in the hearth. A light flickered from Quintus' cubicle. With a heavy sigh, he tossed aside his blankets, and went to find Quintus, on the edge of his bunk, ransacking his saddle bags by a lamp guttering on the floor.

"What're you doing now?"

"You should be asleep. Sleep is a great gift. Make the best of it. I can't, not without wine."

Manius passed a hand over his eyes and yawned. "But what're you doing?"

"Aha… here it is." He pulled his fist from his bag and opened it to reveal a small bottle, half full of red liquid.

Manius remembered. "That's…"

"The potion that brought oblivion to Publius Flavius and now it will bring blessed slumber to me." He uncorked the bottle with a chuckle. "Better than anything our little Greek quack could prepare."

"Quintus!"

He stopped, the bottle half way to his lips. "What?"

"Are you sure it's safe?"

"It did our whispering friend no harm, did it?"

"But he… he's younger than you."

"Then I'll take less." He waved Manius away. "Go back to sleep and leave me to do the same."

Chapter Nineteen

Felix grasped the peel's long handle, but the more he gripped, the more it shook in his trembling hands. He was frightened. He'd taken loaves from the oven hundreds of times for Prudes, usually without mishap, but always remembered the first times, when he'd burned himself, leaving livid red wounds across his forearms, making him cry. His weeping angered baker Prudes more than the dropped loaves and Felix had learnt to suppress his sobs to avoid Prudes' cursing and finger wagging.

Felix eased the peel into the oven's mouth, jiggled it under the loaves and slowly withdrew it.

Then came a shout from outside the bake house. "Hey, Prudes y'lazy, bony bastard, are y'up?"

Felix started and two of the loaves jumped onto the floor.

"Oh, for fuck's sake," breathed Prudes. He snatched the peel from Felix and cuffed him. "See who that is."

Felix gulped back a sob and stepped outside, shivering as he moved from the heat into the freezing air. It wasn't fully dawn but there was sufficient light to recognize the soldiers Syneros and Baccio. He didn't like them; knew they'd jeer if they saw him sniffling, so he sucked his thumb.

"Hello, it's the brains of the operation," said Baccio, a fox-faced veteran. "You got our bread? There's one hungry contubernium waiting with no hard tack, so they'll turn nasty if you don't produce the necessary, young Felix."

Prudes came the door, wiping his hands on a towel.

"Fuck's sake," he muttered. "Look what my ill Fate's brought me now, the cohort's last resort."

"Well, if it isn't the cheery master baker," said Baccio.

"You're early," growled Prudes.

"You're late."

"Bollocks."

"Early or late, are they ready?" asked Syneros, a youth with a porcine nose and wide nostrils. "It's fucking cold out here. Look at 'im." He pointed at Felix. "He's sweating, he's all right. It's a cushy number innit? He's called Felix right enough. Who'd be a citizen and free? Free to freeze your bollocks off while slaves stay cosy. Ain't that right Felix – y'shit-for-brains?"

"Leave the lad alone," said Prudes. "You know what he's like."

"Daft y'mean?"

"I'm not!"

"No, it's us that's daft, freezing on that rampart while you're in there."

"Make the most of it, Felix," said Baccio. "Way things are, they'll be roping you into the galearii."

"What d'you mean?" asked Felix, looking from Baccio to Prudes.

Baccio nodded. "Aye, you'll soon be on that rampart, trying to stop some hairy bastard Briton from carving you."

"No!"

"Leave him be!" snapped Prudes.

The soldiers laughed as the baker handed them loaves. Felix goggled. Was it one of their jokes?

"You'll all need bread and Prudes can't manage without me."

"Dead men don't need bread," said Baccio

"What? I don't understand."

"That's 'cos there's nothing to understand," said Prudes, angry now. He shoved Felix back towards the bake house door and thrust more loaves at the soldiers. "Don't listen, they're just a pair of windy bastards."

"Oh hearken to the bold baker, safe and sound by his oven," jeered Syneros.

"I've served my time, sunshine."

"Not like this you haven't. This isn't friggin' Egypt y'know. Have you seen those bastards? There's thousands, and more of the savage fuckers arriving every day. They've nearly broken through once."

"But we've got the fort!" protested Felix, who regarded the great grey walls with their tall turrets as being of impregnable, almost supernatural power.

Baccio spat. "The fort's cursed."

Felix turned to Prudes for explanation; reassurance. Prudes repeated, in a parodying sneer: "Cursed."

"Aye, cursed, y'floury bastard. Those savages are using magic, their priests cast spells, y'could see the evil buggers if you shifted your fat arse to the vicus rampart. Their women egg them on – witches."

"Bollocks," said Prudes, less vehement, eyeing the trembling Felix.

"Bollocks? Hasn't Roman murdered Roman? And we're talking nobs here, senators and knights. That's the work of magicians. And, if bloody British black magic isn't enough, we've got frumentarii. If those cunts don't bring bad luck, you tell me what does."

"Just take your bread and fuck off. You're scaring the lad."

This provoked jeers, then grumbling retreat as the pair turned to crunch their way back through the snow. Prudes turned to Felix. "Don't listen to that shit. D'you hear? Good, now take this spoiled bread to the pig pen – and don't take all day."

Felix's trembling hands took the spoiled loaves. He was soon shaking as much from cold. He missed his coat but to return would be to try

Prudes' temper. What Baccio and Syneros had said: he didn't really understand. But they'd reinforced recent impressions he'd picked up from other anxious soldiers and an irritable Prudes – that danger was threatening the cohort, which was his family, his provider and protector, the only world he'd ever known.

He hurried, past a granary block, across the street to a barrack block, blinking away lightly falling snowflakes. Light crept over the fort's tall walls where he saw the silhouette of a sentry patrolling and heard him answer the ritual challenge of his comrade advancing towards him along the parapet. On a couple of exciting occasions, soldiers had allowed Felix up there, higher than he'd ever been before in his life, to gaze for miles to the high tree tops of the forest and to look down, with an eagle's vantage, onto the surrounding vicus and onto its own earth walls and rampart.

And now they said that rampart would have to be abandoned. But not the fort. No, never the fort, those walls were just too high. Anyone could see that. Now he'd think of good things, like pigs.

Felix loved the pigs. Whenever Prudes allowed, he'd visit them, lean over their pen, against the fort's north wall, talk to them and feed them whatever scraps he'd foraged. He didn't name them – never. The pig keeper had warned him against that, for they all had to meet a pig's fate. That upset Felix, but there was a regular arrival of piglets to croon and chuckle over.

He quickened his pace in anticipation, then gave a high-pitched titter as he realised how much they resembled Syneros.

"Hee, hee, Syneros is a right pig. Syneros the fat pig," he sang until he reached the pen.

He leaned over the low wall and, seeing no pigs, chirruped over the short expanse of churned mud, snow and shit to the sty's small entrance, from which he could hear a happy snuffling. He waited, but neither pig appeared. Felix frowned. Normally they would come waddling for his treats.

"Silly pigs. You see what I've got."

He stepped over the wall. His feet squelched in the mire. Prudes would be cross if he trod that into the bake house. Better wipe his feet in the snow on the way back.

He stooped and peered into the sty. It was dark, he could barely see movement in the far corner. He stepped inside.

"Here piggies."

No response, no interruption in the frenzied grunting. He shuffled forward. He could see both now, their pink, hairy bodies wiggling, their heads down and ears swinging. What were they rooting at? A boot? Had they found an old boot? Felix drew closer until he could see the leg coming out of the boot.

He screamed, turned, banged his head on the door lintel. He dived out into the enclosure, scrambled over the wall and ran back towards the bake house yelling and gibbering.

The pigs ignored the loaves he'd dropped.

§

Boots woke Manius – running, scuffing and stamping boots, – accompanied by barked commands and all the other din of soldiery. Light trickled through the shutter. He must have slept for more than ten hours. He was easing himself from bed when the door crashed open and Quintus stormed in, his hair wet and on end and his eyes red-rimmed and wild.

"Awake at last!"

"As you see." Manius yawned. "And where've you been?"

"To the baths."

"Aren't they closed?"

"They're not heated. I've been for a cold plunge."

Quintus boiled with some mighty but suppressed emotion – suppressed until Manius asked whether he'd slept well.

"Slept well! I've been pacing through the night with my mind raging; I've been duped, duped, I tell you!"

"Who has duped you?"

"Who? Why, that cur Publius Flavius Fimbria, that's who. But he won't get away with it. I'll have it out with him. Come, let's see him now, the dog, and confront him with his duplicity."

Quintus fretted and muttered as he buckled on his armour and he'd answer none of Manius' questions, only shook his head and urged him to hurry dressing.

"You'll find out what that whispering bastard has done from his own lips."

It took them some time to find Publius Flavius. His century was on the rampart, but he wasn't to be seen. They asked a principalis who directed them back towards the fort. After further hunting, and Manius half trotting to keep up with Quintus' furious pace, they encountered him by the mansio. Publius Flavius was hurrying, his head down, oblivious, until Quintus stopped him with a hand against his breast.

"I want a word with you."

Publius Flavius contemplated them, his expression darkening. He looked at Quintus' hand and tried to paw it away. "I'm on duty, I've no time for you."

"We're frumentarii. You make time. Need I explain? Either come with us now, or I'll have Antonius Merenda arrest you."

Publius Flavius glared, his face burning. He said, in his soft voice: "I'm on duty, I cannot leave the vicus."

"In here then," said Quintus and pulled him into the mansio's deserted lobby. "You remember in Eboracum: you remonstrated with me for drugging you?"

"I've not forgotten. Nor will I."

"Good. Perhaps you'll also remember whether – had it not been for the drug – you'd have obeyed your orders and prevented us leaving?"

"Of course."

"So, you concede that you had such instructions from Caerillius Priscus?"

Publius Flavius frowned, his cheeks reddened.

Quintus studied him then continued."Explain this: I took that drug last night, from the very same phial, and it had no effect on me whatsoever."

Publius shrugged. "It's your drug."

Quintus fastened his fist around the scarf at Publius' neck. "Oh, don't you make an enemy out of me, my young friend."

Publius prised away Quintus' hand. "Of course I didn't take your drug. It could've been poison. D'you think me mad?"

"How did you do it? You exchanged it, didn't you?"

"Yes, yes – I entered your room and replaced it with simple wine."

"How did you know?"

A disagreeable smile spread across Publius' face.

"I had your boy here followed to the apothecary's," he smirked. "The beneficarius Carbo procured me a whore, the German slave girl, and I had the mansio steward employ her at table to get to know your faces and then follow you."

If Quintus' potion wasn't poisonous, the look he shot at a blushing Manius was.

"So, you substituted wine for my sleeping potion?"

"I hope you don't expect me to apologise."

"You weren't drugged, but you still let us leave Eboracum. Why?"

Publius said nothing. Quintus' eyes widened in realisation. He stepped back from Publius Flavius and rubbed his chin. "Caerillius Priscus told you to. Those were his instructions?"

Publius Flavius blustered. "Now, you ask me too much… must protest… attend to duties…" and the rest tailed off, as he sidled past an unprotesting Quintus and onto the street. Quintus' eyes didn't follow him, but continued staring.

"I don't understand," Manius said.

"Eh? No, nor I." Quintus shook himself. "But I do understand this. There's more to that fellow than meets the eye. He's quite an actor for one thing."

"So is he in league with Caerillius Priscus, or even Tita Amatia?"

Quintus blinked. "I'm going to get myself some wine and go to bed. Say I'm ill and that'll I'll help if the Brigantes come calling." He gave Manius a final filthy look, shook his head and muttered: "German whore."

Manius didn't smart for long. He'd forgotten the German girl at Eboracum. No, his mind whirled at the rest of what Publius Flavius had said. They'd believed he was the governor's man. But if Caerillius Priscus had charged him with keeping the frumentarii out of mischief, why'd he allowed them to go to see Tita Amatia, who'd no time for the governor?

Manius had no idea, but suspected Quintus had and wasn't sharing. There could be no question now, he must take care of number one; look out for the interests of Manius Suetonius Lupus.

He wandered out into the vicus. There was the crackle of flames from a bonfire in a garden, where two soldiers stood warming themselves. A goat bleated and a hen clucked, soldiers called to each other but Manius more felt those sounds that were missing. When they'd first arrived, this had been a bustling little settlement, alive with traders, shopkeepers, labourers, pimps and slaves. Now, there was no laughter or chatter between neighbours, no tradesmen calling their wares. Since the desertion, most of that life had gone and, what remained was furtive, flitting through doorways, round corners or briefly and warily appearing at windows. These few shy villagers were largely the womenfolk and the handful of men were the old or crippled. Any attempt to meet a gaze encountered shifty reluctance and an eye swiftly averted. They were withdrawing into their rough homes, into themselves, away from the Romans and from Rome.

This unsettled Manius. And he was unsure what he should do. Report to the rampart? After the previous day's experience that idea made him shudder. He'd tasted blood, he'd killed a man, hadn't he? He'd more than done his duty and had no wish to court death again. But he was ranked with the galearii and should serve with the cohort. Yet he was also a frumentarius and had other duties. And who, other than Quintus, could know what those were? He decided: he'd roam the vicus and fort with apparent purpose and, if challenged, he'd refer vaguely to some affair he was engaged in on behalf of Antonius Merenda.

As it was, the first to question Manius about his business was Birca, who hailed him from the doorway of a trim, single storey building.

"Is this home?" asked Manius.

She nodded. "Yes, there are just two rooms but there's only me and my slave Treva, she sleeps in the kitchen. Well, she used to, she's disappeared now, run off like so many others. And Titus stays when his duties don't keep him in the fort. And they so often do."

"He's second-in-command… and at a time like this…"

"Oh but Manius! How are you? Aren't you stiff from yesterday's battle? Are you returning to the ramparts?"

"I've a few aches." He rubbed his side. "But there's nothing serious. No, I'm not bound for the ramparts, I'm… er, on an errand for Quintus."

"The killing?"

Manius hesitated. He didn't want to commit himself to anything regarding Tiberius Flavius' death which she could report back to Titus. Happily, before he could answer, she added: "You're looking into last night's killing?"

"Last night's killing?"

"I've only just heard. A body's been found in the fort, in the pigsty…" she lowered her voice "… his throat slit."

"Who?"

"A common soldier apparently."

Manius smiled. "That sounds like barrack-room squabble and probably best dealt with by the man's centurion – not something for frumentarii. You see Birca, our work's more serious, it's about the security of the Empire, the discovery of plots against Rome and the Emperor. Tiberius Flavius Fimbria's murder only interests us because the man was a senator."

As he savoured his own words, hoping she's repeat them to Lucia, a recollection of something Quintus had said jolted him: that their ambush by the Wolves only a few days ago, had probably been down to information passed on by some traitor in the fort. Did this pigsty killing confirm that? Was there a Wolf among them? He only half listened to her saying what an important profession he had, until he realised she was looking at him, her eyebrows raised.

"Er… I'm sorry, what did you say?"

"I said, I'm sure your work is dangerous, is it not?"

Manius twirled a carefree hand.

"Oh, I'm sure it is, but I know you're very brave, Manius, after yesterday. And Lucia Antonia Merenda knows it too, because I told her this morning, as I said I would." Her eyes twinkled. "She was anxious to know, before anything else, that you were safe."

"Birca, is that true? Oh, you're not making fun of me are you?"

She placed a hand on his. "No, Manius, I wouldn't joke about that. To do that would be to betray the love Titus and I have. I'm your ally, you see, and I know what you feel."

Manius felt a great affection for her and for Titus. They were both good and kind. He told her he had a message for Titus and she directed him to the vicus gate at the southern end of the settlement where he saw him on the rampart contemplating the few rebel Brigantes who'd issued from the trees.

As Manius breasted the top of the rampart, he flinched at the keen north wind that blew a spray of fine, gritty, stinging snow into his face. He half closed his eyes and pulled his scarf up over his chin. The wind tugged at Titus' cloak and the snow crystals formed a glistening sheen over his hair. He didn't turn at Manius' approach but, hand on sword pommel, he continued to gaze intently at the enemy. It was a fine pose.

"I just cannot understand why they don't attack again – dash it!" he said, without any greeting.

"Perhaps they had enough yesterday.'

Titus laughed mirthlessly. "No, they had a few losses but their numbers are far greater and they did almost overwhelm us – surely enough to encourage them."

"I'm no soldier Titus, for all this gear I'm wearing, but couldn't it be they're planning to keep us cut off and starve us out?"

"If they are, they've miscalculated. Our granaries are full and we could last the winter." He punched his open palm and turned to face Manius. "But this day they've given us – they've wasted – convinces me that I'm right and that the old man wrong. We shouldn't abandon the vicus. The enemy are missing an opportunity and by tomorrow many of our injured will be back in the ranks. But it's no good, I'm convinced Antonius Merenda has made up his mind to pull back into the fort."

"Then why doesn't he order a withdrawal?"

Titus paused a couple of seconds, then spoke, weighing his words. "I'm not easy criticising my commander, especially not to a frumentarius, it's not done." He gave a quick smile and put his hand round Manius' shoulder. "I am sorry, Manius, forgive me if that sounded rude but what I mean is, just as I've my duties, I'm sure so do you. Look, I can see you're honourable. You told me once that I could trust you and I won't insult you by asking you again.' He paused, nibbling his lip. "The truth is I fear he can't reach a decision, or at least that he can't bring himself to order it done, if you get my drift. On the one hand he thinks – wrongly – that abandoning the vicus is a military necessity. But then y'see, on the other, it's handing a victory to the rebels and the news will spread and others will swell to join 'em."

"I suppose, we couldn't fight our way out and march back to Vinovia and the cohort there?"

Titus shook his head. "No, it won't work. The enemy outnumber us many times y'see and to fight them in the open would be to yield the advantage we gain from our defences. Personally, I'd still back our lads but even if we beat the Britons off, we'd still be left with a long march through the snow and we'd be encumbered with those blasted civilians still in the vicus.

"And don't forget," he said, warming to his theme and jabbing a forefinger at Manius, "we'd also be weighed down by the pay."

"Pay?"

"Yes, the pay, the money, in the basilica's strongroom. It's for the fourth stipendia and not just for this garrison but for those of Vinovia and Vindomora too: several hundred thousand sesterces. Ha! Imagine if that fell into the rebels' hands. Worse still, the buggers would seize the fort's grain supplies."

They both stared at the barbarians who were not stripped to the waist for fighting that day but were swathed in furs and sheepskins, tending their fires.

"Manius, we must discuss the general's death seriously. I'm not a fool – well, not a complete fool – I know your father resents my involvement and I understand that. Personally, I'd happily have nothing to do with this ghastly business, believe me, but I've been ordered to help in your inquiries and the old man's certain to ask me about it."

"Titus, this will remain between the two of us, won't it?"

Titus frowned. "Of course, if that's what you want."

"You think Publius Flavius isn't necessarily his brother's murderer. Quintus resists that idea."

"I know the old man wants Publius Flavius to be the guilty party. A family quarrel makes his position much easier – he was supposed to be protecting Tiberius Flavius. Is your father set on Publius Flavius' guilt in order to protect Antonius Merenda?"

"No, I think it's to protect himself."

"Himself?"

Manius spoke in a hurry, committed now. "If the general's death wasn't down to a family quarrel then maybe it was political. Quintus fears that if it was seen as political then some might point the finger at a frumentarius."

Titus stared at Manius, whistled then looked back at the barbarians. Manius was calculating: if suspicion ever did fall on the frumentarii, better that it should focus on just one of them. Yes, let Titus' gaze be directed that way.

"May the gods preserve me," said Titus. "I'm glad I'm just a simple soldier. Take those barbarians – you know where you stand with them. But this business..." He shook his head and turned to Manius. "Look, you don't think he did... well, have anything...?"

An optio interrupted, saluted and told him that the tribune wished to consult with him.

"We must talk of this later," Titus whispered.

§

Tita Amatia smiled her thanks to Gaia Antonia when the slave girl placed the glass of mulsum and plate of honey cakes on the table. She took the glass and held it to the light.

"These are lovely."

The cohort commander's wife simpered. Tita Amatia guessed that the best glassware had been brought out to impress her, that the Merendas' slaves had been worked hard cleaning this light and airy living room. Gaia Antonia was – like any army wife – eager for her husband's advancement and anxious to enlist the support of any who might assist, hence Tita Amatia's invitation for refreshment, which, normally she'd have regarded as a bore, but the preceding days had been eventful enough to provide for interesting conversation.

"Poor Decima Flavia," murmured Gaia Antonia. "But my dear, I was forgetting, you're old friends."

Tita Amatia nodded. "Many years ago. She made a bad marriage, I'm afraid."

Gaia smiled tightly. This was dangerous ground for a knight's wife.

She said brightly: "Well, at least she is in good hands, Antiochos will look after her."

"He's good is he?"

"Oh, my dear. He's among the best. Well..." she tittered, "that's what he tells us."

Tita Amatia threw back her head and laughed. "He is very Greek isn't he?"

Then they launched into eager discussion of Publius Flavius and how awful it was that he should kill his brother so horribly.

"They say he'd reason to hate his brother, but even so," said Gaia. "I do hope this won't reflect badly on Lucius Antonius. Do you think it will?"

"If one brother chooses to kill another, it's hard to see how anyone can blame your husband."

"No... I suppose you're right, but he might be thought unlucky. He lacks influential patrons, people to speak up for him." She gazed at Tita Amatia.

"Doesn't he have the governor's ear?"

Gaia Antonia looked puzzled. "Of course, they frequently correspond; Lucius Antonius is a senior commander. I believe the governor has a good opinion of him."

Tita Amatia sipped wine and held the glass up to the light again, gazing at it as she asked: "But does your husband know the governor?"

"Well... we've met him in Londinium. Lucius has seen him on other occasions on official matters."

They fell silent, nibbling their cakes. Tita Amatia wondered: was Merenda in good standing with Priscus? Was he in his camp?

Gaia Antonia sighed. "I suppose it's stupid to be worrying about such things when we're under siege and the country risen in turmoil." She shook her head. "One lives among these people, thinks one knows them, we bring them all Rome's benefits, and then this, then one realises how little one really knows them. But, I'm forgetting, you've lived among them yourself for many years."

"Indeed, I married one of them."

Gaia Antonia blushed. She cleared her throat and brushed cake crumbs from her lap.

Tita Amatia took pity. "Sometimes I think I know them. At other times I'm not so sure."

Gaia Antonia nodded sagely, said how deeply her husband felt all these things, how he "let things get on top of him". Tita Amatia stretched out a leg, winced and whispered something about stiffness. She stood, apologised, adding, "Do go on my, dear," and walked behind Gaia Antonia to look out of the window, half listening and making sympathetic comments. She preferred this to sitting, it gave her a proprietorial feeling over the room and those in it. She'd used to do it unconsciously, until her husband had begun to copy her, aping another Roman patrician habit.

Her first impressions of Gaia Antonia had changed She'd thought her easy-going and moderately witty. Now her wit had degenerated into sarcasm which informed her querulousness. Tita Amatia could hear her – "I suppose some people might think being a senior tribune in a border province an easy matter."

Tita Amatia sighed. She was being unfair. Gaia Antonia wasn't alone: others were reacting badly to this siege, tempers were frayed, hysteria was near the surface – in men as well as women.

She turned from the window. Not only was she being unfair, she was neglecting her duty. She should be trying to learn about Merenda, Priscus and Cotta. She returned to her seat.

"Surely my dear, your husband can confide in you?"

Gaia Antonia blinked, confused. She must have moved on while Tita Amatia had been daydreaming.

"No... I mean he needs a man to talk to, a man who understands military matters and politics, someone of his own rank."

"Aurelius Cotta perhaps?"

"Spurius Aurelius? Yes, Lucius finds his advice valuable. But he's not a military man."

"What manner of man is he?"

"Intelligent and cultured. The Cottas had a house in Londinium at one time."

"Really? Did they know the governor?"

"I think so."

"Does he correspond with him? Couldn't he plead a case for Lucius Antonius?"

Gaia Antonia brightened. "That's possible."

"It must be hard for Aurelius Cotta – with his people risen in revolt."

"Oh, you're right. Poor man. He's so proud of his citizenship and now must feel that his people have disgraced him."

Tita Amatia nodded but wasn't convinced. In the quadrangle the other day, he'd seemed positively cocksure.

"Doesn't your husband's deputy give counsel and support?"

Gaia Antonia rolled her eyes. "Lucius believes Titus Caelius to be a good enough soldier but he's not thoughtful, he's headstrong and he – oh, I don't know – he's dramatic, he behaves as though he's in some play. Lucius says he sometimes thinks he should have been a poet not a soldier." Another sarcastic laugh. "My husband hardly needs a poet at the moment!"

"Indeed not."

"Apart from that, Titus Caelius has little thought beyond horses and the dice. He has debts you know. Then there's that woman, the Briton, so unsuitable, I..."

Gaia Antonia broke off, horrified by her fresh blunder.

"Then your husband should talk to Quintus Suetonius."

"Talk to a frumentarius? Isn't that like giving one's account books to a tax collector?"

Tita Amatia laughed. "I don't suppose Quintus wants to be overrun by the Brigantes any more than the rest of us – frumentarius or not."

Gaia Antonia shook her head. "I don't know, it's all so difficult. Poor Lucius Antonius. The decisions are his alone and yet, if he weighs them carefully – which is surely his duty – then people say he's indecisive."

"The decisions are his, but he can still take advice."

Gaia Antonia bit her lip, picked up a napkin and wrung it. "What's Suetonius Lupus doing here?"

"I thought he was here to serve Tiberius Flavius Fimbria."

"Frumentarii only serve the Emperor, surely?"

"Don't we all?"

Gaia Antonia didn't look happy at this evasion. She probed Tita Amatia: what was a frumentarius doing in a remote border region, involving himself in some tribal insurrection? Did she think his presence was connected with Tiberius Flavius' murder? Tita Amatia shrugged. Gaia Antonia appeared dissatisfied and sulky.

"What of his assistant, the boy?"

"Manius? What of him?"

"I believe that's his name, yes. Do you know him?"

"What could I know of him? I believe he's Quintus Suetonius' adopted son. He's handsome, seems bright, rather deep I think. Why d'you ask?"

Gaia Antonia pursed her lips. "He pays my daughter too much attention."

Tita Amatia suppressed a smile. "Your daughter's beautiful. Surely it's natural."

"Yes, but she's showing too much interest in return."

Now Tita Amatia smiled openly. "Again, that's only natural. They're young and there's nobody else of their age."

"That's the problem. Circumstances are far from normal and at times of great danger passions run high. I saw that in Egypt."

Tita Amatia nodded. There was something in that. As Horace wrote: `Pluck the day, trusting as little as possible in the future.' Or roger yourselves silly before the Brigantes kill you. To Gaia Antonia, she said:

"You may have a point."

"I cannot be worrying about Lucia in addition to everything else. I've spoken to Lucius."

Aye, thought Tita Amatia, give him something else to fret about, he'll thank you for that. She was framing a more sympathetic reply when the door crashed open. The slave girl Blathin stood staring, her mouth opening and closing.

"What's the matter?" asked Gaia Antonia. "What do you want, girl?"

"My lady. The master wants you, you must come straightaway."

"Why? Where is he?"

"He's at the sick lady's room – Decima Flavia Fimbria. Something horrible's happening."

§

Manius stared after Titus when he left him on the rampart. Had he done the right thing? He'd opened a little distance between himself and Quintus. Should Quintus discover it… Better not to think of that. Manius' options seemed to be narrowing. The Fates were bundling him headlong with Quintus. He had to do something.

His thoughts were interrupted by squealing. It was the Gracchus children: Numerius and Gnaea. Numerius was six with black curls, a querulous, dissatisfied child. Gnaea was two years older and, though her hair was straight and brown, shared her brother's nature. Manius wasn't good with children, didn't understand them and was too self-conscious to feign sympathy. Little wonder, with no brothers or sisters and a father such as Quintus.

But convention dictated he pretend pleasure in their company. He dutifully squatted level with them.

"So, what are you two up to? Eh?" They gawped. "Do mummy and daddy know where you are?"

Numerius bowed his head and thrust out his lower lip. His sister was more forthcoming. "Daddy's sleeping. He was up there all night with the soldier-men. Mummy is helping cook for the soldier-men and she told us we might play on the rampart so long as we didn't disturb the soldier-men." She looked worried. "Are you a soldier-man?"

Manius laughed merrily. "No, no, like your daddy, I'm only a soldier-man until the bad men in the woods have gone away."

Gnaea pointed at the trees. "Do you mean those Brigantes?"

"That's right. But you shouldn't be afraid of them, for other soldier-men will soon come and drive them away."

"Oh, we're not afraid. They're our friends." At this, her brother gave her a vicious pinch on the arm, she howled and they both ran squealing down from the rampart, leaving Manius once more staring and wondering.

"Manius Suetonius Lupus?"

"Hmm?" He realised the fair-haired centurion who'd been at the fateful dinner party was looming over him, Servius Ambrosius Crassipes. He was flustered, apologetic. "I'm searching for Quintus Suetonius on behalf of Antonius Merenda. Do you know where I might find him?"

"I'm afraid he's ill… indisposed."

"Ill!" He looked alarmed.

"Nothing grave, he's tired and has a touch of… of colic."

"May he be disturbed?"

Manius assured Ambrosius Crassipes that Quintus had left instructions that, in emergency, he was to be disturbed and, if the centurion would accompany him, they'd go and do so. They set off for the fort. The centurion, although tall, took mincing steps and every third or fourth pace gave a little skip to keep up. Manius wondered what demanded Quintus' urgent attention.

He entered the barrack block rooms, leaving the centurion outside. Quintus was snoring, an empty wine jar folded in embrace. Manius roused him. Quintus sat up, shook his head and asked whether the Brigantes were attacking.

"No? So what the hell's so important?"

There was a delicate cough from behind.

"Suetonius Lupus, this matter is seriously urgent, it… it concerns the lady, Decima Flavia. The tribune requests you come at once."

Quintus and Manius exchanged a look. Then Quintus was out of his bunk and thrusting his feet into his boots. A minute later they were hurrying into the Praetorium courtyard to be met by Merenda who seized Quintus' sleeve. "Come, come," he whimpered.

They approached the door of Decima Flavia's room, which was ajar and, from which came strange and ugly noises. They entered.

Lying in her bed, on her back, with shocked eyes gazing at the ceiling, was a dead Decima Flavia Fimbria. They turned towards the noises and saw Vibia Rufia, sitting on the bed. She was jerking to and fro, her hands in front of her, with the fingers working as though drumming an invisible tabletop. She gasped, her mouth worked and twisted as she strove to speak, but could only make a harsh, insistent rasping. Her eyes, the pupils dilated, seemed to plead with Antiochos, who sat beside, trying to restrain her. The convulsions lasted a few seconds and then, with one tremendous jerk, she tore herself from Antiochos' grasp and crashed onto the floor, where she lay, convulsing and writhing before she gave one last great, rattling gasp.

Manius looked away and his gaze fell on a spot on the floor by the head of the bed, onto a small, cloaked and hooded clay figure.

Chapter Twenty

Antiochos could do nothing for the women, but he rushed to Antonius Merenda, who had collapsed in a faint.

"Help me with him! You!"

A stunned Manius realised he was shouting at him.

"Help me get him out of this accursed room!"

Antiochos took Merenda's shoulders while Manius grasped his ankles and they hurried the tribune two doors further along to his own family's day room. Quintus followed.

There Merenda's wife and slaves flapped around, twittering questions and squawked at Antiochos' impatient answers. The surgeon ordered them all from the room, insisting Merenda must be in complete peace – did they understand?

When calm prevailed Merenda groaned and sat upright on the couch on which they'd lain him, looking from Antiochos, to Manius and then to Quintus. Antiochos sent for stimulating drugs and for Titus Caelius to be summoned.

Merenda stared blankly while Antiochos fussed, tested his pulse, examined his tongue and felt his forehead. Quintus stared out of the window into the courtyard.

Antiochos had finished administering the drugs when Titus arrived. The surgeon left Quintus and Manius to explain, while he returned to the room of death.

"Dead?" demanded Titus, blinking. "Both of them? Decima Flavia Fimbria dead? Great heavens!" Merenda passed a hand over his eyes. Not only had a senator and general died under his protection, but so had his wife, who was of an even more influential family. Surely now he must kill himself.

Merenda hauled himself off the couch. "This is too much. Where's Antiochos? I must know."

On cue, the Greek returned looking serious and carrying two bowls.

"Well?" Quintus demanded – almost shouted.

"Oh, it was poison, most certainly poison."

"So, we have a Locusta among us,' said Quintus, almost with relish, "a Locusta for our age."

"I say: wasn't Locusta a woman?" asked Titus.

Merenda ignored them. "Why? Why were they slain?"

Antiochos shrugged. "I can tell you it was poison but as to why…"

"There's no difficulty as to why," said Quintus. "Decima Flavia witnessed her husband's death. She'd have named his killer."

Merenda rounded on Antiochos eagerly. "Yesterday, when you told us you were confident Decima Flavia would recover her memory, Publius Flavius was there, was he not?"

"Yes, I believe he was, but it was something I said freely to other people, fellow officers, anyone who enquired. Why shouldn't I?"

"Who heard Antiochos is hardly material," said Quintus. "You hardly need to be a doctor – or be well versed in Galen, for that matter – to know that people recover their memories after a knock on the head." He pointed to the bowls which Antiochos had placed on a table. "The poison was in those?" He picked up one, which still contained some congealed brown stuff and sniffed it, frowning.

Merenda peered cautiously into the remains. "Should we test it? On a dog perhaps?"

Antiochos was dubious. "If it's what I think it is, they say it has no effect on cattle or even on rabbits. On dogs...?" He shrugged, dipped a finger in and licked it. "Not sweet... could be from the leaf or perhaps the roots." He turned to Merenda. "You should instruct your people to bury it."

Merenda took the bowl and opened the door to his wife and Lucia waiting, anxious. "Husband!" "Father!" "You're ill?" "Can I fetch you wine?" They darted at him but he waved them back, told them not to fret and then asked them something in a low voice. Gaia Antonia, her face creased with anxiety, nodded and they exchanged whispers. He returned to the others.

"These are our bowls and we believe this to be the stew we ate last night. I've summoned our cook."

"None of you have suffered any...?" said Antiochos. Merenda shook his head. The cook arrived. Elderly and fat, he looked like a Spanish veteran of the cohort. He stood to attention. Merenda asked him whether he'd provided any food for the ladies Decima Flavia Fimbria and Vibia Rufia Atellus. He confirmed that he had, he believed that it was the food left in the bowl, and yes, it was the stew he'd served the tribune and his family the previous evening.

Quintus paced, his hands behind his back. "Tell us how you came to provide this meal."

The cook's eyes followed Quintus as he recounted how he'd as usual risen before dawn that morning to light the kitchen fire. "I'd only just got the logs to take from the kindling, when the senior centurion's wife – begging your pardon sir, widow – came and said the general's lady was awake and felt she might try some food, so could they have a little something? She said she'd been told I might have some mutton stew for them. It was in the pan so I put it on to warm and said I'd send a slave along with it, but she said, no, it'd only take a minute and she'd take it herself."

"What did you talk of while you waited?"

"In truth, very little, your honour. It was awkward for me, her husband, Appius Rufius having been... well... I didn't really know what I could say."

"This is very strange," said Titus. "How could... the poisoner have got at it?"

They discussed this. Had the murderer met Vibia Rufia on the way back from the kitchen and, without her noticing, administered the poison? Had there been a third person in the sick room?

"Who would they allow into their room at the crack of dawn?" asked Quintus.

"Not Publius Flavius," Manius said, and caught a glare from Merenda.

"Surely the murderer couldn't depend on poisoning their bowls unnoticed in such a small room," said Titus.

Quintus swivelled to face the cook again. "Can you recall exactly what Vibia Rufia said to you?"

The cook screwed his eyes shut and coaxed each word from his memory: "She said she'd heard, or... no, she'd been told that I'd some mutton stew for them."

"You hadn't sent word to anyone to that effect?"

"No."

"Had anyone told you this stew was to be for them?"

The cook shook his head.

"What was it to be used for?"

The cook glanced at Merenda. "In truth sir, I'd been saving it for myself."

"And it was left in a pan, in the kitchen all night?"

"Yessir."

"So anyone could have entered the kitchen during the night and put something in it?"

"I suppose, sir."

Nobody had further questions, so the cook was dismissed. As soon as the door closed behind him, Merenda appealed to Quintus. "What happened here?"

Quintus resumed his position, looking out of the window. The only sound was melting snow dripping from the roof of the portico. He spoke, over his shoulder. "Let's take this slowly. The murderer tells Vibia Rufia – when, where or how, we cannot know – that there's stew in the kitchen for Decima Flavia and herself: stew which he has already poisoned."

Manius made to speak, but aware of Merenda's hostility, stopped himself. Quintus rounded on him. "Yes? You were going to say something?"

"Well... just that... surely that would be dangerous. If only the cook had asked her, 'Who told you that?' we'd now know the murderer's identity, and, surely that would've been an obvious question?"

Titus, Merenda and Antiochos nodded. Quintus pursed his lips and stroked his beard. Titus spoke: "But perhaps the murderer wasn't as shrewd as young Manius here, and took the risk."

"A soldier had his throat slit last night. Who was it?" demanded Quintus.

"Oh, er… Bericus, a storeman. He'd been with the cohort many years, a steady, cheerful soldier. His body was found at first light, in a pigsty." He turned to his commander. "This has done nothing for the men's spirits. We now have more stupid talk of witchcraft and black magic."

"Who found him?" asked Quintus.

"A baker's slave."

"You saw the body? What was its condition?"

"Well… dead."

Quintus spoke through clenched teeth. "I mean, was it still warm?"

"No, but in this weather…"

"Was it stiff?"

"I… I don't know… No, I don't think so."

"So, not long dead. This storeman – Bericus – could be just the man for our murderer to send, to ask after Decima Flavia's health. Or, more likely after Vibia Rufia – he was a soldier, remember and she the wife of the senior centurion – and also to tell them of mutton stew waiting for them in the kitchen. It's unlikely Vibia Rufia would ask Bericus who'd sent him and even if she did, he was no doubt instructed on some pretext not to tell her. Immediately after he'd done this, the murderer kills him to cover his tracks."

There was silence while Quintus' listeners frowned at the floor. Someone coughed. Merenda spoke. "That's all conjecture."

"There is much conjecture in it," conceded Quintus.

"If I follow you, you're assuming that the murderer was an officer, with authority over Bericus?" asked Titus.

"And with intimate knowledge of what the praetorium's cook has in his pans," said Antiochos, his voice tinged with sarcasm.

Quintus snapped: "It would be no great thing for him to look into the kitchen and see what was there!"

"Let's be plain here, Quintus Suetonius," said Merenda, throwing his arms out in supplication. "If you're talking of an officer of the cohort, you're talking of Publius Flavius; are you not?"

Quintus shrugged. "Others could've persuaded Bericus to do their work without necessarily having authority over him. Certainly there's nothing that suggests Publius Flavius' innocence. Where was he this morning?"

"I commanded first watch," said Titus. "He relieved me with his centuries after four hours and he'd still have been commanding this morning."

"And it would've been easy for him to slip away."

"I shall discreetly question his officers."

"Do so," said Merenda.

"What about the hooded spirit? Epaticcu?" Manius asked.

"I hadn't forgotten that," said Quintus.

"I had," said Merenda, massaging his forehead.

"Are you saying one was found in the room?" asked Titus. "Are Wolves involved? By the Unconquered Sun that's a fearful thought. How could they be? Are you saying they're among us?"

"Let's not run ahead of ourselves," said Quintus, holding up a hand. "These figures aren't uncommon and it'd be an easy enough ploy for the killer to leave one as a diversion."

"You're saying it was put there to dupe us?" asked Merenda.

"I'm saying it could've been."

Merenda swore, banged his fist onto a table. He directed Antiochos to have the bodies removed from the Praetorium and told Titus to ask questions about Publius Flavius' movements. "Quintus Suetonius, I want to speak with you," he said, looked at Manius and added: "Alone."

§

Quintus stamped his feet and blew into his cupped hands. He waited with Antiochos, as they watched a couple of soldiers stoop to enter the pigsty.

He regarded the Greek with impatience: he was prattling about poisons and their effects. Quintus didn't want to hear about poisons, he wanted to think. He'd just left his meeting with Merenda and hadn't had time to digest that before he'd come across Tita Amatia, with whom he'd also held a hasty conference. Then he'd had to hurry off for this appointment.

Antiochos tugged his sleeve. "They're bringing it out. We can take a look."

Reluctant, he followed the Greek into sludge and mire of the pen as the soldiers emerged backwards, dragging a body.

The soldiers straightened and knuckled their foreheads.

"Wait over there,"Antiochos gestured towards the gate to the pen.

The soldiers shuffled off squelching and Quintus and Antiochos stepped forward.

"Not pretty, eh?" said the surgeon. "After the pigs have been at him?"

"I've seen worse."

He squatted for a closer look wincing as his knees creaked. "He was identified – how?"

"The top of his left ear is missing. That wasn't the pigs, it was an old wound, according to his comrades. Also here, on his arm, see – a tattoo in honour of Ceres."

"You said his throat was slit – how can you tell?"

"The pigs have gnawed it, but you'll see here, at the side, the beginning of a cut."

Quintus grunted. He contemplated the neck wound and the corpse's staring eyes. He levered himself up. "A miserable end. Better to have died fighting the barbarians."

Antiochos shrugged. "Death is death."

"You're very sanguine about it."

"I'm a doctor and I know you can't avoid death."

Quintus regarded him. He seemed to have lost his bounce. Was the siege getting to him too?

"Of course, I don't tell my patients that."

Before Quintus could reply, Antiochos added: "I could show you something else, if you've time."

"I've nothing pressing."

"Then come." Antiochos headed out of the pig pen, gesturing for Quintus to follow. They made their way to the Via Praetoria through the main gate and into the vicus. Quintus looked up at a sudden noise to see shadows scudding under the low leaden cloud above the east rampart as a flurry of arrows flew in. There were several cries and then shouts of command.

"We must hurry, I have new customers," said the surgeon.

He took Quintus to a building by the corner of the east and south walls. He pushed the door open to reveal a builder's store. Tiles were stacked against the far wall and beams of various dimensions piled in the centre. Quintus followed Antiochos to the far side of the beams and looked down on another male body stretched out. It was in shadow and hard to make out until the Greek opened a couple of shutters.

This corpse bore no obvious signs of violence and the eyes were closed. Quintus contemplated it.

"Why've you brought me here?" he asked at length.

Antiochos drew him by his sleeve. "Look here, at the neck, at that wound."

Quintus squinted at the puncture and the dark scabbing around it, then looked more closely at the face, taking the chin and turning it towards him.

"You know him?" asked Antiochos.

"I know he came from Sicily." He pointed at the neck. "Is this what did for him?"

"Yes, he'd have bled to death swiftly, in seconds."

Quintus looked around. "And yet no blood."

"As you say – no blood. And this is an earthen floor and bears the tracks of his boot heels. He was killed elsewhere and dragged here."

"The wound is tiny. What kind of knife? Something like an awl?"

"Perhaps. Or even a hairpin."

Quintus looked into Antiochos' impassive face. Was he thinking the same? Hairpin? A woman's work? One woman had spoken of revenge on this Sicilian. No! He and she had spoken hardly half an hour ago –

appraising each other of developments and she'd seemed normal enough. Ha, normal and Tita! Not words accustomed to each other. Would she have seemed any different if she'd killed the Sicilian?

Antiochos was speaking.

"What?"

"I must return to the hospital. On the way here I observed my capsarii carrying three men with arrow wounds. Those fools must leave the rampart."

Quintus nodded and the Greek hurried off. He was right: Merenda: couldn't hold the rampart or the vicus. He glanced at Tiro the Sicilian. "You had it easy," he reflected, easier than Gut Crispinus.

He followed the surgeon, but stopped by the mansio's entrance. He glanced around, then entered. He nodded to the steward – still loyally at his post – and climbed the stairs to the room he and Manius had occupied, his steps echoing in a building all but deserted. He left their door open and began throwing the few items they'd left behind into a bag. He tiptoed to the open door. There was no sound from below, other than a low, tuneless whistling from the steward. He crept along the landing to the room Aurelius Cotta and his wife had occupied.

He depressed the latch, then eased the door open, cursing under his breath as the hinges creaked. But there was no break in the steward's whistling, so he entered. There was little – an old brush, a shawl, a couple of towels and two riding cloaks. Clearly they'd also moved most of their gear into the fort. Quintus turned over these few things, feeling the seams of the garments, careful to refold them as he'd found them. He looked under the bed and in the cupboards. Nothing: no clue as to Cottas' character or activities. He'd have to search their quarters in the fort.

Quintus crept back to the landing. His hand was on the latch when he heard voices from the lobby. He opened the door, pivoted himself to the other side and pushed it, leaving a couple of inches ajar. He stood with his back to it, holding his breath, as footsteps ascended the stairs and then paused. Someone spoke: "No, my room." Quintus recognised Cotta's voice. He tiptoed to the centre of the room. If Cotta came in, it would be he who owed an explanation. But the footsteps moved along the landing, to Cotta's door, which Quintus heard open and close.

He gave it a few seconds and then stole back out and stooped to eavesdrop. He heard Cotta's voice, a low rumble, then another, higher, almost a squeak: "But how am I to do it? It's not safe." It was the tax collector Gracchus. "You're known and trusted and you'll have my guarantee," was Cotta's impatient response. "What explanation can I give Antonius Merenda? What shall I say to him." "Just go, damn you! I need you in Corstopitum!"

Quintus stiffened. There were footsteps on the stairs. He strode back to his room as the mansio steward approached. The steward looked at him, eyebrows raised. Quintus nodded and re-entered his room. He sat on his bed rubbing his forehead, thinking, until he heard two sets of footsteps outside. He moved to the door, opened it and inch and watched the backs of Cotta and Gracchus disappear into the lobby.

He darted across to the bedroom window, eased open the shutter and peered down to satisfy himself that they were heading towards the fort.

Five minutes later he followed them, his hood shielding his face to lessen the chances of being interrupted in his thoughts. Cotta and Gracchus: an unlikely pair. What were they up to?

He pondered it as he made his way to the praetorium. He hurried around two sides of the courtyard, his feet padding in the snow and halted at Tita Amatia's room, where he tapped on the door. She opened it.

"Oh, it's you."

"Who else? Isn't this what we agreed?"

"Yes. Well, come in – before all the warmth escapes."

She waited, impatient, while he kicked the snow from his boots in the threshold, then, as soon as he was in the room, closed the door behind him. He took off his cloak, shook it and, noting her glare at the snow it shed, mumbled and hung it on the back of the door. He rubbed his hands. He could feel the heat coming through the floor but was glad to see a fire in the grate. He stood facing her, warming his backside.

"A bad business," he said.

"Decima?"

"Aye."

They both looked down, in unspoken respect, reminiscence and sadness.

Tita Amatia broke the silence. "We must avenge her."

"Like Gut?"

"What does that mean?"

"He's dead – our Sicilian friend."

He observed her from under his eyebrows. She merely raised her own. "Really?" she said, nonchalant. Too nonchalant? "Tell me more."

He described what Antiochos had shown him. She sank onto a couch. "Interesting. What are we to make of that?"

He shrugged. "What are we to make of anything? Mysteries fly at us like the barbarians' arrows. We have Tiberius Flavia's death, his wife's, this Sicilian and now I find Cotta seems to be in league with that tax collector."

"What's that?"

He told her what he'd overheard.

"Why would Cotta want Gracchus in Corstopitum and what guarantee can he give him?" she said, half to herself.

"Where's Corstopitum?"

"Eh? Oh, it's a good-sized town, just short of the Wall."

"This sounds like they're in league with the rebels."

"It does. You found nothing in his room you say?"

"Nothing. And you were to search the Rufius Atellus quarters: how did you fare?"

Tita Amatia went to a small cupboard by her bed. She stooped to remove something. She turned and held out her hand, with a theatricality that irritated Quintus. "I too found nothing – apart from this."

She held one of the hooded spirit figures. Quintus eyed it.

"You don't seem impressed."

"I'm not. These things turn up too frequently. At first I thought they were to throw us off the scent. Now I wonder whether someone's taunting us."

"Cotta?"

"Possibly."

She seemed put out and was terse as she told him about her meeting with Gaia Antonia Merenda: what she'd told her about Cotta's possible connections to Priscus; her curiosity about Quintus' role in the North – Quintus gave a single barking laugh – and her concerns about Manius and her daughter, which made him to shake his head.

"Aye, I've had that from Merenda." He turned so that the fire was now warming his front. He did it to avoid meeting her eye. "Merenda's bound to abandon the vicus. I... er... I believe you should then get out, away from Longovicium."

"Why?"

"Tita! Why stay? If this fort falls to the barbarians..."

He swung round, expecting a familiar look of defiance in angry eyes. He was met by a placid gaze.

"You may be right."

"What?"

"I said you may be right. I'm not sure I can achieve anything here, but I might be able to do something outside, contact some of the tribal leaders, see if I can't put a stop to this madness."

"D'you think you can get out safely?"

"I've spent most of my life passing myself off as a Brigantine. I'll play the part of a cackling old crone and no one will trouble me."

"Aye, that should work." He detected a bridling. "What's wrong? Why're you looking like that?"

"Ever the gallant weren't you?"

"Eh?"

"Never mind."

§

Manius shivered. It was early afternoon but hardly light. The wind had blown in swollen, dark clouds, low and threatening. Nevertheless, Manius returned to his wanderings which had been interrupted barely an hour earlier. Even in that short time, it was evident – the gods alone knew how – that word of the latest slayings had spread. He felt the shock and gloom. Further murders – of the general's lady and the wife of a veteran centurion. Something was deeply wrong, something unnatural. There was much urgent talking between huddles of downcast men, which sank to muttering accompanied by sullen glances if Manius approached: a reminder of the readiness to blame frumentarii for the gods' displeasure.

Their fear was understandable. They were surrounded and outnumbered by barbarians and within their own defences was another enemy, able to strike at will and to take the lowliest storeman or the high-born general. Worse – the chief suspect was one of their own senior officers – a man they'd had no time to get to know, respect, or like.

Publius Flavius was strange, for sure. But capable of that? Manius remembered his display of temper at Eboracum and his fury at his brother's insults at the dinner. These, however, indicated a crime of violence. Not poison. Poison was a woman's weapon. Quintus had mentioned Locusta. But what woman? Manius ran through them – the concubine! Pellia. Could it have been her? She'd no reason to relish the idea of life with Decima Flavia alive. But was there any gain in killing her? Perhaps, if she really believed Tiberius Flavius had freed her in his will, then she could expedite that by getting his widow out of the way, a widow who might challenge that clause in the courts and who could employ lawyers and wield influence far beyond anything a slave whore could match. Pellia could gain access to the kitchen. Hadn't she been helping Birca to serve food the previous day?

So Manius' thoughts ran, as, head down, he paced the streets of the vicus. He didn't notice the figure before him until they almost collided. He apologised and looked up at Publius Flavius, who looked haggard and wild-eyed.

"Manius Suetonius," he whispered. "Is it true: about Decima Flavia and the British woman?"

Manius nodded and said poison was suspected. A spasm crossed Publius Flavius' features and he looked up to the heavens. He gripped Manius by the shoulder. "I didn't do it. Believe me, I didn't do it, couldn't do it. To kill two women like that: that's base… depraved. I do have honour and I can't have that thought of me. Tell Quintus Suetonius." He held Manius' shoulder and his eyes bored into his and then, as if recollecting himself, he released him and looked beyond and behind him and walked on past.

He was a strange man. Quintus had said he was a good actor. That good? He looked so incongruous, as he disappeared around the corner, so implausible in centurion's uniform. Manius remembered how he'd seemed so keen to learn the soldier's profession and studied his Frontinus and his Pliny.

Manius' mind wandered, from the eldest Pliny to the younger, his nephew, and to a strange story of his that Quintus had recounted of the couple who'd committed suicide together because of the ulcers on the husband's private parts. Committed suicide together…

Suicide!

Wasn't it possible that Decima Flavia and Vibia Rufia had poisoned themselves? Why not? Both had just lost husbands; both could have been in despair and decided they couldn't live. They must have discussed that and reached the same conclusion. Vibia Rufia would've been able to obtain the necessary ingredients and to mix them. No problem then about placing it in the stew? No need for Quintus' elaborate theorising on the murder of a storeman? Hadn't he always said that the simple answer was almost always preferable to the more Daedalean?

Manius liked the prospect of embarrassing him by reminding him of that maxim. Or would he? Better to keep that to himself?

Manius hadn't decided when he saw Quintus hurrying towards their barrack block. They met at the door, entered together and, once inside, Quintus shivered and directed Manius to light the fire. As Manius coaxed a flame, he decided that he'd better describe his conversation with Publius Flavius, as it might've been witnessed.

"So, he denies it, does he? Ha, ha. That might not displease Antonius Merenda."

"How so?"

"Merenda lacks many of a good commander's qualities, not least decisiveness and intelligence. However, he has a certain cunning. It must've struck you that the death of Decima Flavia Fimbria, following that of her husband, is hardly likely to reflect well on him?"

"It had occurred."

"Good. Well, as I've said: before today, he thought the best story for his reputation would be that the general had been killed by his half-brother as a consequence of a family quarrel, something he couldn't have been expected to guard against, particularly as Publius Flavius' appointment wasn't his choice. What's changed, you ask? Simple. If it was Publius Flavius, how will Merenda explain allowing him to remain at large, free to poison the only witness and a member of the powerful Valerian clan, who, let me tell you, have long memories and cherish their grudges?"

"You mean that now he doesn't want Publius Flavius to have been the murderer?"

Quintus crouched, eased Manius away from the flames which had begun to lick around the log and held his hands towards them. He chuckled."He can't make his mind up. It's not a good choice either way."

Manius stared at the fire.

"Is that what he wanted to speak to you about? Why didn't he want me there?"

Quintus shot him a sidelong glance. "This is a personal dilemma for Antonius Merenda which he can't find easy to discuss with another and you're a stranger to him." Manius nodded. Quintus gave him another look and cleared his throat. "Yes, you're a stranger to him; he wants it to stay that way."

"What d'you mean?"

"He wants you to stay away from his daughter. He believes you have intentions and he doesn't want to see them pursued."

Manius stared. His face burned. He was prepared to blurt out a hot denial but realised that that could be converted into a promise to abide by Merenda's wish. Instead he blustered. "Outrageous!" "Insulting!" "Ridiculous!"

Quintus replied with asperity: "It is none of those things. It's admirable that he can think about his daughter's welfare at such a time. He has ambitions for her, as any father would, and would like to marry her off to some sprig of a senatorial family. The last thing he wants is you getting in the way."

"What did you say to him?"

"Say? I said I'd speak to you and convey his wishes."

"Is that all? You didn't argue for me?"

"Argue for you! What argument could I frame, you fool?'

Manius stormed out.

So often Manius had been exasperated by Quintus, had been embarrassed and irritated by him but never this – never had he been so furious with him. He felt raw, scourged. His hopes lay dashed and pitifully exposed as having been baseless. Fool! He wrung his hands and blinked back tears. What a cretin to hope! He must've been mad. He raged at Quintus. Rot him! The drunken old bastard had made no attempt to plead his case.

He roamed the fort and vicus, heedless of the snow that had started to fall. Surely Quintus could've made some sort of case for him. Had he no pride?

Should he go to Merenda to plead his own case? He gave a bitter laugh. What could he say? How could he present himself as a worthy match for his daughter? And with what patience would Merenda receive his miserable petition at a time when he faced disgrace and ruin?

He stormed through the streets, snarling at a group of soldiers who bellowed at him – "Step aside! Step aside there!" – as they rushed past, supporting a wounded comrade, deathly white, with an arrow's shaft sticking from his shoulder.

As Manius was passing through the porta praetoria back into the vicus he thought of a representation he could make to Antonius Merenda, an offer of something he might value: a suggestion of how the tribune might avoid disgrace and ruin. How might he regard Manius then?

Merenda could only avoid a charge of failing to protect Tiberius Flavius if the murderer had been his brother, but then he'd be open to an equally serious charge of failing to protect Decima Flavia. But what if Manius' theory was correct? What if Decima Flavia and Vibia Rufia had taken their own lives? Merenda couldn't be blamed for that.

Manius glanced up at the shouts from the ramparts and whistle of arrows. He paid little heed; he was too excited as he savoured his plan's elegance. Publius Flavius could remain as the general's killer, which would satisfy Merenda and would also suit Quintus and himself, by avoiding any possibility of frumentarii involvement and – a satisfying bounty – it would pay Publius Flavius back for that business with the German whore. Yes, Merenda would be grateful to anyone who could provide him with that solution.

As for the truth. Perhaps the women hadn't destroyed themselves and their deaths were also attributable to Publius Flavius. What of it? He could only be punished once.

The question was: should he approach Merenda himself? No, Merenda would regard anything he had to say as the pipsqueak prating of one anxious to ingratiate himself. Manius needed the support of someone else, someone older, with some status.

But not Quintus. No, he'd sneer at his scheme, if only because it wasn't his own, or, because he'd known Decima Flavia Fimbria he might demand justice for her. Or perhaps he would like Manius' theory and claim it himself. Quintus had just proved that he didn't hold Manius' interests dear. Very well, it was high time for him to look out for himself. He'd have to find help elsewhere. There was little choice. It would have to be Titus Caelius.

Manius was never to get the chance.

Chapter Twenty-One

Titus was pacing before the south gate, pounding his fist into his palm. Around him soldiers and officers hurried, shouting. All was urgent and purposeful, yet there was unease. As Manius drew near, an optio also approached Titus with some enquiry and Titus rounded on him with an oath and sent him scurrying. Manius was cautious.

"Titus?"

He swung round with the same look of fury, replaced by an unwilling, crooked smile.

Manius indicated the scuttling troops and asked what was happening.

"So, you've not heard the wonderful news?" Manius shook his head. Titus' eye blazed again. "Our commander, our glorious tribune, has ordered that we abandon the vicus."

"I see," Manius said, at a loss to know why this should upset Titus.

"He has also ordered that..." Titus took a deep breath "... that only those Britons who can and will fight for us will be allowed into the fort."

"So?"

"Manius, don't you see? That means no wives, no sweethearts, no wives-to-be and no – dammit all – no Birca."

"Why in heavens name?"

"The foo..." Titus mastered himself. "The tribune fears Wolves' spies among us. There are no wives and no citizens to abandon as no soldier can have a regularised marriage and I certainly cannot – and... well, I'll only say, some who struggle to take a decision, make up for it by making a stupid one and then insisting upon it. I shouldn't be speaking like this, but... it's just too bad!"

"Have you reasoned with him?"

"He threatened to have me cashiered if I didn't stop arguing." Titus closed his eye and shook his head. "Y'see, I'm worried about Birca. If the Brigantes know her as the lover of a Roman officer... even if they leave her alone, she'll starve, or freeze."

As if to confirm his fears the snow began to fall heavily again.

Titus looked at the sky and swore. There was a cry and Manius looked round to see a teenage girl he recognised as Birca's slave hurrying towards them.

"Sir, Caelius Metellus, please come quickly," she said, breathless.

"What now?"

"The soldiers want to search our house for food and fuel."

Titus' face paled, then flushed wine-red. "If this is Merenda's doing, I'll..."

He stormed back into the vicus, his cloak billowing. The girl ran after him and, after a second, Manius followed, to be on hand to prevent any rash act. A cashiered Titus couldn't approach Merenda on his behalf.

He caught up with them at the door of Birca's house, to find Birca and her slave begging Titus to release the throat of a terrified soldier. Manius ran up and shook him by the shoulder. "Titus, Titus," he implored, adding his entreaties to Birca's, who tugged at his other shoulder. He gave her a wild look, then threw the soldier – Manius recognised as one of the Samartians – to the ground, where he clutched at his neck with rasping coughs. A principalis ran over and kicked the same hapless fellow, lashed him with his cane and ordered him away.

This officer turned to Titus. "Caelius Metellus, sir, my apologies... this man – this half-witted son of a whore – is new to the cohort, didn't know that this house was that of your honour's lady. But I promise sir, he'll know in future, when I've had the skin flogged from his back – the stupid barbarian bastard."

Birca and Manius assured the principalis that no harm had been done and the whole unfortunate incident could remain under the rose. The officer readily and gratefully agreed and, with a final salute for the glowering Titus and a bow to Birca, he fled back into the whirl of bellowing, hurrying soldiery. Birca and Manius exchanged relieved glances.

Titus cursed, looked at Birca. "It shames me. I should be protecting you, not leaving you at the mercy of the barbarians?"

"Oh Titus," she whispered, and they embraced.

Manius turned away, embarrassed, hoping no soldier would see their senior officer exhibiting himself.

Birca rested her cheek against Titus' breast. "My love, you've no choice. You must obey. I'll come to no harm. I know my own people and I'll be safe in my own house."

She gave a brave laugh, took a step back and shook her fist and ample forearm at Titus. "You think they'll dare challenge me?" Titus smiled, his single eye glistening. He made to embrace her again but she held his hands and told him to be off about his duty. Manius felt tears sting his own eyes. He understood their passion. Wasn't he in love himself?

Titus wagged a finger. "Listen to me: lock yourself in and open the door to no one – no one, d'you hear? I swear I'll find some way to safeguard you."

He kissed her and, with a nod to Manius, adjusted his helmet and marched towards the rampart.

"Are you sure you'll be safe?" Manius asked her.

"As safe as in that fort."

"What d'you mean?"

"The evil eye is on it… all those deaths."

She regarded the great turrets that framed the fort's gate and shivered but then brightened and faced him. "You must have no worries for me; you look after yourself Manius Suetonius – and the lady Lucia." His own expression darkened and she looked at him with sudden shrewd curiosity. He told her about Merenda's ban.

She shook her head. "That man's causing so much unhappiness. Don't be too upset. Something will happen for the best, for all of us. I'm sure of it." He thanked her and, not trusting himself to say more without an unmanly betrayal of emotion, excused himself, saying he ought to report for duty, and he made for the ramparts.

These were held by half the cohort's centuries while the others were searching houses in the vicus seizing fuel and other provisions. The soldiers looked truculent and unhappy. Manius watched two driving a squealing pig towards the fort while a woman shrieked abuse and two infants clutched her legs and wailed. Dogs barked, men swore, officers shouted. The light was failing and a number of the soldiers held crackling torches which reddened the gathering gloom. Manius feared he was witnessing something so serious and awful that it would bring its own terrible punishment.

§

At the gate in the southern rampart Quintus stood with Tita Amatia. She was swaddled in a thick British coat, the hood up. Her horse was at her side, saddlebags strapped to it.

"You're confident in your arrangements?" asked Quintus.

"Gaia Antonia's girl Blathin has carried the necessary messages. There are friends waiting for me."

"Friends?"

"Those who remember my husband's name."

"What will you do once you're with them?"

"I told you: I shall use my connections and kinship to meet Brigantine elders and try to persuade them to end this rebellion before it destroys their people."

"Have you much chance?"

She shrugged. "I can't know until I try."

"You're sure you'll be safe?"

"Safer than here."

He opened his mouth, closed it, reached for her hand and stopped himself. She looked at him, curious. He turned, his eyes scanning a cavalry turma who stood by their mounts before the open gates.

"Where's Titus Caelius?" he muttered and approached the troop's decurion. "Where's your commander?"

"Caelius Metellus has been called away, your honour."

"The hell he has! He was under instructions from Antonius Merenda to oversee this lady's safe passage to the barbarian lines."

"I'm to see that the tribune's orders are carried out."

Quintus grunted and returned to Tita Amatia. "All is prepared it seems. Now where are your friends?"

"I do believe he's here."

Quintus peered. From the south, up the road, came a solitary figure riding a walking pony. A few barbarians stepped out of the shelter of the trees, to watch.

"You're sure?" asked Quintus. She nodded. He signaled to the decurion, who mounted his horse and commanded his men to do likewise. They remained stationary until the approaching figure halted fifty paces distant. Quintus squinted, trying to make out features.

"Is that...?"

"Return to the vicus, I'll be fine now."

She swung herself into the saddle. She looked down at Quintus. "Take care of yourself. After all these years I… it would be a shame if…" She gave up but leaned to squeeze his shoulder. Then she urged her horse forward and it trotted down the road towards her adopted people and away from the Romans.

§

Manius watched as a trumpet sounded and the men who'd been looting the vicus formed up in their contubernia and filed through the fort's porta praetoria and the centuries who had been holding the ramparts fell back behind them. Finally, the cavalry, which had been holding the land immediately outside the vicus' south gate, came trotting back through the settlement with a jingle of harness to bring up the rear.

The gates of the porta praetoria shut with a great crash. Then, from the other side of them, in the vicus, came the sound of women weeping. That faded, followed by a terrible, ominous silence. Manius observed the faces of the soldiers who stood close, glowing and fiery in the torchlight, and read in them guilt and foreboding.

Then the officers began bawling orders, dismissing certain centuries to their barracks and ordering others to the fort's ramparts.

Abandoning the vicus made the fort's defence easier. Instead of the earthen ramparts, they now sheltered behind formidable high stone walls, which required only part of the cohort to man and Manius counted just two centuries mounting to take those positions while the others returned to their barracks to eat and to rest.

He stood rooted, reviewing what he'd witnessed over the days and weeks. He made his reluctant way back to his own quarters. His anger with Quintus was still fresh and his absence had been too short for Quintus to miss him, but where else to go? He found Quintus moodily drinking ale, which he must've wheedled out of someone who couldn't provide wine. Manius grunted and sat on his bed.

After some awkward seconds Quintus spoke in a low growl, without looking up. "I hear they've abandoned the vicus at last?"

"Yes."

"Good thing. And overdue."

"Titus Caelius doesn't think so!" Manius spat, and told him how Birca had been abandoned along with the vicus.

Quintus sipped his ale, expressionless. "A harsh decision on Merenda's part," he said, after some seconds. "For Merenda, making decisions is so hard that he has to defend them to the end, however stupid."

"And however dangerous for Birca."

"You seem particularly upset by this, and yet it cannot affect you."

"I like Birca and I like Titus Caelius!"

"You've no need to be so defiant. They're both likeable. Comfort yourself: Birca isn't necessarily in so much danger. She's of these people and no doubt held in some affection."

Manius was neither mollified nor convinced and made this plain. Quintus shrugged and returned to his ale. There was renewed silence for some more minutes until Quintus spoke. "The death of Tiberius Flavius Fimbria and his wife has distracted us from discovering whether Flavius Fimbria or Caerellius Priscus had designs on the Empire."

"Who cares? Flavius Fimbria is dead. Surely that resolves it?"

"As I said: all this has distracted us, and it has certainly distracted you, although you may perhaps have had other matters on your mind." Quintus' voice quickened here, but he mastered himself. "It's surely obvious that if Tiberius Flavius Fimbria was innocent, then his death, far from rendering our task redundant, makes it more pressing."

"But we've always been agreed that if Publius Flavius killed his brother, it had no political implication."

"The killing itself may not, but the death does. Consider: if Tita Amatia is right and it's Caerellius Priscus who's disloyal, then Tiberius Flavius' murder removes the only serious hindrance to his ambitions, which leaves us with a problem – assuming we get out of this fort alive. Also, isn't the general's death convenient for the governor? Did he put Publius Flavius up to it? Was it more than a family quarrel?"

While Quintus spoke, he gazed into the fire, throwing the occasional sly glance at Manius, who wondered: was Quintus sharing his thoughts to appease him over Lucia? "Also," Quintus continued, with another crafty sidelong look, "what of Merenda? As your friend Titus has said: he killed once out of loyalty to one emperor and perhaps Caerellius Priscus persuaded him – as he tried to persuade us – that killing Tiberius Flavius Fimbria would be an act of loyalty to that emperor's son?"

Ah, Manius thought, so Quintus was coming to regard Titus' ideas as not so ridiculous. And, if there was something in Titus' view that

Merenda was implicated in the murder, then should it affect Manius' plan to approach Merenda with his suggestion that the women's deaths could have been joint suicide? Manius wished Quintus would leave him in peace to chew it over.

But Quintus went on. "And yet... this doesn't seem like Merenda. I sense that the killer takes risks and seizes chances as he finds them. How long could he have had to decide to poison stew in the tribune's kitchen, hoping to find someone to persuade Vibia Rufia that it was for her and the general's lady? Merenda would have been pondering that for a year."

But, Manius thought, not a problem if it was suicide.

Quintus drained his ale and tossed his goblet aside. "We need information from outside and there's a chance now. Tita Amatia has joined the barbarians.

"What? She has betrayed us?"

"No, you fool. She has gone – with Merenda's permission and my blessing – to see if she can talk sense into her people. Here's a thing: the man who came from the enemy lines to meet her – d'you know who it was?"

"How could I?"

"I'll swear it was that steward of hers from Cenares, I forget his name, even though the bastard had a knife at my throat."

"Bodvoc?"

"That was it."

"What's he doing here?"

"I don't know, but I swear she's up to something. Let's just hope she can send us intelligence – from Londinium or from the Brigantes."

But the next news of the Brigantes wasn't good. An optio called to tell Quintus that the tribune would appreciate his attendance on the walls. Quintus rose with a grunt and Manius, with rebellious resolve, rose to follow. Merenda had barred him from seeing his daughter – well he could endure seeing him face-to-face. Anyway, Manius calculated, as he followed Quintus into the falling snow, he hoped, sooner or later, to reach some accommodation with the cohort's commander, which would be hard if he was never in his presence.

The optio led them to a turret flanking the porta praetoria. They climbed the steep steps to the rampart. Manius put his hand to the wall's black stone for support but snatched it back as the cold nipped his fingers. On the rampart, lit by a torch burning in a wall bracket, they found Merenda, with Titus and Aurelius Cotta, The three were gazing out to the vicus. Merenda gave Manius that now familiar look of surprise and distaste and only addressed Quintus, nodding in the direction of the vicus and inviting him to listen. They heard the wind and from the dark distance came the drawn out howl of a wolf. Merenda raised his hand. "There!" he whispered urgently.

In the vicus, they heard low voices – British. Door latches were rattled and many footsteps padded through the snow approaching the fort.

"It's the enemy," said Merenda, "they've entered the vicus."

"Well, what did you expect?" asked Quintus.

"Are they moving in to attack us at first light from close against the walls? Should I have ordered the vicus burned d'you think? Should I order a sally now, to drive them off and allow us to destroy the place?"

Manius observed Titus behind him, his one eye rolling.

"It could be a ruse," said Quintus. "Perhaps they're hoping to provoke you to open the gates."

Merenda's eyes darted at him. "Yes, perhaps you're right. No, better not to."

Titus couldn't contain himself. "Look here, I believe we should…"

"We know what you believe!" cut in Merenda. "But I don't propose to imperil this fort and this cohort for your private interests."

Titus flushed angrily but said nothing. Merenda asked Aurelius Cotta's opinion. The British magistrate looked grave, pondering, before saying: "I'm no military man, but isn't it possible that the rebels are only seeking loot?"

"That makes sense," said Quintus. "I doubt there'll be any decisive action by the rebels tonight. Why don't we all retire to the praetorium to take wine and discuss this at our ease and return in an hour or so?"

"There's something in that," said Aurelius Cotta. "We can't…"

"Listen!" hissed Titus.

They craned forward. The footfalls were receding. There was a shout; some seconds later another shout and a laugh. The sounds were perceptibly more distant.

"They're leaving," said Merenda. "A scouting expedition, d'you think?"

They agreed that was probably the case, but also that a few handpicked men should be sent out to confirm that the enemy were not waiting in numbers to launch a dawn attack.

"I still wonder whether we should also have them torch the vicus," said Merenda.

"No!" said Titus.

"There's thick snow on the thatches," said Cotta. "It would be impossible."

They considered this, while the cold ate into their bones, until a dozen soldiers under an optio stood by the gates for their orders. The conclusion was not to burn the settlement. The soldiers were ordered accordingly and the great double portalled gates were opened with such great jangling and creaking that the patrol's subsequent caution in slipping silently out into the vicus struck Manius as absurd, particularly as the gates then slammed shut with a thunderous crash.

They watched the men disappear into the shadows and the settlement's narrow streets. Manius hugged himself and stamped his feet. Aurelius

Cotta cleared his throat. "Antonius Merenda, is our situation a good one, from a military point of view?"

Merenda, Titus and Quintus exchanged glances. Then it was Merenda who gave an embarrassed cough. "As you've told us: the local tribe has been joined by other Brigantes, including those beyond the frontier, so their numbers seem to grow daily and, while withdrawing to the fort has made our position easier, numbers must eventually tell." They each brooded on this before Merenda added: "But, we've food to last the winter. Remember: the rebels are making war in the wrong season and they cannot feed themselves out there for long. They also lack shelter and warmth. If we can hold out long enough, they must disperse."

Aurelius Cotta frowned and rubbed his chin, looking out at the vicus. "You've money in the fort?"

"Why, yes."

"Much?"

"Some hundreds of thousands of sesterces. We've seven hundred effectives in this cohort and we have the pay for their fourth stipendia which is more than two hundred thousand sesterces and we also hold the pay for the cohorts at Vindomora, Vinovia and Concangis. Why d'you ask?"

"Wouldn't it be a great victory for them to take this fort?"

"Of course."

"But wouldn't it be an even greater blow to Rome if they took the fort and destroyed its garrison?" Cotta's voice grew eager. "What I suggest is a political solution, a compromise which would represent a defeat for Rome, but not the worst defeat and it would be one from which we could recover. Bargain with the rebels."

"Bargain?"

"Yes, you have much to offer. They're exposed in a terrible winter and have thousands to feed. You can let them have grain, you can bargain with great treasure and you can offer them this fort itself. With all of that, you must be able to negotiate safe conduct for the cohort to the next fort. You'll have sustained a defeat, but it'll be a defeat you could avenge in spring. D'you see?"

No one spoke. Then Titus erupted. "That's outrageous!" The soldiers stationed along the rampart stared and he dropped his voice to a fervent whisper. "Look here, you cannot be serious. To bribe Rome's enemies with the pay of her soldiers and to give up the fort we're here to defend. Can you imagine the dishonour for this cohort? We'd have a mutiny if we even thought about it, may the gods be my witnesses."

Merenda shook his head. "Titus Caelius is right. I'd be taken back to Rome in chains if I even contemplated what you suggest."

Aurelius Cotta shrugged as if it was of no concern to him either way. Titus grumbled his continued disapproval and Merenda looked downcast and wearied. They stood in uneasy silence for half-an-hour until the patrol passed back through the gate, its leader mounted the rampart and reported that, apart from a few of the vicus inhabitants – mainly the old and infirm cowering in their homes – the settlement was deserted. At this, Merenda declared there was no more they could achieve that night and dismissed them, and so they descended, overhearing Titus heated whispering to his commander about the monstrousness of Aurelius Cotta's suggestion.

Quintus and Manius drew their ration of biscuit and returned to their quarters. They ate in silence. Manius was too troubled by Merenda's appraisal of their situation and irritated by the speed with which Aurelius Cotta's suggestion had been dismissed.

Quintus belched. "There must be some officer in this cohort who has wine to share with one who can bring news of home and memories of lands where the sun shines and where the gods confine snow to the mountains. That little Greek must have a store for medical purposes. I'll go talk to him of philosophy. The Greeks like that."

He went, leaving Manius to undress and climb into bed where he could be warm. What a day! In this one brief period of northern winter sunlight, he'd experienced so much. My gods, if he continued to live at this rate he'd have his life's span, even if the barbarians did soon overrun them and cut off his head.

He extinguished the lamp and, with his cubicle lit only by the dying embers of the fire, closed his eyes. But he couldn't sleep. Thoughts jostled for attention. He lay, as the fire's embers turned to ash and the sounds outside faded to the odd footstep, the occasional command and then to silence. Still no sleep.

Hell! He'd have to rise and go for a walk, until his mind could be more at peace.

He'd just found his cloak in the darkness, when he heard something outside – soft footsteps. Quintus returning? No, never, he'd have been blundering through the snow, with no concern about waking him. A wild idea struck to him. Could it be Lucia? The notion was insane. And yet…

There was a tap at the door. His heart thumped and his stomach fluttered. He smoothed down his hair and unlatched the door – to Titus.

"Titus? What…?"

Titus put a finger to his lips, gently pushed Manius back into the room, whispering: "You're alone?"

"Yes… yes, I…"

"I thought so. I saw Quintus Suetonius leave."

He closed the door. Manius fumbled and relit a lamp, which he held between them, so that it cast a globe of flickering yellow light which encompassed both their faces. Titus was tense and controlled. Manius opened his mouth but Titus held his hand up. "There's no time to talk here," he whispered. "Take your sword. Here strap it on; come with me. I've a proposition to put to you, a favour to ask."

Manius took the belt and began fastening it around his waist. "I... I, yes, of course, but I should leave a note for Quintus..."

"No, the fewer who know about this the better. Here ...' he bent and scrabbled on the floor "... take these clothes, this bag and stuff them under your blankets like so. He won't stoop to kiss you good night, I take it?"

Manius grinned. "That's unlikely."

Titus squeezed his shoulder and ushered him out of the barrack block and into the night.

Chapter Twenty-Two

Titus led Manius through freshly falling snow, to the gate turret by which they'd stood earlier. They entered a room with bare stone walls, in which shields, javelins and other equipment were stacked. A stairway climbed, hugging two walls, to disappear into the floor above. A pair of lamps burned.

"We're alone," said Titus. "I've ensured there are no sentries for fifty paces either side of us."

"Why? What're you planning?"

Titus gripped Manius' forearm. "It's Birca: I can't leave her in the vicus. I have to bring her within the fort."

"But... that's against the senior tribune's orders. You'll be cashiered; disgraced."

"I'll risk that; I have to."

Manius shook his head. This was madness.

"Manius, I know places in this fort where I can hide Birca and the men love me enough to look the other way when necessary."

"But how will you get her in without being discovered? You can't open the gates – that'd be heard in Londinium."

Titus smiled, for the first time that evening. "There, my friend is where you have a part to play, if you'll help."

"How?"

"Follow me."

They mounted the stairs to a similar room with a door leading to the rampart. It too was lit by lamps and in the wall on the vicus side was a shuttered window. The room contained a rough table and a few chairs and there was a hearth in the corner. Manius guessed it was a room for the sentries.

Titus strode to one corner and took up a coil of stout rope which he dropped thudding onto the table. "We'll secure this to that shelf bracket. D'you see? Test it. It's sound, isn't it? Capital. You'll lower me from that window into the vicus and haul the rope up. I'll get Birca. I'll be no more than ten minutes, fifteen at most. Leave the shutters ajar and when you hear a low whistle – like this – lower the rope again and pull me up. Don't worry, the bracket'll hold and I'll be climbing, walking up the wall. D'you see?"

"What of Birca?"

"She can't climb, but the two of us can pull her up."

Manius eyed the rope. Birca was a big woman. And the window was narrow.

"Well, Manius, will you do it? Will you help me?"

Manius swallowed. "Of course."

"Good man! I knew you would. Now, to work."

Titus secured the rope to the heavy iron bracket which supported a long shelf on the opposite wall and which bore the weight of many helmets and other pieces of armour. Titus threw open the shutters, letting in the icy night air. He leaned out of the window looking right and left and below and then fed the rope out. Manius watched it snake away into the darkness. It stopped. Titus turned and whispered: "Now my friend."

He threw a leg over the sill and gripped the rope in both hands, waited until Manius had also grasped it and the bracket was supporting the slack, then gave him a nod, and began to lower himself. Manius planted his feet against the wall and leaned back, taking the strain, until Manius heard Titus drop with a soft thump into the snow. The pain in Manius' forearms eased and he felt the rope jump as Titus shook it as a signal. Manius hurried to reel it in before it could be spotted by a sentry. The situation was fraught with danger. What if some centurion questioned Titus' orders to leave the gate turrets unmanned? What if Quintus discovered his absence and came searching? What story could he concoct to explain his presence here? The best cover he could come up with was sleepwalking.

Oh merciful gods, how had he got into this? He was alone, cold, in a dark cell, in a barbarian land where sun was rare and nights long, where an unknown murderer struck at will, in a place under a black magic curse, where sleepwalking and other terrifying phenomena of the night seemed more than plausible.

These thoughts churned his mind and set his nerves on edge. Then he heard the door opening in the room beneath. Oh shit! Who was it? The guards? Quintus? The murderer? Had Publius Flavius utterly lost his reason and come searching more blood?

"Heaven have mercy," Manius whispered.

He drew his sword. His scalp crawled, as he heard slow, soft footsteps climbing the staircase. He gripped his weapon and readied himself. A head appeared, arising into the room, vague in the shadows, shoulders followed. He made out long, black hair. Lucia!

She was holding a lamp and her other hand clasped a thick cloak tight around her throat.

"Who's there?" Her voice trembled

Manius stepped from the shadows.

"Manius."

"Lucia, what are you doing here?"

"Where's Titus? I saw you both leaving your quarters and I followed. I've a message for him. Where is he?"

"I... we... he is... he's inspecting the ramparts." He waved towards the door.

"Surely he won't be long? I'll wait."

Manius stared. He had to get rid of her before Titus' return.

"Lucia, you can't have come alone, not with an assassin on the loose?"

"Numeria, my slave, is keeping watch downstairs."

Manius closed his eyes. Blood and thunder! Two witnesses to Titus' mad project. "Even so, I think your father wouldn't be pleased."

She said nothing. Was she thinking of her father's ban on them. Hell! If he could've seen them then!

She pouted. "Father can be severe, but it never lasts, not with me. Mother and I can always persuade him to reconsider – and to relent."

Could she mean... could she possibly mean that she'd persuade her father to reconsider him? He had that fluttering in his stomach again. He sheathed his sword and smiled.

"Really?"

"Oh yes, that's what I came to tell poor Titus: that we're in league, mother and I, to persuade father to relent and allow Birca into the fort."

Manius' smile died. Not only were Titus and Birca – not him – the objects of her soliciting, but Titus was risking his career, his life and Manius' well-being on a mad undertaking which might prove unnecessary. And if she did persuade her father to admit Birca, could Titus then tell Merenda that his generosity was appreciated but not required, as he'd already defied him and brought his mistress over the wall?

Manius ran a hand through his hair. "You and your mother are both very good but you mustn't risk your father's displeasure. Let me give the message to Titus, or, if you must tell him yourself, let it wait until morning."

And when Titus returned – with or without Birca – Manius would present him with the situation, return to his bed and let him devise his own tactics. This was his mess.

She placed a fingertip on her lower lip and looked thoughtful. "You're right, I came on impulse. I couldn't sleep, took Numeria and went to the temple to pray and was returning when I saw you and Titus, looking secretive. I wondered what you were up to so I followed to find out and give Titus the good news." She cocked her head. "So, what are you up to?"

He groaned inwardly. Merciful Jove, spare us. He combed both hands through his hair again, cleared his throat, and looked grave. "We're engaged on secret, frumentarius work. Lucia, it's dangerous and secret and... er... very serious."

"Oh, that sounds frightening. Aren't you scared? You don't look scared – except your hair's all on end." She pointed and giggled. He reddened and clawed at his scalp.

"And it's very scary up here, in the cold and dark," she said, and set his heart racing again by pulling out a chair and sitting.

"It makes me think of ghosts. Do you believe in ghosts?"

"What? Yes… no… I don't know. Lucia, you must go."

"I heard the most terrifying ghost story – a true one. I'll tell it, then I'll go."

"Lucia, please. If one of the officers of the guard should come and discover you he'll report it to your father, who'll be furious with you – and me. I implore you."

"Just this one story, then I'll go. I've been dying to tell it."

He heaved a sigh. To argue only meant more delay. He made her promise that once she'd told her ghost story she'd return to the praetorium. Lucia leaned over the table and adopted a dramatic whisper. "Once, in Athens there was a large villa with a fearful reputation..."Lucia's black eyes were unblinking at the terrors of the well-worn story. Her tale wound on with its narrative of the clanking of chains and a spectre, until she interrupted herself.

"Manius are you listening? Why do you keep looking at the window?"

He apologised and bade her go on.

She gave him a sharp look before continuing for some minutes. Finally, she concluded: "And what do you think happened then?"

"Nothing."

"What?"

"Nothing happened. The house wasn't haunted any more."

"You've heard the story?"

"No, in truth, I just guessed."

Lucia looked both impressed and suspicious. "You're right, you're very clever, but don't you think that a most interesting story?"

"Yes, yes, it truly is. You told it well. You ought to set it in verse. Now, Lucia, please – you really must leave."

She pouted and pushed back her chair. "Very well, but you seem anxious to be rid of me."

"No!"

She smiled. "I shall leave you. Give Titus Caelius my message and reflect Manius Suetonius that my father can be persuaded on most points." She rose; turned to leave and there was a whistle from outside. "What's that?"

"Lucia, you must go."

"But someone whistled. There it is again."

"Please go."

"Why?"

Manius pleaded. "Because you'll get me into trouble."

She said softly: "We cannot allow that." And then she left the room.

Manius exhaled noisily, shook himself like a wet dog and rushed to the window, where he began paying out the rope. He felt it taken from him and grow taut and, once more he gripped it and planted his feet against the wall as Titus came hauling himself up and grasped the sill and Manius took his forearms and pulled him in. Titus was alone. There no sign of Birca. Before Manius could ask why, there was a voice behind him. "What is happening? What are you both doing?"

Manius spun round. "Lucia! You promised!"

"I did nothing of the kind. Why Titus, what's the matter?"

Manius turned to see Titus, now sitting under the window, his face ashen and a tear coursing down his cheek.

§

Quintus swirled the wine in his goblet and eyed it. It was poor, though he'd had worse. But was it too poor to justify the company he was enduring for it? For Ambrosius Crassipes was a dull dog.

Quintus had met him as the centurion had been returning to his quarters from the latrines and had larded small talk with heavy hints until Crassipes had invited him back to share a jar.

He had a centurion's suite of three rooms at the end of a barrack block. They sat in the anteroom to Crassipes' bed chamber. Embers still glowed in the hearth.

"You're from Samnium y'say? When were you last there?" asked Quintus.

"A brief visit, years ago, when we transferred from Egypt."

Then Crassipes grew morose and gazed into the hearth. Quintus sighed: this fellow was hard work.

"Tell me..." Quintus leaned forward. Conversation at last. "You've been on a number of campaigns?" Quintus nodded. "Have you been in a fort that was taken?"

"If I had, I wouldn't be here to tell you about it."

Crassipes nodded gloomily and resumed his contemplation of the embers.

"It worries you?" Quintus pressed him. "The prospect of the barbarians overrunning the fort?"

Crassipes squirmed. "If I said it did, I'd be accounted a coward, would I not?"

"Not by me, no. If you said it didn't, I'd just think you a liar. I'll wager what worries you most is how you'll behave; whether you'll face death like a Roman."

"You're a mind-reader."

"I just read my own mind."

Crassipes looked back at the hearth. "That lady – Tita Amatia Aculeo – they say she knows the barbarian chiefs and has gone to treat with them. An extraordinary task for a woman. Is it true?"

"These are matters for the tribune only. I cannot discuss them."

Crassipes turned to him, eager. "Surely you can tell me whether there's cause for hope?"

Quintus frowned. So, he is a coward. "I'm sorry, I can tell you nothing."

The centurion half turned away, annoyed. Quintus made a number of attempts at conversation: about Samnium or Egypt, but Crassipes returned only grunts or shrugs and then gave a theatrical yawn and rubbed his eyes. Quintus resorted to his own play-acting, draining his goblet with much sighing and lip-smacking. He fixed his eyes on the second, unopened jar by Crassipes' feet. He was buggered if he was leaving until that had been broached.

§

Titus sank his head into his hands and groaned. Manius eyed the door through to the ramparts, fearful it might be overheard.

Then Lucia was at Manius' side. "Is it Birca? Is something the matter with Birca?"

Titus removed his hands and glared at her. "Birca… is dead!"

Manius felt a thud in his chest. He exchanged a horrified glance with Lucia and saw tears start into her eyes. She gave a little cry. "Titus, no! What happened? Please tell us what happened."

Titus rubbed his brow with a shuddering sigh. "I went to her house; the door was unlocked; I … found her there… on the floor… stabbed… dead!" He groaned, put his head into his hands once more and repeated: "Dead." A sob. "The barbarians found her and killed her. They hunted her down as the lover of a Roman officer." He beat his fist into his palm. "I knew it! I knew they would!" He looked again at Lucia with anger. "Your father should have let her in!"

Lucia began to weep. Manius looked from one to the other, helpless. He could only hang his head, feeling useless and sick, fervent for this to be over.

Lucia said: "Titus, I'm so sorry…"

"I wanted to bring her back, couldn't bear the thought of her body being left there to those savages. I wrapped her and made her decent and tried to bring her back, but I couldn't… not on my own."

"No!" cried Lucia. "That can't be allowed. I'll tell father; he'll send soldiers to bring her back. I'm sure he will. I'll make him."

Titus looked at her but Manius couldn't read his expression. Was it surprise? Hope? Both? Manius' own reaction was horror. He saw the full awful consequences of what she proposed. Her father discovering that she'd been wandering the fort at night and had been with him; that Titus had been defying his orders and Manius, a frumentarius, had been aiding him. Then he pictured the wrath of Quintus.

"No, Lucia," he said. "Don't do that."

She rounded on him. "Birca can't be left there. It's indecent."

Titus emitted another groan and sank his head back into his hands. A sound distracted them. Lucia's slave Numeria, appeared at the top of the stairs. "Mistress, how long will you be?" Lucia snapped at her to return to her post and wait until she was told otherwise. In the pause that followed, Manius made his decision.

"I'll come with you Titus. I'll help you."

What was possessing him?

Titus stared. "Manius, I can't ask it of you? Are you sure?"

"I'll help you."

Titus regarded Manius and then lunged and embraced him. Lucia started sobbing again. Manius was miserable, feeling controlled by the Fates. Titus held him at arm's length and his eye burning bright again. His voice thick with fervour and barely above a whisper, he said: "You truly are a good and loyal friend." Manius, feared he, himself, was about to start sobbing with Lucia, but Titus collected himself. He released Manius and got to his feet.

"We can do it. We can do it together, you and I, Manius. But we'll not bring her back over the wall. That would be madness to try and… " he glanced at Lucia "… and the senior tribune hasn't authorised it. I'd risk his anger for myself but I cannot do so for the two of you."

"What are you proposing?"

"We won't bring her over the wall. We'll take her to the cemetery."

"The cemetery!" said Lucia. "That's outside the vicus; it has to be, it's the law."

"Only by about a hundred paces."

Manius stared. A hundred paces! Heaven and hell combined! Not only was he to leave the safety of the fort for the perils of the vicus, in which Birca had been murdered within the last few hours, but he was also to venture beyond the vicus ramparts a hundred paces towards the lines of the barbarian horde. He squirmed in terror and cursed his stupidity.

Titus continued, excited and gesturing. "And we won't even have to dig a grave. They're already there for Tiberius Flavius and Appius Rufius before their funerals were postponed. We can put my beloved in and cover her in earth and snow and give her proper burial when this siege is over."

Aye, Manius thought, if we're still alive.

"We'll need tools."

Titus bit his lower lip, frowning.

"You're right Manius. I'm heartily glad I have you with me, but there are spades and a pickaxe downstairs."

He strode to the staircase and went clattering down. Manius marvelled at how the prospect of action and danger seemed to have dragged him back from despair. Manius wished that he could share some of that courage. But then told himself: this is all madness.

He shared his doubt with Lucia. "This is unwise."

Her reply was matter-of-fact: "He's mad with grief." She was gazing into space, somewhere over Manius' shoulder and then her eyes focused on his.

"You truly are very brave to go with him."

Manius thought: if I come through this alive, then perhaps it'll be worth it.

Titus reappeared, taking the stairs in twos, with spades and a pickaxe under one arm. He repeated the instructions to Lucia that he'd given Manius earlier in the evening and reassured her she'd have no need to pull them up on their return as they knew the bracket to be strong enough. Her only duties were to pull the rope up after them and lower it at his whistle. "And if a sentry comes?" she asked.

"There's no chance of that. They've had their orders and – believe me – they know I'm in no mood to be disobeyed."

She nodded, meek and thoughtful, and she looked at Manius and touched his hand. His heart thumped as they went through the window.

They dropped into the snow, crouching until they saw the rope go wriggling back up the wall, giving a final waggling farewell flourish as it disappeared through the window.

They waited. All was quiet. Further along the parapet was the silhouette of a sentry, who turned and continued his patrol. Titus tapped Manius on the shoulder and they ran, their boots making a light crunching, to reach the shadows of the nearest house. At Titus' whispered instruction they waited, crouching. They heard nothing, save the half-hearted barking of a dog somewhere in the vicus and the faint challenge and response between a pair of sentries on the ramparts. There was almost a full moon and, despite some cloud, there was enough light to see by.

They crept around the corner of that building, entered an alleyway and padded to its end, where they waited again. Still no noise: either those few inhabitants who'd remained in the vicus had abandoned it or they were lying low. The silence worsened Manius' nerves. Were there barbarians roaming the vicus, looking for plunder? Were Birca's murderers still at large and were they going to meet them when they rounded the next corner? Another dog barked but it was closer and louder. Manius jumped and Titus shot him an enquiring glance, then signalled that they should move on.

They darted across the next street, hugged the buildings on one side for another twenty paces and then stopped at Birca's timber cottage. The door was ajar and Titus eased it open.

Manius peered into the shadows. He made out a table in the centre of the room and a few more sticks of furniture and then, half under the table, a long shape, wrapped in something like a blanket.

He pointed. "Is that...?"

Titus nodded and gave a sudden loud sob, his head down, leaning against the door jamb for support. Manius gaped, aghast at the noise. Not now, not here! Manius shook him by the shoulder. "Titus," he whispered.

"Please, collect yourself, you'll be overheard."

Titus sniffed and blinked. "Forgive me."

Before his grief could return Manius prompted him: "Shall we carry her?"

Titus wiped his hand across his face and contemplated the figure lying in the shadows across the threshold. "No, it's too far and she is too... heavy. Here, this is what we'll do." And he hefted his pickaxe, turned to the door frame and began attacking the hinges.

Again Manius was horrified at the noise and tried to restrain him, protesting. Titus ignored him and dealt a great blow to the frame, then swore and muttered a quick prayer to the spirits of the hinges and to Father Janus. This worked, for the top hinge gave way, leaving the door hanging and swaying, supported only by the bottom hinge. A couple of strokes detached that from the frame and Manius sprang forward to catch the door before it crashed to the ground.

"Titus, what purpose?"

"You'll see. Wait here. Give me some moments alone with her."

He took the door from Manius and carried it into the house. Manius feared that grief and shock had robbed him of all reason. Now he was stuck in the vicus with a madman. Manius peered after him but could only make out that he was bending over the body and had laid the door to one side of it. Manius looked away, into the vicus, watching the shadows for any movement and straining for any sound above the scrapings and rustlings coming from within the sinister gloom of that house. The dog barked again, causing him to jump and bite his tongue. He shivered and prayed. What was he doing in there?

"Titus," he breathed, "what're you doing?"

He received only a snarling reply, heard more strange sounds, a grunt, then a sigh. Silence.

"Titus?"

"Yes, yes, I'm ready, come here. Help me."

Manius cast a last quick glance up and down the street and entered. He approached Titus, who was standing over Birca's body.

"I've bound her to the door. We can pull her using these."

He handed Manius a piece of harness, which was attached to other straps which bound Birca's shrouded body to the door. "We'll pull her. The door will be a sledge."

Manius' brief admiration for his ingenuity gave way to anger and despair as they manhandled that sledge and its burden out of the house, grunting, swearing and gasping and making enough noise to alert every barbarian in Britannia. Once on the street and on the snow, it became easier. This makeshift sledge had no runners but they achieved some momentum sliding it over the beaten and icy surface, though Manius cursed its awful scraping. They pulled Birca to the end of her street, where they paused for breath and precautionary looks around, before turning west. They soon reached the earth rampart and then spent several gruelling minutes hauling Birca onto the top before releasing her for an ignominious slide down the other side.

They sat on the rampart, watching over the sledge while they fought to regain breath. Then they followed Birca's body onto the plain beyond. Manius could just make out the cemetery and its snow-covered gravestones some hundred paces distant. These, however, were to be the most tortuous of all. Outside the vicus, the untrampled snow was thick and light and the door had to be dragged through it. Soon Manius' arms and shoulders were wracked by an agonizing ache, he was sobbing for breath and his undershirt was drenched with sweat despite the cold. Even so any elation Manius felt, once they finally reached the entrance in the cemetery's low wall, was short-lived.

He'd just moved himself a hundred paces closer to the Brigantine lines. True, the forest was the same distance away and there were no signs of any enemy in the white plain surrounding the cemetery. But he was uneasy in this place of death, with its cold, snow-shrouded stones surrounding him and in a silence so complete as to be almost overpowering. Lucia had told her story badly, but he wished she hadn't told it at all as he looked about, fearful of seeing, flitting towards him, the ghosts of all these black and pitiless dead. He looked at the Moon, scudding between clouds, and shuddered as he remembered when the witches had attempted to steal it, to suck it down from the sky. He'd been cursed ever since then. What if witches should attempt it again now? May the gods forfend. It didn't cheer him to observe that Titus was wide-eyed and agitated.

"Let's find one of these graves," said Manius.

Happily, Titus knew they'd been begun near the entrance and abandoned when the siege had got under way. The excavated earth had been piled into two snow-covered humps. A few minutes of scraping uncovered one of the graves.

"We must deepen it," said Titus.

The earth was like iron and had to be attacked with the pickaxe before it would yield to the spade. Titus worked with wild-eyed frenzy and again Manius was terrified at the noise, but said nothing, suspecting he was seeking to scare away the ghosts or was challenging Birca's killers. Manius tried to comfort himself, reasoning that any barbarians who heard them would never suspect a midnight burial but would be more likely assume the presence of spirits and stay away.

Titus' zeal meant that it wasn't long before they'd excavated about three feet, enough, he judged, to take the body. He unstrapped Birca and bent over her and – as Manius shuddered – kissed her bloodied shroud. Then he put his hands under the door and, veins swelling in his forehead, lifted it so that she rolled into the grave with a dull thump.

Titus remained gazing at her for half a minute while Manius waited, eager, poised with snow and earth ready on his spade. At last, Titus sighed and looked away, and, Manius pitched his spade-load over the body and set to bury her and get back to the fort. Titus joined him and soon they'd filled the grave and piled the excavated earth on top. Titus gave it a dubious look as they patted it down with the backs of their spades.

"I say, d'you think it deep enough? I couldn't bear it if foxes or wolves got at her."

Fond as Manius had been of Birca, he couldn't bring himself to care. He felt he'd done enough and that there was a chance of regaining the fort and his bed if they lost no more time. Anyway, he asked himself, with irritation, why should dismemberment by wolves or foxes be worse than consumption by worms? To Titus, he only said he was sure Birca's body would be secure and that scavengers were unlikely to come foraging between two armies and, even if they did, would soon find plenty of carrion above ground. Titus gave him a black look before shouldering his tools to set off back across the snow to the vicus, leaving Manius to follow.

Without that sledge they made it to the earthen rampart within a minute and Manius' spirits rose. Once in the vicus, they moved more slowly, careful now not to alert the sentries on the fort's looming walls. They stole through the streets, again hugging the shadows. They passed the open door of a wine shop and Manius placed a hand on Titus' shoulder.

"What is it?" hissed Titus.

"May I have a moment to look in here?"

Titus shrugged his assent and Manius entered. Inside it was dark but it was obvious that the place had already been looted. Manius poked about with little hope and was on the point of leaving when he spied something on a shelf. He pulled it down – it was a wineskin, either missed by looters or rejected as being inferior to what was in jars.

"For Quintus," he whispered to Titus, who'd come to the doorway. Manius slung it over his shoulder. "I'll tell him you donated it."

Titus gave a tight smile. They moved on and rounded the corner into the last street before the porta praetoria and their turret.

There, facing them stood four men, with long British swords in their hands and on their heads wolf masks.

§

Quintus shivered as he stepped out of Ambrosius Crassipes' quarters and closed the door. He raised the unopened jar of wine, kissed it and chuckled, a trophy from the yawning centurion who'd realised that he had to buy off his unwelcome guest if he was to regain his bed.

Heartened by this, Quintus felt an uncharacteristic benevolence. But who could benefit? Crassipes had retired and the rest of the fort's inhabitants – apart from those sentries tramping the ramparts – were also, presumably, asleep.

The boy! Aye, young Manius. He'd been down-in-the-mouth with that business over Merenda's girl. He wanted cheering. He'd wake him and treat him to wine – well, a swallow or two.

Quintus made his way carefully, cursing a couple of times when he slipped and nearly fell. Other than that, the scraping of his boots on the ice was the only sound until he gave a short barking laugh at the recollection of Crassipes' anxious probing on their military situation. What kind of bloody centurion was he to ask questions like that? He should know; battles and sieges were a game of dice where everything was staked and if you lost, you lost all. This was only just dawning on Crassipes and probably the rest of the cohort. Egypt was a notoriously soft posting and didn't involve much real soldiering. Thank the gods Tita had got out. Where was she now? Safe and warm somewhere, to be hoped.

He entered their quarters to find the fire had died in the grate. He passed through Manius' chamber and into his own where a lamp still guttered, took it, returned to Manius' room and held it aloft. He regarded the figure curled up under the blankets. Sleeping. No matter, he'd soon get back to sleep after a taste of wine. Quintus shook the figure, gentle at first and then with fury as he discovered and scattered rolled up socks and tunics.

"By the Unconquered Sun! What the fuck is this?"

He looked into the shadows, as though they might hold the answer.

He was gone. In secret. Where? Surely not to the girl? The young fool couldn't be that stupid. Merenda would kill him. Quintus groaned. The irony of it – Manius repeating his own youthful folly.

"I must stop this!"

Quintus extinguished the lamp and put down the wine jar before going out again into the night. He looked down at the doorway where the snow on the pavement was much trodden. A little beyond were distinct footprints. One set – heading off to the right and sometimes overlain by their own return – was surely his own. Aye, press his boot next to one and it made a perfect match. But another set – two sets – went off left. Two people? One pair looked the right size for Manius. But the other? Had Manius been lured from his bed by someone? By a Wolf? By the murderer?

"Hell and thunder!"

Quintus smashed the door of their quarters open, charged back into his own room, threshed about until he found his sword, then he rushed back to follow the trail of footprints.

They were clearly stamped in fresh, clean snow. They led him to the turret by the porta praetoria. The door was ajar and a light shone inside. He kicked the door open and burst in, his sword out. Inside, cowering in a corner under the lamp in a wall bracket, was a girl. She was a slave of Merenda's household. They stared at each other, then she pointed a trembling finger to the stairs. As she did, there came the sounds of shouts, screams and clashing blades. Quintus charged at the steps.

§

Titus and Manius stared at them and the Wolves – eyes gleaming through masks – stared back. Manius, paralysed, hardly breathed. Titus drew his sword and charged with a great cry.

Manius – fearing to be left – followed a few paces behind, skipping tentatively, his voice shrill. There was a clash of steel and then a break as the four circled warily round them, snarling through their masks. Then another shout from Titus who feinted at one before driving his blade into him and then slashed the throat of a second Wolf, who collapsed to his knees. A third rushed at Manius with sword raised but Manius ducked and lunged, missed but followed through to grapple. They wrestled for a panting, grunting minute. The other was stronger than Manius and must prevail. Desperate, Manius clawed his face, seeking his eyes, but only dislodged the mask to reveal the face of Spurius Aurelius Cotta, magistrate of Conganis and Roman citizen.

"You!" Manius gasped.

Cotta pushed Manius away and swiped at him with his sword. Manius jumped back, heard a scream and saw another figure fall. Then a body crashed into his side, winding him and knocking him to the ground. There was a whirl of figures, Manius scrambled to his feet and turned to retrieve his sword. He gasped at an agonising blow to his kidney. He clutched his side and took another blow to the back of the head and lights danced and the white snow came up to greet him. He thought how cold it would be. And then all was blackness.

A widening stain seeped out from under his body, colouring the snow red.

Chapter Twenty-Three

Even through the mask, Titus detected fear. He feinted right, left, then drove his sword into the Wolf's stomach. As the man fell, Titus spun, crouching, ready.

He saw Manius grappling, but then came a third from the left. Titus side-stepped, slashed and a spray of blood hissed and steamed into the freezing air. Again he turned to Manius, only to see the lad's attacker stab him and – as Manius yelled – strike him on the head with his pommel. Titus shouted "No!" and ran at Manius' attacker and the two remaining Wolves. They gave way and Titus recognised who'd downed Manius.

"Cotta," he breathed.

Titus' sword snaked out and took him in the throat. As Cotta fell choking, the last Wolf fled, skidding on ice. Titus watched him, his chest heaving. He wiped his brow then, gasping, knelt by Manius.

The lad's face was as white as the snow on which he lay and Titus could detect no breath. He saw the crimson oozing from Manius' tunic and shook his head. He looked to the turret window.

"Lucia! Drop the rope, it's me, Titus."

He moistened his lips and whistled. Then the shutters opened, a head was silhouetted, and the rope came curling down.

§

Quintus burst into the turret's upper room. A girl – Merenda's girl – stood by an open window, looking fearful.

"What...?" he began, then saw a rope running taut through the window. They were betrayed! He rushed, sword raised to hack at it.

"No!" shouted Lucia, seizing his cloak. "It's for Titus and Manius."

He looked at her, then at the window as Titus' face appeared. Titus reached for the stonework and Quintus dropped his sword to haul him into the room where he leaned against the table his chest heaving. Quintus took him by the shoulders.

"What's happening? Where's the lad?"

"He's been hurt – badly."

Lucia gave a cry.

"Where?" shouted Quintus.

"Outside, by the gate."

Quintus stared at Titus, then turned and pelted down the stairs, roaring.

Quintus' bellowing faded. Titus became aware of Lucia.

"Lucia, listen to me. Oh merciful gods! Stop crying and listen!"

She gulped, sniffed and wiped her eyes with the heel of her hand.

"Go! Take your slave and go. Tell no one and no one will know you were ever here."

"But you said Manius is hurt I must… I want to…"

"Do what? What can you do? If your father finds you were here tonight with Manius all hell'll be let loose. Even if Manius is… Look, your father will impose fearful punishment on him and on me – even your slave will be in for a terrible whipping. Just go and let us mend things. Please."

She shook her head, began sobbing again and, head down, her hands clasped, descended the stairs. Titus shook his head, strode to the window and hauled in the rope. He could hear Quintus shouting to call out the guard and open the gates. There were answering calls and soldiers running. He untied the rope, coiled it and dropped it in a corner, then he headed down the stairs and to the porta praetoria where Quintus stood before a group of soldiers, demanding that they open the gate.

"Do as he asks," ordered Titus. "And fetch the surgeon. Quickly! Where's Moravius Scapula?"

A centurion stepped forward. Titus drew him to one side. "When the gates are open, take two conturbia and secure the street. There are bodies to bring in."

The centurion barked orders as other men, driven by Quintus' curses, opened the gates. Quintus made to stride through, but Titus held him.

"Wait for them," he said and nodded to Scapula's men who were forming into their conturbia. Quintus snarled and wrestled to free himself, but Titus held him while the troops filed by. Then he released Quintus and followed him at a run into the vicus.

Four bodies lay in the snow, which the moonlight showed stained black with blood. Quintus knelt by Manius and raised him by the shoulders. The head lolled lifeless. Quintus closed his eyes and moaned. Titus placed a sympathetic hand on his back.

"What's the meaning of this? What in hell's name's going on?"

Titus stiffened at his commander's voice.

"Antonius Merenda, this is my fault. I went over the wall to rescue my woman, Birca. I took the lad – the frumentarius. We were attacked by Wolves." He coughed. "I'm… awfully sorry."

Merenda goggled. Before he could speak, Antiochos appeared, sleepy and irritable.

"I've been summoned. What do you want with me?"

Titus pointed at Manius. "The boy… I fear…"

Antiochos touched Quintus, who looked up, his eyes glistening. He lay Manius down and stood to make way.

"You can do nothing."

Antiochos knelt, pulled back Manius' eyelid, placed two fingers to his neck, laid his ear to his chest, muttered, then rolled Manius over.

"He lost too much blood, I fear," said Titus. "We're too late."

"I think not," said the surgeon. He poked the red snow, sniffed his finger and tasted it. He grimaced. "He has lost cheap wine – rotgut – no more." He pointed. "This wineskin took the blow, maybe saved him. He still breathes, though it's faint. Get him inside my hospital before he freezes."

Quintus gave a shuddering sigh which ended in a sob.

"Oh, thank heavens," said Titus. He gripped Quintus' arm. "Let's pray you have no cause to grieve."

Quintus eyed him. "I do grieve – for the wine."

§

In the hospital, Quintus paced the length of Antiochos'office, His boots squeaked on the stone flags: four steps one way, four back. At one end, a whitewashed plastered wall and at the other a shuttered window. But all Quintus could see was Manius' white face against the white snow.

The surgeon was next door, in one of the smaller sickrooms, where he'd had the unconscious Manius taken. Antiochos had shooed everyone out, while he examined him.

Curse and damn the man. Why was he taking so long? Quintus had really thought the boy dead. That had been hard – hellish hard. Dare he now believe he could live? Quintus gnawed his knuckle, alert for any sound from next door. But how the fuck could he hear with this arsehole prating on? He threw a furious glance at Merenda who was raging at Titus.

"You defied me! You disobeyed me and placed this garrison in danger in pursuit of your own private concerns." Merenda quivered while Titus stood head bowed. "Well? Do you deny it?"

"I cannot deny it. I've already admitted it."

"I swear, if we weren't under siege I'd have you arrested."

"Sir, I admit I was frightfully stupid and irresponsible. I only felt I couldn't leave Birca in all honour…"

"Honour! What's your honour compared to that of this cohort? To Rome's honour?"

Quintus rolled his eyes. "Pah!".

Merenda rounded on him.

"And you? What've you to say? How do you account for a frumentarius in this business?"

Quintus returned a cold eye. "For now, I've nothing to say."

Merenda blinked. Titus spoke. "It was absolutely all my doing. Manius is young, I persuaded him."

Quintus contemplated Titus: a dangerous halfwit, no question, but at least he was ready to shoulder blame. He'd also kept Merenda's girl out of it, though that could be self-interest – why incense her father more?

But Titus' intervention only fuelled the tribune's anger. He smashed his fist onto Antiochos' desk.

"Young! He's a frumentarius for fuck's sake!"

Titus mumbled: "I suppose…" and Quintus glowered and tugged at his beard. Antiochos entered and closed the door behind him. He regarded them with disapproval.

"There's too much noise in here. My patients need tranquillity."

Merenda laughed bitterly. "Tranquillity!"

§

Antiochos contemplated the tribune whose face was a dangerous colour. Could he be on the verge of a seizure? He realised Quintus was addressing him.

"I'm sorry. What did you say?"

"Dammit, I asked you how he is."

"The lad?"

"Yes!"

"He will fare better if you keep your voice down."

Quintus gave him a venomous stare.

"There are no obvious wounds other than the blow to the head. I've made him comfortable. There's no more to be done for the present."

"Oh forget the boy!" cried Merenda. "There are more important things." He flapped an impatient hand at Titus. "What happened out there precisely?"

Halting, Titus described how they'd met the Wolves, the fight and how he'd slain Cotta.

Merenda stared. "I don't understand this."

"It would appear Cotta was a traitor," said Quintus.

"What?"

"He was a traitor, a Wolf, a rebel. As to what he was doing with his fellows tonight, we can only guess. Perhaps making his escape, or maybe he was in the vicus to prepare a night assault. Somehow he got out and into the vicus unseen and perhaps he was preparing to lead an enemy party back into the fort by the same route, to throw open the gates."

"You mean… he was a traitor all along?"

Quintus sank into a chair behind the desk, picked up a bone lever toying with it. Antiochos bridled. He valued that implement. Who did this bear think he was?

Merenda elbowed past the surgeon to stand before Quintus.

"So, does this mean…?"

"That he killed Tiberius Flavius Fimbria and his lady? I think we can be confident of it. He was a rebel and had an opportunity to kill a Roman general. He then killed Decima Flavia to silence a witness. Easy enough for a man who's ruthless. Come upon Rufius Atellus unsuspected, your weapon concealed; then, once in the room, stab Flavius Fimbria in his bed, knock the wife on the head and be back out into the night. It'd take only a few more minutes to change your bloody toga and return to the dinner party."

"The man must have had nerves of ice."

"Yes… that's so," said Quintus.

Antiochos detected a hesitancy but Merenda seemed to notice nothing. He was staring at the floor in thought.

"So… Publius Flavius is innocent?"

"It would appear so."

"Hmm." Merenda rubbed his nose.

"You should also consider it likely Cotta had accomplices to help him over the rampart."

"That's so!" said Titus, who'd been standing morose in a corner.

Merenda shook his head, as though it were all too much for him.

"I shall question the sentries," said Titus and left.

Once the door was closed, Merenda scowled at Antiochos, took Quintus and led him to the corner, where he spoke in urgent whispers which Antiochos couldn't follow. He busied himself by taking up the bone lever and replaced it safely in its small leather case. Better take it into the sick room, safe from the bear's fiddling. Antiochos began to edge towards the door but paused as Merenda raised his voice.

"You say we know Cotta was a Wolf. But his secrets have gone with him, haven't they?"

Quintus nodded.

"What of his wife – Aurelia Cotta?"

"What of her?" asked Antiochos.

The two regarded him as though an imbecile and Quintus said caustically: "It's probable – is it not – that she had at least some knowledge of her husband's treason and might have some useful information?"

Antiochos' cheeks burned. Did this bear, this oaf, take him – Antiochos – for some stinking frumentarius that such a thing should occur? "So what do you propose? That she be tortured?"

"We can't do that, you Greek fool! She's a Roman citizen."

Antiochos stiffened and pursed his lips. "You must excuse me, I must see to my patient." He turned to the door but Merenda stopped him. "Wait! Antiochios, we may need you."

"Me?"

"We'll be dealing with a woman, informing her of her husband's death. Isn't she likely to become hysterical? It would be well to have a medical man present."

Antiochos winced but sighed: "Very well"

He summoned a capsarius to keep an eye on Manius. Then, as he Merenda and Quintus left the hospital, he closed the door, anxious to conserve precious heat. He shivered and looked at the moon and stars. With little cloud the night was even colder. Surely it must soon be dawn? Would there be any point returning to bed?

He scurried after the other two to overhear Merenda explaining that the Cottas' quarters were in a barrack block near the porta decumana, in the suite of a cavalry decurion. "Hirtius Glabrio – the fellow whose head was thrown over the wall."

"And so badly mishandled by Manius Suetonius," murmured Antiochos.

"What's that?" demanded Quintus.

"Nothing."

"Here,' said Merenda, pointing to the end of a barrack block.

Antiochos saw a light flickering behind shutters. Quintus and Merenda strode to the door, stern-faced. Merenda took a deep breath and knocked.

"Sexta Aurelia Cotta, it is I, Lucius Antonius Merenda!"

There was silence. Merenda turned to Quintus, who shrugged, raised the latch. He stepped over the threshold, followed by Merenda and then Antiochos.

They were in the apartment's day chamber. It was furnished with a plain table and chairs. Most of the room was in shadows, but Antiochos could make out pieces of harness hanging from hooks, some armour and other items of kit stacked by the door. What light there was came through another door, open opposite them.

They exchanged glances. Merenda coughed. He called: "Sexta Aurelia."

Nothing.

They made their way to that door and crowded on its threshold, looking into a bed chamber. There was a fire in the hearth and a lamp burned on a table by the bed. Kneeling against this bed – as if in prayer – was a female in a plain white nightgown with her back to them.

"Madam," said Merenda. "We must speak with you."

Still she neither moved nor spoke.

"Come, Aurelia Cotta, this will do you no good."

Merenda turned to Antiochos and nodded at her, indicating that here was an awkward woman with whom the surgeon must deal.

Antiochos frowned, approached her and said: "Lady…"

He touched her shoulder. As she turned, he thought she was looking at him in surprised affront, but her gaze slid to the ceiling, as her whole body turned to sink to the floor. Antiochos saw a sword pushed well up into her guts, her hands still clasped around the bloody hilt, the sightless eyes still staring.

Chapter Twenty-Four

Manius could hear snatches of conversation:

"How is he?" "Has he woken?" "He's weak." "His condition is worrying."

Then Quintus' growl: "'You should always look on human life as short and cheap. Yesterday sperm, tomorrow…'" a sob… "'a mummy or ashes.'"

Then another voice – Antiochos? "And remember Heraclitus," he switched to Greek, "'The death of earth is the birth of water. The death of water is the birth of air. The death of air is fire, and back again.'"

To Manius, these voices were less real than the place where the gods had sent him after death, where mortal concerns were so banal. There, on the Island of the Blessed, the sun blazed in a cyan sky, warming his bones and dazzling his eyes as it bounced from white sands caressed by a lapping sea and which were soft and welcoming to his feet. Those voices drifted away, growing fainter, carried out to sea with the tide, as he slept on the warm sand with the waves as his lullaby.

Then they were closer and loud. He half opened his eyes to see, in an unfamiliar white room, Quintus and Antiochos standing over him. Then those concerned faces receded into mist, which cleared to reveal again the beautiful beach, which he saw ended in a headland of black rocks, beyond which he knew something lurked that would judge him. In the other direction, where the sands curled away into the far distance, he could just see the breakers meeting trees that grew down to the shore and that way lay something wonderful. Manius walked towards it. Lucia. He could see her in the distance, white and radiant, and beckoning. He hurried, but the sand became heavy, making the going hard and tiring, his steps grew shorter and his limbs heavier and she drew no closer, until, eventually, he had to lie down and close his eyes.

§

When Manius woke he felt not sand beneath his head, but a pillow. He tried to return to his dream but couldn't. He sensed a presence and opened his eyes to see Antiochos standing over him.

"You're awake?"

Manius' eyes followed him as he reached for a goblet. He placed an arm around Manius' shoulders and raised him, putting the vessel to his lips. Manius sipped a bitter draught and coughed. Antiochos encouraged him to drink more, then shouted an order towards the room's open door. The surgeon fussed over Manius for some minutes, while he became accustomed to his bed and to the small, whitewashed room.

"Where is this?" Manius could barely hear his own voice.

"You're in my hospital and have been for several days. You've had a fever, prompted by injuries and lying in freezing snow. We feared for you my friend. Even I, Antiochos, almost despaired, but with a little judicious bleeding and a copious dosing of borage and violets, at morning and night, I've saved you. I shall document this and correspond with Galen, for he values my letters. Ah, but now you have your first visitor."

Over Antiochos' shoulder Manius saw Quintus hurrying into the room, wild and dishevelled.

"One of your capsarii summoned me. What is it? What's happened?"

Then Quintus' eyes lit upon Manius and he rushed to the bedside. "You're awake? You're well?" He seized Antiochos' arm. "Is he well?"

"With Aesculapius' blessing, and with rest and nourishment, he will do well."

Quintus sank onto the edge of the bed and covered his face in his hands, muttering some prayer of gratitude. That reacquainted Manius with fear and care and hauled him back from the Island of the Blessed. Back to bloody Britannia.

"Quintus," he croaked. "What's happened?"

Before Quintus could reply, Antiochos was back, eager. "What do you remember?"

"I… I remember going over the wall with Titus. I remember Birca and burying her and… coming back. I… remember the Wolves. Quintus, Cotta is a Wolf! He…"

Antiochos eased him back onto the pillow, murmuring: "Remarkable. No loss of recollection. The borage perhaps."

"We know, boy," said Quintus, "We know all about that."well."

"So, I haven't betrayed Titus? I spoke foolishly, I…"

"Have no fear, you've not betrayed your doltish friend. However, all is known about your stupid escapade. As for Cotta – he's dead."

"Dead? How?"

"I say, can I tell him?"

Quintus turned at the voice and Manius raised his head. Titus stood at the foot of his bed, smiling. Quintus contemplated him, then rose, gesturing Titus to his place. "Suit yourself," he said and leaned against the wall, arms folded, scowling, while Titus told Manius about Cotta's death and the discovery of his wife's body.

"Did you get into trouble?"

Titus smiled wryly. "The old man wasn't best pleased. He reprimanded me and harped on about responsibility and duty and judgement – hell, what a lecture, Manius! But in truth, I think he felt a guilt over poor, dear Birca so he didn't push it. He has other things to worry about – our situation's too serious, it..." He trailed off.

"What do you mean, why... "

"That'll be enough," said Quintus, elbowing Titus aside.

"Yes, yes, you must let him rest," piped up Antiochos and they ushered Titus out.

§

Tears coursed down Tita Amatia's cheeks. Before she could dash them away, they were shaken from her face as a hacking cough seized her.

"Here, drink this and sit there."

She took the proffered beaker, glanced down and perched on a wobbling hassock of stuffed sacking, so that she sank below the worst of the smoke that billowed up from the fire and towards the roof. She sipped the warm ale and drew a tentative, wheezing breath, then blinked and peered through the fumes.

Opposite, in this rough pyramid shelter of branches and hide, on the other side of the fire, sat a squat muscular figure with a horseshoe of wild grey hair framing a bald pate above the kind of rugged face that would suggest a peasant or field slave, but for the shrewd authority in the eyes. She'd heard that this Drustan was nobody's fool. He, legs apart, elbow on his knee and chin in hand, contemplating Tita Amatia.

"So, you're Epillus' Roman wife?"

"I am... or was, until he lost his life in a fruitless rebellion."

"We're kin then, you and I?"

She nodded.

"You're far from home, Tita Amatia, in winter, in a land at war and with only one servant." He waved at the shelter's entrance, outside which stood Bodvoc who'd shadowed her from Cenares. "Why're you here?"

"I heard you'd brought your people out from the Lopcares, led them to join the other septs under Iovir. I'd like to meet this Iovir."

"Iovir?" Drustan raised his eyebrows.

"Iovir... whoever leads you."

A smile crossed Drustan's lips, a smile she'd difficulty reading.

"He's not an easy person to see."

"He needs to speak to Rome. Even while he fights Rome, he needs a line of communication. I gather he lost his last one."

"Cotta?"

"Aye, Cotta."

Drustan looked at the wall of the shelter, thoughtful, as though he could see through the branches and hide to Longovicium only a quarter of a mile distant.

"Some say victory is ours and that we've no more need for talk. You speak of fruitless rebellion, but this isn't like the last time, this time Rome is divided – between those who'd crush us and those who'd use us."

"Who'd use you?"

He kept his gaze on the wall and waved her question away.

"You know that fort is about to fall don't you? The whole Brigantine nation knows it and is gathering for the spoils – and the blood. You should go, you're a Roman, you don't want to see it. Go back to Cenares, Tita Amatia Aculeo."

"I have business here."

Drustan looked at her and shook his head.

§

The hospital was noisy with the groans, cries, and the boots of the harassed capsarii running along the corridor. Antiochos wore an increasingly careworn expression.

Manius now had visitors; one afternoon he'd just finished a bowl of porridge and lay propped on his pillows when Titus returned.

"Manius, you're looking much better; and I see you've been eating. Good show! I'm sure Antiochos must approve."

"Antiochos seems busy with the demands of the hospital," said Manius, with a weak smile. "No time for talking to me."

"He's one of our busiest officers. The Brigantes keep his hands full."

"How's that?"

Titus frowned. "Their strength increases. Fresh bands from the various septs are joining those besieging us. The buggers attack our walls at least once a day."

There were shadows under Titus' eyes, his cheeks were unshaven and his voice was dull as he described how the cohort was under strain, the men exhausted and, although repulsing attacks, suffered a steady stream of casualties. His voice died, he stared at the floor, then seemed to recollect himself and jerked his head up and smiled. "But we'll be all right, Manius. These rebels are no match for the First Vardulli and we only need this awful weather to improve for a few days and relief will surely arrive from our neighbouring forts."

Antiochos entered, stopped and stared.

"He needs rest," he said with a stern look at Titus, who, sheepish, mumbled about having to return to his duties. He embraced Manius and, promised to visit again. Manius uttered some awkward words of commiseration for Birca. Titus flinched, with his eye screwed shut, squeezed Manius tighter and left, head bowed and his hand to his brow, shielding his face.

Antiochos shook his head. "He hides his grief, but it's there."

Manius sighed and nodded. The hospital walls couldn't protect him from life's grief. If only he could sink back into unconsciousness.

He started. Antiochos was speaking. "I'm sorry, what did you say?"

"I asked how you're feeling. Are you having trouble hearing?"

"I was daydreaming."

Antiochos grunted and dosed him with a bitter-tasting tonic. As he wiped the spoon Manius studied the careworn face of the normally jaunty Greek.

"You seem tired."

Antiochos shrugged. "The men are uncomplaining and I must be no less phlegmatic." Then his black eyes flashed with uncharacteristic ill-humour. "Some officers would do well to emulate me. That great clown Ambrosius Cressipes is forever whining about his piles – at a time like this! It's like being back in Rome, tending such spoiled creatures. But now I forget myself – I should never have told you this, but you doubtless noticed yourself how the great fool takes such abbreviated steps: an unfailing symptom." His eyes widened. "Please: you won't repeat it?"

"I promise."

"Good, then I shall reward you."

"How?"

Antiochos leaned over and whispered: "I gather that when the lady Lucia heard that you were killed, she screamed and swooned."

"Swooned?"

"Clean away my friend."

Manius sank back into his pillows, smiling, his melancholy gone.

§

"What are you smirking at?" Quintus asked a couple of hours later.

"Nothing," said Manius, composing his features.

Quintus grunted. "I'm glad somebody has something to smile about."

He sank into the chair by Manius' bed and rested his elbows on his knees, frowning at the floor tiles. Manius asked airily: "I understand Lucia Antonia was ill. I trust she's recovered?"

"Ill? First I've heard of it."

"Somebody mentioned… I forget who… that she fainted on the night of Cotta's murder."

"Oh that! Yes, I heard something of the sort. Bloody good job she didn't faint in the turret. Merenda still has no idea his daughter was consorting with two halfwits."

Manius changed the subject. "How has Merenda taken the discovery of Aurelius Cotta?"

Quintus shrugged. "He's understandably keen to know how he got over the wall and whether he had accomplices but he's content that the assassin's identified. It's not as convenient that the general wasn't killed by his own brother but it must gratify Merenda that Aurelius Cotta was also trusted by the governor."

"And Publius Flavius?"

"Oh he's strutting around, looking smug but hard done by."

Quintus moved away from the bed and paced, forcing and rubbing the fist of one hand into the palm of the other. Manius, still intoxicated by Lucia's fainting, prattled on heedless. "So Antonius Merenda made no mention of his daughter and showed no suspicion of..."

"To hell with all that!" roared Quintus, in a Vesuvian eruption. He rounded on Manius, eyes afire and spittle gathering on his beard. "You went behind my back, you young turd! Playing stupid, dangerous, fucking games with some lovestruck cavalry dolt instead of reporting to me. Heaven help us! You're a frumentarius, with an empire in your care!"

Quintus – quivering, eyes bulging – bellowed, expounding Manius' immaturity, stupidity and duplicity. Manius gazed, helpless and frozen but some part of his mind worried that this must be heard throughout the hospital.

"Can't you see – damn you – how vital it is, as frumentarii, that we can trust each other? How proper it is, as father and son, that we trust each other? How can I, if you go behind my back?"

He raged on: how he trembled for Rome in the hands of such a generation and finished, in quavering Greek: "'They will pour scorn on their aged parents and sting with their abuse.'"

Manius was still weak. This was too much. He began to weep. Not from guilt. Remorse seldom troubled him. It was his misfortune and the weight of unease and uncertainty which settled back upon his shoulders like a familiar burden. Everything was so... unfair.

Quintus blinked.

"What? What now? Oh, this is insupportable." He strode to close the door, more anxious, Manius realised, about this sobbing being overheard than his bellows.

Between snivels, Manius acknowledged his foolishness and begged forgiveness. Quintus knitted his great brows and cursed some more, but with less conviction. He darted glances at Manius while subsiding into a gentle grumbling.

Manius finished sobbing with a trembling sigh. "I'm truly sorry. I wish... I wish none of this had ever happened. I wish I'd never seen Tiberius Flavius Fimbria. That bloody bastard. If he hadn't come none of the murders would've happened – and we wouldn't be bound up in it."

"Nonsense! Your illness makes you unreasonable. Cotta – a Wolf and a fanatic – would've killed him somewhere and Decima Flavia would doubtless have been with him and, sooner or later, you and I would've been bound up in it. That's our function, remember – to get landed in the shit. As for the rest – wouldn't the Brigantes have besieged this place anyway? Or are you suggesting that his assassination and the rebel attack were of a piece in some plan?" He paused. "Interesting. Is that what you propose?"

"I... I don't know, I'm too tired to think what I might mean."

Manius felt suddenly exhausted, as though his very spirit was draining from him. Quintus strode to his bedside, staring, then he was back to the door and bawling for Antiochos. Manius was aware of the little surgeon scurrying into the room with Quintus wide-eyed behind him and then Manius left them again.

§

Quintus lay on his bunk, hands clasped behind his head, gazing at the ceiling. It was half an hour since he'd left Manius and he was brooding. The lad had wept – like a girl. Quintus hadn't expected that; that had taken him aback. Then, he'd assumed it had been because of Manius' injury and his weakness. Now, he wasn't so sure. The lad had shown himself – yet again – to be capable of dissimulation. Had his tears been forced? Had his faint – which the Greek had dismissed as trifling – been genuine, or a ploy? The heavens knew he'd shown himself capable of it.

Quintus gave a mirthless laugh. He could hardly condemn Manius for dishonesty. Hadn't he been training him in a trade that demanded lies and repaid deceit?

But Manius had been disloyal – to him.

That rankled.

Truth be told, it should be no great surprise. As a child Manius had been sly and self-centred. "And I turned a blind eye; wouldn't see it," reflected Quintus. Yet Manius' father had been such an open and ingenuous man. Truly, there was no telling. Tita, of course, had seen something of it – straightaway. No fooling her. What was it she'd said?

Whatever it was, the fact remained, Manius was out for himself – always had been, always would be. That made his infatuation with the Merenda girl so surprising. Of course, at that age you were led by your cock, but his starry-eyed obsession seemed more than lust. Not that there wasn't a fair measure of lust there. The girl was beautiful. Stupid, but beautiful. May the gods help her when the Brigantes got their paws on her.

Hell, what a bloody mess!

That prompted a shadow of an idea, just beyond reach. Manius had said something. Something about Tiberius Flavius. Something that struck a chord.

Quintus tried to concentrate but his thoughts were shattered by a blare of trumpets and shouting. With a groan, he swung his feet onto the floor and sat up. Another fucking attack.

He slipped into his boots, buckled on his sword, picked up his helmet and walked out into the fort where he stopped Ambrosius Crassipes and asked him where he'd have him serve. The harassed centurion directed Quintus to the northern wall. There, an optio ordered him onto the rampart where, breathing heavily from the climb, he found himself next to a portly man, past middle age.

"I know you don't I?" said Quintus peering.

"Aulus Irminius Ambustus, sir – cook to his honour the tribune."

Merenda's cook. He'd questioned him after the poisonings.

"So you're with the galearii?"

"That's right sir. I did my twenty-five years in the ranks. I might be long in the tooth now but I can still hold a sword."

That was less useful than an ability to keep below the rampart wall, as the enemy began to send arrows and slingshots whistling over their heads. This had been their tactic for days. With the defenders cowering behind the battlements, the Brigantes then sent parties forward to place scaling ladders against the fort. To force these back, or to hack at those climbing them, the Romans had to expose themselves and this brought a stream of losses – men reeling, with an arrow in the throat or a slingshot in the eye, to plunge off the rampart and land with a thud in the fort below, or to be led down bleeding and cursing to the hospital. Slowly, remorselessly the garrison's losses grew and the ramparts thinned as Antiochos' patients multiplied. The patch of ground in the shadow of the eastern wall could accommodate few more shallow graves.

The Brigantes didn't attempt to rush that section of the rampart where Quintus and Irminius Ambustus served. The pair sat, their backs to the battlement wall, contemplating the roofs of the fort's buildings ranged in successive rows below and before them. They watched the arrows and slingshots sail over their heads to land on those roofs in eruptions of powdery snow, occasionally exposing the red tiles beneath.

After an hour the cold stone was too much for Quintus' backside. He shifted.

"Watch yourself!" cried Ambustus, clutching his sleeve to pull him down again.

Quintus grunted his thanks, then was distracted by noise below. Merenda came into sight from around one of the barrack blocks, striding, with a couple of centurions skipping beside him.

His voice, high and angry, carried to the rampart. "Do as I say! Do as I tell you! Any man who can stand must be back in the ranks." He faced the officers and shrieked: "Obey me!" Then he stormed off toward the north gate, leaving his centurions to exchange shrugs before dispersing.

"Heaven help us," whispered Quintus.

"Oh dear, oh dear," came a voice from his left. The soldier next to Ambustus, thin, with a sharp face, tapped his temple and nodded towards where Merenda had stood. "All proving a bit much for the tribune."

"Shut your noise, Baccio!" Ambustus shouted. The other subsided into muttering about fucking galearii and fucking frumentarii.

"Ignore him sir," said Ambustus, loud and precise. "He's just a cunt." He followed this with a glare at Baccio.

"So I see," said Quintus. To change the subject, he added: "I dare say you'd rather be back in your kitchen?"

"I'd only be worrying what these nob heads are up to." A venomous look at Baccio, who sneered back. "Anyway, things aren't much quieter in the praetorium. What with the Flavius Fimbrias and then the Cotta lady, I'll take my chances up here."

"Poor woman."

"In with the Wolves, they say."

"But one must admire her fortitude. She died a good Roman death."

"A hard death, mind you. I heard her squeal."

"What d'you mean?"

"I heard her – when she done it. I think I did."

"What did you hear?"

"A cry from her quarters."

"What sort of cry?"

"I dunno… just a cry."

"Of pain? Of fear?"

"I… I suppose."

"Tell me what happened – everything."

"It was that night when all hell let loose. There's been some fight outside the gate, the lady Lucia has a fainting fit and the tribune's lady sent me to find him."

"And?"

"I went to the north gate but somebody said he'd gone to the hospital. So I – fucking hell!" The cook ducked as an arrow passed within an inch of his ear.

"Never mind that. Go on."

"I went to the hospital, going back past the praetorium and the Cotta's quarters. That's when I heard the scream."

"Did you see if anyone wanted help?"

"No! There was screaming and shouting all over the bloody place. Anyway, I reckoned it was some private business."

Quintus signalled him to go on.

"So I got to the hospital to see you and the tribune and the surgeon coming out. You all looked so severe I thought better of interrupting. You were heading for the praetorium anyway. I hung about for a minute. Then his honour Caelius Metellus came along from the praetorium. He looked like he'd got plenty on his mind too, so, to be honest, I thought 'sod it' and went back to bed."

Quintus regarded Ambustus but his mind was elsewhere. Again, that sense of something significant, right before him. What the hell was it?

"Apart from the scream – did you see anything? Can you remember?"

"Oh, there was plenty to see that night."

"What?"

An optio came running at a crouch along the rampart. He slapped Baccio's shoulder. "Five!" Next on to Ambustus. "Six!" Then he turned to the men he'd counted. "Follow me, at the double. Reinforcements needed at the south wall."

Swearing, the six rose and followed the optio down into the fort. Baccio's voice drifted up: "What's wrong with you, Ambustus? Talking to a fucking frumentarius – that's not on."

Quintus rubbed his beard. He needed to think. He needed peace and quiet and...

"Ladder!"

The enemy assaulted and Quintus' section of the rampart, having just lost six men, was hard pressed by three ladders against their battlement. There followed half an hour's desperate hacking and thrusting at the attackers with missiles whirring past them and – in three cases – into them. When the attack was beaten off and the ladders withdrawn, Quintus and his comrades sank back exhausted. An hour later, they were relieved by a rested conturbium of bandaged, limping soldiers.

Back down in the fort, Quintus made for the south wall. He must find Ambustus. He had more questions. He stopped a couple of officers and asked for him, receiving only angry, impatient shrugs. A soldier overhead.

"He copped one. I saw him carried off."

"To the hospital?"

Another shrug.

Where else? Quintus hurried there and found it overflowing. A capsarius directed him inside where he found Antiochos bending over a body. Quintus approached as the surgeon closed the cook's staring eyes.

"Dead?"

"You knew him?"

"How did he die?"

"What kind of question is that? It wasn't the plague. He was stabbed."

"Where?"

"Does it matter? In the kidney, the left kidney."

"In the back? How?"

Antiochos shook his head. "I've no time for this nonsense." He pushed Quintus aside and hurried into another room.

Quintus rolled the cook's body over. The tunic was stiff with blood and there was the rent, into the kidney. Stabbed in the back. And shortly after it had been broadcast that he'd been talking to a frumentarius.

§

"So, she killed herself?" said Manius.

"Yes," said Lucia. Her eyes shone an even more dazzling black, as they moistened with tears. "Forgive me; I was fond of Sexta Aurelia, she was kind. My mother was her friend."

Manius could say nothing. Glib consolation didn't come easily and he was breath-taken by Lucia's visit. He'd had a long sleep to recover from Quintus and had barely woken when Lucia had come gliding in bearing a basket of her little barley cakes. Stuttering, he'd asked about the death of Aurelia Cotta – the first thing to come to mind – but then could only nod in sympathy and nibble on a cake in response to Lucia's sadness.

She told how her family and the Cottas had seen much of each other, how her parents had found them a cultured and genteel couple, who'd brightened the humdrum routine of garrison life.

"Your father must also be dismayed."

"Poor father. He has so many responsibilities and so much to worry over. He fears it can't reflect well on him that the killer of Tiberius Flavius was a family friend, but he can console himself that Aurelius Cotta was also respected and trusted in Londinium."

Her eyes widened, as though shocked by her own words. "But that sounds terrible, as though father was only thinking about his career. That's not so. He liked Aurelius Cotta and trusted him and now he feels betrayed."

Manius nodded and murmured something sympathetic.

Lucia went on: "I'm angry towards Cotta for the trouble he has brought us, but I must admire Sexta Aurelia. She'd such strong feelings towards her husband that she couldn't bear to live without him and took her own life. I must admire that."

"Perhaps she only feared arrest and punishment."

"You're a cynic."

Manius shrugged. "My trade inclines me towards cynicism."

"Perhaps you should change your trade."

He gave a wry smile. Behind it his teeth ground. Change his trade! Jove weeps! Few things could make him happier. But his plans to find himself a patron – Tiberius Flavius or Merenda – had turned to shit. He wondered: was there still any way to win her father's approval, or at least avoid his bad opinion?

"Did your father discover that you'd been in the turret or that you'd any involvement with what happened?"

"No. Numeria got me back to the praetorium unseen and unsuspected. I must be a deceitful and undutiful daughter." She sat in sombre contemplation, but then her eyes shone and she rubbed her hands. "But it was exciting, wasn't it Manius?"

"I understand you fainted?"

Those eyes betrayed momentary shock. She looked down and coloured. "They said you had been killed and that upset me."

Manius made a bold move. He stretched out his hand, took hers and pressed it. She looked at him with surprise but he'd the feeling that this was as much at herself as at him, for she made no attempt to withdraw. Neither spoke. Manius thrilled. He'd vaulted to a tremendous height, from which he might fall with one ill-considered word. It lasted a minute. She sighed and he felt a hint of movement in her fingers, sensed she was signalling "enough" without an actual pulling away. He released her.

"I must be leaving. Mother's expecting me."

"She knows you're here?"

"Father and mother both know I'm here."

"They don't mind? Your father doesn't mind?"

She stood and shook her head and, as she turned, he saw her eyes glistening again.

"Father's indulgent at the moment. He doesn't say it, but mother and I know what he thinks. He's afraid we're all going to die."

§

Manius worried over that. It confirmed his impressions. He'd been increasingly aware of the noises around him – of groans and cries and of Antiochos' dark-rimmed eyes and the absence of his usual jauntiness.

Her words were still preying on him a little later when a thoughtful Quintus returned. Manius taxed him with them.

"She's right, of course. That's the fate that awaits us. As the late emperor had it: 'Mortal man, you've lived as a citizen in this great city. The laws of the city apply equally to all.'"

Manius swore at him. Quintus only looked surprised. Manius wondered whether he still thought he was too unwell for argument or perhaps he agreed with Merenda's defeatism and had no stomach for reprimanding him.

Manius pointed. "You've blood on your tunic."

"Eh? Oh yes… yes."

"Not yours?"

"What? No… Merenda's cook. You remember him?"

"Is he dead?"

Quintus nodded, as though more in answer to a thought than to Manius' question.

"Were you with him?"

"Yes… no… after he was killed… in the hospital."

"I gather it's bad out there?"

Quintus drew a deep breath and sat on the foot of Manius' bed. "Our situation isn't good."

"So the barbarians show no sign of weakening?"

Quintus shook his head. "If anything, their numbers increase. They attack the walls several times a day. They rush at us and they gain footholds with ever greater frequency. Oh, we force them back – but only with ever greater difficulty. We lose men and we can't make up those losses. You can imagine: our troops grow weary and dispirited."

He ran his fingers through his hair and rubbed his face. "To tell the truth, I'm feeling the strain myself. You know I'm numbered with the galearii. We form a reserve to be deployed wherever we're needed. We're called upon more every day. Thank heaven it'll soon be dark. These

Brigantes show no stomach for fighting after sundown."

Quintus was weary, wearier than Manius had ever seen him. He'd always been indifferent to hardship but this siege was taking its toll; he was looking his age.

"No hope of relief?"

"How can we know? We're cut off. We've no way of knowing how the insurrection fares elsewhere or the situation of our neighbouring forts and of the Wall. The snow still lies thick and any relief column would struggle to reach us. But I can't believe the Brigantes aren't suffering. They must be short of food supplies. If we can hold out: who knows…?"

He fell silent and his great shaggy head sank onto his breast. Manius was afraid he'd return to their quarters for sleep and abandon him to the dark loneliness of his hospital room, to lie awake with the moans of the wounded and thoughts of barbarians pouring over the walls.

"So," he said, to revive conversation, "Cotta killed Tiberius Flavius and his wife?"

Quintus head jerked up. "Hmm?"

"Aurelius Cotta was a Wolf and killed Tiberius Flavius Fimbria. Do you think he could have been Iovir himself?"

Quintus waved a hand airily. "Who knows?" He sat up and shook himself. "Yes, it's undeniable that Cotta was a Wolf and a traitor. It's reasonable to assume – as he had good political reason to kill a Roman general and the opportunity – that he murdered Tiberius Flavius, Decima Flavia and Vibia Rufia Atelus. His attack on you and Caelius Metellus was an attempt to escape discovery. That failed and he's dead, and now it's important to know whether he acted alone or had an ally within the fort."

This jolted Manius. With the barbarians outside the walls, it had been his only comfort that, with Cotta's discovery and death, there were no longer enemies within. This prompted him to share his store of information. As though just remembering, he told Quintus about the Gracchus children and how they had described the barbarians as their friends.

Quintus raised an eyebrow; rubbed his beard. "Interesting, or perhaps only infant babble. If I'm right that Gracchus is a Christian or a Jew, his loyalty must be suspect. Was he in league with Cotta and helped him over the wall? Still so many questions. Also this one – does this in any way touch on Caerellius Priscus and his loyalties? Hard to see how, but I'll ponder it more when my head aches less."

"How can we gauge anyone's motives? Isn't it extraordinary that Cotta, a respected Roman citizen and a magistrate, should be a barbarian rebel?"

"Perhaps that shouldn't surprise us. Cotta was an aristocrat of the dispossessed Brigantes. Yes, he seemed reconciled to Rome and seemed – no, was – a civilised man. He would've been educated in a city such as

Eboracum, or even Londinium. He would've been a senior decurion on the ordo and elected senior magistrate, and we know he had extensive estates to support him in that position. Perhaps he valued other things more highly than wealth, as we Romans once did. Perhaps he had loyalties we can no longer comprehend."

"We'll never know; now that Aurelia Cotta has taken her own life."

"Yes, that's all neat, isn't it?"

"What d'you mean?"

"It makes such a tidy bundle: a nice parcel no one will think to unravel."

"I don't understand. What's to unravel?"

Quintus shook his head and struggled to his feet, grimacing.

"I don't know; probably nothing. But Aurelius Cotta seemed a judicious man who'd weigh things carefully. Surely not one to react so recklessly – only think of that poisoning."

"But he obviously was such a man."

"Doubtless you're right." He made to leave, then paused. "But his wife – are we to believe that she was also a Brigantine at heart, unreconciled to Rome? Yet, she chose that most Roman of deaths, fell on her own sword – strange."

"I still don't understand."

"No, neither do I. I'm too tired yet have thoughts that won't leave me in peace. One in particular: something you said. If only Tiberius Flavius had never come. It's not a problem, nor a question, merely a premise, but it keeps nagging away here." He tapped his forehead. "Enough, I must away to bed."

He made for the door but stopped when Antiochos came hurrying in. They regarded each other with heavy lidded eyes.

"Oh, you're here," said the surgeon wearily. "That's good."

He asked Quintus to wait while he examined Manius. He held his wrist and tested his grip, peered into his eyes and at his tongue and enquired after the functioning of his bowel and bladder.

"That's good," he declared. "You may leave, with your father's help. In better circumstances I'd have had you here for another day or so, to rest more and to move you from grain to meat – if we had any meat. That's the proper way, that's my way, but I can no longer spare the bed. There are others in greater need than you, young man."

He gave Quintus instructions that Manius was to rest and be limited to light duties avoiding exertion or excitement. He might report back to the hospital tomorrow, where he could assist.

Quintus grunted assent and Manius thanked the little Greek for all his diligence and care. Antiochos acknowledged this with a weak smile and a wave and left.

Manius stood and wobbled, until Quintus darted to support him and Manius dressed himself with his help. Then he leaned on Quintus back towards their quarters. At first Manius felt light-headed and thought he might faint, then the cold air revived him.

They limped through the fort's streets lit by the flames of an occasional torch, passing soldiers, alone or in small groups, who moved listlessly without their usual military urgency and whose faces were unshaven and grubby with sweat besmeared grime, making their eyes seem large and white. Manius was seeing the ghosts he'd feared in the cemetery.

One figure surprised Manius by approaching to confront him. Manius looked up into the face – under his centurion's helmet – of Publius Flavius Fimbria – a face as grubby as those of the men he commanded. His eyes were bloodshot and glassy.

"Manius Suetonius." His evident exhaustion rendering his voice even more of a whisper. "You're well, I trust?"

Surprised, Manius stammered that he was and thanked him. Publius Flavius nodded and moved on. Manius exchanged a glance with Quintus. These were the first friendly words from the centurion since Eboracum. Clearly things were desperate.

They returned to their quarters which were lit by one oil lamp and Quintus told him there was no wood left for the hearth.

"Have you eaten?" he asked.

"Recently enough."

Quintus nodded and chewed on a piece of bread while he fumbled with his other hand to undo his belt. He'd just dropped it, with his scabbard and sword to the floor, when there sounded a trumpet blare and harsh shouts.

Quintus closed his eyes, groaned and reached for his belt.

"You told me they didn't attack at night," Manius said.

"They haven't – until now. Perhaps this is the end."

Chapter Twenty-Five

Manius stared at the door after Quintus left, listening to the turmoil outside. Should he join Quintus with the galearii? Out of the question. He wasn't afraid. While he'd no stomach for more combat, he knew it would come sooner or later. But not now. He was too weak. But what to do? There was no chance of sleep while events unfolding a few score paces away would determine whether he ever saw another morning.

He groped under the cot for his sword belt and buckled it on.

He put on his boots and cloak and walked out into the night. He wandered aimless and his unsteady legs took him to the Principia where he saw a group of about thirty armed men. They stood in loose ranks, feet shuffling and heads down, talking in low voices.

"What're you doing here?" Quintus stepped forward.

"I… don't know, I feel I must do something."

"You're not fighting, you're not strong enough. Just look at you."

Manius nodded, not displeased. This seemed to satisfy Quintus and, as they stood in silence, Manius recognised Arrius Gracchus among the galearii, his fingertips together before his face, his eyes rolled up to the sky, while his lips made frantic, whispering, loquacious appeal to his own singular god.

They looked at the ramparts, at the soldiers hacking frantically down at their unseen foes and heard the roars, screams and clash of metal. Quintus grasped Manius' arm.

"You're shivering. Are you cold?" The entreaty in his voice said he so much wanted Manius to be cold rather than afraid. Manius was both.

Before Manius could answer, there was a great crash followed by a shuddering echo. The galearii greeted this thunderous boom with eyes wide and mouths agape while from the ramparts came a cry of dismay.

"What… what is it?" Manius asked. There was a second thunderclap. Quintus swore.

"A ram: a battering ram."

It came again, and again and with each blow against the Porta Praetoria the galearii flinched. Then a centurion came running, shouting: "Galearii, follow me! To the Porta Praetoria!"

Quintus held Manius by the shoulders. "Go to the hospital, go to the Greek and report to him."

Manius watched Quintus rejoin his comrades as they jogged behind the centurion. Then he made his way towards the hospital. As he approached, he met four soldiers who came trotting around a corner, carrying a man, each supporting a limb. Manius recognised the bloodied face of Titus, his features twisted in pain.

Manius ran alongside, demanding to know his injury, but they gave no reply, intent only on getting their burden to the hospital. They were met by Antiochos, who ushered them along the corridor to the room Manius had occupied, where they laid Titus, with great care, on the bed.

"Titus!" Manius elbowed his way to Titus' side, but the surgeon rounded on them all.

"Give him air! Leave the bloody room before I have you whipped from it! You infernal fools!"

The soldiers trooped out. The little Greek's eyes still flashed, so after one last look at Titus' white face, Manius also left.

He paced the corridor. He remembered Titus' words: "A cavalryman who's still alive at thirty is a blackguard". His throat tightened. He would've wept, if the centurion Ambrosius Crassipes hadn't come hurrying down the corridor, panting. He had a cut from nose to cheekbone and the blood was caked into his beard.

"Titus Caelius?" he asked and Manius had just nodded towards the door when it was opened by Antiochos.

Crassipes turned to the surgeon. "Are his wounds serious? The tribune must know. The men are upset to see him carried away."

Antiochos wiped his hands on a towel. "He'll live. He needs rest. In truth he needs days of rest, but some few hours will see him back on his feet. He has a minor wound to his knee and a blow to the head, but his helmet saved him." He turned to Manius and said gently, as though apologising for his earlier anger. "It's nothing like as serious as yours."

Ambrosius Crassipes relaxed.

"We couldn't lose him. He's worth another century to us."

Antiochos nodded and made to move on, but Manius stopped him and stammered that he couldn't remain idle and wanted to serve in the hospital. Antiochos gave him a searching look, nodded again, and handed him over to the supervision of a passing capsarius.

Manius passed the next hour in a blur, carrying bandages, water, messages and pails of vomit. He helped limping men through the hospital which was now full of groaning soldiers lying on floors, in the corridors and even in the hospital courtyard where they lay in the snow with only blankets to protect them from the cold.

Among them, Manius recognised Lucco, who had manned the scorpion. He had an ugly wound to his belly and Manius gave him water and a weak smile and passed on, unable to do more. All the while he could hear the crashing of the enemy's ram against the gate and, at each stroke, even the wounded in their pain, and the capsarii in their bustling preoccupation, rolled fearful eyes in the direction of the Porta Praetoria.

As Manius ran down a corridor with a message for Antiochos, the distant blows of the ram merged into a pounding in his temple, becoming one painful, pulsating boom. He put a hand to his head, leaned back against a wall and slid down it.

Hands grasped him and hauled him upright and he was staring into Antiochos' intense black eyes. "Are you all right? No, of course you're not. Can you hear me? Good. Go back to your quarters and rest as I told you. Have I not enough sick to tend?"

Manius staggered out into the cold night air which revived him enough for the pounding in his head to subside to a dull, aching throb, but he promptly forgot the surgeon's order and wandered towards the Porta Praetoria, drawn, like Ulysses to the Sirens, towards the sound of the ram.

§

Ambrosius Crassipes saluted Merenda.

"The surgeon reports that Titus Caelius' injuries aren't serious and that he should return to duty in a few hours."

Merenda frowned. Quintus read conflict between satisfaction that his deputy would live and annoyance at losing him even for a few hours. The surrounding galearii and the troops all cheered.

Merenda snarled at Crassipes: "Keep these men quiet!"

The centurion bawled and the soldiers sank into sullen silence. Quintus reflected: Titus Caelius was an idiot but at least he had his men's love. Merenda moved on, into the shadows beyond the torchlight.

There was a warning shout from one of the turrets flanking the Porta Praetoria.

"They're back!"

Quintus and his fellow galearii shambled towards the gates and braced themselves against the two great beams, hastily fashioned by the cohort's carpenter, propped one against each gate.

The ram struck and the shock shuddered the gates and rocked them a couple of inches and then passed into the beams and the bodies of the galearii.

"Hold firm!" shouted Crassipes.

The blows were renewed and the galearii gripped their props, muscles straining and teeth gritted, resisting as the doors swayed on their hinges.

Quintus was at the right-hand prop, with feet planted apart, his arms wrapped around the beam, leaning into it, his cheek against it, absorbing the repeated shocks of the ram. To his right one galearus, somebody's teenage slave, leant, both palms against the beam. Another galearus was to his left, and yet more put their backs against the gates.

Quintus sought distraction from the rhythm of the blows, the stiffness in his arms, back and legs and from the rough beam chafing his armpit. He thought about recent events.

The dead cook – Irminius Ambustus – what the hell had he seen that night? He'd said he'd seen something. Was it anything worthwhile? He'd never know now. But he had said something significant, he was sure of that. But what? Bah, his thoughts were going in circles. Fretting over what might have been – where was the profit in that? Where did that ever end? What if Tita hadn't been exiled…? Hell, don't go down that path again.

Aye, what might have been. That's a many forked road. What was it the lad had said? What if Tiberius Flavius Fimbria had never come? That was like a tune he couldn't get out of his head. Oh for pity's sake, what's that fool shouting about now?

He turned and peered into the early evening darkness to make out Merenda who strutted by, yelping querulous, pointless commands. He was followed by his new second-in-command, Publius Flavius, who spoke some words of gentle encouragement to the galearii.

How he's coming along, thought Quintus. Ha! His brother would be proud.

Then Quintus was jolted back to the immediate by a particularly hard blow against the gates.

"Fuck!" breathed the young slave.

Then another, even stronger blow struck, rattling their beam, catching the young galearius off balance so that he stumbled into the man on Quintus' right, bringing him down. Quintus hugged the beam but its far end no longer rested against the gate but wobbled inches away. It fell from Quintus' arms as a new blow hit the gate, driving its top hinge from the masonry and leaving it hanging.

There was a great groan from the defenders.

"Heaven defend us," whispered Quintus.

The galearii gazed at the damaged gate and a triumphant roar came from its other side.

§

Manius swayed. He staggered, almost fell, then recovered and contemplated the great gates bulging inward. The bar that secured them was splintered and the right gate hung with its top hinge torn from the wall's crumbling mortar. Silently surveying the damage were some thirty soldiers and Merenda, Publius Flavius and Quintus. All looked utterly spent and held their helmets in their hands to reveal hair tousled and stringy with sweat.

Manius approached. Publius Flavius saw him and tapped Quintus on the shoulder. Quintus turned and his brow creased as he took Manius by the arm.

"I'm fine," said Manius, noting Merenda's irritation at his arrival. Publius Flavius produced a small leather flask, which he uncorked and offered.

"Manius Suetonius, drink this."

Under Quintus' envious gaze Manius took a pull of the rough army wine, choked, and took another swig. The wine burnt his throat but spread warmth through his innards and revived him.

"What happened? Where are the enemy?"

"Back to the forest in their hour of victory," said Quintus.

He and Publius Flavius explained how, instead of exploiting their breakthrough, the barbarians had marched off singing.

"But why?"

"They're ignorant barbarians," said Publius Flavius and then with a sudden smile added: "You see, I'm now quite the veteran."

"You joke, but you've shown yourself a credit to your family," growled Quintus.

Publius swelled at that and his eyes regained some spark. Merenda, however, made a petulant gesture. "Ignorant barbarians! They're sporting with us, don't you see? In a few hours they'll be back, with a full day before them to finish us."

"Cannot the gate be repaired?" Manius asked.

Merenda gave an exasperated snort.

"Not in the time we've got,' said Quintus. "Not to stand up to the Brigantes."

"If the gate was refashioned from solid brass the enemy could still pour over the walls!" burst out Merenda. "I've not the men to hold them and those I have lack the strength to wield sword – look at them!"

They avoided his eye, silent. There was nothing to say. For himself, Manius was too tired for fear and only yearned for some resolution.

Merenda's voice was anguished. "The situation is hopeless, I..." He checked himself with a wary glance at the soldiers, as he turned to Publius Flavius. "See the gates have whatever can be found piled against them and make sure the men get what rest they can." Publius Flavius saluted and marched away and Merenda turned a cold eye on Manius. "Quintus Suetonius, your... assistant also ought to rest."

"I think not, Antonius Merenda," replied Quintus. "I may have been playing the common soldier but I remain a frumentarius, and my long experience whispers that I might soon need a witness. Am I wrong?"

Merenda stared breathing hard through his nose. "May the gods blast you. Can you see inside my mind?"

"I do believe I can."

Merenda looked as though about to weep.

"We've no chance, Quintus Suetonius," he said, covered his face and groaned through his fingers. "No chance."

Quintus betrayed nothing.

Merenda dropped his hands and implored him: "It's not me, or the cohort... it's my wife and my little Lucia. I can't let them fall into barbarian hands. Merciful heavens man, I've already armed my chamber slave and ordered him to..." he choked "... to do his duty... if the barbarians break through."

"I understand your distress, but that's not what you wish to share with me, is it? You believe you see a way out of this, don't you?"

Merenda stepped toward Quintus, his cheeks and eyes burning. "For heaven's sake, Cotta made us a proposal. We know he was a Wolf and we must take seriously what he suggested. It was the enemy suggesting it."

"Suggesting we buy them off?"

Merenda winced. "Yes... if you put it that way. We give them money; provisions, even the fort, in return for free passage."

This was a shocking proposal from a tribune of the Roman army. But Manius liked the sound of the plan. It gave a chance that Lucia and he might live. To hell with Rome's honour and dignity.

"Could you trust any promise of free passage?" asked Quintus. "They could cut us down in the open as easy as gathering snails."

"What have we to lose? They'll cut us down for sure here. Anyway, I hope to keep the fort by satisfying them with money and grain. What's your view?"

"My view? You want my cover for this? No my friend, this is your decision alone."

Merenda looked wretched.

"I only say this – as an observation, you understand," continued Quintus. "If they overwhelm us, they get everything: the fort, the money the victuals and the cohort's destruction. Your way – Cotta's way – might just mean that we lose less. Rome probably won't see it that way, but..."

"I don't have to give them all the money," said Merenda eagerly. "These savages will have no idea of value. Fifty thousand sesterces might satisfy them and surely Rome would consider that money well spent? It would be seen as a cunning stroke, worthy of Fabius Maximus himself."

Manius remembered Cotta and his wife and their talk of land investments: one pair of Brigantes with a shrewd idea of money's value. But Manius kept quiet.

Merenda looked towards the East. "It'll be dawn in a few hours. Will you accompany me to the strongroom and be my witness while I count out some money? You'll do that for me at least?"

"Yes, I'll do that for you, but don't expect the barbarians will furnish you with a receipt."

Aye, Manius thought, and he wants to get this done before Titus is back to denounce this stain on Rome.

As a detachment of soldiers came shoving a cart against the broken gates they took a couple of torches and made their way to the Principia. Manius summoned by a jerk of Quintus' head.

There were no rigid sentries guarding the colonnaded courtyard. The cohort had no men to spare even for this sacred duty. The three of them entered the great basilica and their tentative steps echoed while the dancing shadows cast by their torches added to the daunting majesty of the place. As they passed the statue of the late emperor, Quintus bowed. By the shrine, Manius thought Merenda hurried his pace past the reproach of the cohort's spirits. They reached the trapdoor to the strongroom.

"The key's in my office," said Merenda.

He strode to the door of his room. Manius whispered: "Can this scheme work?"

Quintus shrugged and quoted the emperor whose statue they had just passed. "'Gladly surrender yourself to Clotho: let her spin your thread into whatever web she wills.'"

Manius bit back a retort as Merenda came hurrying back with two great keys. He handed Manius his torch while he bent to unlock the door. Neither the lock, as he turned the key, nor the hinges, as he opened the door, made any squeak.

Their torches revealed a steep flight of six steps down to a solid oak door.

"You, wait," said Merenda to Manius and indicated Quintus should follow him. They descended, Quintus still holding his torch. Merenda took the other key and unlocked the second door into the cellar beyond.

Manius watched them, their backs towards him, on the threshold of that strongroom, staring in, neither speaking nor moving. Then Merenda made such a sound that Manius nearly dropped his torch onto him.

"Aagh," he cried. "Aagh, no… No!"

He would have collapsed, hadn't Quintus seized him with his free hand and lowered him to sit on the steps. Quintus looked up. "Here boy, help me with him."

Manius trotted down to join them. His eyes were drawn to follow Merenda's horrified stare into the strongroom, a room of perhaps five paces by three, plastered and whitewashed – and which was completely bare of any object, not even a single coin.

Chapter Twenty-Six

They helped Merenda back up those steps and out of the basilica. There, he wrenched himself from their arms and threw up. He remained bent for some moments, then straightened, wiped his beard and coughed.

"Forgive me," he said, looking across the street but his eyes seemed unfocused. "What's happening is clearly not of this world. This is the work of the evil one, Ahriman, or a test from Mithras himself. This cannot be cured by devotions at the lararium or even by offerings. No, the only worthy sacrifice is of myself, by adherence to my duty."

He gripped Quintus' forearm. "Farewell. I go to die with my soldiers." The warmth in his expression was swiftly replaced by a venomous glare at Manius. "I only ask that you keep this" – a quivering forefinger was thrust into Manius' face – "away from my daughter. I'll not have her defiled before she dies."

Manius recoiled, then quivered with fury. He could have borne Merenda's unprovoked dislike but not speaking of Lucia and himself in that debasing way – that was too much. He advanced, his face burning, his fists bunched.

Merenda, oblivious, was already turning, as Quintus, with a quick furious look at Manius, put an arm around the tribune's shoulder and reassured him that he'd do everything in his power to protect his daughter's honour. Merenda nodded absently and headed towards the Porta Praetoria with an uneven gait, as though his feet couldn't anticipate the ground.

Manius would have shouted some insult, but Quintus took him by the shoulder and walked him to the south rampart. They sat there while Manius raged. The dawn turned the black sky to dark blue, then to grimy grey, and still Quintus listened. Manius cursed his fate: his lowly status, his prospects and the way the gods were tormenting him with Lucia, driving him insane with a longing thwarted by her father's animosity, by their difference in station and – were that not enough – by death.

Manius paused, exhausted by his own grievances. Quintus opened his mouth but before he could speak Manius rounded on him. "Do not – I beg of you – do not quote the late emperor."

Quintus held his peace. Silence ruled the fort. The soldiers around them slumped on the walkway, their backs against the wall, chins on chests and eyelids blinking to stay awake. Now and then optiones would give orders, but in low voices, as if in reverence. Once or twice Manius looked over his shoulder through the wall's crenellations at the vicus and the open ground beyond, over which the road ran, back to Eboracum and thence Londinium. There was no sign of the barbarians. But they were surely coming.

They were given bread and even a little wine and while they ate and drank Manius asked for Quintus' thoughts on the empty strongroom; not that he cared, but he needed conversation. Quintus put a finger to his lips and motioned towards the soldiers.

"Keep your voice down. It's hard enough that they're to die; knowing that their pay has been stolen into the bargain would be too much."

"Who stole it?" Manius whispered. "Cotta?"

"I don't know. I've many confused thoughts. No, if you press me, I don't believe Cotta took it – how could he? Nor do I believe he killed Flavius Fimbria, but if you ask me why, I can't explain. What you said: if the general had never come, would the money still have been stolen? I rather think it would."

Manius shook his head. He was too tired. "Does it matter? The money's no good to anybody in this fort now. Do we care?"

"Yes, I care. It's a riddle and I must solve it. That's my nature. About the only thing I'm proud of." He smiled. "Didn't the late emperor say: 'The pride that prides itself on freedom from pride is the hardest of all to bear'?"

"Sorry," he added, at Manius' weary sigh.

Manius' mind returned to Lucia and the imminent barbarian assault. Quintus stared at his boots and pulled at his beard.

Manius heard voices. It was Publius Flavius Fimbria walking along the rampart, checking that his men had eaten, and even attempting jokes. Manius reflected how recently this man had been anxious that he wasn't cut out for the military life, yet the soldiers seemed appreciative and there was no eye-rolling when his back was turned. Had his brother's death freed him to be his own man?

His musing was cut short by Quintus. "Ha, here's the fellow who can help me with my riddle. Publius Flavius Fimbria! Over here!"

Fimbria approached, his expression guarded.

"Publius Flavius Fimbria," said Quintus, with – Manius was glad to see – the grace to get to his feet. "I ask a favour. Would you approach the tribune and request that I be allowed to examine the cohort's adjutant records and rosters?"

"What? Now?"

"I fear I may never have another opportunity."

"But… why?"

Quintus only smiled. Fimbria shrugged. "If that's what you want."

"Perhaps it would be fitting to ask Antonius Merenda."

Publius Flavius drew closer and adopted his lowest whisper. "I'd rather not bother the tribune. He's somewhat… absent."

"You mean you can't find him?"

"No, he's at the Porta Praetoria. I mean he's somewhat absent in his mind and I think it best if he concentrates on as few things as possible."

"So, I've your authority to examine the records?"

"You're a frumentarius; you're your own authority. You once made that clear." A wry smile. "The records are in the Principia, in the room by the tribune's. I only ask that when you hear the trumpet you return to your position immediately."

Quintus nodded and, after one last curious glance at him, Publius Flavius passed on.

"What can you want with the cohort's records?" Manius asked.

"You may accompany me and then you'll find out."

Despite imminent death, Manius was curious. There was also the proximity of the Principia to the Praetorium, where Lucia was confined.

They made their way to the Principia and into its basilica. They entered the office next to Merenda's and found it lined with shelves of documents. Quintus peered at them.

"The great thing about the army is that everything's so undeviating. Yes… y'see, the adjutant's clerk in Longovicium arranges his files in the prescribed manner, just as his counterpart does in Nicomedia or Emerita Augusta and just as they did in my day. Here we have the sick sheets, here the granary rolls, here the punishment rolls and – aha – here the duty rosters, all in date order."

"What are you looking for?"

"It'll be easier to explain when I've found it. Now hold your tongue."

He took a sheaf of documents, spread them across a table and pored over them, leafing through while, muttering: "What a ridiculously crabbed hand this clerk has." He called to Manius to find a tablet and stylus, that he might make extracts. Manius had to go to Merenda's office where he soon came across what was required. He had just stepped back out when he saw a man hurrying towards him across the basilica. He recognised one of Antiochos' capsarii.

"Sir, what a relief. They told me I'd find you here; you're wanted at the hospital, the surgeon needs you."

"Why?"

"It's his honour Caelius Metellus who calls for you sir."

"Titus wants me? Then I'll come at once."

Manius stuck his head next door to explain to Quintus and to hand him the tablet and stylus. Quintus waved him away without looking up.

He trotted with the capsarius to the hospital where Antiochos met them at the entrance and gave Manius a searching look as the young man leaned, one arm outstretched against the door jamb.

"You're very pale. You're still not well?"

"The run from the Principia has set my head pounding again but it'll pass."

The throb and ache did recede as he leaned panting while Antiochos told him not to be so foolish as to attempt running again. "You need several days more rest before you try such an exertion."

Manius managed a harsh laugh. "Several days? You think we have even one?"

"I'm a doctor and sworn to do what I can for my patients. Truth be told, I never know whether they have one day or one thousand, but I must treat them all as if they had a tomorrow."

This was a rare professional humility. Was he, in facing a final grim reality, recognising his limitations?

"Are you sure you're well?"

Antiochos' concerned face drifted came back into focus.

"Titus Caelius, I was told…"

"Ah yes… I understand you're his friend."

"I am."

Antiochos drew Manius inside the doorway. "Titus Caelius' condition is more serious than I first thought. I confess to an error there. As for his head wound, there was no mistake: that was trivial. But he also sustained a severe blow to his knee and that damage was initially hidden from me. I understand that was received earlier. Men report they saw him limping for much of yesterday. On close examination, it's a bad wound… the bones… the tendons…" Antiochos shook his head.

"Is his life at risk?"

"The leg is poisoned… if nothing is done…"

Manius groaned.

"If only he'd come to me earlier…"

"Not Titus. He'd never leave the fight."

The surgeon nodded in sad acknowledgment and squeezed Manius' shoulder. "He's feverish and calls for you. Go, see if you can steady him. We've only minutes. All's prepared."

"Must you? Is it necessary now? How long do any of us have?"

"If we don't act he'll surely die. I know my duty and I'll do it until the end."

He led Manius along the corridors, once so spotless, but now soiled with blood, puke and shit. They arrived at Manius' old sick room where they'd taken Titus. Outside waited four capsarii, grim and weary.

Antiochos again pressed Manius' shoulder.

"Comfort him as best you can. You only have a few moments."

Reluctant, Manius opened the door. Titus lay, his head slightly raised. His face, as white as the pillows supporting him, shone with sweat and his curls were darkened with moisture and lay flat. His shirt was sodden and the rest of his clothes, with his armour and sword belt, still lay on the floor. Manius closed the door and approached. Titus gave a weak smile and croaked: "Manius, old man, it's good to see you."

Manius couldn't speak for the knot in his throat.

Titus moistened his lips. "Tell me: how are the men, how's the cohort?"

Manius swallowed and with an effort said: "In good heart… but they miss you, Titus. To hell with the cohort! How are you?"

Titus gasped, then composed himself. "Not good, my friend. One of the Brigantes caught me on the knee with some sort of scythe. Aye, I've been felled by a peasant's tool. Here, see."

He peeled back the sheet. Manius fought to remain impassive as the hair stood up on the back of his neck. Titus' right knee was livid and grotesquely swollen.

"Not pretty eh?" Titus said and – to Manius' relief – covered it.

Manius searched for something comforting. Before he could speak, Titus clutched his sleeve and pulled him down and raised himself up so their faces were inches apart and his blue eye burned into Manius.

"Manius, don't let them cut it off. I'm a cavalryman, you mustn't let them…"

"Titus, they'll only do what's best, they…"

"No Manius! Don't let them! Fetch Birca, she knows herbs, she'll mix me a potion. Fetch her!"

This was awful. Delirium was taking hold. Manius made soothing noises, as to a child, but Titus' eye continued to blaze. Then he looked over Manius' shoulder, terrified. Manius turned to see Antiochos and his capsarii entering.

"No!" shouted Titus. "Manius, you promised!"

He released Manius who stepped back, his hand over his eyes to shield them from this.

"Seize him," said Antiochos. "Quick now!"

The capsarii moved. Titus shouted another protest, then lunged down to the side of his bed before, sword in hand and, his face twisted, he thrust at Manius.

"Stop him!" shouted Antiochos and a capsarius grasped Titus' wrist, almost as his sword blade reached Manius' stomach. Manius jumped back and the capsarii crowded around and over the shouting Titus, each holding a limb, forcing him down and Antiochos, approached, bearing knife and saw.

Manius fled. He ran down the corridor, tears streaming and, in his ears, coming from that room, was a mighty roar, which rose and blossomed into an echoing shriek.

§

Manius staggered down one of the fort's streets and then another until he reached a quiet corner by the farrier's, where he could weep. But that was soon done. Things were beyond tears. He made his way towards the Praetorium.

By the Principia he bumped into Quintus as he was leaving.

"Where're you going?"

Manius didn't reply, but a flickering glance towards the Praetorium betrayed him.

"The girl?" Quintus shook his head. "No, don't be a fool. That won't end well. Come with me, back to the rampart. That's your place. At a time like this don't let it be said you were skulking in a girl's room."

Manius had neither the strength of mind nor body to argue. He let himself be led, like a truant to the schoolroom, back to the rampart, where they sat.

"You've been weeping. Is Titus Caelius dead?"

Manius shook his head and told him what had happened.

"What! He tried to kill you?"

"He didn't know what he was doing. The pain and the fever have taken his wits."

Quintus nodded and squeezed Manius' arm. Manius wished he hadn't, for his tears threatened again. Angrily, he turned and looked over the wall. "Still no enemy. Why do the bastards delay?"

He watched a brown dog lope round the corner of one of the buildings in the vicus. It slunk, its tongue lolling and teeth bared in a grin, and its ribs showing under its matted coat. It disappeared round another corner and Manius shuddered: what would it scavenge after this day was done?

He flopped back beside Quintus. "Did you find what you were looking for?"

Quintus' eyes narrowed. "I believe… yes, I believe I found most of what I expected. I have the solution and I only need to think some more."

"Will you tell me?"

"When I've everything in its place to my satisfaction."

"How much time do you think we have? The Brigantes…"

"That's in the hands of the gods. Let's hope they haven't brought me so close to the truth – as I believe they have – for it to die with me. No, I can't believe that they'd sport so."

Manius didn't pursue it. He was past caring. Quintus squinted into the body of the fort and called out: "Hey you! Arrius Gracchus. Yes you. Come here, if you please."

Manius saw the upturned face of the tax collector, who smiled, half raised a hand and made as if to speak and then headed for the nearest steps and began to climb. Quintus watched him with a sly eye and said from the side of his mouth: "Here's one matter we can settle easily enough."

Gracchus stood, rubbing his hands and bowing, and he'd barely returned their greeting before he was pleading the necessity of resuming his place on the rampart.

"My… my optio only excused m… me reluctantly," he stammered. "For the latrine."

"Orders must be obeyed," conceded Quintus and, as Gracchus

beamed and turned to make off, added, "and mine rank before those of an optio. Stay where you are. I wish to speak to you. I order you – as a frumentarius."

Gracchus froze. His eyes darted and his tongue flicked over his lips. "Oh, I didn't know."

Quintus smiled. "You surprise me. Usually, when I arrive at place such as this, it's the common gossip of the garrison within hours. Isn't that so, Manius Suetonius?"

"Invariably the case, Quintus Suetonius," Manius said, too weary to point out that he'd informed Gracchus of their status.

"Furthermore," continued Quintus, "I'm sure Aurelius Cotta would've told you. You were well acquainted, weren't you? Enough for you to help him leave the fort on the night of his death."

Gracchus' lips peeled back in a terrified grin.

"You seem to be unable to speak. No matter, I've a little more to say yet, but when you do find your tongue, I advise you not to deny what I'm putting to you. That you're a Christian, or a Jew. That you and your family have been seeking to win the local people over to your beliefs. Cotta, as a magistrate and a Wolf, would've learnt that and no doubt he threatened to expose you if you didn't help him.

"Now, I want you to tell me the truth; if you don't, I'll haul you before the tribune and insist that you make sacrifice and obeisance to the Emperor and deny your god. I shall treat your wife and children likewise. Will you so deny your god, with death so imminent? If you refuse and defy the law you will all be executed. Isn't that so Manius Suetonius?"

"It cannot be otherwise Quintus Suetonius," Manius dutifully intoned.

"But this needn't happen, Arrius Gracchus and, believe me, I've no wish that it should. Trust me and just confirm what I already know. There now, a nod. That'll do. Well done. Now, find your speech: how did you help Cotta?"

The grin was still on Gracchus' face. He stared, he trembled, but he managed to stutter. "We… we… put a rope over the wall when the sentries had passed. He had… had accomplices in the vicus. I took the rope up."

"Heaven help us, there must have been more ropes over the wall that night than from the vestal virgins' windows. Were you to help him back over again?"

Gracchus shook his head. "No, he… he'd no intention of returning."

"So, he was to have led an assault from without," mused Quintus. "He wanted to send you to Corstopitum – why? Don't look surprised, your conversations weren't as private as you might have hoped. Well, why?"

"He wanted me to take messages to the tribal leaders."

"What messages?"

"I don't know, I never received them."

Quintus stared at him. "Have you anything more to tell us? No? Go, take your place at the rampart and don't bring yourself to my notice again."

Gracchus gibbered and fled along the rampart.

Quintus looked at Manius. "So, there's Cotta's accomplice. I wonder: did Aurelia Cotta know her husband was leaving her?"

Manius shrugged and a hoarse cry came from his left. A soldier was pointing out over the parapet.

Manius reached for his sword with resignation. "The bastards must be upon us."

Before he could rise, there was a ripple along the ramparts as the soldier's cry was taken up. The shouts had an energy about them and then there was laughter and cheers. Manius struggled to his feet.

He looked in disbelief. The road that ran down into the valley to the south was no longer a barely discernible ribbon in the snow. Now it was black with a long column of marching troops, whose tail disappeared into the dip of the valley. They marched, relentless and synchronised, growing steadily nearer, the crunch of their boots growing louder and the weak sun caught their helmets and armour. On their flanks were cavalry auxiliaries, picking their way through the snow, a moving line that stretched out to the forest's edge. At the column's head rode a general in glorious scarlet cloak, and around him were his staff and trumpeters.

Manius rubbed his eyes. Had his fever returned?

"A little tardy," said Quintus, at his side. "But welcome, none the less. Behold Sixth Victrix."

The cohort's little remaining strength was being spent cheering and waving at the advancing legion, some thousands strong, which made no acknowledgement, but marched with stern discipline towards them.

"Come," said Quintus, and dragged Manius along the wall, elbowing past joyful soldiery and Arrius Gracchus who was wringing his hands, his eyes streaming. Manius allowed himself to be led to that corner of the rampart where the south and east walls met, beneath which the road ran to the Porta Praetoria. They arrived as the general, at the column's head, reached the fort. One of his staff officers shouted a command, repeated down the ranks and the whole formation came to a halt with a smash of boots and rattle of leather and iron.

The general looked up at the beaming faces lining the rampart. He rose in his saddle, smiling from under his great crested helmet. "Well, where's your commander? Where is Antonius Merenda? Will he not open the gates and welcome Sixth Victrix? Hey? Hey?"

Manius recognised the bony, ruddy face of Gaius Caerellius Priscus, governor of the province of Britannia.

Chapter Twenty-Seven

Quintus was summoned barely an hour after the governor's arrival at the head of Sixth Victrix, an hour of turmoil and of weary jubilation from the besieged as rescuers crowded into the fort and as officers barked commands to try to bring order to the mayhem.

"My dear Quintus Suetonius, how are you?"

Priscus beckoned him into Merenda's office where he stood behind the desk.

"It's even fraying him," thought Quintus, for, while Priscus beamed, there were signs of strain: the eyes wandering and the voice a touch brittle.

"Much better – after your arrival."

"You're surprised?"

"I shouldn't be. There was a revolt and you have moved to deal with it."

"You make it sound easy. Well, let me tell you, it's been infernally difficult. We've had forced marches from Eboracum, in this appalling weather. We left Vinovia two days ago and had to camp last night just three miles short of here."

"That explains it."

"What?"

"The Brigantes must've seen your camp fires. They abandoned the siege, even as our gates were broken."

"Well this morning they'd drawn up to oppose us, but they took one look at Sixth Victrix and then melted away into the forests."

"They're unlikely to attempt open fight."

"Good. This business is getting out of hand."

"So it would seem."

"Yes," drawled Priscus, "I've much to do here, to restore some sort of order. Merenda's of little use, seems to be in a state of collapse. But I had to see you urgently. Where's Cotta?"

"Dead?"

"Dead? How?"

"He was with the rebels. He was discovered."

Priscus stared. Then his gaze dropped to papers on the desk. "Did he... er... say anything... before he died?"

"Nothing."

Priscus nodded. "I shall need a full report – on Tiberius Flavius and Cotta."

"In writing?"

"Great heavens no! We'll dine this afternoon and you can tell me everything."

"May I bring my assistant?"

"Don't tell me you want a witness?"

Quintus smiled. "I doubt that'd help. No, he may recall details that slip my mind."

"By all means let him come." He took up a document. "Now, I really must get to grips with all this..."

"Of course. One last thing..."

Priscus looked up, eyebrows raised.

"Have you spoken to Merenda?"

"Not in any detail, but it's one of my many priorities."

§

"Why'd he want to see you so urgently?" asked Manius.

Quintus shrugged and sat on Manius' bunk. "He wanted to know where Cotta was. Once I told him, he wanted time to think."

"Why didn't you mention the empty strongroom?"

"Let Merenda tell him himself. The money was in his keeping."

"Isn't it our responsibility to report it?"

"Our responsibility is to the emperor not the governor, and the interests of those two parties don't coincide."

Manius considered using the money's disappearance to his own advantage? Be first to inform Priscus? Win his appreciation?

"By the way," continued Quintus. "Priscus has invited us to dine at the praetorium. He wants us to brief him."

"Today?"

Quintus nodded. Manius swore. This left just a few fraught hours to arrange their washing, shave and render their togas fit to be seen in a fort turned upside down.

And to think whether, and how, to approach Priscus.

§

Tita Amatia was at a party, in the villa of Voconius Romanus. They'd all returned from the source of the Clitumnus and were now gathered in the garden, enjoying the balmy evening, drinking, laughing immoderately. "How priceless!" There was a sudden chill. She regarded the waning moon, a vanishing moon. She shivered and looked over to see Quintus staring back. They exchanged a smile, then somebody was trying to attract her attention, touching her shoulder, shaking her, insistent...

"My lady, my lady."

Bodvoc was standing over her bed, looking earnest.

"Ugh, what is it?"

"My lady, there's news."

She groaned, sat up and rubbed her eyes. She'd slept badly last night and had been making up an hour's lost sleep. Now her head was heavy.

"What news?"

"The siege is over." She winced, but he added: "The fort stands. The legion has marched from Eboracum and now the cymru are dispersing."

"So, Sixth Victrix have come to the rescue, have they?"

"They say the Roman governor himself commands it."

"Priscus! The dog! He's got wind of Flavius Fimbria's death and has thrown the dice. I must stop him!"

She threw the covers back and swung her bony legs out of the bed. "Where's Drustan?"

"In the camp, on the other side of the valley."

"Get me a horse."

Tita Amatia began dressing. She was lodged in a one-roomed cottage that formed part of Drustan's estate, a hovel, but without lice and by the road and less than a mile from Longovicium.

Five minutes later she had her coat on and was in the scrubby pasture that separated the cottage from the road. Bodvoc held the bridle of a sturdy, dappled pony, He cupped his hands to receive her foot as she hoisted herself onto its back.

"Wait for me here."

Once she was in the saddle, she kicked the pony into a walk, then a canter, as she headed across the road and down into the valley and the trees that cloaked it.

§

"And you, my dear boy – Manius isn't it? – splendid to see both of you, safe and well."

As they entered the dining room, Manius congratulated the governor on his victory.

He guffawed. "Victory! I doubt they'll grant me a triumph for that little affair. No, it was hardly a great battle, but that's perhaps no bad thing. I… oh, what is it now?"

Manius looked over his shoulder and to see one of Priscus' staff officers, a haughty young blueblood. He approached to hand Priscus a note and whispered.

"What? What?" said Priscus, flapping an impatient hand. "Yes, see that it's done as the legate suggests and tell him I'm not to be disturbed again, unless it's a matter of importance – importance – you understand."

The officer gave a stiff bow and marched out, his eyes gliding over the frumentarii. Priscus watched him go.

"You see how these fools plague me. Military life can be a bore, young man, as your father will agree. Marches to plan, camps to be made, latrines to have dug, rations to provide, reports to be written. Oh no, it's not all battles and glory, whatever the histories say. Now, I must house the best part of a legion and a cavalry ala in a fort made for a milliary cohort. More than five thousand men, where there should be less than a fifth of that number; and then they want feeding. And every tiny thing referred to me."

"You have your staff," said Quintus.

Priscus rolled his eyes. "They're hopeless. And the legate of Sixth Victrix, Julius Valerianus, seems to think my presence renders it impossible for him to make the smallest decision himself. As for Antonius Merenda – what's wrong with the fellow? He appears bereft of all initiative."

"Have you spoken to him?"

"I can hardly get any sense out of him."

Manius watched Quintus. Was he going to raise the missing money?

"He's had much to tax him recently."

"What? Well... perhaps. At least I've had working parties out collecting wood and the bathhouse furnace is stoked – that's something, hey, hey? Anyway, that's enough of... oh no, here's another."

He broke off to shoo away a centurion, telling him that he'd take no more interruptions and if Julius Valerianus was wondering what boots to put on he must decide for himself.

The centurion made a hasty retreat and Priscus shook his head. He wasn't the same urbane politician Manius had met in Londinium. He seemed preoccupied as he signaled them to take their places. When they were on their couches, he clapped and slaves trotted in bearing food and wine. After days of hard tack and porridge, Quintus and Manius smiled at the radishes, eggs, dried sardines, duck, hare, sausage.

"I congratulate you on your commissariat," said Quintus.

Priscus gave a thin smile. "Military life can be tiresome, but it doesn't have to be unbearable. I brought some comforts. But here" – and he relieved a newly arrived slave of a wine jar – "see what we have. It's been cooling in the snow."

They took the proffered glasses. Manius sipped while Quintus took a greedy swallow and smacked his lips. "Ahh."

Priscus rolled the wine in his mouth. "Good, isn't it? Yes, it has travelled. In the words of Silius Italicus: 'Reserved for the table of Lyaeus himself.'"

Quintus raised his glass in salute. "'The Setian wine that drowned the grey embers.'"

Priscus smiled. "That's what I respect about you, Quintus Suetonius: you're cultured, well-read. So many other frumentarii are... let's not circumlocute – crude, even inclined to boorishness, whereas you're... no, I won't make you blush. But you study him Manius, he has much to teach you."

Manius simpered while Quintus growled and crammed a handful of radishes into his mouth. They ate.

"So," said Priscus, dabbing a napkin to his mouth, "you were surprised to see me today?"

"Few things surprise me anymore."

"Of course you were surprised. Admit it. I'm only sorry I couldn't get word to you, but this accursed weather – what could I do? It was fortunate that Aurelius Cotta did succeed in getting a message to me weeks ago – and you'll appreciate just how labrynthine the channels of communication were – informing me of Flavius Fimbria's death. If necessary, he was to have accomplished that himself, but you, of course, pre-empted him. You acted with such dispatch too. You can picture how this changed things in Londinium. Tiberius Flavius Fimbria's party is utterly collapsed and his one-time creatures fawn around me." Priscus gave a wolfish grin and rubbed his hands together. "You've done Rome proud."

Quintus helped himself to duck and chewed under Priscus' approving gaze. Manius stared, in horrified realisation.

§

Tita Amatia held her pony to a canter along the rough path through the trees. She dared not gallop, the way was too narrow and there must be hazards hidden under the snow. Even cantering invited a fall but was easier on her protesting muscles than a trot and she'd no time to lose. She must find Drustan, speak to him and convince him.

She grew uneasy. The path didn't look familiar. Had she taken the wrong one? Hell! The way took a turn to the left and, as she rounded it, she had to haul on the reins.

"Whoa! Whoa!"

Three men faced her: Britons, one middle-aged and two younger. They had swords hanging from their belts and wore helmets. The elder spoke and one of the others seized her pony's bridle.

"Fine lady. Out for ride?" said the elder, in broken Latin, but with a plain leer.

Tita contemplated them, wishing she had a whip.

"I seek Drustan," she said in Celtic. "He's kin. Where can I find him? Quickly now!"

The man released her bridle as though it was on fire. The older started, then shuffled, coughed and pointed down the path. "This leads to the camp, perhaps half a mile, my lady. Lord Drustan was there."

Tita nodded, ignoring them as they knuckled their foreheads in salute. She urged on her pony, relieved to be on the right path but anxious to reach Drustan. If she missed him at the camp, if he'd already left, she'd no idea where to find him. He was her best acquaintance among the tribal elders. Without him, it'd take too much time to follow up other names, seek other kin. And that time was working for Priscus.

The path took another twist. Something moved to her right. She caught a glimpse of a boar blundering through the undergrowth. She looked back to her front – to see the branch that struck her in the face and sent her crashing from the saddle.

§

"With that business taken care of I came north with all speed," continued Priscus. "I had to secure a now leaderless army and – with Cotta's help – bring these over-enthusiastic Brigantes to heel. This atrocious weather slowed us and it seems our rebellion has got out of hand.

"Now I learn Aurelius Cotta is dead. You must give me the details. His loss is inconvenient and we'll have to find another intermediary. I'm not pessimistic. Cotta did leave me names of some supposedly close to this Iovir, and these people know and approve the bargain struck. You'll take up these threads."

Quintus positioned a duck leg on his plate, wiped his fingers, raised his glass and surveyed Priscus over its rim. "In `taking up these threads', I'll need to know the terms of this bargain."

Priscus flapped his hand. "You'll have guessed the outline, the detail can be laid out later."

"The outline is? In case I guessed wrong."

The governor's eyes narrowed. "Very well. If you must. The Brigantes are to regain their lands with this Iovir as their king, a friendly king of a friendly nation which will guard our frontier – this barren, worthless wilderness. This is policy Londinium has been urging on Rome since Antonius Pius. It would safeguard all of value in this province, at a fraction of the cost of that absurd wall."

"And there's a more immediate advantage?" prompted Quintus.

Priscus swung his feet to the floor and sat forward on his couch. "We come to the essence, don't we?" He pointed at Manius but kept his eyes on Quintus. "The boy? Do you still want him here as witness, or would you rather he preserved his virginity?"

Quintus looked at Manius for an answer: would he remain while treason was under discussion? Manius had no doubt. Remote, hypothetical dangers weren't going to outweigh his determination to know, finally, what Quintus was about. He nodded.

Priscus chuckled. "Very well, Quintus Suetonius, let's put into words what we both understand already. With the Brigantes securing the frontier, the legions can be taken to Gaul, to march on Rome, to remove those corrupting the emperor and to restore his father's ideals to the governance of the empire."

"So you fomented rebellion to achieve this?"

"Matters weren't intended to reach such as pass. As it is, this can be contained."

"And Tiberius Flavius Fimbria is no longer an obstacle."

"You don't need to remind me of your valuable service there."

"Caerellius Priscus, there'll be some – who warned Horatius Buteo, for example – who'll say they were right and that Tiberius Flavius was loyal to the Emperor in trying to thwart your… less than loyal designs."

"Those such as Tita Amatia Aculeo? You're surely not so naïve. Don't tease. Flavius Fimbria only cared about his own interests. Yes, he wanted to thwart me, but not for the Emperor Commodus' benefit. The choice was between Fimbria ruling the empire – probably as emperor himself – or of me, guiding Commodus. Me and others who loved the late emperor – people like you, Quintus Suetonius. That's why I trusted you – and was right to trust you."

"Trust me!" Quintus laughed. "If you trusted me so much, why send Publius Flavius Fimbria along to nursemaid me?"

"Oh come, I thought you were the wiliest of frumentarii and you ask such a question." Priscus leaned back onto his couch. "Nobody trusts anybody completely. Rome wasn't built on trust. I established that Publius Flavius' famous hatred for his brother was genuine and so who better for the task – and such a quiet young man, don't you find?"

"And the play-acting in Eboracum?"

Priscus raised his eyebrows. Quintus described how Publius Flavius had permitted their departure to see Tita Amatia while pretending to succumb to a sleeping potion.

"He did that, did he? How remarkably enterprising of him. Yes, he was following my instructions – in enthusiastic spirit, if not in detail."

"Why? Why did you so instruct him?"

Priscus concentrated on carving some hare before answering. "Let's go back a little. The young emperor has several faults, among which is a tendency to believe every man's hand's against him, if not actually, then potentially. He trusts no one, which can be a strength in an emperor, but with Commodus, it goes too far. Encouraged by that creature Saoterus, he sees conspiracies around every corner and this could – if left unchecked – make him another Domitian. And I do not – and I emphasise this – I do not intend any oblique reference to that emperor's unhappy fate.

"Of course not."

"No, indeed." Priscus' eyes glinted. "Where was I? Ah… yes… the emperor suspects everyone; he suspects me, naturally, but also, he suspected Tiberius Flavius, could see through his overdone protestations of loyalty – a child could. He thought he was plotting with elements who'd been devoted to his late father and that made him very distrustful of Tiberius' proximity to Tita Amatia. I must confess that I encouraged his suspicions with one of two judicious letters of my own. After all, I had to counter whatever poison Tita Amatia dripped into the Emperor's ear concerning myself."

Priscus chewed looking at the ceiling; swallowed, took wine, then added: "So foolish really, given that I, Tita Amatia and yourself, all loved the late emperor.

"Anyway, put yourself in my position. Could I be sure of you? Would your loyalty to Marcus Aurelius give you a misplaced loyalty to his son? I couldn't know for sure. I did know that Tita Amatia, had recommended your posting to Britannia through her old friends at court. You suspected it? I suppose... yes... naturally, you would. Well, that would've made Commodus suspicious of you too. So I insured myself. I knew you'd try to meet Tita Amatia and, if you chose to oppose me, I could always tell the Emperor I'd made every effort to prevent it and instructed your escort not to permit it but that you circumvented the barriers I put in your way. Had things gone awry, it would've given me a weapon of sorts. Perhaps I was being over-subtle."

Quintus shrugged and helped himself to more wine. "Do you know anything about a man called Tiro?"

Priscus paused, a piece of hare halfway to his mouth. "Should I? Who is he?"

"A Sicilian desperado. A dead desperado."

Priscus' eyes widened in recognition. "Oh him. He's just some thug that Flavius Fimbria kept in tow. My information is he was working for Rome. Didn't they tell you?"

"They neglected that."

"How very like them."

Quintus pursed his lips. Priscus opened his mouth to speak but Quintus, his eyes still fixed on the table, pre-empted him.

"And Horatius Buteo?"

"What of him?"

"Did you kill him?"

The corner of Priscus' mouth twitched.

"I believe his steward, a man called Theon, was responsible. He confessed."

"And did he confess who paid him to do it?"

"Sadly not. He hanged himself in his cell before we could get that information."

"Convenient."

"Wasn't it."

Quintus made as if to speak again but Priscus cut in. "Quintus Suetonius, you seek explanations and that's your job. However, we've no time to waste on history. You must work with me now to deal with the present – for the good of the Empire. Now I'll ask the questions. Tell me about Cotta."

Quintus sighed and took a draught of wine. "There's little to add to what I've told you. We were besieged and believed the Wolves had someone in the fort. Cotta was discovered in the vicus in the company of rebels and he fought and was killed. He is, by the way, generally believed to have been Flavius Fimbria's killer."

"Is he, by Jupiter? Well let's leave it at that, shall we?"

They ate in silence. Manius' mind raced. Quintus had killed Tiberius Flavius Fimbria? Is that what Priscus had said?

"How is Tita Amatia, by the way?" asked Priscus.

"Surprisingly little changed."

"Splendid. Don't worry, I shan't ask for any account of what she had to say." He held his hand palm out. "That would be impertinent. You and she were… well, yes." He smiled, almost a leer. Quintus glowered. "Remember, old friend, all that was part of my youth too. Heavens help us – can it really have been so long ago?" He shook his head. "There's a natural alliance, isn't there, among the members of a generation? Aye, we're allied against young bucks here like Manius, who'd seek to supplant us and put us out to grass; hey hey?" He beamed at Manius, then shook his head again. "No, Quintus Suetonius, to probe would be to betray and sully my own youth. We were all together then and must honour each other now."

Then, Priscus' expression lost any trace of good humour and his voice grew heavy with sibilant sarcasm. "Also, while I yield to none in my admiration for Tita Amatia I fear she overrates her own importance these days. Oh, she still has many friends and corresponds with many of influence, but things have truly moved beyond her."

Silence fell, as they toyed with crumbs and wine glasses. Quintus observed Pricus from under his eyebrows, while Priscus stared at the table, his thoughts seemingly elsewhere. Manius, his mind boiling, darted covert glances from one to the other.

Finally, Priscus sighed, declared that he had to rise insanely early and so he must retire.

"I'm sorry we've had so little time today, Quintus Suetonius. There's much to discuss and we'll repair that in the coming days. It hasn't escaped my notice that I've spoken much and you very little. Oh yes, young Manius, he's a cunning old dog. You've much to learn from him."

§

Manius smiled politely. Yes, he'd much to learn from Quintus and he was determined to learn it that evening.

§

Tita Amatia came to. The pony nuzzled her. She spluttered, pushed it away and groaned. Her head ached. She raised a hand to her temple and flinched as she found a lump and a graze. How long had she been insensible? She heaved herself into a sitting position and from there rose by stages until standing. Her forehead pounded and she felt dizzy and nauseous. She leaned against a tree and closed her eyes until the feeling passed. Then she took the pony's reins in one hand and hoisted herself with a grunt so that she lay stomach-down across its back before swinging her right leg over its croup. With a groan, she settled in the saddle, eyes closed again, collecting herself, before she urged it to a gentle walk.

At this pace, less than ten minutes later, she reached a large clearing, which had been a camp for a hundred Brigantes besieging the fort. Now they were leaving and Tita Amatia watched a score of young men, assisted by some women and children, stuffing belongings into bags and rolling blankets. She studied their faces. They glanced back – furtive, curious. She'd spent the best part of her life among these people, but still found them hard to read. What were they feeling? Resentment? Resignation? Defiance? Probably all three. They were mercurial enough.

She sniffed the air and looked at the leaden sky. There was a change coming in the weather, she was sure. Nor was rain the only thing she could smell. To the west, across the valley, were Longovicium and several thousand soldiers. Even over more than half a mile she could detect the smoking fires, the sweating horses and the damp leather. She shifted in her saddle and, wincing at her bruises, raised herself so that she could just make out, through the highest, leafless branches of the nearest trees, the black turrets of the fort. Priscus was there – and she was damned sure she could smell him too.

She sank back and patted her pony's shoulder. It whinnied and pawed the ground which was a mess of slush, ash, dung and bones, the detritus of a camp. Well, no matter, it would manure the earth, feed the grass for whatever grazed here – goats probably.

She looked around with relief as she saw Drustan approach on a large, heavy roan.

He pointed at her forehead. "You've been hurt?"

"It's nothing." She nodded at the fort. "I hear Priscus has brought his legion."

"You're well informed."

"Better than you know." She gestured at the Brigantes. "They're breaking camp. Where will they go?"

"Many will go home – those with families. The young men will head west, into the hills, until spring."

"Over the winter? They'll die!"

Drustan shook his head smiling. "No. There are plenty of hidden glens where the Romans won't find them and people will take them food."

"Will the Romans even look for them?"

He raised his eyebrows. "Isn't it the Roman way to hunt down rebels?"

She gave a mirthless cackle. "Let's not play this game again, Drustan. We know this has been manufactured by some Romans for their own ends."

Drustan shrugged.

"Priscus has used you – and he'll continue to use you." She pointed at a group of Brigantine warriors loading gear onto an ass. "They believe they were simply in revolt against Rome?"

"They believe they were fighting for the Brigantes – and they were right."

"Aye, well they'd be wiser to stop now. I told you, this scheme of Priscus' will fail, sooner or later, and the sooner you and your people – our people – leave him to it, the sooner the Brigantes' part in it will be forgotten."

They both stared towards the fort before she added: "And what are Priscus' intentions now?"

Drustan shrugged again. "We cannot know. Cotta was our link. We need… Iovir needs… to talk to this Priscus."

Tita Amatia leaned and seized his wrist and he turned in surprise. She fixed him with a glare.

"It would be best for the Brigantes if you and I were to arrange that meeting Drustan. D'you follow?"

He stared back, holding her gaze.

"Well? Do you?"

He lowered his eyes and nodded.

Chapter Twenty-Eight

Quintus and Manius returned to their rooms without speaking. Once there, they circled each other like gladiators, but they feinted and probed with heavy silences, punctuated by inconsequentialities. A fine meal, yes a fine meal; we've no fuel for the hearth; no we must get some; will you have some wine? Yes I'll take wine.

Somehow, Quintus had had three jars delivered. Also, Manius noticed a note addressed to him. He took it over to the window.

"It's from Antiochos. Titus is doing well and I may see him tomorrow."

"That's good."

"So," said Manius, as if throwing out a casual observation, "Tita Amatia was right – in her estimation of the loyalties of Tiberius Flavius and Priscus."

Quintus grunted. "Not for the first time. She has her own, strange, woman's way of thinking but it can hit the mark as surely as any logic."

He added nothing, but Manius couldn't hold his tongue.

"Well, did you do it? Did you kill Tiberius Flavius Fimbria?"

Quintus bent to remove his shoes. "D'you think so?"

"How can I know? Priscus said you did and you didn't say otherwise."

Quintus looked at him with curiosity. "Kill Tiberius Flavius and Decima, like that? No, boy, you disappoint me. The solution to this riddle lies in the nature of the creature who performed those acts. D'you believe me to have such a nature?"

"Priscus said you did. Why didn't you deny it?"

"You'll recall he dropped heavy hints in Londinium that I should rid him of Flavius Fimbria. Remember, he said Merenda had served the late Emperor in slaying Avidius Cassius? I held my tongue then as I did this afternoon. Let Priscus believe what he chooses. By all means let him think I'm supporting his cause."

"Are you?"

Quintus sighed, and lay down on Manius' cot, his hands behind his head, staring at the bunk above. "Support his cause? I throttled one civil war in its cradle and I won't help Priscus be midwife to another. No, Rome is greater than me or Priscus. But I'd be lying if I said I know how I stand. We're cut off at the moment, are we not? We're in Daedalus' labyrinth without Ariadne's thread."

"And what's our mission now?"

"A ticklish question. It should be to serve the Emperor, though, for reasons so eloquently given by Priscus, that isn't an appetising option. I don't support Priscus, but I'm not out of sympathy with his motives. Tita Amatia now... well... I believe she'll side with the young emperor, if only to honour his father's memory. We must make contact with her somehow. Let's hope she stays safe from Priscus. He had Buteo killed."

He took a reflective gulp from his cup.

"So, if you didn't slay Tiberius Flavius, who did? His brother?"

"Back to him again? He's Priscus' creature, isn't he? If he did it, wouldn't he now be taking the credit? No it wasn't him."

"You're very sure."

"I am."

"How can you be?"

"Because I know who did do it."

Manius sprayed wine over his chin and down his toga. "What!"

Quintus eyed the crimson stains. "I'd soak that if I were you. As for the killer, I'm not going to tell you. No, however much you splutter and flail about, I'm not. Why? You demand why? You're impudent! At the moment, the less you know the better – for you.

He took another drink as Manius continued to protest.

Quintus propped himself on one elbow and faced him. "Listen, I'm sure I know who did it, but I must settle some things in my mind first."

"Oh, this is ridiculous!" Manius shook his fists and stamped, making the lamp tremble in its socket

"Think for yourself, it'll be a good exercise. I'll start you with this: Tiberius Flavius' death wasn't the main purpose, it was a feint. There! Ponder that and I'll go and pursue my own thoughts."

He stood, took a jar of wine, belched and stepped into his own room.

Glaring at the closed door, Manius grew angrier. Spitting oaths, he kicked off his shoes and threw off his toga, whose stains only worsened his temper. He lay on the bed Quintus had vacated. What had he meant? Tiberius Flavius' death a feint? How? On whose part? The concubine Pellia? What had happened to her? Other names occurred, but none seemed likelier than any other, apart from Quintus, Cotta, Publius Flavius, and Merenda...

Merenda? No, he was buffeted by events not directing them. To think: Manius had planned to win him over by arguing that Decima Flavia and Vibia Rufia could've committed suicide. Aye, that had been one of his great plans; as had the idea of impressing the general Tiberius Flavius. How the gods loved to sport with him!

As a child he'd once tormented an ant on the kitchen table, blocking it, by placing a knife across its path. He'd watched it scurrying along the edge of that blade, seeking escape, but, failing, turning to scuttle in another direction, to find its way blocked again by the knife. Were all his attempts to escape from a life without promise to be similarly thwarted? Was he stuck with Quintus forever?

Damn the old bastard! Manius was no ant. The gods weren't sporting with him, only testing him and there was yet a way out – Priscus.

Yes, he could go to the governor and place himself at his service. Join him against Commodus, share his triumph, and be rewarded with high office and great estates under the new imperium. What prizes: a villa and land in Tuscany; a house in Rome; slaves, power and the respect of men – and the hand of Lucia.

But how to approach Priscus without distancing himself from Quintus? This wasn't a matter of loyalty. Heavens knew the old goat had stretched that to breaking point and beyond. But to join Priscus would provoke conflict with Quintus, a conflict which Manius might lose.

And, if Priscus' rebellion failed and he shared the fate of Avidius Cassius, then, as a supporter, Manius could anticipate a grisly end, nailed up outside the Esquiline Gate, citizen or not. But if he didn't side with Priscus, wouldn't the governor view any who weren't with him as opposing him? And if the governor then triumphed? Oh, his ant had had it easy.

He needed someone to discuss this with. Lucia? Could he talk to her? No, to discuss such things with a woman would show weakness. That wouldn't be a good way to secure her respect and admiration.

The lamp flickered and flared, making the shadows swell and jump before it died, its oil exhausted. The darkness embraced him, like an even greater shadow over his future. His thoughts circled until he sank into sleep, in which he became a scurrying ant.

§

In the middle of the night the young slave was awake when he heard tapping at the door. Saoterus, slumbering in the bed beside him, was breathing steadily through his open mouth, whistling with every exhalation.

The young slave slipped from the bed and tiptoed to the door, which he opened noiselessly to one of Saoterus' house slaves. He stepped out to join the other in the corridor.

"What is it?" he whispered.

"The messenger."

"Wait."

He stole back into the room, took a tunic from the back of a chair and returned to the corridor, pulling it over his head. He accompanied the house slave down long passages, through the inner hall, skirting the courtyard and to the entrance hall. There sat one of Saoterus' people, Sabo, a hard, young blade, a regular visitor with messages, usually at night. He lolled on a bench, not rising to meet the young slave.

"Where is he?"

"Asleep. Do you need to speak with him?"

"No. Just give him this." He handed him a letter. "Make sure he reads it. Wake him. It's from the usual route and hasn't been seen by the frumentarii."

The young slave bowed, saw Sabo out and returned to Saoterus bedroom. The emperor's chamberlain was still asleep and he had to shake his shoulder before he opened his eyes. He looked dazed, then petulant.

"What is it?"

"Sabo brought this. To be read it immediately. He said it came by the usual way, unseen by the frumentarii."

Saoterus sat up and snatched the letter. "Light another lamp. No, don't bother. Here, you read to me."

He thrust the letter back and the young slave took it to where the wall lamp cast some light. He unfurled the document and brought it close, his lips silently framing the words.

"Well? What does it say?"

"The writer gives no name."

"I know who it's from, I asked you what it says."

"Er… Londinium is alive with rumours that Tiberius Flavius Fimbria has been killed in the north of Britannia; that Priscus was behind it. Priscus is moving north to quell the rebellion and take command of all army units. Tiberius Flavius Fimbria's supporters have either gone into hiding or have thrown in their lot with Priscus."

The younger man looked up from the letter to see Saoterus now standing by the bed, a night robe pulled around him. His face was pale and he passed his tongue over his lips. He stared into the darkness.

"So, the legions are his," he whispered.

He stood motionless a full minute, then came back to life.

"Light more lamps," he ordered and gathered up the clothes he'd discarded hours earlier and began dressing, muttering. "The Emperor must be informed. He'll take it badly. He'll want somebody to blame."

The young slave saw to the lamps and the darkness receded into the corners and outlines grew clearer. Saoterus froze again.

"Nobody else must know," he said, as though in sudden realisation. "If the praetorians – or any of the patrician families – get wind they could move against the Emperor, pre-empt Priscus; put in their own man. Nobody must know."

His gaze came to rest, unblinking, on the young slave. "But you know."

"I… I won't tell anyone."

Saoterus shook his head. He turned to a low cupboard and opened it. He stooped, his back to the room, but the young slave heard a clink of glass and liquid being poured. Saoterus straightened and turned, a glass of wine in hand.

"Here, take this, drink it."

"I… please… I don't want to… please."

Saoterus gave him a stinging slap across his face.

"Do as I tell you! Drink it!"

Sobbing, the young slave put the glass to his lips. Saoterus took the base in both hands and tilted it, making the wine flow into the young slave's mouth, overflowing, choking him. He coughed, wiping his mouth with the back of his hand. Fascinated, Saoterus stared, as he choked again, clutched his throat, gasped, sank to his knees before pitching forwards onto the floor, where he lay writhing, then twitching, then was still. Saoterus wept like a child.

§

Manius' dream was still vivid for some seconds when he awoke, until it was interrupted by a great banging. He opened his eyes to see light trickling through the shutters and realised that someone was beating on the outer door. He rolled out of bed and groped for his cloak.

"Wait a moment," he croaked. The knocking ceased. He pulled his cloak around him and staggered to the door, opened it and blinked down at Lucia's slave Numeria.

"What..what is it?"

"Oh sir, you must come. My mistress needs you, and she asks you to bring the old one – your father."

"What's the matter?"

"Mistress Lucia and her poor dear mother are beside themselves. It's her father, the tribune – he's been arrested by the governor."

Manius told her to wait and, while he dressed, shouted through the closed door that it might be take too long to rouse Quintus. But she called back that her mistress had insisted that the old one should also be summoned.

Manius swore. A chance to rush to Lucia's aid, to serve her and her father, but Quintus was called for the lead role.

Balancing on one leg, pulling on a boot, he hammered on Quintus' door.

"Wake up!"

Manius heard the usual grunts and oaths, followed by the creaking of his cot and the shuffling of feet, more oaths and coughing, before Quintus squinted at him through his tangle of hair. In a few words Manius explained and asked whether he should go on ahead.

"No, wait. I don't suppose Priscus is going to summarily execute him."

He closed the door and Manius listened to gushing and sighs as he emptied his bladder into a jar. Minutes later, Quintus reappeared, clothed, but with hair and beard uncombed.

"Let's see what we can do for Antonius Merenda this morning."

They were leaving with the impatient Numeria when Quintus tugged at Manius' sleeve, whispering: "D'you have money about you?"

"No. Why? D'you think we'll need some?"

"It's possible. Get some – I may make a repayment. I've no time for explanations."

With another curse Manius fumbled in his bag for a purse which contained a few hundred denarii. He handed it to Quintus who, from within his tunic, took out one of the thick woollen socks Manius had bought in Londinum. He slid Manius' purse into it, winking and tapping the side of his nose, before secreting it again.

Numeria, almost dragged them to the principia, where Lucia was pacing before the basilica steps. She ran to them and Manius' heart raced and he balled his fists to prevent himself from embracing her. There were tear tracks on her cheeks and her eyes still glistened.

"Thank you for coming." She turned to Quintus and placed a hand on his forearm. "And you too."

Quintus' face creased in avuncular kindness as he took her hand.

"Calm yourself, my dear. Things can't possibly be so bad as to warrant such distress in one so young – and so beautiful."

A glint shone behind the tears as she withdrew her hand, replying, with an edge to her voice: "It was bad enough for my father before. Now he's been arrested."

Quintus smiled, opened his mouth, but she stamped her foot and shook as her voice rose. "My mother, who's been living in fear of rape and murder at the hands of the barbarians, now faces her family's ruin and disgrace. She's distraught! How could she be otherwise?"

Quintus cleared his throat. "Yes… er… where is your father?"

"In there, with the governor." Her voice cracked and she waved at the basilica while turning away.

Quintus nodded to Manius who, with many backward glances followed him up those colonnaded steps. They arrived in the great hall to find Caerellius Priscus and Publius Flavius in conversation, their heads bowed. Priscus looked up.

"Ah, Quintus Suetonius, your arrival is timely. I was going to send for you."

"I hear you've arrested Antonius Merenda?"

"Have you, by Jove? You heard correctly."

"His offence?"

"Embezzlement of imperial funds." Priscus made a sweeping gesture towards the strongroom trapdoor. "Empty! It should contain some half a million sesterces and it's empty! But you know this, or at least Merenda tells me you do."

Quntius acknowledged it and, in answer to Priscus' angry enquiry as to why in the name of hell he hadn't informed him the previous evening, said that under the shadow of the highly important matters they'd been discussing, it had slipped his mind. Priscus shot a glance at Publius.

"Rubbish!"

"I believe Merenda knows nothing of this," said Quintus.

"What? Oh come, what do you take me for? A sizeable treasure is taken from a strongroom in a fort guarded by eight hundred men and their commander knows nothing of it?"

"The gods forbid."

Priscus contemplated him, stonefaced, then sighed. "I'm not pretending outrage or playing the stern paragon of republican virtue. Heavens knows these are strange times and the usual rules cannot always be followed. Ha! What a hypocrite I'd be to say otherwise; hey, hey? I'm willing to believe that Merenda – who never struck me as venal – has taken those funds for some… political reason. That can be looked into later, but now I've troops to pay and the Brigantes to treat with, and I was counting on that money."

"I see your difficulty."

"Difficulty!" spluttered Priscus, then gave Quintus a searching look. "Did you have anything to do with this?"

"I did not. I take it Merenda denies all knowledge?"

"Eh? Oh yes. I can hardly get any sense out of him. He babbles about sorcery."

"Where is he?"

"He has just been escorted back to the praetorium where he'll remain under guard. I had him taken out through the back. The longer we delay barrack-block gossip the better."

Publius Flavius coughed. Priscus wheeled round.

"Sir," said Publius, "I'm afraid there are already rumours. There has been trouble between the cohort and Sixth Victrix. They mock us as murderers and harbourers of murderers. Now, they've taken to calling us thieves too; blows have been struck and…"

"Enough!" barked Priscus, holding up his hand. "You're acting tribune of this cohort now. Restore discipline. Order beatings and scourgings and whatever else is required and I shall command Julius Valerianus to do the same – that's one decision I'll happily make for him. And, whatever you do, scotch these rumours. Put it about that Antonius Merenda had the money hidden for safekeeping, that the men will be paid and that it'll snow coins tomorrow. Tell them anything, but just keep the swine quiet."

Publius Flavius saluted and marched away. How he'd changed, thought Manius. Even his voice had grown louder.

Priscus faced Quintus who, rubbing his beard and staring at the floor, spoke. "This is all coming to a head sooner than I'd anticipated."

"What d'you mean?"

Quintus began pacing and Manius noticed that he'd taken out the sock containing his purse. He held it in his right hand, beating it into his left. "Yes, it's now time to tell you something you should know Caerellius Priscus."

Priscus and Manius stared.

"First, Merenda didn't take that money and knows nothing of its whereabouts." The sock thumped into his palm. "Second, I didn't kill Tiberius Flavius Fimbria for you."

"Then... who?"

"Who was the killer, or the thief? One and the same."

"Who? Who, man?"

Quintus smiled, with the sock dangling in his hand. "Come, let's go speak with our little Greek friend Antiochos."

"Antiochos?" gasped Manius. "How?"

He faced a whirlwind as Quintus rounded on him, his voice boiling and his hands shaking.

"What the fuck's it to you?" he shouted. "Don't think you're coming with us, you little worm, you viper? Don't think I'm having you spying and plotting against me. Don't think I don't know what you've been up to you, you little shit!"

His twisted face was inches from Manius' and his spittle flew. Manius recoiled from his onslaught, appalled and, even as he wilted under it, was embarrassed by the presence of Priscus, whose eyes were goggling, his mouth opening and closing.

Quintus continued flaying Manius. "Oh yes, don't think I don't know what you've been doing behind my back: undermining me, working against me, looking out for yourself. What? You deny it? Why the evidence is plain boy and it's right there – behind you."

Manius turned and Quintus dealt him a tremendous blow to the back of the head, rendering him unconscious.

Chapter Twenty-Nine

Manius felt pain: a persistent throbbing, centred on the back of his head. He tried to feel it, but neither hand would move. They were tied above his shoulders.

He opened his eyes. He was lying in a darkness relieved only by a glimmer from a shuttered window up to his right. He could only raise his head a few inches. He was tied to a bed. He strained, but fell back, his head pounding.

Quintus had hit him! The old fool had gone mad!

It must've been Quintus who'd had him strapped down. Or perhaps this was Hades. He was condemned to an eternal prison of shade, forever immobile among shadows.

No, he was alive and he must think. What had Quintus said in all those angry, hurtful words?

He'd mentioned Antiochos.

Antiochos! That's where he was – back in his room in the hospital. He craned his neck as far as he could now that his eyes were accustomed to the dark.

But why? Quintus had attacked him. Hence his presence here. But why bind him to the bed? He felt nauseous. Was he delirious? Had his illness returned? Perhaps his recovery had been only a dream, and he'd never left his hospital bed.

Something was different. By straining, he could just make out, against the far wall, something new. A table covered with a dark cloth. Also a sound: A low rhythmic breathing.

Manius peered to his right, into the shadows. There was another bed within arm's reach and a figure on it. He remembered: Titus had been placed here.

Manius swallowed, moistened his lips and whispered: "Titus, Titus."

No change in that soft breathing. He cleared his throat and spoke louder. "Titus, is that you?" Still no response. Manius swore. If it was Titus, he had to wake him. He had to penetrate whatever drug Antiochos was dosing him with.

"Titus!" he repeated, louder.

Thank the gods, he stirred.

"Titus, Titus."

"Hmm... wha... hmm."

"Titus. Oh for heaven's sake! Wake up, Titus."

With a grunt Titus sat up, his one eye staring. Manius called him again and Titus turned, searching. "Manius? Is that you?"

"Yes, it's me," Manius almost sobbed.

This was met with silence, except for Titus' rapid breathing and a low moan. Then Titus spoke, as if to himself. "My knee: it still hurts, merciful gods, how it hurts."

Then, an abrupt change of tone. "What're you doing here? Are you injured? I don't understand. I was told the siege was over. Your illness has returned?"

"No. Quintus attacked me and now I'm tied to this bed. He's gone mad, the moon must've got to him. You've got to help me."

Titus struggled to stretch and push open the shutter in the window above. Daylight flooded in and Manius blinked and saw a death-white Titus, leaning on one elbow, panting with his recent effort. He looked seriously ill, face twisted in pain. Only his shining, staring eye held life.

"Titus, there's a knife by your bed. Cut my bonds?"

Titus regained his breath. "I… I don't know Manius, I daren't strain the dressing on my leg. Oh hell, it hurts."

"You're little more than a foot away. If you could just free this near hand and give me the knife…"

"Give me a moment and I'll try, I swear."

Manius lay back onto his pillow. He explained how Quintus had raged at him; how he'd suggested that they see Antiochos and asserted that the assassin had been the one who'd stolen the money.

"What money?" asked Titus, plainly exhausted, staring at the ceiling. Then, with more interest: "What money's been stolen?"

"You don't know? Of course."

Manius told him about the empty strongroom and Merenda's arrest. Titus said nothing, staring.

Manius added: "And Quintus is convinced that whoever murdered the general stole the money."

"Who does he say that is?"

"He mentioned Antiochos."

"Antiochos? I… I suppose he would've had opportunity to poison Decima Flavia, but her husband… what motive?"

"And, if Quintus is right, he must've stolen the money. Why did he do that?"

Titus laughed. "Why steal half a million sesterces? My dear fellow, that would buy a decent estate and qualify a man for a knight. You'd get a tidy income from that at twelve percent. Oh, that'd tempt any man, Manius."

"Quintus always says Greeks care only for money."

"Talking of Antiochos," Titus' tone became conversational, "why d'you think he left me this knife?"

He had the knife in his hand, his thumb testing the blade.

"I don't know. Perhaps he forgot it."

"I don't think so."

"Then why?"

"Oh, surely that's obvious? So I might kill myself."

"Titus, no! Why would he do that?"

"I've nothing to live for. I believe I said something of the kind to him. I'm a one-legged man now. Ha! They were going to throw old Appius Rufius out for a bad foot. No, Manius, soldiering's my life and the cavalry my passion. Antiochos knows that and he's a compassionate man."

"You shouldn't talk like that."

He smiled. "I won't. Come, let's cut those bonds of yours."

With evident pain, he eased himself to the edge of his bed, knife in hand. He bent over Manius, who saw that his face – now right above his own – shone with excitement and that his fist gripped the knife overhand, to stab, not cut.

"Titus, what ?"

"I'm sorry, Manius, I truly am."

"Titus, in heaven's name, no!"

"No!" This erupted from the covered table which burst into the air and crashed to the floor. The black cloth which had covered it stood, waving like a ghost, uttering muffled oaths. It twisted and stamped and the cloth was hurled aside and there was Quintus spitting thread and fluff, sword in hand.

"Not this time!" he roared and stumped over to a stunned Titus, knocked aside his knife and thrust him down on to the bed, his blade to his throat.

"Here we have him, boy. He's our quarry."

§

Manius stared at Titus, who was regaining his poise, even after the door crashed open to admit Priscus, Publius Flavius and Antiochos. They joined Quintus to stand before him.

Antiochos acted as though on a routine call, easing Titus back onto his bed, adjusting his covers and relieving him of his knife which he then used to cut Manius free. Manius sat up, ignored by all, apart from the surgeon who examined his wrists.

"So, Titus Caelius, what was the story to have been?" boomed Quintus. "What would you've told us about this? Would you've had us believe that you'd acted while in the power of some delirium, or claimed to have been insensible throughout and have us fear our mystery assassin on the loose again? Which was it to be?"

There was a sheen of sweat on Titus' brow but he looked back at Quintus unwavering.

Then he grinned. "To tell the truth, old man, I hadn't yet decided."

Manius started, jolted from his daze. "Why?" he shouted.

Titus ignored him.

Manius, Publius Flavius and Quintus all tried to speak, but an indignant Priscus cut across. "Am I to understand that this man killed Tiberius Flavius Fimbria? On whose orders? For whom was he acting?"

Titus opened his mouth, but Quintus held up his hand. "No, Titus Caelius, let me explain. It's the only reward I seek – or ever receive."

Titus gave gracious permission with an ironic twirl of the hand.

Everyone was silent. Manius heard the purposeful tread of capsarii in the corridor.

Quintus spoke. "Tiberius Flavius Fimbria was unfortunate, wasn't he, to be in Longovicium at a convenient time to give cover for the death you really wanted to accomplish – that of Appius Rufius Atellus?"

"Who?" asked Priscus, looking at everyone in turn.

"Appius Rufius Atellus was the senior centurion and a man of no account to any but his cohort. He was assigned to guard Tiberius Flavius. He was a long-serving soldier, but was to be retired – cast aside, as he doubtless saw it – without a pension. A commonplace circumstance but fated to have far greater import."

Quintus stroked his beard and paced the space at the end of the beds. "It's easy to imagine conversations between this aggrieved veteran who faced destitution and the penniless but ambitious second tribune who'd diced his way into debt. How many evenings in the tavern did it take? How many night watches together on the ramparts? Eh Titus Caelius?"

Titus only smiled. Quintus continued. "I'm sure the agreeable, highly respected young second tribune played on Appius Rufius' pride, arguing that the army owed such a distinguished old soldier much and he owed it nothing."

Quintus pointed a quivering finger at Titus. "You must've studied his character and weighed the strengths and weaknesses of the man. I don't doubt that he was devoted to you. I observe men are. How easily the self-serving can charm and bend others to their wills."

Quintus looked at each of them, like a lawyer addressing a court. "They'd need and they'd motive, and they'd a fortune sitting in the fort's strongroom. They also had opportunity. As second tribune, Titus Caelius had access to the key and Rufius Atellus, as senior centurion, was responsible for guard rosters. Rosters which I've examined and which record that two soldiers: Varisidius Nepos and Celestius Piro were guarding the principia one night only weeks before the murder of Tiberius Flavius. Easy enough for the four of them to remove the treasure while the fort slept. How coincidental that those same two soldiers were killed while on patrol with Titus Caelius and Rufius Atellus. You must have thoroughly corrupted Appius Rufius to achieve that." Quintus jabbed his finger. "You bewitch people." Then he rapped: "Less to share, and two fewer tongues to wag – wasn't that so?"

Titus started at this, then gave a hint of a shrug.

While Quintus surveyed him, Priscus took a chance to speak. "I don't understand this at all. What's any of this got to do with Tiberius Flavius?"

Quintus ignored him but continued to study Titus. "I don't know everything. I wonder whether you planned it all along after the killing of those two soldiers gave you the idea, or whether the arrival of Tiberius Flavius seemed like a sudden present from the gods. Here was a great chance to have all the money by killing Rufius Atellus in such a way his death would appear merely incidental to that of a general notoriously loathed by his own brother, on whom suspicion would be bound to fall. Indulge me Caerillius Priscus, I shan't detain you much longer. Yes, Titus Caelius, you're a true cavalryman, a fast thinker. I suspect you only made this decision on the very night of Tiberius Flavius' murder, even while we were all at dinner in the praetorium. Probably the original plan was for Appius Rufius to retire far from here and be on his way before the fourth stipendia revealed the theft. But suspicion would naturally fall on the retired senior centurion and, vast as the Empire might appear, there was always a risk that he'd be discovered, questioned and would name names. Surely better to kill him and, of course, keep all the treasure."

Priscus, now beside himself, stuttered. "But... but..."

Quintus still ignored him. "Of course, such spontaneity and reckless courage weren't without their dangers. You can't have foreseen the snow that would keep you prisoner in Longovicium when you should've been on the road to Londinium with the money. Did you?" Quintus' accusing finger shot out again with such violence Priscus recoiled and Antiochos raised an eyebrow. "Well? Did you?"

A faint head shake from Titus.

"I thought not. Then, there was the problem of Decima Flavia Fimbria and what she might've witnessed. But, again, the gods smiled on, for you were able to take her life and that of Vibia Rufia, who might've been told heaven knows what by her husband. Did Birca help? Did she have that knowledge of potions and poisons so common among the Britons? It was you, of course, who ordered that storeman – what was his name? Ah yes, thank you Publius Flavius – Bericus. You ordered the unfortunate Bericus to tell Vibia Rufia that the stew was in the kitchen for her and Decima Flavia. Then you killed him. To divert attention: after the poisoning you left a hooded spirit to make us think it was Wolves' work. Cotta's involvement with the Wolves was also fortunate, wasn't it, and your chance to kill him; for then the whole mystery was solved for us. All that remained for you was to destroy his wife before she could insist that her husband hadn't had any part in those deaths. That leaves one unaccounted for – the Sicilian Tiro. Was that your work too?"

"Birca actually."

"A formidable woman."

Titus only smiled.

"The rest were all the work of a man who could gallop hard and still turn his mount in the space of a wagon's wheel."

All goggled at Quintus, apart from Antiochos who regarded him with curiosity and Titus, whose expression was inscrutable. Manius had only one question.

"Why did you try to kill me?"

"Yes, surely the boy deserves to know that," said Quintus. "You could attempt to deny all this, but there's this failed attack on Manius' life to explain away. I was sure you'd attempt it. You've already made two attempts, haven't you? Oh, yes Manius, this was his third essay on your life. I believe he would've killed you in the vicus that night, hadn't Cotta's blow split the wineskin and made him think you already dead and then he made that other trial on his sick bed yesterday. So come, Titus Caelius, tell us why."

Titus shrugged. "No purpose in throwing the dice again I suppose?"

"No."

Titus turned a sorrowful face to Manius. "Remember the night you helped me bury Birca?" Manius nodded, his throat too tight for speech. "When I went in for her body, I noticed – too late – that she'd left Publius Flavius' spew-stained toga in full view. I couldn't be sure you hadn't seen it, you see, or might not remember having seen it at some future time. You do understand?"

"Of course! Publius Flavius' missing toga!" exclaimed Quintus. "I'd quite forgotten that. The toga he couldn't produce the morning after Tiberius Flavius' murder, which we believed Publius Flavius must have destroyed because it was covered in blood."

Titus shook his head. "I told Birca to burn it. Poor Birca, she could be niggardly – like a peasant – and couldn't bring herself to destroy such fine wool from which a tunic might be cut. Stupid to rely on others. I'm sorry Manius, please don't think there was any animosity; I just couldn't be sure you hadn't seen that toga."

"I hadn't," Manius said, choking.

"I'm sorry."

Publius Flavius lunged toward the bed, Quintus wrapped his arms around him and held him.

"Sorry? You monster! You… you had me accused a… murderer… of my own brother. You're not human."

"I promise you, there was nothing personal in that either."

"And I believe you," said Quintus, placing Publius near the door. "I suspect there are many feelings you're incapable of. You know, I think you might even have killed Birca."

"No!" cried Titus. "You go too far, old man! And spare me the hypocrisy. You're a frumentarius, don't tell me you don't kill in the Emperor's service?" He grinned. "And where's the Emperor's service got you? Nowhere – and me neither. I thought it time to look out for myself."

"What!" exclaimed Priscus. "Hear him! He's brazen! He admits it! The rogue! He was recommended to me and he was to have commanded my mounted singulares."

"Eugh!" said Quintus. "Recommended! A knight, a class corrupted by love of money. I tell you: I tremble for Rome."

Priscus paid no heed, but leaned over Titus, his voice urgent. "Where's the money? Tell us what you've done with the money."

Manius saw indifference from Titus. He observed Quintus frowning, Publius whose knuckles were whitening on his sword pommel and Antiochos, his brow furrowed.

A shudder ran through Titus and he fell back on his pillow, sweat pumping from his hairline and down his white face. Antiochos stepped forward to feel his brow and his pulse.

Titus closed his eyes and whispered: "Gentlemen, I'm tired. Tomorrow I'll tell you everything, I swear it."

Antiochos straightened. "He's not shamming. I cannot answer for it if you don't let him rest."

Quintus exhaled heavily and took the knife from Manius' bed. "Very well, but I'll take this." He pointed at the surgeon. "Leave him no other means of self-destruction this time. He must have no easy way out."

Chapter Thirty

Manius was reeling as he and Quintus left the hospital. He'd been knocked insensible and almost murdered and then he'd learnt that a man he'd respected had tried three times to kill him.

His thoughts chased each other. "So, there was no connection between Caerellius Priscus' schemes and the murder of Tiberius Flavius Fimbria?"

"Only in the corruption of our empire, in a generation lost to all sense of duty, in men who care nothing for the state, but only for their own gain. I tell you: the greatest threat to Rome comes not from the barbarians, but from ourselves."

Manius couldn't take any more of this. He seized Quintus. "You hit me! You struck me!"

"Oh that! A necessary ploy. To lure Titus Caelius into one last rash act that could be witnessed. I doubted you'd have played the part willingly and wouldn't have been convincing!"

"You might've killed me!"

"Rubbish! I've learnt to judge such a blow. I did once misjudge... but Septecius Clarus was thin-skulled."

Manius spluttered: "The things you said... accused me of – and in front of Caerellius Priscus!"

"I needed you to convey some motive for my actions to Titus Caelius, so he might believe things were still be in play. I accept that I was perhaps guilty of some self-indulgence."

This didn't placate Manius, who continued raging even when they joined Priscus and Publius Flavius in Merenda's day room in the praetorium. Priscus frowned.

"My dear boy," he said, when Manius paused to draw breath. "This is disrespectful. You've had a knock on the head, but you're a frumentarius – or aspire to be? Ah, here's Antonius Merenda – my dear fellow: how are you? I'm delighted to tell you that the whole unfortunate misunderstanding is resolved."

Antonius Merenda, shoulders bowed and looking ten years older, eyed the governor without enthusiasm and, at his invitation, dropped into a chair. With Quintus' help, Priscus explained how Titus had been exposed as the fort's assassin and the looter of the strongroom. Merenda's only reaction was to shake his head, as though nothing more could surprise him. His silence created an awkward hiatus which Publius Flavius filled.

"Tell us, Quintus Suetonius, what led you to Titus Caelius?" He moved close, dropping his voice to its familiar low timbre. "You must appreciate how to be suspected affected me. I wracked my brains as to who might've been capable… I even, for a while…" He paused, then coloured as his gaze slid momentarily from Quintus, and coughed,"… but I never suspected Titus Caelius. How did you?"

"Yes, do tell us," said Priscus, with cheery disregard for Publius Flavius' embarrassment. "At the moment, it looks like sorcery." At that, he cast a quick apologetic look at Merenda.

Quintus sighed. "There was no sorcery. From the beginning I pondered the character of a murderer who could act with such decision and take such risks; Titus Caelius plainly was such a man, but I'd no reason to question his virtue and I'd no motive to attribute to him. Then Manius here prompted another thought; didn't you?"

Manius, taken by surprise, nodded, uncomprehending.

"Yes, Manius remarked that none of this would've happened but for the presence of Tiberius Flavius and that set my thoughts on another path. Was it true? Would there have been no murders had he not been here? I amused myself by wondering: what of Rufius Atellus? Would he still have been killed? What if he was the true victim and the great general was only incidental to the death of a lowly centurion? The idea led me nowhere and I rejected it – until we discovered the empty strongroom and then I returned to it. The disappearance of a fortune had no obvious link to the murder of Tiberius Flavius, but it was worth examination. And, when one looks for who had opportunity and need of money, then the mystery isn't so great.

"The fog cleared a little more a few days ago. Antonius Merenda: your cook, I forget – his name?"

"Irminius Ambustus," said Merenda wearily. "He's dead."

"I served with him briefly on the ramparts. He shared some interesting information about the night Cotta died. He heard Aurelia Cotta cry out, which doesn't preclude her taking her own life, but is suggestive. More important, he then saw us – Antonius Merenda, Antiochos and myself – heading from the hospital for the praetorium and, shortly after, saw Titus Caelius coming from the praetorium. Why? What business had he there?" Quintus shrugged. "Possibly legitimate business. But why didn't we see him? We were going towards the praetorium. I can only conclude that he saw or heard us and hid in the shadows until we passed. He didn't want to be seen and so, whatever he was doing, he was up to no good."

"The murder of Aurelia Cotta," murmured Publius Fimbria.

"I believe so."

Quintus sighed once more. "My conscience troubles me about Irminius Ambustus. He was seen speaking to me and later that day he was stabbed in the back."

"Caelius Metellus again!" said Priscus.

"One must suspect so."

"The fellow's a demon!"

"Indeed," said Quintus. "Anyway, my theory was forming and then my examination of the duty rosters gave the hypothesis substance."

"Ha, you're a cunning fox Quintus Suetonius," chortled Priscus, "I've always said so."

"There was one other thing: on the night Cotta was killed, I was in that turret when Titus Caelius came climbing in and I saw that his face wore the expression of a man who was looking for more blood. I truly believe, Antonius Merenda, that he intended to slay your daughter and be rid of one last witness. Without her, he could've claimed ignorance even of Cotta's death and what he thought to be Manius' killing."

Merenda sat bolt upright and looked as though he might faint. Manius' own skin crawled and he offered a swift prayer of gratitude.

"I couldn't be sure," continued Quintus. "But now we know just how little regard Titus Caelius has for the laws of man and heaven. Character is the key to everything. The late emperor said: 'To pursue the impossible is madness: and it is impossible for a bad man not to act in character.'"

"Yes he did," said Priscus and, after suitable pause for reverential homage, clapped his hands and added briskly, "but now, Antonius Merenda, we must consider the whereabouts of the money. I want you to turn this fort and vicus upside down. Use men from Sixth Victrix if necessary."

As if conjured by the legion's name, its legate Julius Valerianus was announced. He was a short, bluff man. Priscus introduced him, explaining that he had called him to confer on military action. There followed animated discussion between them, with swift agreement on a march north to Vindomora, but disagreement on what to do then.

"A methodical advance to Corstopitum and the frontier, I think," said Priscus.

Julius Valerianus shook his head. "Sir, I'd advise a move to Pons Aelii to outflank any barbarians who crossed the wall."

Priscus frowned and raised his fist to his chin, thinking, then he summoned Merenda and Publius Flavius to join them at a table, where they sketched their possible moves. Manius remained with Quintus, some distance away, forgotten.

§

Titus took a fistful of his damp sheet and bit into it hard. Fierce pain had gripped the stump of his leg and it rippled throughout his body. His teeth ground the sheet until the agony receded. The pain was still there and insistent, but no longer overwhelming. He lay back gasping.

His pores pumped sweat, his shirt was soaked and his hair plastered to his head. Since Quintus Suetonius Lupus and the others had left, he'd felt worse. Fever was burning him, his wound was turning bad.

He didn't care.

What tormented his mind, while the pain tortured his body, was remembering Suetonius Lupus' triumphant exit – as though he'd won. The old fool!

It was he – Titus Caelius Metellus – who'd won. It had to be. It would be – so long as they didn't get the truth. He, not the corrupt placemen who'd kept him down. Oh no, not this time. He must secure victory.

But this infernal fever could betray him, make him delirious and tell them things.

Then there was the lad Manius. Would he still be too stupid to see the truth? Of course he would. No young nonentity could steal victory.

There was only himself left to be silenced. He just needed courage. It had never failed him before – and it wouldn't now.

"Come on Titus, old son," he whispered. "Just this last time."

He leaned forward, reaching for his stump.

§

Antiochos rubbed his eyes. They were gritty and a headache nagged behind them. He sat in his private chamber, gathering energy to check on the scores of wounded who filled his hospital's rooms and corridors. At least he'd had assistance from the Sixth Victrix surgeon, an oaf and an incompetent, but he'd allowed Antiochos a couple of hours of sleep.

The Greek groaned. He'd enough patients to deny him a proper night's rest for an age. But at least – may the gods grant it – there shouldn't be any more wounded. His head nodded and he jerked upright. Heavens above, he needed sleep. Galen taught that only in sleep did the brain's reviving juices rush back into it from the body. Without that, it would grow desiccated. Yes, it would become like a dried walnut… a walnut… when had he last had a walnut? Mother had loved walnuts… she…

He sat bolt upright. Enough! He must rouse himself. He rose, supporting himself with one hand on his desk.

He froze at a cry from next door. "Ahhh!"

It began as a shout, a roar of defiance that became an ululating scream.

Titus Caelius!

Antiochos lurched across his chamber, sending his chair flying. He scrabbled at the door latch, hurled the door open and stared.

Titus lay back, his features twisted, and yet with a triumphant light in his eye as he contemplated his wounded leg from which blood pulsed and jetted onto the floor at Antiochos' feet.

§

"Julius Valerianus, your suggestion ignores broader political considerations," argued Priscus, wagging his finger. "I wish to treat with the Brigantes. There's little to be gained by embroiling myself in a full-scale campaign against them, to end in burning their villages and crops, driving away their cattle and selling them into slavery. The lives lost and treasure expended would make Rome insistent on terrible retribution. Hotheads would gain the upper hand on their side – and on ours – and wise counsel would be despised. No, this must be avoided at all costs."

Manius heard Valerianus murmur something, but Priscus continued: "So far, we've had mere skirmishing, a large-scale riot. Let's not drive them into outright rebellion. Quintus Suetonius! This is your sphere."

He took a document from the table and hurried over. "We must advance cautiously, show our strength and give the Brigantes every opportunity to reach terms. Don't you agree?"

"That seems the sagest course."

"Good. Then you must plot your campaign. Here are some of the names furnished by Cotta. Let me see: Prasutagus; Cataurus; Segovax; Dumnonix; Drustan… ah, good here's a civilised name – Novius Maximus. These I take to be tribal chieftains or other men of influence, who're party to the bargain I outlined to you. They're men with whom we can treat. See, here are their septs – Lopocares and Gabratovices and so forth and here the places where they're believed to reside… no, I can't hope to pronounce these outlandish names. Read it for yourself."

Priscus made to return to the table but paused. "So, you're quite sure: that young man Titus Caelius was acting purely for his own gain?"

"Isn't everybody now?"

Priscus frowned, then leant over Quintus. "Quintus Suetonius, sometimes your humour can be misplaced. I'd intended that, after you'd completed this matter – " he gestured at the list " – to return you to Londinium to secure my position. Now, I'm beginning to think I should keep you close."

Manius took a sharp intake of breath and winced. Priscus shot him a sharp look.

"Forgive me," Manius said. "My head..."

"Yes, yes," said Quintus. "Go lie down for a spell."

With his hand to his brow, Manius left the room. Once in the courtyard, he straightened and looked to confirm what he'd glimpsed through the window.

She was there.

Lucia stood across the quadrangle, under the portico, sheltering from the steady rain. He hurried over to her and she looked up at him.

"It's raining," he said.

"Yes, it'll melt the snow."

"That's good."

"Yes."

She fiddled with her cloak broach. Manius cleared his throat. "Your father's been released."

Her eyes shone. "Yes! Was that your doing? Thank you."

"We were able to satisfy the governor that he'd no part in the theft."

"How? Do we know how the money disappeared?"

Manius told her what had been discovered. She gasped. "No! Titus Caelius! I can't believe it." She wrung her hands and took a pace away, then turned back to him. "Surely no man can be that wicked. Oh, how could he betray my father's trust?" She grasped Manius' hand and tears started in her eyes: "He tried to kill you! Oh the villain!"

Manius' heart swelled. She was holding his hand! She was gazing at him, her eyes sparkling, her mouth open revealing a delectable little gap between the two front teeth. He leaned into her, then recollected himself. He patted her hand. "But he didn't succeed, Lucia, and I'm safe."

"But you put your life at risk again, to lure him into a confession. Manius, you're so clever and brave – braver than Horatius."

He squeezed her hand. "It was the only way I could see of clearing your father's name."

"Oh Manius! Does he know this? I shall tell him."

Manius was about to agree. Her father was a broken reed but a knight was still a knight and a tribune still a tribune and – best of all – as Lucia's father, he could bestow the greatest gift of all. But then he remembered that Merenda had already received an account which differed substantially from his.

"No Lucia; that's not possible. I'm a frumentarius and I must act in the darkness – that's my curse."

She opened her mouth and he put a finger to the lovely bow of her lips. "Listen: tomorrow the governor marches. He wants me with him and I must do my duty, although it's never been so painful for me. But I'll return to you, I swear it – if you tell me that would be agreeable. Would it?"

She looked down, nodded and whispered: "Yes."

"You know I've no fortune."

"I don't care; you're brave and resourceful and will prosper."

"Yes, but your father…"

He was interrupted by a delicate cough. Furious, he looked round and saw Antiochos a few paces away. The surgeon wasn't his usual cocksure self and his normally merry black eyes wouldn't meet Manius' gaze as he shuffled.

"Forgive me, Manius Suetonius, I've something to tell the governor and Antonius Merenda."

"You'll find them in the day room."

He remained, the rain glistening in his hair and trickling down his cheeks. Manius glared.

Antiochos coughed again. "They won't like what I have to tell them. I wonder, my friend, whether you – or your father – could help me to find some way of making my news more palatable."

"What news?"

"It's... Titus Caelius Metellus, I'm afraid he... is dead. Yes, it's so. I just found him. He has ripped the dressings from his stump and torn open the wound. He's bled himself to death."

§

"Jupiter's temper dictates the weather," reflected Manius the next morning.

Jupiter must have been in a truly foul mood, for it rained – hard – without sign of relief in the iron dawn sky. Everyone was in bad humour. The legion and the cohort's cavalry turmae were formed up outside the porta praetoria, roused long before first light, dripping and irritable, while trumpets blared and braying officers, bawling orders, strutted along the ranks of thousands. But, for all this bustle and badgering, nothing seemed to happen. To Manius, it was an infuriating mess of urgency and inertia, while the troops grew soaked and cold.

And the men seemed infected by the irritation of their officers, who, in turn, mirrored the evident displeasure of their commander Caerellius Priscus.

Antiochos had been right. The governor hadn't been happy about the death of Titus and even less so when the search had failed to turn up the half million missing sesterces. All that had been found had been an empty hiding place under the flagstones in Birca's cottage. With Titus' death, there was little prospect of discovering the missing treasure. So, Priscus' normally benign face wore an expression of determined dissatisfaction and, as Quintus and Manius walked their horses behind him to take their places at the head of the column, Manius observed a legionary optio nod at the governor's red-cloaked back and mutter from the side of his mouth to his tesserarius: "Watch out today, Old Hey Hey's right peevish."

Manius grinned but Quintus was oblivious, his eyes small and bloodshot from the wine he'd drunk yesterday. Only Manius was content, buoyed by his conversation with Lucia and by his new plan.

The trumpets gave a final blast, the officers screamed orders and the column moved off, thousands of boots crashing and splashing on the road's paving. From the head, Manius watched the cavalry in open order, commanded by Publius Flavius, probing through the heathland, picking their way through the fast-receding snow and slush. How this wicked British rain dissolved the snow which had lain so thick.

There was no conversation, except the occasional exchange between Priscus and his officers. Manius was glad. The silence allowed him to savour thoughts of Lucia and that blessed understanding they'd reached. True, their talk had been cut short by Antiochos and his news of Titus' suicide. This had upset Lucia and made her weep, which allowed Manius to comfort her and to steal a kiss while Antiochos looked away.

He smiled. He was sure – sure – that he was on the cusp of some great thing. His fate lay in his own hands now. For once, he'd knowledge that no one else shared – and he was going to use it.

His mood made even that barren land less awful, as the rain turned it from white to drab green and brown, the road rising and falling over its succession of sodden hills and valleys and the dark forest never far from their flanks. His heart almost sang when a herd of deer went springing across the front of Publius Flavius' troopers, and headed, in leaping train, for the trees.

They tucked their chins onto their chests against the driving rain, which ran off their helmets and soaked cloaks and chilled to the bone. But this drove them to put the day behind them, so that the column ate the miles. Shortly before midday, in answer to a querulous enquiry from Priscus, an officer said they were within two hours of Vindomora.

Soon there was a cry from ahead. A number of horsemen gathered around Publius Flavius, who, after a short conference, cantered back towards them. He saluted and wheeled his mount to ride by Priscus' side.

"Sir, there's a handful of Brigantes on the road. They're unarmed and seek to speak with you."

"Do they, by Jove? Did they ask for me by name?"

"They did, sir."

Priscus turned in the saddle to face the frumentarii. "Well Quintus Suetonius, this is what we've been waiting for, don't you think, hey, hey?"

Quintus shook himself out of some deep, solitary reflection and grunted agreement. It made sense that the Brigantes' leaders – given their understanding with Priscus, through Cotta – should seek to re-establish communication.

An order was given for the column to halt and Priscus, Publius Flavius, Quintus and Manius rode forward to where four Britons sat on horseback under the wary eyes and javelins of a decurion and six troopers. These Brigantes didn't look too wild: no extravagant moustaches and plaited hair. Their beards were trimmed and their cloaks and tunics sober. They also spoke good Latin, or at least their grey haired, leather-skinned leader did, as he introduced himself as Novius Maximus, Roman citizen.

"Novius Maximus!" cried Priscus. "There's a name from our list, is it not? Aurelius Cotta gave me your name. He's dead, you know?"

Maximus inclined his head. "A great loss – to Rome and to the Brigantine nation. He worked hard to bring friendship between us."

"True. But that work needn't be in vain."

"I am here to try to ensure that it is not."

"Splendid, splendid."

Quintus cut in. "What are your credentials, Novius Maximus? For whom do you speak and with what authority?"

The Briton surveyed Quintus. "I'm only a messenger, to invite you to treat, to finish this business under terms already agreed."

"Where do you invite us to? To treat with whom?" demanded Priscus.

Maximus pointed to the forest's edge, some hundred paces from the road, where a thin column of smoke was rising just within the trees. "There waits Iovir."

"Iovir himself, king of the Brigantes. This is…"

"Why doesn't your Iovir come out here?" interrupted Quintus. "A Roman governor isn't summoned."

Maximus laughed and his companions beamed.

"Indeed he is not," said one, stocky and bald. "Rather he sends me, Drustan, to humbly invite you to where we can provide some shelter and fire and even some hot wine, more comfortable and seemly than negotiating in the rain. And more private."

Priscus smiled. "Well, there's some sense in that. Come, Quintus Suetonius, let's go with them, just into the woods. Flavius Fimbria, bring a troop and order the rest to come at the first sign of trouble." He faced Maximus. "You realise – any treachery and you'll have a legion at your throats?"

Maximus only nodded, then turned his horse towards the forest, followed by his companions. Manius and Quintus exchanged glances. Publius Flavius and his trooper led the way and he ordered his men to ride after them.

They approached the trees to where a narrow track led in. Maximus took them down this. Here it was darker and the only noise was the steady dripping from the trees and their horses' hooves squelching mud and sodden leaves. When they had gone twenty paces and Manius was looking for the promised shelter and fire, there was a whistle and then a shout.

Quintus was first to sound the alarm.

"Ambush!" he bellowed. "We're betrayed!"

Maximus and his companions spurred their horses and galloped into the forest without a backward glance while a score of armed Brigantes materialised from the trees and dead undergrowth.

Priscus' horse reared and Manius saw him fall. Publius Flavius seized the bridle but had to release it to draw his sword and hack down at a barbarian who darted about his horse's legs.

"Help!" he cried. "We're attacked! To me!"

Manius' own horse skittered and whinnied and he fought to control it, shouting his fear and surprise. He was aware of Quintus, roaring and laying about him with his sword. Then there were more shouts and oaths from behind and Manius and his horse were forced off the track, as Roman cavalry thundered through, javelins lowered.

There were cries, whinnying, rearing horses; men grunting; blades clashing – then it was over. There were anxious questions and breathless orders, men dismounting and horses being calmed. The shouts receded into the woods. Then came swearing and urgent enquiry. Manius, sword in hand, still wrestled to bring his horse under control as he cast around for any enemy. He saw only Quintus and soldiers moving, cautious, swords outstretched, eyes searching the trees.

Quintus dismounted to join Publius Flavius who was bent over a prone figure clad in a scarlet cloak. Manius leapt from his horse to join them. He looked down on Caerellius Priscus' staring eyes and open mouth, from which bubbled blood.

"Is he…?"

"Dead," groaned Publius Flavius, rising. "And I was his escort."

Quintus placed a hand on his shoulder. "You're not to blame. He walked into this trap himself. If blame must be laid elsewhere then it should be on me, I should've suspected."

"We must have revenge. We must pursue them."

"No! On no account send troopers into the forest. They're sure to lay another ambush and you'll have a troop cut down for your pains. The woods belong to the Brigantes. Anyway, don't we have half a dozen dead at our feet, as vengeance?"

"It's poor payment for a Roman governor."

Quintus wrapped his arm around Publius' shoulder, whispering: "This is one governor Rome may be happy to see the back of." He slapped him on the back. "Go! Inform Julius Valerianus of his new command."

Publius nodded, white-faced and miserable. He gathered his men, ordering them to take the body – "With respect curse you! With respect!" – of Priscus Caerellius. Manius made to follow, but Quintus pulled him back, his own face now ashen and his eyes darting, alarmed.

"What?"

Quintus flapped his hand to silence him. He pointed down at a dead barbarian who'd lain closest to Priscus and who had likely slain him. Manius stared at the dead man, a red-haired Briton with the characteristic moustaches, his eyes closed in peace. Manius looked, not understanding and then with a chill of recognition.

§

"It's…"

"Bodvoc, Tita Amatia's steward. Oh that crazy bitch! What has she done now?"

§

Long after night had fallen, Manius was alone in his own room, in another mansio, in another vicus, outside another fort.

After their melancholy arrival at Vindomora, bearing the body of Priscus, there had been hours of fretful conference where Julius Valerianus, Quintus and the prefect of Vindomora's garrison had swapped views, questions and proposals. They agreed: the situation was desperate – a frontier in arms and a province with no governor and no direction from Rome. Quintus, Manius noted, was withdrawn and said nothing of Priscus' machinations. When the council finally broke up, the only resolution was to send urgent word to Londinium and to Rome for instruction and to meet again the next morning to decide on immediate measures.

Quintus and Manius had then gone to a vicus tavern to eat. There Quintus hadn't shared his thoughts on the death of Priscus, nor the involvement of Tita Amatia. But Manius could see that he was worried, for he drank steadily, tugging at his beard and gazing into the fire.

Manius was beyond caring. These would no longer be his problems. To hell with them all. He'd be used no more. No, now was finally the hour for Manius Suetonius Lupus to pursue his own interests.

§

That was an hour ago. Manius had lain awake until he heard Quintus' steady snoring through the wall. Then, he rose, wrapped his cloak about him, took his bag and stole from the room. As he passed Quintus' chamber, he opened his door with great care. The light from the corridor's lamp dimly revealed Quintus, on his back, his mouth open and chest rising and falling with his stentorian snores. Tears pricked Manius' eyes.

How would he fare without this contrary old sot? For ever, so much of what Manius had done, or said, had been for his approval – usually withheld. Life would be barely conceivable without that. But it was time: Manius must look out for himself – and Lucia. With a painful swallow, he raised a hand in valediction. Farewell Quintus.

He closed the door.

§

He made his way to the neighbouring stables, found his horse and reassured it over this midnight disturbance. He led it through the dark streets of the deserted vicus to the gate. The rain had stopped, and the moon reflected in the shimmering black puddles. He approached the sentry.

Manius deepened his voice. "I'm a frumentarius with urgent despatches for Londinium."

The sentry gave a hurried salute and, flustered, opened the gate. Manius nodded his thanks and set his horse at a steady trot out of Vindomora towards Longovicium.

For all his resolve, he was nervous. He twitched at every noise – the hoot of owl and wind-rustled branches – alive to the possibility of enemy patrols. His horse beat a rhythm for anyone to hear and, while the moon lit his way, shimmering the rain-soaked paving, it was a treacherous light, silhouetting a lone rider. He fortified himself by thinking of Titus. Aye, Titus had taught him the importance of the bold stroke, of seizing the initiative. Only thus could an ant escape.

Titus: a remarkable man. What speed of thought and reaction. Naturally, that had meant detail left to chance. That preposterous story about Publius Flavius' toga!

How could Manius possibly have seen it in the dark of Birca's house? Even if he had, what importance would he have placed upon a soiled toga? Absurd! No, Titus hadn't wanted him dead because of that, but because he had much more important information, of which he'd been bound to realise the significance – sooner or later.

Oh sure, Birca had been a big, heavy woman, but not half a million sesterces heavy.

No, it wasn't she who lay in that Longovicium cemetery. It was a fortune, and Manius, following his road by the light of the moon, was determined to recover it before she did.

Lightning Source UK Ltd.
Milton Keynes UK
UKHW011113151021
392226UK00002B/21/J